RECKONING

A TWISTED LOVE STANDALONE

This is a work of fiction. Names, characters, businesses, places, events, and incidents are either products of the author's imagination or used in a fictious manner. Any resemblance to actual persons, living or dead, or actual events is purely coincidental.

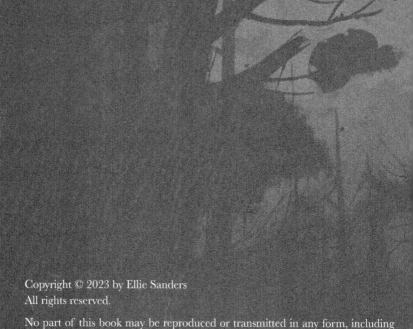

Published: Ellie Sanders 2023
www.hotsteamywriter.com

RECKONING

A TWISTED LOVE STANDALONE

ELLIE SANDERS

TRIGGER WARNINGS

This book is a dark revenge romance. There are a lot of triggers so please be aware of this before embarking down this road as it's labelled 'dark' for a reason.

Ideally, I'd prefer for you to dive into this book blind so as not to spoil the twists and turns but I know some people like a warning. Below are the main triggers.

For a full list please visit www.hotsteamywriter.com

Triggers include: familial abuse, emotional abuse, sexual assault, somnophilia, rape play, CNC, non con, sexual penetration by objects "beyond the norm", BDSM vibes, spanking, torture, kidnapping, detailed rape scenes, physical violence, human trafficking, organ trafficking, drug use, fertility issues and the inability to conceive, historical child abuse (hitting of a child) and murder.

There are also a lot of extremely explicit sex scenes so if this is not your thing, then this book is not for you.

Reader discretion really is advised because you have been warned.

Playlist

The Sound of Silence — Nouela
What I've Done — Linkin Park
Sleepwalking — Bring Me The Horizon
Tourniquet — Evanescence
Kill or Be Killed — Muse
Closer — Nine Inch Nails
Uprising — Muse
A Little Wicked — Valerie Broussard
Me & the Devil — Gil Scott-Heron

Long is the way and hard, that out of Hell leads up to light.

—John Milton, Paradise Lost

CHAPTER

SOFIA

I shouldn't be here. That's the thought that keeps echoing in my head.

That I have to stop. That I need to stop.

Turnaround, Sofia. Turnaround you utter fool.

Only I don't. I just keep my pace, creeping through the darkness like I'm some sort of avenging angel.

But that's not what I am, is it?

I'm not anything remotely close to angelic anymore. Not after what they did to me. Not after what they put me through. I used to be a good person, kind, considerate, despite how my family and I suffered, I still believed that the world was a good place.

And then Otto Montague happened.

I grit my teeth, burying the wave of emotion that rises up at the mere thought of that man's name.

Ahead a street lamp flickers. I pause, watching as my would-be target comes to a stop and I press myself flat against the damp brick of a building.

I had to take this chance. I didn't know when I would see the bastard again. If I would see him. I didn't even know his name, we'd never been introduced. After all, who makes introductions in the kind of situation I was forced in?

No, I wasn't going to let him slip through my fingers. Wasn't going to let him continue to live his life like none of it happened.

As soon as he starts moving, so do I.

Around the corner, into the yard of some construction company.

It's hard not to smile. It's hard not to let out a laugh because I couldn't have picked a more perfect place if I tried. It's away from the street. Away from any would be bystanders or witnesses.

I grip the knife firmer in my hand. My eyes fixed on him. One firm strike will be enough to bring him under my control and after that I can take my sweet time. The way he did with me. The way he brutalised and tortured my drug addled body as my monster of a husband stood by and laughed.

I take a bigger step. Then another closing the distance. Just as I get within striking distance he turns and our eyes connect.

He must recognise me. He must.

Only he doesn't speak. He just stares at me, running his eyes over my body before fixing on the blade.

Footsteps echo behind me. I drop my focus on the man in front for a millisecond and someone behind me laughs.

"Did you come for another round?" The man in front taunts. "Drop the knife and we'll all have some more fun."

"Fuck you." I spit, raising it instantly, pointing it right at his face.

They both laugh. The one behind stepping closer, making this feel like this was all done as a set up. That they knew.

My heart rate turns erratic. Sweat starts to moisten my palms and it feels like the handle of the knife is suddenly so slick.

I've lost the element of surprise. I've probably lost this entire fight and I know it's not going to end well but then, it never has for me, has it?

I charge, without hesitating. If I can gut one of them, kill one of them, just do something before I once again lose then maybe this might ease the incessant, continuous, all-consuming pain inside me.

Maybe it might make the voice in my head shut up.

Maybe, just maybe I might be able to look at myself in a mirror and not feel disgusted with what I see.

The man's eyes widen. He makes a grab for my wrist and I knee him in the balls before jabbing wildly with the knife. The other man grabs me, trying to pull me back but I'm manic now, feral. I lash out, I thrash in their arms, slicing the blade through the air not caring where I cut, where I hurt, just as long as I make contact.

And I do.

I feel the knife hitting something solid over and over. The handle no longer just wet with sweat but with blood.

One of the men fall. He collapses. And I realise I've actually hurt him.

My heart leaps.

I can do this. I can kill them both.

The other man wraps his arms around me locking my body against his and as his smell washes over me I get a flashback, a memory so vivid I lose sense of myself. I let out a whimper, trying to fight it but the trauma overtakes me and I can't focus. I can't do anything.

"Stupid fucking whore." The man spits swinging me around, throwing me forward.

My eyes widen as I see more men surrounding us. This *was* a setup.

"Drop the blade or we fuck you with it." One of them says.

I shake my head. I'm not that stupid.

"Little bitch wants another lesson."

Every voice, every man here that I look at makes a new vision echo in my head. One of pain. One of violation.

"It's been a while, Sofia." One of them says stepping closer. "I'll admit I missed your cunt but I missed the way you cried as I was fucking you more."

I snarl, holding the blade out like my life depends upon it but I guess in a way it does.

They all start moving, closing in on me and I turn swinging the blade, trying to force them to keep away but I can't hold five men off. I don't stand a chance.

Just as that thought hits me I see more. They're rushing in, only they're not joining this sick soirée, they've got bats, wrenches and they're attacking the men who seconds ago were all but attacking me.

I stare about, not understanding what the hell is going on and someone grabs me, trying to use me as some sort of human shield. I scream, I flail, instinct taking over as I bury the knife over and over and the man slumps, releasing his grip while I'm covered in his blood.

He falls to the floor, blood now gurgling from his mouth but he's not who I'm staring at. Not who I've got my attention on.

All I can see are the pitch black eyes of a man so big, so domineering it feels like this entire world has to bend to fit him.

He stares back at me but there's no brutality in his eyes right now. There's something so much softer.

"Sofia."

The way he murmurs my name feels w
react to it, shouldn't respond the way it do

This man should petrify me more than
does the complete opposite.

I shake my head, dropping my eyes and
in the blood that's covering me. It's soaked m
my skin.

My breath hitches.

I killed him. I killed that man. I know it's w
now that I've done it, it feels so different. It feel

I have to get it off. I have to get his blood of

Koen steps closer to me, not touching me b
he is.

"Sofia." He says again, more softly, as if he ca
to break completely.

I shake my head, shut my eyes. I don't wa
I don't…

"Reid." Koen growls and a man crosses the spa
us. "Get her out of here."

"Yes boss." The man says.

I shake my head once more. I don't want to leave, I
that every one of those bastards are dead but I can't
My legs are shaking, my body is losing itself in a dark sp
get out of and I can't focus on anything.

I let out a whimper, my head feels too dizzy, my heart
too rapidly. I take a step back but it feels like my feet aren'
the ground anymore and as I start to slip into darkness I k
Koen's arms that catch me.

That it's him who carries me away. Not the man he calle
one of the five men who raped me so long ago.

And worse than that, I don't fight him, I don't even try,
let the darkness take me and let this man carry me away, tru
that he won't hurt me.

Trusting that he will keep me safe.

CHAPTER

SOFIA

Two Months Earlier

They say what doesn't kill you makes you stronger. Well, I've never heard more bullshit in my life because it certainly didn't make me stronger. It didn't make me tougher.

It broke me.

They broke me.

Otto Fucking Blumenfeld broke me.

I let out a ragged breath, feeling my anger mixing once more with my panic. Even after all this time I still can't seem to get any rational grasp on my emotions. I still can't get any rational grasp on anything.

But I'm good at pretending. Really good in fact. So good the entirety of Verona thinks I'm fixed. It's only my family that know otherwise. And to be fair, I'd much rather it that way. Much rather the world think that I'm capable of healing than them realising what was really going on and how damaged I truly am.

How utterly, irreparably damaged my soul is.

My feet crunch as I take another step. The glass beneath my boots makes a satisfying noise as it shatters more. My eyes skim about the place, and I walk from one luxurious room to the next reliving every horror that I endured, every awful violation my husband put me through, all whilst letting the petrol pour freely from the canister in my hand.

The smell makes my nose wrinkle.

The fumes fill the air.

But it masks the stench of what this place is. The walls Otto twisted around into my prison cell.

I haven't removed a thing. I've kept all his possessions here. The priceless art, the jewellery, the furniture that could gain me a fortune at any decent auction house. All of it became mine when that bastard died, only I don't want his money. I don't want to profit from any of this.

No, there's only one thing I want.

One thing that would at least begin to sate the agony inside me.

I want to wipe away every last living memory of that man. I want to destroy everything he ever owned, everything he ever touched. I want to make sure this city learns what happens when they cross the Montagues, but not just us, what happens when they fuck with *me*. I want this city to stop seeing me as some poor innocent girl and to finally accept that I have changed. I have grown. I am no longer the baby-faced victim they all read about a year ago.

I am so much more than that.

I draw myself up, pouring the last of the fuel onto the bed that I technically shared with my late husband. If it were possible this is where I'd set the fire, this is where I'd start the inferno, only I know if I do that I'll burn with the house and I don't have a death wish.

But I'll admit it irks as I make my way back through the house and to the front. I liked the poetic justice of burning our bed. Of burning that room - I guess torching his entire house will have to make up for it.

My lips curl as I pick up the flash bomb. Yeah, I like to be dramatic and let's face it a simple match just wasn't going to have the same effect. There just wouldn't be enough drama.

I pull the pin tossing the thing inside. The blast is limited, small, I did my research when I snuck this out of Roman's stores. I don't want to blow the house up. I want to burn it to the ground. I want to burn every last fucking thing of Otto's.

As the bomb sparks it makes a tiny crackling bang and my skin erupts in goosebumps.

I stand, feeling the cool autumn wind against my back and watch as the flames catch, as they slowly rise and spread and then the heat, the fire, it lights up the night sky, illuminating it for the entire city to see.

My soul seems to stir.

That numbness that has clung to me for what feels like forever is replaced with fire. With brimstone.

I cross my arms, my face lit up not only by the blaze but by the smile that's gracing my lips.

I don't move.

I don't even think I blink.

I just stand there, watching.

Until the sound of sirens becomes too loud to ignore.

Oh I knew they'd come. I knew that even in this moment this damned city would try to stop me.

Well, I guess now is time for part two of my plan.

I turn, picking up the assault rifle, and step out into the road blocking the engine that comes hurtling towards me.

The tyres screech as it comes to a stop and half a dozen men jump out.

They try reasoning with me. They try to persuade me that I need to let them pass, that if I don't the whole house will be unsalvageable, as if this is all just some simple mistake. Like silly me merely left a few unattended candles and whoops look what happened.

I laugh in their faces because nothing they say will make a damned bit of difference.

"This is my house." I state. "Mine. And if I want to burn it down there's nothing you can do to stop me."

They exchange looks like they think I've gone mad. I can feel the heat of the inferno at my back, I can hear the cracks as the fire ravages through the wooden structure of the house.

Just a little longer and the whole thing will be reduced to rubble.

More sirens ring out. Another engine arrives and the city's militia arrives with it.

My eyes widen when I see the Governor getting out of the car, his eyes fixed on me as he makes his way over.

"Sofia." He says once he's within speaking distance.

I grip the assault rifle tighter. If they think they can put a stop to this then I'll make them see how far I will go.

He eyes the weapon with obvious concern. "You don't want this to turn nasty," He says quietly.

"No?" I muse. "As far as I can see it's you making it nasty. Here I am just trying to have a nice, quiet bonfire, when all of you lot show up and ruin my evening."

His lips quirk. "Bonfire?" He repeats glancing to the flames that must be fifty foot high behind me.

"It's a private party." I reply. "I didn't invite you."

He lets out a chuckle and half the men around us side-eye him like they can't understand why he's not simply tackling me to the ground and handcuffing me already.

"Alright." He murmurs. "You want to raise it to the ground, that's your prerogative."

"So you're not going to stop me?" I question.

He glances at the weapon again. "No, Sofia. Besides, I'd say it's a little late for that don't you think?"

I look over my shoulder and gasp as I see he's right; the walls are collapsing in. It barely looks like a house anymore. Give it another ten minutes and I don't think there will be anything but just a crumbling mass of burnt out bricks.

He moves to stand beside me making me feel like he's some sort of bodyguard. Some sort of protector.

"You never replied to my messages." He says quietly.

I arch a brow. Really? Now he wants to have this conversation. It's been over a year for Christ sake. "There was nothing to say." I state.

He shakes his head. "We both know that's not true."

I jerk my chin, feeling a flash of irritation. "This was meant to be cathartic, Hastings. Don't ruin this for me."

He lets out a sigh that feels so weighted. "Then promise me you will talk."

"I have nothing to say." I snap.

He folds his arms, letting out a huff of irritation but we both know I'm not lying. There is nothing to say.

It's over. It's in the past. All that they did to me, all that I endured, why the fuck would I want to divulge any of it? Why would I want to file police reports on the men that are still out there and stir up all that shit?

Besides, I was drugged most of the time, and those few memories I do have – no, I don't want to visit them, I don't want to relive them just so Verona can close off another sordid chapter. I refuse to become even more of a victim than I already am.

This city already knows I was forced to marry Otto, I'm sure plenty of them have spent many evenings imagining all the ways in which Otto himself hurt me. I don't need to divulge the actual horror of it. I don't need to make it publicly known what else he and his mates did. What further abuses I suffered.

No, I want my justice to be private. I want my vengeance to be mine. Only mine. I just need to bide my time and then I will have it on the terms that suit me.

I look back at him. The reflection of the flames makes his skin take on a strange orange hue that clashes with what little hair he has left. He must be in his late fifties. Every flicker of light catches in the deep set wrinkles on his forehead. Verona is so plastic fantastic that it's odd to see a man who doesn't try to hide his age, who doesn't try to mask it.

"Are you planning on burning anymore of his properties down?" He asks.

The other properties all went to his previous two wives to be held in state for his two children. This house of horrors was the only one left to me, though we all know that wasn't by Otto's hand. No, a judge decided this would all be split 'fairly'. My mind flickers to the ridiculous court date I still have to face, the one his other two wives are forcing. Both of them apparently *do* want all of his money and are willing to fight tooth and nail for it.

I shake my head, focusing my eyes back on the burning wreck in front of me. "I don't own them." I state. "Besides this was where..." I gulp swallowing those words. I can see from the look on his face that he understands what I was about to reveal.

"Good fucking riddance then." He says.

And I can't help it, I grin, staring back at the flames.

Good fucking riddance indeed.

CHAPTER

KOEN

It shouldn't be this easy. It really shouldn't.

And yet apparently these fuckers really do believe they're untouchable.

The night is still early, I can hear the drunken laughter of tourists out enjoying the summer delights of this city.

There's a carnival going on. Music is playing. The street is filled with performers dancing, twisting their half-naked bodies, while the crowd around them ooos and awwws accordingly.

But that's not what's got my attention.

Ahead, I can see a man, with a string of fake flowers hanging around his neck making his way through the crowd, pushing his way through like he's on some sort of mission.

He doesn't realise that I'm following him.

He doesn't realise that he's taking his very last steps of freedom. His last breaths of free air.

As he rounds the corner, I can see what's got his attention, why he's removed himself from all the fun of the carnival. Danny Boy has his sights on a different kind of fun.

The girl stumbles, leaning heavily against a brick wall as she stops to puke for what is undoubtedly not the first time. She gasps, wiping her mouth, and then continues onwards. I'd put money on her being a tourist. I'd put money on her drink being spiked too.

Her heels are so high that every step she makes seems to force her ankles to bow and I wonder how the bones don't simply snap from the pressure.

But Danny keeps close.

Close enough to keep her in his sights without her yet realising what danger she's in.

I guess somethings haven't changed. Leopards really don't change their spots do they?

As the noise of the crowd dies, I pause. I don't want him to know I'm here yet. I want to ensure the bastard is cornered, contained, that there's no way he can get out of my trap.

Behind me, Colt and Reid appear. They've been doubling back, making sure none of Danny's mates have decided to come along for the ride. In truth, a part of me wanted them too, though technically they don't have anything to do with this, anything to do with *her*.

I've done my research. I've spent months tracking down every single one of them. Of course it helped that one of the first I caught had video footage. It certainly made it easier to identify them even if watching the thing, hearing her screams, seeing what she actually endured, was the most horrific thing I've ever witnessed.

Danny comes to a stop. I can see him. I can see her too. The tourist. She's slumped against some bins so I guess the drugs finally overloaded her system. Danny wastes no time in pulling her around, manoeuvring her body into a more beneficial position.

It's when he undoes his trousers and gets his cock out that we make our move.

Colt steps out first, blocking the only other escape route. Reid stands between him and Danny, making it clear he'd have to take them both on if he wants to try and run.

Only Danny boy doesn't even realise we're here. He's too focused on his prize.

I prowl towards him, grabbing him by the scruff of his neck and toss him back onto the ground far enough away from the girl to no longer be a threat.

"What the…?" He groans, his bare arse hitting the tarmac with a thump.

"Playtime's over." I say.

He gulps, looking up at me then back at the girl who still hasn't moved an inch. Whatever he gave her must have knocked her out cold.

"She's my girlfriend." Danny splutters.

"Is that right?" I reply.

"This is a scene."

"A scene?" I repeat.

"Yeah, you know, roleplay. We pretend I'm stalking her and then…"

"How come she's drugged up, huh?" I snarl.

His lips curl. "She does it. Makes it more realistic."

I shake my head at the utter shit he's spewing.

"You can have a go." He says, glancing from me to Colt.

"Excuse me?" I snarl.

"Come on man, I'll even let you go first."

"What a gentleman." I deadpan. "Real fucking noble of you."

He grins nodding. "Yeah, yeah I am. She's hot, you should feel her cunt. She's so good when she's wrapped around…"

My fist silences the rest of his sentence. The impact sends him back, slamming into the tarmac again and, as he groans, I can see he's not gonna put up any more of a fight.

"Reid, take the girl to the hospital." I order.

Reid nods moving quickly to cover and carry her away while Colt and I drag our new toy out by his arms, with his trousers still down by his ankles.

By the time I'm done with him, he'll wish he'd left this city. He'll wish he crawled away like the piece of shit he is and disappeared forever.

I CAN SMELL THE STENCH OF HIM. THE SWEAT AS IT POURS OFF HIS body. The ammonia from where he's pissed himself – they always piss themselves.

He's been hanging here for only a few hours. If I had more patience I'd leave him in the dark for days.

I usually like to play with my toys, I like to torment, to torture. But when it comes to this, when it comes to *them*, by the time I catch another I'm so riled up I don't care to make it last. I just want to make sure it hurts. That every moment up until their last breath is one of agony.

His body sways from the shackles that keep him suspended high enough off the ground to ensure his feet can't relieve any of the pressure.

His head hangs down with his chin resting on his chest. I pause watching him for a moment.

And then I raise my hand slapping his face hard enough to wake the bastard up.

He lets out a groan, jerking, his legs kicking wildly like he's forgotten where he is, what this is.

"Wakey, wakey." I murmur and the two men by the door snigger.

Old Danny boy starts whimpering. "Please." He begs, "This is just a misunderstanding. You've got the wrong man."

I grab his face forcing him to look me in the eyes.

"I don't think so." I reply.

"You have." He shouts. "I'm not who you think I am."

"And who do I think you are, Danny Campball?"

He gulps, his face paling as he realises I know his name.

"Please." He says his eyes darting wildly from me to Colt and Reid like they have the power to step in. Like they'd do anything to help a man such as him.

I pull the knife from my belt, running the tip down his cheek, seeing as it slices through his flesh so perfectly, spilling his blood the same way he spilt hers.

"How does it feel?" I murmur. "To be on the receiving end?"

He shakes his head, acting like he doesn't have a clue what I'm talking about.

"She's my girlfriend." He splutters like I'm still focused on the tourist he was about to rape.

"It's not about her." I reply.

He frowns his eyes staring at the blade I've got pointed right at his eye.

"Then who..?"

"You know who."

He starts breathing faster. His eyes dilating as realisation hits him. "I have money." He cries. "I have a lot of money…"

My laugh cuts across his pathetic pleas. "Not this time. You can't buy your way out of this."

I run the knife down, slicing his other cheek.

"Every bit of you that touched her, every miniscule scrap of your piece of shit body, I'm going to hack it out."

"Please." He screams out, throwing his head back and kicking those useless legs more. "I didn't do anything. I didn't…"

I slam my fist into his side, feeling his rib facture so perfectly beneath my hand. "That's a fucking lie." I growl. "You touched her. You put your hands all over her."

"It wasn't my fault."

"No?" I muse.

"He told us that's how she likes it." He gasps.

I pause, gripping his throat so tightly he splutters. "What did you say?"

"Some bitches are into that."

My anger flares more. He's trying to pull that one? Trying to act like it was consensual?

"She enjoyed it." He says.

Those words make me pause. I stare into his eyes, holding his gaze long enough that he starts physically shaking.

"She did. She…"

My fist breaks his jaw as it makes impact. The howl he lets out does nothing to appease the fury inside me. He knows that wasn't the case and yet he thinks he can fool me?

He starts murmuring, his words no longer quite making sense because he clearly bit off part of his tongue when I punched him.

I tilt the knife, getting the angle just right and then I bury it deep into his eye socket, twisting it, turning it to mush.

"Know why I'm taking your sight, Danny?" I murmur as I pull the knife back out.

He's whimpering, howling, his mouth drooling from how I've broken it.

"You saw her, you looked at her, when you had no right. Did you really expect to get away with it?"

I take his right eye next, letting the blood from both pour down his cheeks. Blinding a man always feels a strange move. On the one hand I like the psychological torment, I like that removing that sense not only heightens all the others but it also means I can't see the fear in the eyes when I make my final move.

Blood streams down his cheeks, they look like tears. He's blubbering, spluttering and then he starts repeating the same name over and over. "Christian, Christian, Christian,"

I know who he's referring to. I know who the bastard is. He was there too, he also touched what wasn't his.

"You need to see this…" Colt says getting my attention.

I force my gaze from Danny and see Colt's holding a phone out. He must have used Danny's face to unlock it before we beat him to a pulp.

He holds it up, right in front of my face. "I went through the videos." He says but I'm not really listening.

I'm staring. Transfixed. On the screen I can see her, tied down, immobile. I can see the rope around her wrists, around her ankles – there's slack for her to move and yet she's not. She's just lying there, like she's not even alive. She's wearing some dirty underwear but nothing else. Six, no, seven men are surrounding her, their faces all on view.

As someone rips her bra off she seems to wake up from whatever drug induced stupor they put her in.

And she's screaming, jerking, trying to get free.

The men around her are laughing. One of them grabs her hair, yanking her violently to the side.

Above their jeers, above their insults, I can hear her pleas. She's begging them to stop. Begging them to let her go.

Someone slams their fist into her face and that silences her. How they haven't broken her jaw I don't know.

"Boss?"

I look up, snatching the phone, needing that awful noise to stop.

As I turn back to Danny, my rage seems to take a new form. He kept this video like it was some sort of trophy. Did he get off watching it? Did get off seeing the way they'd hurt her?

"You piece of shit." I snarl, grabbing Danny by the throat once more. I'd planned to slit his throat, to watch him bleed out, but that feels far too impersonal now.

My hands wrap around his neck, he kicks out, pleads for mercy as if he deserves any. And I'll admit I enjoy the feeling of his fighting, of his heart beating furiously under my grip, of his body slowly dying beneath my grasp.

When he finally does slump, we cut him down, before throwing him in the incinerator. If there's one thing I did learn from Darius, it's that. You clean up your crimes in a way that they can't come back to bite you in the arse.

Colt sticks by my side. I still have the phone in my pocket and it feels like a ten ton weight - I want to go through it myself, see whoever else is on there, what more evidence there is.

All the faces were new. Men we didn't know. I'll print them off, add them to the board. They're on my kill list now and I won't stop until every one has been eliminated.

CHAPTER

SOFIA

"Daddy?"

My eyes dart about the room, from my father sat behind his colossal desk to the stranger, leaning over it, getting right in his face. Maybe I should have turned and run at the sound of raised voices but I guess I'm not that smart.

They both turn and while my father's face is one of shock and annoyance, the other man's twists in a smile.

He's taller than my father, his face is harsher, his eyebrows seems to point down like he's some sort of picture book villain.

"This is your daughter?" He asks.

"Yes." My father says quickly, springing to his feet, grabbing me roughly enough that I yelp.

"You're hurting me." I say indignantly.

Either he doesn't listen or he doesn't care because he pulls me further behind him as if there's some sort of threat.

The other man lets out a low laugh. "You know we don't have any interest in little girls." He murmurs.

"I'm not little." I pout. "I'm six."

My father hushes me, but the man laughs more, squatting down, like he wants to get a better look at me. "Six?" He repeats. "Then you're practically a grown up."

"That's right." I state, though it feels like he's mocking me and I don't know why.

"Come here," He orders.

Maybe my sense of self-preservation kicks in, maybe my sense of survival does but a voice in my head screams that his man is dangerous and I shrink back, into my father's leg, clutching his trouser for good measure.

The man looks from me to my father and I can tell he's getting annoyed.

"Horace," He says in a tone that's more than threatening and to my absolute horror he leans forward, yanking me from his protection.

I cry out, at least I try to, but as he lifts me up, as he hauls me off the ground all my fear turns to paralysis.

"You look just like your mother." He states. "Same face, same eyes, only your nose is your father's."

"Mummy is in heaven." I reply.

His lips quirk like it's some sort of joke. "Would you like to join her?" He asks.

My eyes widen, is that possible? I've never even seen her, I don't even remember her. She went to heaven when I was still a baby but I've stared at the framed picture on my shelf, imagining what she would sound like, what her laugh would sound like, how tightly she'd squeeze me when she gave me a hug.

"Daddy?" I gasp, "Please can I, please?"

The man chuckles more and as I look at my father I can see a sickening sweat appear on his brow. "That's enough." He snaps moving to grab me but the man is quicker. Far quicker.

"Ah, ah, ah." He says, moving his hands, grabbing my throat and pressing me back against him. "You want to play games, Horace, then these are the consequences."

"Daddy?" I whimper. His hand feels so tight I'm afraid he's going to snap my neck.

"Let her go." My father snaps.

"We had a deal." The man replies. "You think you can back out of it now?"

"It's not me who's backing out."

"No?" The man says. "Then give me the jewel and I'll be on my way."

"Let my daughter go."

"Give us what you agreed, Horace."

My father's eyes drop to mine, I can see it, for the first time, I don't see the strong scary man I know him to be, I see sorrow, I see fear. He's afraid. Does he think this man is going to take me? Does he think this man is going to kill me?

"Daddy," I plead, and my tears start to roll down my cheeks.

"Oh, sweetheart," The man holding me coos, "Your daddy's going to play ball, he's going to do exactly as expected, aren't you, Horace?"

My father nods, quickly, like one of those plastic toy dogs.

The man laughs again, before putting me down. He turns me to face him and I'm so petrified now I don't even struggle. As I stare up into those ice cold blue eyes I think he might actually be a monster.

He strokes my cheek, wiping away the tears. "Be a good girl, Sofia."

As soon as his grip loosens I fling myself at my dad. He catches me, holding me tightly.

"Be good, Horace." The man says, striding to the door. "Behave and no one has to get hurt."

As the door shuts I erupt into tears, sobbing against my father's chest. "I'm so sorry," I cry, like this is my fault.

"You should be." My father says, yanking my head back, forcing me to look at him. "I told you to stay in your room, didn't I?"

I gulp nodding. He did say that. He always says that.

"I told you bad things happen when you disobey me. But you didn't listen, you don't ever listen, Sofia."

"I just…"

"What?" He snaps, all but dropping me onto the floor at his feet. "You're a child. Learn to behave."

I don't know what I expected, I don't know why I thought he might be kind.

I stumble to my feet, but he pulls me back. His hand is wrapped around my arm as I struggle.

"Daddy, please," I gasp. "I'll be good. I promise."

He snarls, opening the draw and I know he's getting the stick before I even lay eyes on it.

"Please," I scream. Surely that man was punishment enough?

"You need to learn." He says grabbing me by my hair, forcing me to bend over the desk, only I'm not big enough to fit so he has to haul me up, and hold me down with my legs dangling off the edge.

As the lash comes down I scream more.

"Say you're sorry." He orders.

"I'm sorry, Daddy."

He strikes me again.

"Say you won't do it again."

"I won't, I promise." I sob. I'd say anything now, do anything to make him stop.

He hits me three more times, it's brutal and it burns, it bites into my skin - I doubt I'll be able to sit down properly for a week.

When he's done, he lets go of me and I slump onto the floor in a heap. I know he beats Roman when he's been naughty but it feels like I'm always the one on the receiving end of his punishments. That I never do anything right in his eyes.

He storms to the door, hollers for my governess who comes running, clearly flustered.

"Mr. Montague?" She says dropping a curtsey like he's a king.

"You weren't watching her." He says pointing in my direction with the stick.

Her eyes dart to me, "I'm sorry, sir, she must have slipped out."

"You need to do better." He says shoving the stick right in her face like he might hit her too.

"I will, sir, I promise I won't let her out of my sight."

"You better not." He snaps as she rushes past and hauls me to my feet.

I can't walk properly, my legs seems to refuse to work and she has to drag me out of the room, but as we pass the threshold my father grabs my head, pulling me back.

"Not a word of this, Sofia." He says in my ear. "Never mention that man to anyone, you hear me?"

I gulp, nodding.

"If you do, you'll get a lot more than a simple lashing."

I whimper, scrambling out of the room, unsure who I'm afraid of more, my father or that man with the dead eyes.

IT'S AMAZING HOW MUCH LIFE CAN CHANGE IN A YEAR. HOW YOU CAN go from existing in the very pits of hell to suddenly being transformed into a world where happiness exists, where the dead come back to life.

Where everything is supposedly back to normal as if none of it ever happened.

I stare up at the big white house that my brother and sister-in-law now call home. For a few weeks I lived here, no, I existed here. I barely remember all that much of that time. I don't want to remember. It's easier to blank it all out, and start afresh now.

The man on the security gate inclines his head and opens it enough for me to drive in. When I come to a stop I can see there are more cars on the drive than I expected. Roman's flashy new range rover is parked besides Rose's. And the classic Defender tells me that Ben is also here.

But there's a G Wagon alongside them. All black, with tinted out alloys. It looks like it's armoured as if that's a thing.

I squint as the realisation hits me of who else is in the house.

As I walk up to the front door, it opens and I step back taking in the enormous bulk of the man coming out. He stops immediately as our eyes connect.

I know him. I know his face. A memory stirs from what feels like forever ago.

'I was the one who made him pay'

His words echo in my head, reminding me of that awful moment, that awful time when I was still so weak. When I didn't even have the strength to defend myself.

"Sofia." He murmurs my name like it's a secret. Like it's forbidden. Like he savours every syllable.

His hair is up in its usual topknot. Dark stubble covers the lower half of his face and tattoos crawl up the skin along his neckline beneath his leather biker jacket. Everything about his screams danger and yet when I look into those dark, intense eyes they seem to hold me captive in a way that's thrilling, not petrifying.

My skin turns to goosebumps. Something visceral seems to take over everything, like I've suddenly taken leave of my senses. "Why are you here?" I ask quietly.

His lips curl as if me merely talking to him gives him some sort of pleasure. "I had business with your brother."

The wind swirls around us, whipping at my hair, I quickly tuck it behind my ears but it feels like he takes that moment to step closer to me, to close the gap between us as if he wants to block even the elements from harming me but I must be imagining that because it's a ridiculous notion.

I steal my breath and though even just the thought of it, of being in such proximity to a man should make me panic, for the first time my heart doesn't flutter in fear. My adrenaline doesn't spike. I just stare back at him.

As if I'm a creature of calm.

As if I'm a creature fully in control of myself.

"You look good." He says softly, keeping his eyes on my face. "You look well."

As I open my mouth to reply, my head jerks with the realisation that someone is stood watching us both.

"Ben." I murmur.

Koen narrows his eyes, glancing towards him, before a scowl covers his gorgeous face.

"Don't you have somewhere else to be?" Ben says stiffly walking up, physically putting himself between us like I need guarding, like he'd be able to stop Koen if he did decide to do something.

"Ben." I snap in reproach.

He grabs my wrist, pulling me away, and it feels like Koen watches us both, watches intently where we're now connected until we disappear into the house leaving him outside.

"What was that about?" I ask as soon as the door slams shut behind us.

Ben shrugs. "He's dangerous."

"You don't say." I reply sarcastically.

He fixes me with a look I can't read. But it's not just Ben, it's all of them, Roman, and Rose too. They all act like there's some big secret, some conspiracy I'm not privy to when it comes to Koen Diaz.

I wish they'd just say it. I wish they'd just admit whatever the hell is going on because clearly there is something. Do they think I'm too fragile? Do they think I wouldn't be able to handle whatever awful truth it is? Like I haven't faced enough shit already, like I haven't had to fight my way out of the very circles of hell.

"If he is so dangerous why is my brother still be working with him?" I bristle.

"Why don't you ask him that yourself." Ben grumbles.

I huff, following him through the house. I wish they'd all stop treating me like I'm a child. That I need protecting.

My brother is in his office, just like usual. We walk in and he's stood, staring out the window like he has the weight of the world still on his shoulders.

For a moment I just stand there taking him in, it still doesn't feel real. It still feels like this is all some drug induced dream and any minute I'm going to wake up, with Otto's disgusting face leering over me and Roman will be dead. He'll be gone. All of this will be gone too.

"Roman." Ben says pulling me out of my head.

My brother turns, his face going from a slight frown to a smile when he looks at me.

"Sofia."

I smile back, putting on that false brightness I'm so good at. "You summoned me."

He lets out a chuckle as I pull out a chair and sink into it.

Summoned isn't quite the word I'd use. More like demanded. But now I'm here it doesn't feel quite like the confrontation that I'd imagined in my head. The one I'd prepped for.

Roman pours himself and Ben a drink of whiskey and then puts a glass of water in front of me. I murmur my thanks, taking a sip. I haven't drank a drop of alcohol. Haven't been tempted too. Not since it all ended.

I don't like the thought of losing control. I don't like the thought of what else could be lurking in the glass. Water is safe. Water is clean. It's hard to hide a drug in it, it's hard to disguise the taste.

Roman watches me for a moment and I'll admit, I keep my eyes down, letting him. He's still the protective older brother, he's still looking out for me and I know he has my best interests at heart. Besides, after what we all went through, it's to be expected that he's jumpy.

"How's the therapy going?"

I arch an eyebrow. That's what he wants to talk about? My eyes glance towards Ben. I might lean on him, I might depend on him, but it doesn't mean I want him privy to my every secret.

Ben looks back with that same look he always has. One of love. Of devotion. One that says he would willingly die if it made me happy for just a moment. I don't know how to deal with him. How to deal with his feelings. Yes, I know he's in love with me - I'd be damned stupid not to notice. But I don't love him, at least not the way he wants or deserves.

"I can go if you want." He says.

"Why don't you go see Lara, I'm sure she's eager to see you." Roman replies not looking at him. Just keeping his eyes fixed on me.

Ben gets up, taking the bait because that's what he does, that's how he is. He's the nice guy. The good guy. He'd do anything for me, right?

I wince as that thought hits me. God, I'm a bitch. A heartless, nasty bitch.

"Sofia."

"Roman." I murmur as the door shuts.

"Talk to me."

"About what?" I half snap.

He lets out a sigh. "You burnt the house down."

I get to my feet, crossing the room, staring out the same window he was when we entered. The view is unbelievable. The sweeping garden looks like something out of paradise. I can see Lara running around, with the nanny chasing her, and then Ben as he approaches them both.

God, they really have sorted their lives, haven't they? Everything is just as it should be for them. I'm not jealous, I'm not bitter. It's just hard not to feel something akin to grief when I come here, when I see what I could have, what I could be if I wasn't so fucked in the head. If I could just love Ben, if I could just convince my heart that he was what I wanted, then I could have this too.

This happiness.

This peace.

Only I can't.

I can't love him.

And I hate myself for it.

Roman walks up behind me, staring out at the same picture perfect scene.

"Where's Rose?" I ask.

"Asleep." He replies.

I nod. Her pregnancy isn't exactly an easy one. It makes me wonder how on earth they managed to hide her last so well. But then, her parents locked her away, practically chained her to a bed by all accounts until Lara was born.

"Hastings was here." He says.

"When?" I ask, turning to look at him.

"First thing. He wanted to talk about you."

I narrow my eyes. "If he wants to talk about me then he should talk to me." I snap.

"He tried, Sofia, but apparently you keep ignoring him."

I bristle more. "It's none of his business."

Roman shakes his head. "I want to help, I want to…"

"What?"

He grits his teeth. We've never argued, not properly. I don't know why but we've always just understood one another, understood what the other needed. But that was before. Before everything went to shit, before I lost who I was, before they broke me, before I became nothing but a figure of sympathy to this city, a victim to feel bad for, and whisper about behind my back.

"You burnt the house down." He says again.

I let out a chuckle and the tension that's been slowly festering seems to subside. "What did you expect? I had to do something."

He shrugs. "You could have sold it. It was worth a fortune."

I jerk my chin. "I don't want his money and besides, selling it gives the wrong message."

"What message is that?"

"That my forgiveness can be bought."

His eyes flash. His hands move to grip my shoulders and I feel that awful twist at the contact. "Nobody thinks that, Sofia."

"No?" I murmur.

"If you speak to Hastings, we can bring them to justice."

I scoff. Like hell I'm going to do that. "I don't want that sort of justice."

"Then what do you want?"

I step back, pulling from his reach. I'm not his little sister anymore, I'm not the sad little girl who grew up without her mother, who needed her big brother to protect her. I need him to understand that. I need him to see who I am now. Who I've become.

"I want revenge, Roman."

"Hastings can give you that."

"No, he won't." I spit. "I go to him and the entire city gets to hear what really happened. They get to revel in all the horror of it, they get to feast on every nasty little detail."

"It won't be like that."

"No?" I snap. "Like it wasn't for Rose? You saw what they did, you saw what happened after Paris died. The gossip columns went wild with all the juicy details of how he abused her. What do you think they'll do when they hear what Otto and his mates did to me?"

Roman's eyes flash. "Darius was behind that."

"It doesn't matter who is behind it, Roman, this city hasn't changed." I state.

"I want to help you."

I let out a ragged breath. My heart is thumping, that awful sickening feeling is telling me how close I am to a full blown panic attack. I dig my nails into my palms using the pain to focus my headspace. I won't lose it now. I won't let him see me as weak.

"I know." I say as calmly as I can. "I know you mean well but I have to do this my way. I have to figure this out in my own head."

"We have to be careful, Sofia. Hastings won't turn a blind eye if we do something that draws his attention. He'll be forced to act."

"Right, because you all got your revenge. Darius is dead. The Capulets are dead. This city is back to its fully glistening majesty like the riots never happened but me…" I trail off as my anger ebbs and my mind tells me to shut up before I say something that would hurt Roman. "It won't be *us*." I state drawing in one long ragged breath. "It will be me, only me, so you don't have to worry about the repercussions."

He tilts his head. "I won't let you do this alone."

"Roman," I murmur, wanting so much to reach out and touch him but I can't. "Please just leave this alone."

He lets out a huff and I can see I've won whatever this is. He won't push me. He sees me as too fragile now.

A part of me hates that. I want him to rage, to scream, to prove that it's not the case. But he doesn't. He just accepts it, like I'm some broken pot put back together and he knows if he applies too much pressure all the gold covering my cracks will melt and I'll crumble back into tiny pieces.

"Why was Koen here?" I ask, changing the subject.

His look is everything I expect. There's a flash of something unreadable as he meets my gaze.

"We had some business to sort."

"Sure." I smirk.

I know they've been working together. They've been keeping it on the downlow but their alliance didn't simply stop when we reclaimed this city. No, I know the pair of them have been up to something. Plotting if you will.

"If you must know we're going into partnership." Roman states.

"Partnership?" I repeat.

He nods. "He has contacts and I have supply."

"Supply of what?"

He shrugs. "Weapons, guns, you name it."

"You're becoming an arms dealer?" I say half-shocked.

"Our father's businesses weren't legitimate enterprises. With Hastings in charge we have to be above board or he will take us down just like any other family in Verona."

"But arms?" I repeat. He's becoming one of them. A warmonger, a profiteer?

"The world is cruel place, Sofia. You know that more than anyone, if I simply stay on the peripheries, enjoying my millions as they slowly deplete, then our family will become weak, we'll become a target, just like before."

"Being an arms dealer makes you a target." I state.

He shrugs again. "Perhaps, but with Koen on our side it very much lessens that risk."

"So you're using him for protection purposes?"

"Protection, opportunities." He shrugs. "We're both bringing something to the table."

I let out a sigh. He's right about us becoming weak, our enemies are still out there. They may not be shouting from the rooftops the way the Capulets did but now is not the time to rest on our laurels. We have to be strategic. We have to be smart. Verona is still a vipers nest and we'd be fools to think otherwise.

"What are you doing for the rest of the day?" Roman asks.

I pull a face. I didn't have plans. Not concrete ones. I was simply going to go back to my penthouse and hide out.

"Stay then." He says. "I know Rose will want to see you. And Lara misses her aunt."

That comment makes me wince. Truth been told I've been avoiding them. Keeping away. When I'm with people I have to put a happy face on, to be the person I was before. But doing so, pretending all the time, it's exhausting.

And being around Ben, seeing the way he looks at me, the way he tries to do whatever he thinks will make me happy, all that does is make me feel more guilty.

The door crashes open. I physically jump so high I'm surprised I don't hit the ceiling.

"Aunty Sofia. Aunty Sofia." Lara screams barrelling into me and thank god she doesn't feel the way my body flinches at the unwelcomed contact.

"Larabell." I smile, pretending that I've not just had a complete adrenaline spike, pretending that my heart isn't now racing at a million miles an hour. That I'm not on the verge of a complete meltdown.

She grins up at me as Ben walks into the office with that sheepish look on his face and Bella is there, circling at my feet.

The little dog is a cross breed but clearly she's been recently groomed because she looks far more like a pug than usual, with her big bug eyes poking out and her crooked teeth on display.

"Stay." Roman mouths at me.

My shoulders slump, not enough for them to notice, not enough for anyone to see. But I give in. I nod. Reminding myself that I can't always be selfish, I can't always put my needs first. Family is about making sacrifices, about working together. If I want to get back to where I was, then maybe a bit of faking it till you make it could help - I mean it certainly can't make it any worse, can it?

CHAPTER

SOFIA

The hotel foyer is buzzing with people by the time I get back. There's been a four day carnival and the entire city is rammed to the rafters with all the extra tourists.

I don't mind the noise. I don't mind the commotion. Most of these people have no idea who I am as I make my way across the polished marble floor so I slip by like I'm a ghost, but then that's how I prefer it.

My driver dropped me off at the grand entrance so, thankfully, I didn't have to wander through the dark carpark alone.

I get to the lifts just as they ping open and behind me someone shouts out. Instinctively I turn in the direction of the sound.

There's a man staring right at me. He's running, all but sprinting in my direction. I step back, press myself against the back mirror. My heart is racing, my throat is constricting tighter and tighter as he gets closer.

I can't move.

I'm frozen paralysed as my fear engulfs me.

I want the lift to shut. I want whatever the fuck is happening to stop.

He rushes in, smiling. "Thanks." He says slumping against the wall in a way that tells me he's definitely drunk.

Reality hits me as I stare at him. He wasn't attacking me. He was just asking me to hold the lift.

He glances at me and I wonder if he can see the sweat on my brow or the fact that I'm as white as a damned sheet.

Maybe he can hear my breath, maybe he can hear how ragged it is.

"What floor are you?" He asks.

I gulp, unable to form any actual coherent words.

He glances at the row of buttons. "Oh, penthouse. Nice." He says flashing me another smile.

I give him a weak one back and then mercifully the lift stops. The doors open. Freedom seems to lurk just ahead of me.

"This is mine." He says and I nod like that's even a normal response. He gives me a strange, confused look that I don't doubt I deserve.

And then walks out, disappearing down the generic corridor to wherever his room is located.

As soon as I get into my place, I slump against the door. Christ, I really have lost it, haven't I? The poor man was simply trying to get to his room. He was simply doing what every normal person in this hotel does and yet I acted like a total freak.

I let out a groan, kneading my forehead.

My stomach rumbles, reminding me that though I had dinner barely an hour ago I didn't really eat all that much, I more picked at it. I don't like eating in front of others. I don't know why, I don't even know where the issue came from exactly but I feel so self-conscious, like I'm being judged.

But when I'm alone I eat just fine.

Maybe that's one of the reasons I still stay here. In this penthouse. I like the fact that I have twenty four hour room service. And I like the fact that they know to simply leave it by the door and not make a big deal of it.

I all but crawl over to where the phone is and order my favourite meal; cheeseburger with extra fries and a large strawberry milkshake. Yeah, I know I said I only drink water but this is the one indulgence I allow myself.

It's not healthy.

It's certainly not classy.

But I don't care.

Within these four walls no one is judging me. No one is watching me. I can completely and utterly fall apart and the only thing that witnesses it is the flickering faces of the TV that I keep constantly on like it's some kind of lightshow because I can't be in the dark. Not for a second. Not at all.

I kick off my boots, toss my bag, and force myself to go take a shower. By the time I'm out, dried, and wrapped up in the fluffiest bathrobe to exist the food is there, ready and waiting.

I grab the tray, carrying the entire thing over to the soft leather couch and I snuggle down, tucking my feet under me and slowly, deliciously, I devour every mouthful.

My phone buzzes with a notification but I ignore it, sinking back further into couch and I shut my eyes, feeling a moment of peace. A moment of contentment.

I survived another day.

I got through another twenty four hours of pretending that I'm normal. That I'm doing fine. That everything is just dandy.

And then a taste hits the back of my throat.

A metallic, bitter, nasty taste that I know only too well.

My heart suddenly lurches. I let out a cry as my eyes open so quickly.

This can't be happening.

No way.

My body trembles as I move. Already my muscles feel heavy, weighted, as some awful drug seeps further into my body. I reach out and everything on the tray beside me goes crashing to the floor.

My phone falls with it, landing oh so tauntingly just beyond my reach.

I all but roll off the couch landing in a heap and my hair soaks into the spilt remnants of my milkshake. I throw my hand out, frantically reaching for my phone and just as my hands find it, I hear the sound I've been dreading.

The one I knew would come.

Footsteps.

Someone is here. Someone is coming for me.

My fingers slide all along the screen. My eyes keep blinking like they want to close and never open. I don't know how I do it, if I even do it, but I try to dial Roman's number and just as it connects my eyes meet those of the hooded man who's now standing right over me.

I can't see his face. I can't make out any features. My vision is blurring. My head feels so heavy and all I want to do right now is just give in, just sleep.

But I know I can't do that.

If I let the drugs win, then I'll be powerless, defenceless.

He crouches down, brushing my hair from my face just as my brother speaks through the phone.

"Help." It's the only thing I can say. The only word I seem to manage to speak.

And I scream it hoping my brother hears, hoping he understands how scared I am, that I'm in danger, that I need him.

The man tilts his head, taking the phone from my weakening grasp and he hangs up.

I want to fight, I want to lash out, to kick, to scream, to do something.

But I'm so beyond that.

I blink. Then blink again. And that awful darkness takes me like a friend welcoming me back into the pits of hell.

"Sofia?"

I groan, turning my head at the sound. My body feels so stiff. I'm lying at an angle with one of my legs suspended above me and as I come around more I realise it's resting on the couch like I simply fell off it and forgot to get back up.

"Sofia?"

My brother calls more urgently.

I try to sit up, to force my arms to work and they do for a millisecond before they give way and I land back in the spilt milkshake.

Roman rushes to me, helping me up. Thank god the bathrobe covers me enough that I'm not indecent.

I mumble his name. My mouth feels so dry. My tongue feels almost scratchy.

"Jesus." Ben murmurs standing behind him and my face heats more with shame at the fact that he's here.

"What happened?" Roman asks.

I screw my face up trying to remember. Forcing myself to remember.

The metallic taste, the haziness, the man.

"I was drugged." I say.

Roman and Ben exchange a look.

"How is that possible?" Ben asks.

"Someone was here." I state. "A man. Dress, dressed in black."

Roman struts over to the phone, picks it up and starts barking orders to whoever is on the other end. Within minutes the hotel manager is there, in my room, trying to answer the barrage of questions my brother is half shouting at him.

Ben sits beside me, wrapping his arm around as if what I need right now is comfort. But I'm so tired I lean into him anyway, ignoring the way my body hates the physical contact, the way it protests against it.

"Do you want to go to the hospital?" He asks quietly.

I shake my head. I don't feel like anything happened, although it's hard to explain that out loud.

Roman all but grabs the manager, forcing him out of the room and while they're gone I just sit there, in silence, trying to calm the panic that even now, is right there, all but consuming me.

When he returns, his whole demeanour has changed.

"What is it?" Ben asks.

Roman glances at me then sinks down onto the other end of the couch.

"There's nothing in the footage." He says quietly.

"You mean they got in another way?" Ben replies.

Roman frowns more. "Sofia, are you absolutely certain you saw someone?"

I feel my anger spike. "Of course I did." I snap. "One minute I was fine and then next I was passed out."

Ben looks down at the plate, at the tray, at the drink that's still lying on its side on the rug. He picks it up giving it a sniff.

"How many of these have you drunk?" He asks.

I shrug. "It was just one milkshake."

He narrows his eyes. "Single or double?"

"Excuse me?" I reply before staring at the glass in his hand. Is that what happened? Is that how they drugged me? They simply slipped something into my drink? I curse myself for being so stupid. If I'd stuck to water then none of this would have happened. That's what my little treat cost me.

"There's alcohol in this." Ben says more to Roman than to me.

"No." I say. "I don't drink. I don't…"

Roman takes the glass from Ben and sniffs it before fixing me with a look.

Does he think I got drunk, is that it? Do they both think that I what, came back here, got wasted, and imagined the whole thing? That it's simply a projection of my wild imagination?

I get to my feet, trembling more. A wave of nausea hits me and I know it's a side-effect from what they gave me. Thank god it was only a sedative and not the other stuff Otto used to control me because that would not be so easily undone.

"Sofia." Ben murmurs.

"You don't believe me, do you?" I say. My voice high pitched with both panic and hurt.

"We didn't say that." Roman replies.

"You think I got drunk and it's all in my head?"

"No." Roman says getting to his feet.

My eyes are filling with tears. I never once questioned him, never once stopped supporting him.

Christ, it's happening again. Just like the last time. He thinks I'm lying.

"It's okay." He says.

"They drugged me." I state, hearing my voice catch, hearing myself start to give into the sob.

"I believe you, Sofia." Roman says. "I believe you."

"But you said…"

"Listen to me." He replies, tucking his hand under my chin, lifting my face to look at him properly. "If you say someone was here, then I believe you. If you say someone drugged you, then I believe you."

I can't look at him. I can't think straight in this moment. The fear of rejection, of betrayal, of all of it is spiralling inside me.

I pull myself away, stumbling back.

"Sofia." Ben murmurs.

"I…" My voice trails off as my head seems to spin once more.

I don't know what to do. I don't know how to convince them.

My brother catches me before I hit the ground and he sweeps me up into his arms.

"I'm taking you to the hospital." He says.

I whimper back as my hands dig into the fine fabric of his shirt. I don't want to go. I don't want to leave this space even though I know it's been compromised. But he's carrying me out, barking orders, already taking control and I'm helpless to do anything to stop him.

CHAPTER

SOFIA

I *stare up at the fluorescent lights as they whizz past my head.*

My father sticks to my side, his hand firmly on the metal rail of the bed they're transporting me in. His presence should be comforting, his presence should make me feel better - only it doesn't.

The corridor is empty beyond the occasional person in scrubs who passes us by without even looking our way.

"Daddy?" I whimper.

He shoots me a look, one that tells me to be quiet. To behave.

We reach another sterile looking room and I'm transferred across, laid out like a sacrificial lamb while something is clipped onto my thumb and they connect a tube to the needle in my hand.

"Daddy?" I cry louder.

"Stop that." My father says, slapping me around the face.

If the nurses in the room are shocked they don't react.

A man walks in, with a strip of fabric covering his hair and a pair of the weirdest looking glasses hanging from his neck.

"Hello, Sofia," He says smiling. "Are you excited for your surgery?"

I don't know how to reply. I don't even understand why I need surgery. I'm not sick. I'm not injured. There's nothing wrong with me.

"She's ready." My father replies, doing his usual trick of talking for me.

The doctor looks across at him and inclines his head. "I know my colleagues have been through the risks already, considering she's only nine years of age, and this is highly experimental…"

"It doesn't matter." My father cuts across him. "If you can fix her, if it will make her normal."

The doctor glances at me with a look that's full of sympathy. "We'll do what we can."

I flinch back, that word echoing in my head. Normal. I'm not normal.

"What's wrong with me?" I gasp. Am I dying? Surely I'm too young to die? Surely I'd know if I was? I'd be in pain. I'd be unwell. But I feel fine.

"There, there," A nurse says quickly, patting my hand. "You're going to be fine. We're going to put you to sleep and when you wake up it will all be done."

"I don't…" My eyes well up as I start crying. "I want to go home. Daddy, please, I want to…"

"Shut up." My father snaps, smacking me again. "You should be grateful. Most girls with your condition never get fixed, never get cured. You're lucky you're a Montague. You're lucky that these doctors even want to treat you."

"But I'm not sick." I repeat.

My father growls, turning his back on me. "Put her to sleep already." He instructs.

Again, the nurses exchange looks and the doctor nods his head.

I watch as they produce a plastic mask from what feels like nowhere. They press it to my face, covering my mouth and nose and though I don't want to breathe whatever it is in, I do it, I gasp, gulping in the gas. My eyes grow so heavy. My body feels like something is pressing down on it, but it's comforting, soothing.

The last thing I think before I drift off is that maybe my father is right, maybe I am sick.

Maybe this surgery will make me normal.

And that maybe, just maybe, doing this will be enough for him love me.

"Her bloods are clear."

I don't know what I expected. Did I think that I'd be vindicated? That these strangers in their clinical white coats would come to my defence?

Roman stares back at me and I can't tell what he's thinking in this moment.

I'm huddled up in the bed with the blankets pulled around me like some sort of shield. They put me in a flimsy gown that doesn't feel nearly covering enough. The bed seems to squeak every few seconds from how much I'm shaking and it's not doing my nerves any good.

"We can give her something to calm her." The medic murmurs to Roman as if he doesn't want me to hear.

I shake my head snarling. I don't want that. I won't have that. No way are they going to drug me now.

"Roman…" I plead.

He looks at me before shaking his head. "No." He says. "That won't help."

"You're sure?" The medic repeats, like he's all for strapping me in some straight jacket and throwing me into a padded cell.

Roman snarls, pushing him back. "Get the fuck out." He says.

Beyond the door I can see Ben pacing back and forth. Every few seconds he passes the glass window obscuring the light with his face all contorted into one of concern.

Roman sinks onto the edge of the bed and I steal my breath ready for whatever this conversation is about to be.

"Tell me what happened." He says gently. Calmly.

I shut my eyes, talking slowly, explaining how I came back, how everything was fine and then it really wasn't.

He frowns when I finish. "Why did you order food when you had dinner with us?"

I wince, not wanting to admit the truth, but if I lie now, if I withhold anything, he'll only see it as more evidence of me being duplicitous, me being the addict my family is starting to convince themselves that I've become.

"I didn't eat." I mutter. "Not properly. I don't like eating in front of people. I hate it."

His eyes react, he lets out a deep sigh like he's only just realising how truly broken I am. "Why didn't you tell me?"

My tears start falling before I can stop them. I let out a sob that sounds half choked. "I didn't want to disappoint you."

He grabs me, wrapping me into one his big bear hugs and though on some level it's so comforting the contact still makes my heart race, still makes me panic.

"You've never disappointed me, Sofia."

His words are meant to be soothing, reassuring, but all they do is make me cry even harder.

"Tell me what I can do to help." He says.

I reply the same thing I say every time. The awful truth that I know he hates. "There's nothing you can do."

I feel his shoulders slump. I feel the way he physically deflates. He's so used to fixing everything, only he's starting to realise he can't fix me. No one can fix me.

"You do believe me, don't you?" I whisper it.

He looks at me nodding. "Yes."

"You didn't last time."

I see the flash of pain, of regret, but it's clear he still thinks last time was my doing. That I intentionally relapsed. That I went on some massive drug binge like I was a crack-whore.

"Sofia…"

"I didn't do it." I hiss. "I wouldn't do it."

"I don't know what you want me to say…"

"Tell me you know. Tell me you believe me."

He lets out a sigh running his face over his hand. "No one is judging you, Sofia. We all make mistakes."

I fold my arms, scowling. He thinks that's what that was? A mistake? That I just woke up one day decided to add a little spark to everything, to get so fucking high I almost died?

"I'd never do that." I state. How can he not see? How can he not understand? I'd never put myself in that position again, I'd never let myself ever lose control.

"Okay." He says. "Okay."

"Are we done here?" I ask looking about the stark, sanitary space.

"Yes but you're not going back to that penthouse."

My eyebrows raise. "Why not?"

"If someone got in, if they drugged you then it's not safe there."

"If?" I repeat, narrowing my eyes.

He shakes his head like he's pissed at himself for slipping up. "You're coming back to mine."

"No." I snap. I won't do that. I won't be back playing happy families.

"Just for tonight. We'll figure something out tomorrow."

"I don't want to live with you. I don't want to be around…" My face heats as I trail off.

"I know. I get it." He says. "You need space and I'm not trying to take that from you but I'm not willing to compromise on your safety. You'll sleep at mine until we can figure something out."

"I'll get my own place." I state. "Tomorrow. I'll find somewhere."

He pulls a face like he wants to object.

"You can surround it with guards." I add. "Put a damn watchtower up if that's what it takes."

His lips curl at my tone. "Fine. Tomorrow we'll get you a place. It's about time you left that hotel anyway."

"I liked that hotel." I huff. "The room service was good."

He rolls his eyes. "Tonight it wasn't."

Yeah tonight it definitely wasn't. Maybe I should have seen that coming. Maybe I should have realised that was a weak point. God, do I need to hire a taster now? Someone to make sure none of my food is poisoned from now on? Could I even trust such a person to be truthful?

"Come on." Roman says getting up and holding his thick wool coat out for me to wrap myself up in. "Rose will be beside herself."

"You told her?" I hiss.

"You think she wouldn't notice me racing out in the middle of the night?" He replies as he wraps his arm around my shoulder protectively and leads me out to where Ben looks like he's torn between smashing the place up and cradling me in his arms - like he alone can protect me from all the worlds hurts.

"I'm okay." I say, giving him my best stoic smile.

He glances at Roman who nods just enough for me to notice.

"Let's go home." Roman says.

Ben's eyebrows raise but he thankfully keeps his mouth shut as we walk out into what is now the beginnings of morning.

CHAPTER

SOFIA

Lara wakes me up. She comes bouncing into my room and I groan, pulling the covers over my head hoping she'll get the hint to piss off and leave me alone. Only she spots me, in the far corner, and runs over to me.

"Wake up. Wake up." She cries in a far too cheery voice for my liking.

"Go away." I grumble.

"Did you sleep on the floor?" She asks frowning.

"I fell out of bed." I lie.

Her face calls bullshit but she doesn't say it. She just yanks on the covers again. "Come on, Aunty Sofia. Daddy's making pancakes."

My stomach grumbles like the traitor that it is and I give in, kicking the duvet off and feel the cold air hit me. I shudder despite the borrowed pjs I have on.

"Why don't you go down and I'll see you there?" I say.

Lara shakes her head, putting her hands on her hips. "No." She says. "Daddy asked me to check on you."

"Of course he did." I mutter, grabbing the spare robe and I wrap it round like it might just protect me from all the merriment I'm currently exposed to.

Lara grabs my hand, pulling me from the room and down the stairs so fast I almost trip.

I can hear voices from the kitchen. I can hear the sound of pots and pans and the smell of something delicious cooking.

Roman looks up surprised as we walk in.

"Lara." He says in a very dad-like tone.

"Daddy?" She says innocently.

"I thought I told you that Aunty Sofia was asleep and not to disturb her."

She grins, biting her bottom lip. "Is that what you said, Daddy? I thought you said go and wake her up?"

I let out a laugh before he can answer. Rose shakes her head but I can see the grin on her face too.

"Lara." She says after a moment, no doubt reminding herself that parents are meant to parent.

"It's okay." I said sinking into the nearest bar stool, lowering my hand to scratch Bella's soft ears and she leans into it appreciatively. "I was awake anyway."

Roman gives me a doubtful look and I do my best to ignore it. Besides, I'll admit it's amusing to watch Lara run rings around him the way he did our dad when we were growing up. It's almost cathartic.

"You okay?" Rose says quietly, once Lara is out of earshot.

"I'm fine." I say back.

She tilts her head, scrutinizing my face before nodding.

I know she gets it. I know she understands better than Roman, better than anyone. We weren't all that close before everything kicked off. In truth, I used to think she was a stuck up, prissy bitch. But then I learnt a few things. Realised a few things. They say appearances can be deceptive and that's never more the case than with my sister-in-law.

Roman starts dishing up pancakes like they're going out of fashion and Lara pours half a jar of maple syrup on top of hers before anyone can stop her.

"Not a chance." Rose says pulling the plate away, ignoring the protests of a eight year old and carefully scrapes the copious amounts off into the sink.

"You don't have to eat any if you don't want to." Roman murmurs.

I let out a sigh, pick up a fork and eat some anyway. He may say that but Lara will notice if I don't eat.

Ben will notice too - and he'll fuss.

It's easier to just comply. It's easier not to make a situation.

"But it tastes disgusting now, Mummy." Lara moans.

Rose gives her a deadpan look that makes even me cringe and then Lara gives in and stops protesting.

"So, you're going to get your own place?" Ben says quietly to me.

I look across at him and nod. "It's about time, don't you think?"

He smiles encouragingly. "Want someone to come house shopping with you?"

I can hear the hope. I can hear the kindness in his words too. He doesn't want to be pushy. He's just so desperately trying to support me in whatever way he can. So much of me wants to say no. I should say no. Giving in, being nice back isn't doing him any good is it? It's just hurting him.

"Sure." I say because somehow, for some illogical reason it feels like if I'm careful I can let him down gently. That soon he will give this all up and this way is so much better than carving his damn heart out.

He grins back, like I've agreed to go on a date and I wince ducking my head, spooning another mouthful of pancakes, forcing myself to chew, wondering if it might be better if I just choke and end it now.

"What are you grinning about?" Roman asks.

"We're going house shopping." Ben says.

Roman glances at me and I shrug. If it wasn't Ben then Roman would insist on coming anyway. This way I'm not monopolising all his time.

"Have you looked any up?" He asks.

I pull my phone, sliding it across to my brother. I don't want to admit that I spent half the night unable to sleep, unable to shut the thoughts whirling in my head and looking for somewhere to live felt like the best way of compartmentalising.

"These are nice." Roman says. "The one by the marina is beautiful."

I smile like I need his approval but my heart seems to react like I'm a six year old being praised for a shitty piece of art I did at school.

"Might be harder to keep secure though."

"Yeah." I reply, staring back at the screen. He's right. Anyone could sail right up to it. I doubt, despite our wealth, that we can afford an entire navy's worth of ships to guard me.

Rose gets up, collecting Roman's plate and piles it up with her own carrying them over to the sink. Technically they have maids, and chefs too, but they seem insistent on keeping themselves grounded. I'm not complaining one bit, I'd much rather it was just us than have a bunch of strangers constantly fussing around the way my father did. Breakfast is always a family meal, cooked by

Roman. The rest is more ad hoc. But dinner, they always have the chef cook them dinner unless they go out.

Rose lets out a murmur, running her hand along her back. Her belly is swelling enough now to show she's pregnant if you know her figure.

Roman is there in an instant, massaging her shoulders, soothing, and her face heats with whatever he says.

I love watching them and I hate it. They're so happy. They're so content. They've gotten everything they deserve and I know in many ways this pregnancy, though not planned, is like a dream because they can both enjoy the experience together the way they were never able to with Lara.

But watching them, seeing how normal they are, it only reminds me of everything I don't have. Everything I can't have.

How can I trust a man? How can I even be near a man in *that* way?

Otto's face seems to stir in my head. I can taste his tongue as he forces it into my mouth, I can smell his sweat as it covers me. Nausea races up and I swallow the vomit because I don't want anyone else to realise what just happened.

"You okay, Sofia?" Ben murmurs.

"Just a bit of reflux." I lie. Like that's it. Like I simply ate too many pancakes.

He glances at my plate, seeing how much is still left there and I think he might say something so I cut across him to make sure he can't.

"Shall we get ready?" I say brightly.

A micro expression crosses his face and then he gives in and nods.

"I'll be ten minutes." I say, getting up and disappearing, because the need to rinse my mouth out is overwhelming me.

We traipse from one house to the next. I don't know what exactly I'm looking for, it's not like I have a 'dream house list' or anything, but I guess I expected to feel something, to walk through the doors, and get a sense that one of these overpriced monstrosities felt like a home.

Only none of them did.

They were all too fancy, too fussy, too somebody else.

In the end, I settle on the most basic of them simply to be done with it. Ben side-eyes me as I fill in the paperwork and I can see he knows this house is merely a stop-gap, a temporary solution, just as the penthouse suite had been.

Luckily, it's fully furnished so I don't have to worry about fitting it out. The entire space is a mix of off-white, black and beige, as if the interior designers forgot that they had an entire rainbow worth of colours to work with. When I point that out, Ben is more than eager to suggest how we can brighten it up and, if only to stop him from ordering an shop worth of scatter cushions, I ask him to take me back to the hotel, to help me pack what little belongings I have and make this official.

By the time we get back, Roman has already sorted out what seems like an entire army of guards.

They stand, two abreast, either sides of the gate and as we drive through it feels like they're even suspicious of me.

I don't have any kitchen items. I don't have any real belongings beyond my clothes and I dump them in the walk-in closet, leaving them in the bags because unpacking them feels like far too much energy.

Ben loiters.

He produces mugs from god knows where and makes us coffee. Perhaps Roman left me a care package, emergency supplies, bread, milk, eggs, that sort of thing. If he did then Ben was the one who put them away.

When I walk into the kitchen, it feels stark, clinical. The white polished marble countertops gleam. The oven looks like something worthy of a Michelin star chef. A flash of guilt hits me because I doubt this place will be used for anything more than cheese toasties and takeaways – although now I'm worried about eating even those. Would someone go so far as to poison that? I doubt it would take long before whoever is behind this realises I'm no longer at the hotel. In fact, I suspect they're already more than aware. They probably had eyes on the place, probably watched every move I made, every time I left, every time I returned, maybe they even had someone on the inside, taking note of every order for room service.

I chill runs down my spine. Was I really that stupid? To put myself in such a vulnerable position?

"You okay?" Ben asks.

I sigh, looking at him. "Fine." I reply.

He narrows his eyes, seeing the obvious lie but like always he doesn't call me out on it.

"What do you want to do about dinner? We could order pizza?" He says.

Food. It's always food. That's my biggest weakness, isn't it? If I didn't need to eat, if my body could go without, then I'd be in a far safer position.

"Pizza is good." I state, feigning the enthusiasm I used to have. Pizza used to be my favourite. I used to live off it.

Ben disappears off, no doubt to talk to the guards and sort it out. In my head I figure I've got at least one days reprieve, one day of risk-free meals before *they* figure out where I am.

When he comes back he has a bottle in his hand, champagne no less, and he pops it while stating we should celebrate my newfound independence. I smile, I nod, I take the glass he hands me and I force down the drink because it's Ben, because he's trying to be kind, to be considerate and to refuse him now would be an insult.

The bubbles catch in my throat. The taste is far too sweet and it makes that feeling of nausea multiply.

When the food arrives I'm grateful to actually line my stomach but I still only manage a few slices.

Ben chats away merrily, he fills the empty room with that bright optimistic charm of his that I both admire and hate.

The house came with a huge cinema room. It seems ridiculous to have such a thing when I'm going to be living alone but for anyone else, such a place would be a luxury. Ben declares we should try it out and we end up, sprawled on the floor, with the pizza boxes around us, watching some action movie that I barely pay attention to.

I feel exhausted.

I feel drained.

I feel like days ago I had some sense of control – when I burned the house down, I felt like an avenging angel, I felt powerful, untouchable even. But now, now I feel like I'm back to me, the scared, fearful creature Otto created.

I don't mean to cry. I don't even realise I'm doing it until one silent tear becomes two. Until I'm silently sobbing.

Ben doesn't notice at first, he's too fixated on the massive screen in front of us but when he does he tenses, turning to ask if I'm okay.

"I'm fine." I lie.

He tuts, shaking his head and he pulls me into a hug. I can smell his aftershave, I can smell that light, sporty scent and it's so different from the one that haunts my nights. I shut my eyes, wishing that this felt more, that this was more. God, if I could just love Ben, if I could feel for him what he feels for me then maybe that would help heal this horrific pain inside me. It would fill that void.

"You're okay." He murmurs, stroking my back and I can hear it, the tone, the soothing way he's comforting me.

He's never felt like a threat, I know he would die to protect me, and what more could someone ask for? What more could someone want in a partner? He's strong, he's capable, he's good looking even with the scar that covers one part of his face, so why isn't that enough?

I pull away, blinking, staring at his face. His grey gaze meets mine and maybe it's the alcohol that makes me do it, maybe it's because I really am fucked up in the head, but I lean forward, I close the distance between us, kissing him slowly as if I'm testing this moment, expecting some sort of fireworks to go off, some cataclysmic explosion that will change everything I feel inside, that will fix everything.

He tenses, his hands rest of my shoulders and though he's kissing me back, I can feel he's not really committing to this.

Gently, he pushes me away, shaking his head a tiny bit. "Sofia," He murmurs.

"I, I shouldn't have…" I begin, feeling the heat rise in my cheeks. God, I've made this so much worse now. I'm such a fucking idiot.

"It's okay." He says in that understanding tone of his.

"No, it's not." I snap back. "None of it is okay."

His hands grip me tighter, he draws in a deep breath. "I love you, Sofia, I always have but I know you don't love me. Not like that. And it's okay..."

I sob more, I cry both from the shame of this moment and the fact that his words are true. I don't love him, I will never love him, and it hurts so much when I know that if I did, perhaps I'd find some peace, perhaps I'd find some happiness.

"…I understand it." He adds, as if that makes it better, because I sure as hell don't. "I'm not what you need. I never have been. I've accepted it. I can't change how I feel for you, I can't alter it, but I want to be a part of your life, even if that means I'll only ever be a friend."

I want to rage, I want to scream, perhaps it would be easier if he was angry with me, perhaps it would be easier if right now he called me out for my behaviour, but he doesn't, he's just so damned considerate, so reasonable.

I palm my face with my hands and he hugs me again, he comforts me as if I'm not the biggest arsehole in the world, and I bury myself in his chest, too embarrassed to look at him.

CHAPTER

KOEN

I'm on edge. Agitated. Roman told me to stay clear, that it was none of my business, like she means nothing to me. Like he believes she *is* nothing to me.

Yet it was my men guarding her, my men ensuring that even now, she is safe.

Except someone fucked up. Someone got close, too close. And Sofia almost paid the price for that ineptitude.

I like to think I'm a rational man, a logical man. Violence is delicate beast to control. As is fear. You create too much, you have anarchy. You don't create enough and you get this; failure, incompetence.

In my line of business, neither of those outcomes are acceptable.

Neither of those outcomes result in anything but death.

As I walk down the concrete steps, I can hear the noise, the bustle of a thousand people, all living their lives underground. I bought this house for one particular reason. One feature. It matches almost like a jigsaw to the tunnels beneath Verona. We had this hall added, these steps connecting the subterranean fortress to my now home.

Oh, I knew we could have moved everyone above ground, could have moved everyone into a military style complex but then we'd be visible, countable, trackable. This way no one knows the strength we have. No one understands the power we have. No one realises that I've turned myself from a hypothetical ruler of the underworld into a real one.

While Verona's elite walk in the sun, with their polished pavements and designer bullshit, we exist here, in the darkness, surrounded by our own treasure, protected. Un-fucking-touchable.

In the main hall I can see a bunch of them, off duty, drinking and gambling. I don't give a shit what they do with their time off, as long as they're not endangering us they can do as they like, but when my eyes spot the four men I'm looking for I make a beeline, crossing the room, hauling them off their chairs.

No one speaks. No one dares argue with me. Down here my word is law.

I pull my gun, point it right at the first man's temple. To his credit he doesn't try to argue, he doesn't try to justify why he failed. He just meets my gaze like he already knew he was a dead man walking.

I pull the trigger, blasting his brains out. Then I take aim, and pull again.

All four of them lie in a heap, their blood pooling around them.

"This is the price we pay for failure." I bellow. "You fuck up, you get us all killed."

It's that simple. It's that damned obvious. Sofia might be my biggest concern but she's not the only one. One mistake will mean the death of all of us. Failure is not an option.

"Clean this mess up." I growl.

We've got shit to do. We've got more names now, more locations. This isn't over until every last one of them is dead.

Sofia

The house is silent. Too silent.

Since Roman was exiled my father will barely even look at me. I think in total we've exchanged less than five words.

He eats alone in his study. He spends his time hauled up there, like he's trying to pretend I don't exist, like none of this is happening.

I normally keep to my own wing - that's a lesson I learnt a long time ago and it's worked for almost six years, it's kept me safe, but when I went down to the kitchens the staff said that he hadn't eaten anything all day.

It might not mean anything. The old codger could just not be that hungry but my gut tells me something is wrong.

So I do it, I break his cardinal rule and I step over the threshold, crossing into what I know is forbidden territory.

Every step I take feels like I'm condemning myself but, as I move steadily closer to the colossal oak door of his study, I tell myself that I'm not six years old anymore, I'm not a child, if he raises his hand then I will damn well raise mine back.

To my surprise the door is ajar. I tighten my grip on the silver tray, the food might be lukewarm at best now but it gave me an excuse, a justification for being here. He can hardly accuse me of snooping when I'm acting like I care about his wellbeing.

"...It's done." My father growls, making me pause. I wasn't aware anyone else was in the house. That anyone was visiting.

"You're certain?"

"Of course I am."

I gulp, recognising the other voice more from the telly than anything else. So Darius is here. The great Governor himself has deigned to pay us Montague's a visit.

I lean forward, sneaking a peak through the gap. My father is sat at his desk, no surprise there, a puff of smoke is emanating from the oversized cigar in his hand and the room is foggy with it.

I can't see Darius, but as he moves, a shadow tells me that he's close, that he's right by the door.

"I want proof." Darius replies.

"You know I can't provide that."

"No?" Darius sounds almost amused, but I can tell under that playful tone he's not messing around.

"We agreed the steps." My father states. "And I have done my part. It's time for you to do yours."

Darius seems to bristle, "They'll get the second half when I decide."

A bang makes me jump. My father's hand remains on the leather top where he smacked it. "They are not fucking around."

"You think I don't know that?" Darius sneers. "You think we're not a match for them?"

"You have resources, Darius, but you know full well I do not."

I can't see the Governor's face well enough to judge his reaction but it feels like he doesn't seem to care all that much.

"You fucked that up when you sided with the Capulets." My father states.

"You fucked it up yourself." Darius retorts. "We were doing fine until you got greedy."

"Greed had nothing to do with it."

"No?" Darius muses. "Why else did you try to bring in new partners? You tried to sideline me, Horace, that wasn't a smart move."

"You think I wouldn't act?" My father spits. "You think I'd just let it all go?"

"She's dead." Darius snaps. "She's been buried and rotting for more than a decade."

"Aye, and don't we know why?"

I don't know for sure but my gut tells me they mean my mother. That her death started something, or ended something, only I thought she died of a stroke, so how could that possibly be the case?

The door opens.

I blink, stepping back, only just managing to keep the tray straight and to not pour the entire contents onto myself.

"Sofia?" Darius says surprised, with a smile that I'm sure is meant to be disarming. I know he's a 'lady's man' as they say, I know half the city's population is in love with him. I just don't know how to react to such attention, I'm too awkward, too shy.

"What are you doing here?" My father snarls. Yeah, he's pissed at me.

"You didn't eat breakfast, or lunch." I state, trying to avoid Darius as I step into the room. "I thought you might be hungry, or sick…" I add.

"You are lucky to have such a devoted daughter." Darius murmurs.

My father narrows his eyes, grunting, like can't even bring himself to pretend that he cares.

I can't help the shake as I carry the tray and I know the Governor sees it. Does he think I'm afraid of him or does he realise it's my own father that scares me shitless?

"Here," Darius says, taking it off me. "It looks far too heavy for you."

I smile politely, folding my arms. A voice in my head tells me I should go, that I should leave them to it. I've seen he's alive and well so there's nothing else for me to do. Besides, if I can get out now maybe my father might just let this go, though that's unlikely.

I take a step back, then another, but Darius is quick to put the tray down and to grab me. His hand latches onto my forearm and he guides me back. "Don't rush away." He says in a tone that sounds almost seductive.

I glance at my father and he's glaring at me but we both know Darius holds the power here.

"You don't go out." Darius says to me. "You don't come to any of our balls, or events."

"I prefer not to." I mumble. Jesus, I'm barely eighteen, does he really think I'd be out partying all the time? My cheeks heat at the way he's looking at me, the way he's almost devouring me.

"She's a loner." My father says in a manner that shows his disapproval. "She always has been."

I try not to react, not to wince, but as usual he knows exactly how to hurt, how to cut me down. Roman was the popular one. Roman was the society darling. I've always been an outcast.

"Maybe we should change that." Darius says, placing his hands on my hips.

I jolt, something seems to sliver down my spine and I step back to escape him, only he steps forward.

"A beauty such as yourself, you shouldn't be hiding away." He looks across at my father who is now on his feet, clearly pissed. "Horace, you should have done better, you should have introduced her to…"

"She's hardly neglected." My father snaps. "She had the best governesses, clothes, jewels, I even got her a damned horse, though it cost me a fortune in vets bills."

Yeah he did, he did all of that but it wasn't for me. No, it was to pretend to the world that he didn't love his son and hate his daughter. But more importantly, it was that no one would realise the truth; that no one would realise I wasn't worthy of being a Montague. That I was faulty. Diseased.

"Pfft," Darius says dismissively. "What the girl needs is a bit of fun. I doubt being cooped up in this house all day gives her that."

"I'm happy here." I say, though happiness is not exactly the word to define it. More like I'm comfortable here, as long as I stay in my rooms then no one judges me and I'm free to do as I please. I go to the club house most days, I read, what more could I want?

Darius frowns, dropping his gaze, and I swear he's staring at me, at my body but he's at least three my age, why the fuck would he be looking at me like that?

"Is there anything else you need?" My father asks, cutting through the tension, making it ten times worse.

"No," Darius replies, mercifully letting me go. He turns to face my father and I step back, far enough away that if I need to I can run from both of them. "I'll be in touch." He murmurs.

Once he's gone I let out an exhale. Apparently I am afraid of him, but not as afraid of the raging monster now focused on me.

"You stupid bitch." My father growls.

"I'm sorry." I say quickly. "I didn't mean anything, I was just…" His hand slapping my face silences me.

I fall backwards, flailing and I only just manage to stay on my feet.

"You never learn." He states and then he seems to deflate, like he doesn't have the strength to beat me properly anymore.

I blink back at him, seeing the way his hand is now pressed against his chest.

"Father?"

"Get away," He bats my hand off like I'm contagious, and then he slumps against the desk.

"You need a doctor." I say.

"I need no such thing." He retorts.

I know I shouldn't care, I know this man has shown me who he is enough times that I should just walk away and leave him to it, but he's my father, my only parent, and with Roman gone, who else do I have?

I grab the pills from the drawer. He thinks I don't know about them but he's not exactly subtle when it comes to taking them. I looked them up when I managed to learn the name. Apparently my father has heart failure – I'll admit I find that somewhat ironic considering he never seemed to have a heart. Perhaps it grew weak from lack of use.

"It doesn't matter now," My father mutters. "Roman is lost and you…"

"What about me?"

He gives me that same look of scorn, of disappointment. "What will you ever amount to?" He asks. "You don't have friends, you don't have allies, once I'm gone this city will tear you apart and feast on your corpse."

I narrow my eyes. It's not like I intentionally ended up this way. He's the one who kept me apart. He's the one who kept all but locked away from the world. "If I'm such a failure why don't you let me leave?"

Oh, I've begged him, I've pleaded with him to let me escape this house, to let me have some form of independence, but he won't have it.

He scoffs. "You think Roman wants you? You think anyone wants you? He's probably happier in exile than he ever was growing up with you as sister."

My eyes sting, I shouldn't cry, I mean, it's not like I haven't heard his insults before. I know I'm a disappointment to him, I know because of my condition I'll never be the daughter he wanted but I'm still his flesh and blood. Why isn't that enough?

He pushes me aside, shuffles to his chair and plonks himself into it before shoving a load of pills into his mouth and taking a long swig from the bottle of whiskey he keeps stashed away. I doubt his drinking is doing him any favours but I keep that opinion to myself.

As he puts the bottle down he fixes me with a look. "They'll be coming soon."

"Who?"

His eyes drop, he stares at what I assume is the fireplace behind me.

"If Darius doesn't deliver his end then we'll be the first to fall."

"What are you talking about?" I snap.

He grins at me, looking almost manic. "You may well wish Alistair killed you all those years ago." He says. "Better to have died as a child than to live through what they'll do to you now…"

My heart lurches. Neither of us have spoken about that night, about any of it since. Sometimes I wondered whether I imagined the entire thing, that perhaps I'd just had an overactive imagination.

"The man with the blue eyes." I whisper.

He nods. "They'll come. And if I'm dead, then they'll take their pound of flesh from you."

"What the fuck is this? What is going on?" I hiss. Only he doesn't answer, he just sits there, broken and defeated.

"...And how did that make you feel?"

I blink back, staring at his almost nondescript face. With his horn-rimmed glasses, and his neatly parted hair, he looks the exact image of what a therapist would be if you googled it. He's practically a cardboard cut-out, with his brown tartan knitted jumper and his beige, boring slacks.

"Sofia?"

I grind my teeth. My anger spiking enough that I'm contemplating picking up one of the thick leather bound books from his shelf and smacking him with it till he shuts the hell up.

On the window the stick of incense is churning out a steady stream of smoke, filling the room with what I guess is meant to be a calming hint of lavender, vanilla, and something else I can't quite put my finger on.

I don't know how many sessions I've had now. I used to keep count, but when the numbers got above twenty I stopped caring. If I had my way I wouldn't be here at all - but these are court-ordered, though there's no legal paperwork to state that. No, this was a deal Roman and Hastings thrashed out after my last 'incident' hit the headlines.

Neither of them believed my side of the story.

Neither of them believed that someone drugged me, that someone set me up. I guess it was a hard story to sell when one minute I was walking through the ruins of the old Montague House and the next I was lying in a street, high as kite, as if I were just another addict.

So here I am, stuck with Martin. God, even his name irritates me though I can't pinpoint why.

Most sessions I barely speak, what right does he have to pick through my trauma anyway? To determine how I should correct my behaviour as a result of it.

But the few times I have - the few times his probing questions have broken down walls I know were crumbling - I've come away a complete mess and it takes me days, weeks even, to get over it. And then I have to see him again. Like a bad record on repeat.

"They recorded you." He says. "That must have felt violating."

I blink, registering the words, feeling another flash of rage. Violating? He thinks having a camera shoved in my face was the worst of it?

"Was there no point in which you decided to play along?" He asks.

My nails cut into my palms. My heart suddenly stops as something close to actual fury engulfs me. "Play along?" I repeat.

"Many in your situation might have chosen to do so…" He smiles gently.

"My situation?"

"Abusive marriages."

I'm on my feet, I don't even realise I'm stood up until I'm towering over him. "They drugged me and raped me, over and over and over." I snarl. "They tortured me, they…." I lose my words as a wave of trauma so sharp cuts through my thoughts. "You think I should have played along? You think I should have smiled sweetly while they queued up to fuck me, one after another?"

"That's not what I meant, Sofia." He says moving to stand.

"You have no idea what you're talking about." I hiss.

"Sofia,"

I gulp as he stares down at me. He's only a head taller than me, but something, some fear in me stirs.

I step back, trying not to stumble over my own feet. "Don't touch me." I snarl as he reaches out as if I need a hand.

"Maybe we should call it a day." He says gently.

"Maybe we should call it entirely." I snap back.

He fixes me with that disappointing look I think he must practice in the mirror because he's got it down to perfection. It's one I've dreamed about wiping off his face. "I'll see you in a week."

I grunt back, grab my bag, and practically sprint as quickly as my legs will carry me.

As the door slams shut behind me all that tension, all that fear and panic subsides. Maybe it's because that room is becoming as much a trigger for me as my memories are. Maybe it's because my therapist is a man.

I asked to see a woman, but apparently Martin was the 'most qualified', though I have no idea who made that decision.

I let out a sigh, a breath of air that isn't full of lavender and vanilla, and I turn, wanting to be away, to be back, safe in my own four walls.

The lift is broken, has been broken for some weeks – you'd think they'd get it fixed considering it's an access point, but apparently it's not high on their list of priorities, so instead I take the stairs. It's only three flights so not all that arduous but the space is cold in a way that makes you wary.

Every step echoes on the beige vinyl covered floor.

I'm wearing heavy boots, doc martens, ones that would hurt if I needed to fight but even they make a racket as I make my way down.

My skin starts to prickle. My hair stands on end. I glance around but there's no sound, nothing – it's just me. I readjust my bag, picking up pace, once I'm out, once I'm in the car, I can relax but until then I feel more than a little jittery.

As I reach the door, I yank it open, but someone is there, taking up the entire space beyond. He looks like a giant. An actual fucking monster.

I let out a cry, stepping back, my logical brain telling me I'm overreacting just like I did before, but my heart, my fear is telling me to get away, to run for my life.

He's quick to close the distance, quick to pounce.

I sprint back up the stairs but I barely make it halfway before I'm slammed into them, shoved down by the weight of a man twice my size. I kick out, I scream as a hand clamps down around my mouth.

"Stop fighting." He growls in my ear, as if I'd do such a thing, as if I'd just give up.

The needle bites into my skin. I scream more, I jerk, not caring what the consequences are – *they're* drugging me. *They're* doing it again.

And I can't have that.

I can't go back there. I won't let them turn me back into that shell of a person.

But it's too strong, too powerful. I can't fight it as it takes over my system.

My eyes roll back in my head, my body goes limp, and I'm useless, helpless, completely and utterly fucking defenceless.

HANDS.

Too many hands.

Touching where they shouldn't. Holding me down. Preventing me from moving.

I groan, trying to get my bearings. My head hurts like I've drunk the entire contents of a wine cellar. My body aches as though I've done ten rounds in a ring with someone far more capable of boxing than I am.

I can hear a radio, chattering, sirens.

There's too much noise. I feel dizzy. Sick. Completely confused as the world around me does somersaults.

I blink, trying to focus on the now.

And when I register what's happening, that I'm being carried, I freak out more.

"Calm down." Someone says, as if I'll just obey and become docile.

I snarl, I jerk, trying to get free.

"Put her on the gurney."

"She's drunk."

"We might need to strap her down for her own safety."

"No," I gasp but no one is paying attention to me.

As my eyes focus, as the horrible blur seems to fade, I realise I'm in a woods, no, a park? There's police everywhere, a crowd too. Lights are flashing, cameras are flashing. It's evening. Where the hell have I been all day?

My heart is racing, my body is shivering from the cold. I had a coat on this morning but apparently that's gone now.

I don't know how I got here. I don't understand what the hell is going on. As the person holding me places me onto the gurney, I take in their uniform, the fact that they're EMTs. Have I been in an accident? Am I hurt? I don't feel hurt, at least not seriously but then my body is so used to pain I wonder if it'd even register it.

"How much have you drunk?"

My eyes, my head turns to the other one, the other EMT with the scowl on his face, who's looking at me like I'm total trash.

I shake my head. "I don't drink."

Raised eyebrows and disbelief is the response I get.

"I need my brother." I state. "I need Roman."

They don't reply. No one replies. They just begin moving me towards the waiting ambulance.

And then my mind whispers that this is all a trick, that they're not really EMTs, that this isn't a real accident. This is a ploy, a way to kidnap me again. Afterall, they faked my brother's death didn't they, they went to such lengths to silence us Montagues, who says they won't do it again?

My fear twists, my panic rises, I start fighting, I start screaming. I'm not even sure of the words coming out of my mouth, I just know that I can't trust these people, I can't trust anyone.

"Sedate her." Someone yells.

I scream out. I lash out. I won't let this happen, not again, I'm not going down without a fight. I refuse to be that weak person again.

A needle jabs into my neck. I feel it tear my skin as I try to pull myself away. Someone swears. Straps suddenly pin me in place and a voice that's meant to be soothing is telling me to calm down. To be reasonable.

Sure, I'll just lie back down and let them kidnap me.

I can feel my tears streaming down my cheeks. I can feel my body turning sluggish, and as the supposed ambulance pulls off, any fight I have left is gone.

CHAPTER

SOFIA

"Jesus fucking Christ."

I hear the voice but I don't respond. No, I can't. I feel dazed, confused. My limbs are heavier than ever and I can't seem to break out of whatever this awful exhaustion is.

A machine is beeping and that should be enough to tell me where I am.

But it's Roman, his questioning, his terse voice that tells me that something really bad has happened.

"It's all over social media."

Ben. So he's here too, is he?

I groan, turning my head, feeling the coolness of a pillow making contact with my cheek. I'm so thirsty. It feels like I haven't drunk anything in forever.

"Can you take it off? Get it removed?"

This voice is higher, a woman's, and she's closer to me.

"No, you know that, Rose."

I try to sit up, I try to move but my body won't respond.

"Her blood alcohol level was through the roof." Ben states.

"She doesn't drink." Roman replies.

"So, how do you explain this?"

I hold my breath, waiting for the words, for him to admit that he can't, that obviously I've gone on a binge again, that I've gotten so drunk I've caused an accident of sorts. That I'm out of control. That I need help, real help.

Someone takes my hand, my adrenaline spikes at the sudden skin to skin contact and the machine starts beeping more and more rapidly.

"Sofia will wake soon enough." Roman says and I realise it's him, he's holding my hand. "She'll tell us what she knows."

"Roman," Ben begins.

My brother snarls, and whatever he does, however he moves, it causes his arm to jerk and my own with it. "You didn't see it, you didn't see the look of betrayal on her face, the hurt too."

"When?"

"Last time we were here. Last time the doctor suggested she'd made it all up." Roman states.

I don't hear the reply. I don't hear anything. That darkness takes me again and I fall into it, waiting, dreaming, seeing flashes of memories that make no sense whatsoever.

I WAKE WITH A GROAN. RELIEF FLOODS THROUGH ME AS I REALISE I can move, I can sit up. I'm no longer trapped.

"Easy," Roman murmurs and I blink staring at him.

He looks dishevelled. His hair is messy, his clothes have creases from where he's been leaning on them and his eyes have bags under them like he didn't get much sleep, like he's been keeping watch.

My eyes dart to the door. I know I'm in the hospital. I know something happened. I just can't quite connect all the dots in my head.

"Can I have some water?" I ask quietly.

Roman stands, crosses the room to where the trolley is and pours one out. I clasp the plastic cup with both hands and gulp down the contents. My head still hurts but it's a dull ache now, the kind of hangover you get on the second day.

"How are you feeling?" He asks gently.

"Off." I reply.

He sinks back into the blue, spongey looking chair and crosses his leg, placing his ankle on his knee. "Tell me what happened."

I gulp, staring at the now empty cup. "I don't remember."

"None of it?"

I can hear the tone, just enough, just a little edge to give away how close to losing control he really is.

"I only remember leaving the therapist's office, coming down the stairs. Someone was there, waiting for me. They jumped me, they jabbed me with a needle and then there's nothing."

He narrows his eyes, studying my face as if he expects to see a different truth written there. "So you don't remember going to a garage and buying a Ferrari?"

"What?" I frown. Why the fuck would I do that? I can technically drive, I have a licence, I just never saw the point when my father always had men to drive us around.

"You bought a three hundred thousand dollar car, drove it halfway across Verona then crashed it into a tree while twice the legal limit."

I stare back at him, barely registering the words. Why the fuck would I do any of that? Why would I even get behind the wheel of a car, let alone buy one?

"I didn't…" I begin, then swallow. "There must be some mistake."

He lets out a sigh that sounds far too close to a snarl. "There's CCTV footage. You used your own bank cards, and the blood tests have come back proving you were intoxicated."

"Roman,"

He gets up and starts pacing.

"Roman," I say louder.

"What?" He snaps back.

"I didn't do it."

He shakes his head and that anger flashes across his eyes. "Jesus, Sofia, I can't protect you if you keep doing shit like this."

"Like what?"

"Like…" He waves his hand in exasperation and I think in that moment I truly lose control.

I kick off the covers, force myself to stand. "I didn't do it." I scream. "I didn't fucking do it."

He slams his fist into the wall, and because this hospital is apparently made of cardboard it goes almost the entire way through. The door crashes open, two uniformed men come rushing in, and pause on the threshold, assessing us both like they can't tell which one of us is the threat.

"Get out." Roman orders.

The one on the right begins to object and Roman all but hauls them out, stating no one is allowed in until Hastings gets here.

Hastings - so this all hinges on him again.

I stare back at my brother as that sinking feeling in the pit of my stomach gets worse. "You don't believe me, do you?"

"I want to." He replies. "I want to believe you, Sofia."

"But you don't." I gasp. "You think I'm an addict, you think I'm a drunk."

He moves to touch me and I flinch back, all but slamming into the equipment that I'm still technically hooked up to.

"Stay the fuck away from me." I cry.

"Sofia, I will never hurt you."

My anger spikes, my pain, my agony seems to twists, and I know I shouldn't say the words but I do, I say them anyway, hurling them at him like daggers. "You already have, every time you choose not to trust me, not to listen to me, every time you look at me and believe that I would willingly go down such a path…"

"No one would blame you." He says cutting across me.

"Excuse me?"

"After what you went through, after everything you endured, no one would think less of you. Trauma fucks with people's heads."

I see red. I don't stop to think of the consequences. I don't stop to think how he might react. I hurl the plastic cup that's still somehow inexplicably in my hand.

It smacks into him and he curses.

"You bastard." I hiss. "You bastard."

"Sofia,"

"Get out." I can't calm down, I can't get a hold of my anger, it feels like an explosion that's been building for so long that now that it's gone off, now that it's finally broken loose, it's a tsunami threatening to destroy everything in its path.

Roman blinks back at me like I might just change my mind, like I might just apologise and say he's right all along, and that this is all some misunderstanding. Silly me, drunkenly buying a car and forgetting all about it.

Only, that's not what I think. Not how I feel. I grab the pillow hurling it at him, then the blanket, then anything I can get my hands on.

He might not have been the cause of my trauma, he might not have been responsible for how badly our plan turned out, but I did it for him. I sacrificed myself for him, for Rose too. And now that they have their happy ending, it feels like he doesn't want to see the horrible truth of what it took to get it. What this world, and what Otto Blumenfeld in particular, extracted from me as the price.

When I'm alone, I sink onto the floor, yanking out the damned plastic needle thing that connects me to the drip – it's not like it was doing anything anyway.

I huddle up in the corner, my head racing as I realise *they've* done it again. They've set me up and this time, this time it's way worse.

Will I go to prison? Will Hastings see this the same way Roman does, that I'm out of control, drunk, a true addict now? Will they send me back to rehab? Fuck, I hope not, last time I was there I considered ending it more because of the people around me. I'm trembling, shaking, fearing the worst and hating the fact that there's nothing I can do, that whoever is behind this is winning a game I don't even understand.

The door opens. I glance up, convinced it's Roman and open my mouth to tell him exactly where he can shove it – only it's not him.

"You look like shit." Hastings says stepping inside, shutting the door behind him in a way that makes me wonder if there's a throng of people jostling to get a glimpse of the 'Heroin Heiress' as the press likes to name me.

"I feel like shit." I reply.

He draws in a deep breath, making a point of studying the strewn items as he raises his eyebrow. "I take it the bedding was not to your high standards?"

I narrow my eyes, waiting for the teasing tone to change. Hastings always seems to be wary of me, like he knows something I don't, but whatever it is, whatever horrible thing he discovered, he doesn't seem keen on divulging it. Maybe that's why he pisses me off.

"Where's your brother?" He asks.

"Hopefully he's fucked off." I snap.

He tilts his head, understanding registering. "You two had an argument, I take it."

I draw myself up, force myself to stand, placing my feet wide enough apart that it feels like I'm about to do battle. "I don't need him."

"Yes, you do."

I snarl, clenching my fists, "Whatever you think…"

"Sofia, you are not a child so do not act like one."

That makes me pause. He thinks I'm the one being childish? That I'm simply having a temper tantrum like some errant teenager?

"Verona is not safe." He says. "You of all people know that. Do you think losing Roman's protection will do either of you any good?"

"What do you care?" I hiss.

His eyes soften, that stern, fatherly looks seems to ease just a little. "Not everything is a fight."

"Maybe not for you." I mutter. My entire life up until this moment has been exactly that. One bitter fight after another and I'm exhausted by it. I'm utterly drained.

He runs his eyes over me, in that same, careful, assessing manner and then he walks back to the door muttering to the officer just beyond.

When he comes back in, he waits for a moment, until someone appears with two coffee cups. He hands one to me, stating that he hopes I don't decide to toss this at him.

I scowl, taking a sip, relishing the hit of caffeine before that voice whispers in my head that even this could be poisoned, that the very cops outside my door could be in on it. I gulp, staring down, refusing to take another mouthful.

Hastings leans against the wall, watching me in that silent judgey way and then Roman walks back in like I didn't send him running with his tail between his legs.

"Get out." I cry.

"Enough." Hastings says before Roman can speak. "We need to have a conversation and Roman needs to be here."

I narrow my eyes, putting the coffee down, just in case. "Why?"

"Roman is a part of this, you both are."

"A part of what?" Roman asks.

"Whatever is going on with Sofia."

"I didn't do anything." I state.

Hastings holds his hands up. "I know. You misinterpreted what I was saying. What I meant was, I believe you, I believe someone is playing games, but what I don't understand is why."

I stare at him. My mind repeating that line over and over. He believes me. He doesn't think I'm an addict. I look across at Roman and he meets my gaze with no show of emotion.

"They want me to look like an addict." I state. "They want the world to believe it. That my trauma is so much I decided it was easier to just give up." My last words come out like venom, I aim them right at my brother and he winces enough to tell me they hit home.

"I'm sorry." He says, like that makes up for it.

I don't reply. I don't say a word. I never once second guessed him, never once doubted him. I gave everything I had, I sacrificed everything for him and this is how he responds?

"I'm putting some people onto it. It's hush hush obviously." Hastings says.

"You think you can figure it out?" Roman asks.

Hastings looks from my brother then to me. "Is there anything you want to tell me, anything you're keeping to yourself that might explain this."

"Like what?" I ask.

He shrugs. "You burnt his house down, a lot of secrets went up in smoke."

"You think I'm hiding something? That I'm, what, protecting them?" I snarl.

"Not protecting them." He says in that same calm, reasonable manner. "But a lot of the evidence was destroyed. Tell me you don't have something squirrelled away that you're planning on using for revenge."

"I don't." I huff. God, if I actually had something does he really think I wouldn't have used it already? Do I really look like I'm that patient?

He sighs with frustration.

"You think they're after something in particular?" Roman guesses.

"What else could it be?" Hastings says. "We haven't prosecuted any of them, your sister can't even give us any names beyond her late-husband, right now, they're all sitting pretty so why would they rock the boat?"

"They want Verona to think I'm a mess." I state. "They want to discredit me, to undermine me."

"That's what I believe." Hastings replies.

I let out a huff. It's not a bad plan. In fact, it's a pretty smart one, after all, how believable can I be when Verona thinks I spend my life either drunk, or high, or both?

"So what do we do?" I ask. There's still the matter of a wrecked Ferrari and my apparent DUI.

"Leave it with me. If they're out there…"

"I meant about me." I cut across him. "I meant the car, the supposed drink driving."

He scowls. "That is where things get tricky."

"In what way?" Roman asks before I can.

"By now, most of Verona would have seen the footage." Hastings states, giving me a sympathetic look. "We can't deny it was you. We can't deny you were over the limit either."

"But I didn't do it. I didn't choose to get in that car…"

"I know." Hastings says. "But we also have to play the game, thanks to Darius we're all now under a lot more scrutiny."

"So what, I have to pay the price regardless?" God, is he saying what I think he is, that I'm going to jail for this?

"You'll be banned from driving for the next year. And you'll have to submit to regular drug testing."

I should feel relieved. I should feel like this punishment is okay, I mean, it's not like I drove before so who cares if I can't get behind the wheel again? But I do care. I feel fucking furious. Especially given the fact Hastings knows as well as I that this was a setup.

"What if they drug me again? What if I fail the test?" I ask, voicing the other concern I have. What if I agree to this and it only comes to bite me in the arse further down the road?

He narrows his eyes. "We'll make sure that doesn't happen."

"How? They can still get to me, you can't guarantee…"

"The test will not come back positive." Hastings replies giving me a hard look.

My jaw drops. Hastings is always so damned straight I'm not sure I believe the unspoken words. That he'll fake the results if necessary.

Roman crosses the room, standing beside me but far enough to not touch me. "I've got your back, Sofia. I'll do whatever is necessary to protect you."

"Yeah?" I retort and my anger flares once more. "Maybe start remembering who I actually am first."

CHAPTER

Ten

SOFIA

"We're so sorry Mr. Montague…"

I stare out the window, at the blank, desolate landscape beyond the clinic.

I've been back to this place more than a dozen times over the last year. I've been poked, prodded, examined more than I can count.

Apparently the surgery didn't work again. Apparently I can't be fixed.

My father snarls.

"What good is she to our family?" He asks. "What use is she to anyone?"

No one replies. No one seems to have an answer.

Maybe now they'll all leave me alone. Maybe now I can return back to my life of hiding away, pretending I don't exist.

"She's not dying." One of the nurse says. "This won't affect her life in any way."

My father turns, sending the entire contents of the side scattering to the floor. "You may be a nobody." He snaps. "But my family, our name means something. I won't have people believing that our genes are defective, that we are tainted…"

"It's not hereditary." The doctor replies. "It's an incredibly rare condition…"

"And yet my daughter has it." My father shouts pointing at me. "My daughter."

"There really is nothing further we can do at this stage."

I'll admit those words have the complete opposite effect than they do with my father; they give me relief.

I let out a puff of air, leaning back into the chair. My feet don't even touch the ground, they just dangle above it. Maybe all this surgery has stunted my growth. Maybe now that this chapter is closed I'll be left to be a normal nine year old, at least as normal as someone like me can be.

"You'll try again." My father states. "One more time."

"Mr. Montague…"

"You will do it." My father growls. "Don't forget who owns this facility, who owns all of you…"

"Daddy," I whisper, shocked.

He turns his head, narrowing his eyes at me. "Tomorrow. We'll try one more transplant."

It's been a week. A week of unbearable attention. Every newspaper, every magazine, every damned social media channel is posting images of me, old images, ones where I'm stood beside Otto, where I look exactly like the crack-whore they're already declaring me to be now.

One even has a two page spread on the impending court case, on how it would be reckless to let me have my portion of Otto's wealth because all I'll do is spend it on drugs. Like I want his money. Like I don't have enough of my own. Sure, Otto was rich, but the portion I'm supposedly getting pales in comparison to what I have in my own accounts. Besides, I have no intention of keeping that money. I never wanted to marry him, I wanted nothing to do with any of it. It's his damned second wife that insists on 'playing fair'.

I barely leave my room. I hide in the semi-darkness, with all the curtains perpetually drawn, and the TV constantly on but silent.

I'm unable to sleep but unable to stay awake either.

I know they didn't drug me this time. That they simply sedated me and injected me with alcohol but I can't get over how easy it was for them. How pathetically easy.

I still don't believe it was me that went to that garage, I don't believe I drove that car, that I did any of it – surely I'd remember? Surely I'd have flashbacks? And why the hell would drunk me do any of that anyway? It makes no sense.

I skip my therapy session and I don't give a fuck what anyone thinks. I'm not capable of discussing my feelings, of picking over more of my past. And especially, I'm not willing to put myself back in that space, in *that* stairwell.

Ben comes to check on me, he brings a bunch of grapes as if I'm sick, and I force myself to be friendly, to be sociable, while he acts like I never tried to kiss him, like that night of shame never occurred. I guess I should be grateful for that, no, I *am* grateful. By doing that, by pretending the way he is, he's ensuring we can still be friends, that I haven't wrecked everything between us.

He orders takeaway and once again I can't take a bite, I don't dare too. We watch a movie, watch a comedy that at least makes me laugh a little but I can feel the way he keeps glancing at me. I can feel the way he's studying me, trying to figure out if I've returned to that broken creature I was when I was first rescued.

As the credits load, I let out a sigh. It'll be nighttime soon. When the minutes turn into days and the hours turn into decades.

"Can I say something?" Ben murmurs.

I turn my head, bite my lip, readying myself for whatever he needs to unload.

"You hiding like this, you shutting yourself away, you're only letting them win. Letting *him* win." He states.

I curl my hands into fists, but I wince all the same. I know he doesn't understand, I know he can never comprehend the fear of being trapped, caged, hurt the way I was.

"You're better than this." He adds.

"Am I?" I reply.

He tilts his head, his eyes flashing, for once not in sympathy but in frustration. "The Sofia I knew was brave, bold, defiant."

"Yeah? The Sofia you knew is dead." I state, folding my arms. She died a long time ago.

"No, she isn't. She's just afraid. She's been beaten so badly she's forgotten what it feels like to live. So she got used to hiding in the shadows, existing there…"

"The shadows are safe." I cut across him.

"But you belong in the real world, Sofia, otherwise what is the point in any of this?"

I stare at him, blinking. What *is* the point? I guess he's right. There is no point. There is no point to any of this.

Perhaps he's not expecting a reply. Perhaps he knows he won't get one but he sees himself out while I stay there, alone, caught up in the swirling anger in my head.

I deserve better.

I deserve to be happy.

I deserve to live, and to smile, to not just exist the way I am right now.

After everything I've been through, by god, do I deserve all of that and more.

But I'm so damn afraid.

Even now, in this room, where I'm the safest I can be, it feels like any minute the walls are going to crumble down and my enemies are going to swoop in. Otto is going to swoop in. And I'll be back, in that room, in that house, chained, bound, completely helpless while he and his buddies do whatever they want.

My stomach reacts. I scramble to my feet but I don't make it. I barely get out of the room before I'm vomiting, puking up bile because my stomach has no food in it. If I was back in the old house, back with my dear husband, I know what he would do. Every time the drugs made me sick, every time I pissed or puked over myself from what they did, they rubbed my face in it. Like I was vermin. Like I was less than an animal.

But right now, all I've done is construct my own kind of cage, one meant to make me feel safe – but it doesn't.

I get to my feet, resolve strengthening as I take one step after another. I can't fix myself overnight. I can't put on a smile and pretend none of it happened, but I can't hide here forever either.

Otto didn't kill me. He might have broken my spirit, might have hurt me in the very worst ways imaginable but I survived. I survived.

"...You're only letting them win."

Ben's words repeat in my head. And I repeat them. Over and over. I grab a pen and scrawl it onto the stark white walls, like it's some sort of mantra.

I'm letting them win. I'm letting those bastards still terrorise me. I've become my own torturer now and I'm certain I'm doing a far better job of it than any of them ever did.

Maybe I'm suicidal. Maybe I have a death-wish but it's like something in my head clicks and I need to prove to myself that I'm not back there, that I'm brave, that I'm free.

I grab my cloak, wrapping it around myself and shove on a scarf for good measure. It's a cold night, cold enough that you can see your breath in the air.

When the snows come, it'll feel worse, this feeling of being trapped.

I need to get out now, I need to break whatever this hold is on myself. I need to do this before the cold weather gets to that stage.

The street is deserted.

I jumped over the wall, sneaking past the guards though I'll admit I'm impressed I actually managed it. They seem to be constantly on watch, constantly loitering around; not that I'm complaining.

But I don't want them with me.

I don't want to be guarded right now.

I don't want to be watched.

For a few precious hours I want to be alone, out in the world. I need to prove that not everyone is out to get me.

And as I tighten my grip around the knife in my pocket, I also need to prove that if someone is out there, if they want to try, then I am ready. I will defend myself.

And this time, this time I'm coming out on top.

CHAPTER

KOEN

Christian Moran.

Now he was a tricky one to track down, to get alone. He's more jumpy than his mate Danny. More aware of the fact that there's a target on his back and his days are numbered.

He's never alone, at least not in public. He keeps a pack of security around him at all times.

Of course it helps that he's a multi-millionaire so he has the funds to pay for it. And no one blinks an eye when a rich man effectively armours himself. No, they see it as normal, necessary.

My lip curls as I watch him. He thinks he's so damn smart. He thinks he's got all his bases covered. That he's untouchable.

But tonight he's going to learn that's far from the case. Tonight he's going to learn a lot of things. And most of them will be delivered by my hand. My fists. My fucking fury.

A girl struts past me. Her sleek walk doesn't give away the fact that she's underage. No, with her tight dress and her immaculately done makeup you'd think she was early twenties and not mid-teens -at least that is until you get up close because there's no denying it once you're right next to her. She's a walking honey trap. But that's why she's here.

Christian glances over, eyeing her arse up as she leans over the bar to flirt with the man behind it.

And then she claps eyes on him, blushes, and looks away.

It takes a full hour for him to take the bait. He's good, I'll give him that. He waits until he knows he can get away with it. He's watchful, careful. The way he moves, the sleight of his hand as he drops the drug into her glass – it's so subtle you'd miss it if you weren't watching everything he did.

And I am. I have been. Christian has been my sole focus, day after day, since we tracked him down. I know more about this bastard than I want to know. I know what he eats for breakfast, how often he works out, how often he shits, all of it.

And after tonight, I'll never have to know about him again.

Honey trap starts to falter, to slump, Christian, like the kind, decent man he is helps her up and within seconds he's whisked her out of the bar and to somewhere more private. Somewhere away from watchful eyes.

We give him five minutes. Five long minutes before we silently deal with his bodyguards, unlock the door and slip in behind him.

Christian is too busy indulging in his prize to notice us as we creep in.

The girl is laid out, half on her side. Her dress has been completely removed and he's busying himself with her bra, trying to unclasp the thing and get it off. Only, he's clearly too excited and his hands keep fumbling.

"Want a hand?" Colt asks.

Christian cries out, jumping back, landing on his arse at the foot of the bed. "What the…?"

"Get the fuck away from her." I growl.

He glances at her, then at me, and to his credit, he doesn't make excuses. He's smart enough to keep his mouth shut.

I'm almost convinced he might be a good pet and play nice… and then he smirks. He fucking smirks.

My fist connects with his face. I feel the satisfying crunch of his bones beneath it. As he falls back unconscious, Reid grabs the suitcase opens it, and begins taping him up, folding him up so that he fits in like a neat little package.

I glance at the girl and she's still out cold. Thankfully she knew what would happen – we were more than clear what this assignment was, what was expected and she was paid handsomely for her participation.

Colt scoops her up, carries her out. She'll wake up with a bad head in the morning but no harm done.

Reid leaves first, walking out the door, heading for the elevator with Christian rolling beside him in that suitcase.

I leave after him, ensuring there are no prints, no evidence, nothing that connects any of us. Tia has by now already hacked into their security system and once we're out of the building all visual evidence will be erased too.

The only thing that gives away that something went down here are the two bodyguards left outside the door. They put up a better fight than Christian did. I almost felt sorry for them when my bullet smacked into their skulls, except, they knew what a piece of shit he was, they'd witnessed his crimes enough times to have blood on their own hands.

The only mercy they get is a swift death. A painless one.

The same won't be said for Christian.

Maybe it's to appease my soul. Maybe it's simply to prove that she's safe, but I don't go back with the others.

Instead, I get on my bike and I ride across the city, in the complete opposite direction.

I stop one street over, not wanting the noise to alert anyone. Not wanting my guards to start talking either.

I dismount, secure the Harley, and walk in silence towards the nondescript house.

It's a nice street. A fancy one. Every house is worth tens of millions. All the others are flamboyant, extravagant, but not hers. No, hers seems to fade into the background, as if it doesn't want to be spotted - not unlike its current inhabitant.

I climb over the wall, sinking down low behind a bush. When she was back at the hotel I used to sit there for hours, silently waiting, not that I expected to get a glimpse of her, not that I ever did. But it felt good to know she was there, she was in the same building as me. That if necessary, it would take very little to reach out my hand and just take her.

I clench my fists. Not in anger but in frustration.

It's been a year. A year of watching. A year of doing nothing. I've seen as she's slowly come back to herself, I've witnessed her gradual recovery, but she never seems to get beyond a certain point. It's as if something is holding her back.

She doesn't smile – at least not properly. She doesn't laugh. She's still in so many ways like a statue, a robot, pretending to be human.

Christ, what I wouldn't give to just touch her. To just once, reach out and show her that this world is not the fucked up place she believes it to be.

A shadow moves. A flicker in what I know is the kitchen. I see her face - pale, drawn. She even tiptoes in her own house, like she's scared of making noise and disturbing the dust.

"Sofia,"

I murmur her name. Not loudly. But it's enough. Just seeing her is enough. My dick comes to life, I groan, palming my jeans, reminding myself of all the promises I made, all those ridiculous things I agreed with her brother.

He thinks she's still too broken, too damaged.

He thinks she needs to be boxed up and kept safe but when I look at Sofia that's not what I see. I don't see someone fragile, I see someone fierce, someone deadly, she just hasn't realised her power yet. She just hasn't had a chance to experience it. To taste it.

If I had my way I'd be the one to show her, I'd be the one to teach her.

She moves, walking from the kitchen through to the living room. I follow her, stalking through the bushes, keeping to the shadows, making sure she doesn't spot me.

Apparently neither of us are going to get much sleep tonight, but while I'm content to stay here, she looks torn, upset, just not in a good space. She pulls a book out, starts flicking through the pages like she can't focus and then she flat out launches it across the room.

My lips curl. Something about the way she is, the way she acts, she's so fucking perfect. Like a little dragon that's only just learning how to breathe fire.

I sink down, settling in, making myself comfortable. It's a cold night but I'll happily freeze to death if it means I get to stay watching her.

She grabs a new book. I guess this one is better because she doesn't toss it, instead she pulls the blanket around and hunkers down.

It feels like a date. Like our two souls have arranged this.

She's there, reading away, waiting until the terrors that woke her subside, waiting until the darkness fades and the sun comes up.

And I'm here, waiting too.

Soon, she'll be ready. Soon, I will carry her away. It's just not tonight. Tonight, I have to be content to just watch.

CHAPTER

SOFIA

The needle slides into my vein.

I grit my teeth, clenching my other fist, trying to stay relaxed. They tell me to look away but I find it more reassuring to watch as my blood starts to flush out, as it fills the little plastic tube so merrily. Maybe it's seeing the proof that I'm still alive.

It never gets easier. I don't know if it's meant to. If this is something normal people in this situation just accept as part of life.

And then the needle comes out. I think that's the part I hate the most – the feeling of that metal coming back out, the way my body seems to tense more, as if it's preparing for the hit, preparing for the effects of some disgusting drug that's going to hijack my system.

I have to remind myself that that's not what today's about. This isn't about losing control, this is about keeping it, supposedly anyway.

"All done." The nurse smiles brightly. Too damn brightly.

She pushes a blob of cotton pad against the tiny wound and then tapes it up.

"It might bruise a bit but it'll go down in a few days."

I nod as though I don't know that fact. As though I haven't been jabbed, and injected so many times I'm surprised my veins haven't actually collapsed.

I roll my sleeve down quickly, hiding those tiny round scars that the nurse openly gawped at before she collected herself.

"We'll have the results in a few days." She says like I care.

Hastings has already told me what they'll be. That they'll come back negative. And I already know that I've not used anything, that my system is clear so all is this is simply a tick box exercise, a way to keep all those people vying for my blood happy.

But I'm done, done for another month.

The car is waiting for me right outside the clinic. I secure my sunglasses, step out, and an onslaught of paparazzi snap away like this is the highlight of their damned week.

It takes all my effort to push past. Even my security struggle to hold them back as they jostle for the perfect picture.

My chest seems to close up, my body starts to shake. I clench my fists, forcing myself to move, to keep going. I can't have a panic attack now, I can't fall apart in front of these vultures. They won't see it as a sign that I'm human, they'll see it as weakness, failure, another thing to taunt and humiliate me for.

It feels like I'm climbing a mountain, it feels like I'm wadding through quicksand and I can't get free. The car is barely five metres away but every step feels like a thousand.

Once I'm inside, once the doors are locked and we're driving away, I give in, I collapse, shutting my eyes, palming my face, and all that fear, all that panic consumes me like a raging fire and I can't put it out.

I can't stop it.

I can't do anything but let it burn me.

When we pull up outside my lawyers office, I'm in no fit state for anything. Once more I have to fight my way through an army's worth of press.

You'd think they'd have a more private entrance but I guess they gain from this too. They're the best in the city. Roman instructed them on my behalf.

As I sit one side of a massive, wooden conference table, they lay out all documents, all the papers, everything for this damned case. All of this feels like a farce, a complete and utter waste of my time.

I've stated over and over again that I want nothing to do with this. I've told them I don't even want to be present but I don't have any choice. I've been subpoenaed, and apparently if I don't show I'll be held in contempt of court.

The judges are determined to have this play out. The city wants its circus and who am I to deny them?

CHAPTER

KOEN

It's that last breath. That last intake of air.

That's what does it. That's what eases the fury inside me.

Not their pain – although that certainly helps. No, it's knowing that he'll never move, never breathe, never do anything ever again.

I watch as his body is cut down, as he lands in a heap of broken bones and blood.

He lasted far longer than Danny. Turns out he had more stamina.

When the men start hauling him away, I stop them. I don't want him to burn, I want him to be a message. A warning.

He's unceremoniously chucked into a van. Only Colt and I take the journey, driving out past the bright city lights and the streets full of happy, smiling people, and we pull up to the derelict, boarded up remains of what was the new Barn.

It feels like poetic justice to leave Christian hanging here. Afterall, he didn't just take from Sofia, he didn't just rape and abuse her. He got more, took more, stole more.

Two people died for Christian to live. Two people had their organs removed and transplanted so that he could continue his life of partying and drugs.

Those who know will make the connection. Those who know will realise exactly what this means; that this isn't over. That none of this is over. They want to play games, they want to try and come for Sofia, then fine, I'm ready for them. By leaving Christian like this, they'll realise that they've got a far bigger fight on their hands. They might see her as an easy target but after tonight they'll know she's anything but.

I drag his corpse from the van, drag him through the dirt, right up to the front gates. Together Colt and I strap him to it, securing his arms so that he's practically crucified. Then I take my knife, cut into his chest, removing the heart that wasn't his, removing the liver too.

I leave them both on the ground at his feet.

And then I turn around, step back, admire my handiwork.

Yes, this will send a message alright. This will ensure those fuckers understand exactly who they are now dealing with.

As we drive away, we don't speak. We don't exchange a word. My head is spinning, my hands are bloody. I need to get back, to get clean, and then more than anything, I need to see her.

I KNOW I DON'T HAVE TO HIDE, THAT I CAN WALK RIGHT PAST THE damned gates and up to her front door but I doubt that'll reassure her if she checks the security footage.

No, I don't want her to know I'm here. I want her to believe this house is safe, secure, that it's her sanctuary.

And besides, walking up to the front door takes all the fun out of it.

So instead I quietly unlock the latch to the downstairs toilet window. My men passed me a key so it's not like I'm actually breaking in.

And it's not like this is my first time inside. I've been here, every night this week, I've snuck in, watched her, unable to stay away.

Back at the hotel I couldn't even get close but now that she's moved it's an entirely different story. I guess I should thank her for that. God, I'm itching to give her a reward - but I won't. Not yet.

I step inside, careful not to knock over the soap dish. The window is so small and I'm not exactly pocket-sized so it takes some effort not to rip out half the wall.

It's quiet. Eerily so.

I oiled the hinges a few days ago so the door doesn't creek when I open it.

Moonlight pours in, illuminating the stark almost minimalist space.

I creep up through the house, up the stairs, walking from room to room, studying her space, soaking it all in. I don't need to rush now. I don't need to hurry. I've learnt that despite her trauma, Sofia is a damned heavy sleeper, it just takes her a while to actually fall asleep.

When I get to her bedroom, the bed is empty – not that I expected otherwise. She doesn't seem to sleep in it. She sleeps on the floor, curled up, like it's some sort of den. I can't say I understand the reasons behind it but right now it doesn't overly matter.

Her eyes are shut, she's curled up, looking so damn perfect.

And then she moans. A soft, quiet moan that practically forces me to step closer.

She curls her fists, her expression going from peaceful to anything but. She mutters something under her breath and she starts fighting, kicking, jerking, like her life depends upon it.

I know I shouldn't do it, I know it'd be far safer to just walk away, but I can't .

I bend down, scooping her up, holding her in my arms. The last time I carried her like this she was practically naked, beaten, completely and utterly petrified. And yet she'd clung to me then. She'd stared up at my face, with those beautiful dark eyes, pleading me for mercy as if I were the sort of man who knew of such a thing.

"Sofia,"

She doesn't wake. Thank god, she doesn't wake.

I lay her down on the bed and I watch her again, watch as her breathing seems to ease. As the horrific things she's dreaming of seem to fade.

She's wearing pyjamas but they don't exactly cover. They're certainly not going to keep the chill away.

I go to grab the covers and she moans again making me turn back.

I shouldn't do it.

I know I shouldn't.

And in my head I'm telling myself that this is to soothe her, to comfort her, that right now it's her needs I'm putting first. But a part of me knows that's a lie. A part of me knows that this has nothing to do with her and everything to do with me.

I've watched her for well over a year. I've stayed away, or as away as I can. Her brother has been more than clear that she is off limits but here, right now, she is mine.

So I creep back into the bed, pulling her into my arms. Her mouth opens slightly but still she doesn't wake.

From the angle I'm at, I've got a fucking perfect view of her cleavage. She's put on some weight since her bastard of a husband died but it's not enough, not nearly enough. Sofia used to be curvy, used to have a proper waist, and thighs that could crush you. Sofia now looks like she's trying to fade away entirely. She's skinny, far too skinny - her ribs poke out, her hips jut out. Half her skeleton is on display.

If I had my way, I'd lock her up for her own good. I'd ensure she ate three good meals a day. I'd ensure those delicious curves returned and that smile, that old smile graced her lips.

Only, Roman won't let me.

I let out a growl then instantly regret it. Thankfully Sofia doesn't react. She just lies, limp in my arms as if she too is waiting for me to cross the line. As if she wants this as much as I do.

"You're so fucking beautiful." I whisper, stroking her hair. It's soft, too soft.

Like all of Sofia it feels fragile.

My hands skim down her body, I don't think of the rights and the wrongs. I just know that I want this. That Sofia would want this if she was awake, if she wasn't caught in her trauma. If she were truly present.

I know from that look she gave me the other day, I know that she wants me.

She just doesn't realise it yet.

When I get to the waistband of her shorts a voice tells me that I'm a monster, that I'm just as bad as Otto. Only I didn't whore her out. I didn't rape her repeatedly, or let my mates rape her too.

No, this isn't rape. It's the complete opposite. What I'm doing right now is an act of love. What I'm doing right now is teaching my woman what pleasure feels like, reminding her body of everything it should yearn for.

She's not wet. I guess I should expect that.

As my fingers slide between her folds, she shifts, opening up more for me and if that isn't an invitation, I don't know what is.

"Such a good girl." I praise, even if it's just her subconscious reacting.

I take my time, enjoying the feel of her, as I explore she lets out a tiny gasp and I feel it, wetness covering my fingers. She's aroused. She *does* want this.

"You want me to play with you?" I say. "You want me to make you come, isn't that right?"

She doesn't reply. She just lays there, fast asleep.

I slip a finger inside her. Only one. Two would be too far. Two would stretch her too much and risk her waking. She's so tight, she feels incredible. I can't help thrusting, teasing, revelling in the way her muscles grip me. Christ, how would it feel if my cock was inside her? How much would she grip me then?

I'm dying to do it, to rip her panties off entirely and just fuck her the way I want to.

But that *is* too far. That is crossing a boundary. No, when I fuck her I want her to be begging me for it. I want her to be awake, to be staring into my eyes, to have made her already come on my fingers so many times she can't even think straight.

My thumb finds her clit. I don't know how she likes it. I don't know the way she touches herself, if she touches herself, but I find a rhythm that her unconscious body seems to enjoy. I circle that little nub over and over.

She arches her back, her breathing picks up, steadily I can see she's getting closer to where I want her.

"Such a good girl." I praise. "You're enjoying this, aren't you?"

Her only response is to leak more arousal, to cover my fingers in her juices.

I wish I could turn the lights on. I wish I could lean down and taste her, but I don't dare.

Her muscles start to tighten around my finger still buried inside her.

I should stop. I know I should. If she does come there's a high chance she'll wake up. That she'll open her eyes and see me and then I'll have some serious explaining to do.

But I can't stop. Not now. Not when she so desperately deserves this. When I deserve this.

"Come for me, Sofia." I murmur. "Prove that you want this."

She moans, Christ, does she moan. I thrust harder, too hard. And I pinch her clit almost delirious for what's about to unfold.

It feels like her body doesn't know what to do. How to react. She kicks out, she jerks. Her body goes so tense and then she is coming, right here, all over my hand.

I don't dare move. I don't dare do anything for fear she'll awake. She lies there, panting, and I slip my finger out from where it belongs.

My cock is so hard it's difficult to move. It's difficult to think straight.

I force myself to step away, to leave.

My little devil is laid out, sprawled on the sheets and I'd give anything to lay down beside her. But I can't stay. I have to go.

CHAPTER *Fourteen*

SOFIA

I shouldn't have done it, but my nerves got the better of me and I needed some Dutch courage to ensure I didn't fuck this up before it even starts; so I necked back half a bottle before I even got here.

The vodka seems to ease the shyness, the awkwardness, as I smile and kiss Otto's cheek.

We're in a bar, one of Verona's finest. Around us is half the city's big hitters, designers, celebrities, influencers. You name it.

But no one is looking at them.

No, every eye, every camera, they're all pointed at us. At me and Otto.

I guess I should have expected that. Should have prepared for that. If I had my way we would have gone somewhere quieter, less flashy, but that's not Otto Blumenfeld. No, he's all about show, all about making sure Verona sees him with the best that this city can offer – and apparently I'm the best woman now.

I almost laugh at the irony of that. Christ, if my father could see me would he be turning in his grave or proud that I've actually achieved something? In truth, the fact that I still care irks me. That man showed me little love, little affection, once he realised I was flawed, he pretty much locked me up, locked me away, like a dirty family little secret that had to be buried and forgotten about.

Well, it's worked out well for me now. Well for us. For me and Roman. The fact that I've stayed out of the limelight, the fact that Verona barely knows me beyond my name and my face, has made me a high prize indeed.

Otto takes my hand, leading me over to the best table in the house.

He pulls out my chair, helps me to sit down and in every way acts like the perfect gentleman.

If I were a fool, I'd believe all this, I'd look at him and see just a kind, rich older man and not the wolf he really is beneath that expensive suit.

He orders for us. I'm quickly learning that he likes to be in charge, to make all the decisions. And, seeing as I'm trying to appease him, why would I bother to challenge that?

He does most of the talking, again, that's how he seems to like it. I'll admit it makes it easier, far easier. All I have to do is smile, and simper, and respond accordingly. It takes little effort on my part. And he's trying to charm me right now so it's not like he's saying anything that gets my back up or offends.

Once the meal is done, I make a point of offering to split the cheque. I don't want him to think I'm a gold-digger. Of course he refuses and I smile, blushing, saying I'll pay for the next one. He takes the bait, he fucking loves that, and he holds out his hand guiding me past all those noisy little onlookers.

Once we're in his car is where everything starts to change, where it feels like the mask slips and the real Otto comes out. Maybe it's because he drank most of the wine by himself, maybe it's because there isn't anyone to observe us.

He starts to get handsy, grabbing me, kissing me, evidently expecting this date to end with us fucking despite it being our first.

Only, I'm not giving him that.

He can look but he absolutely cannot touch.

I won't not going to cross that line. I'm not going to turn myself into any more of a whore than I already feel.

I push him back, gasping, as though I'm loving his attention and not feeling sickened by it.

"I," I drop my gaze, playing that shy, bashful creature he seems to enjoy so much. "I haven't been with anyone like that..." I whisper.

The way he reacts, the way his entire body language changes tells me everything I need to know. That my value just went up. That in his eyes I'm an even greater thing to possess.

"Fuck," He groans, running his hand up my thigh. "I truly am lucky to have you then."

I nod, battering my eyelids, ignoring the twisting emotions inside myself. This is for the greater good. This is for my family. It doesn't matter what my feelings are, it doesn't matter what I want. I have to do this, I have to prove myself.

"I don't believe in sex before marriage." I say, playing my trump card.

His eyes narrow, he grits his teeth in obvious annoyance and then that charm comes back. "Then let's go to Vegas now." He replies and it sounds like he isn't joking.

I let out a little giggle. A flirty one. Like I'd just walk down the aisle and marry a man I don't even know because I'm that desperate to fuck him.

He tightens his grip on my thigh, sloppily kissing me again before he stares into my eyes and says, "You're going to be mine, Sofia. And I'll take care of you. I'll protect you the way only a husband can."

I can't help the chill that runs up my spine because those words, they feel like an omen. It feels like right now, Otto is making some sort of prophecy and that my fate is already sealed.

I WAKE NOT ON THE FLOOR, NOT WHERE I KNOW I SHOULD BE, BUT ON the bed. My sheets are sprawled about me but that's not the most concerning thing.

No.

I feel wet. I feel… surely not, surely that's not possible?

My eyes dart about the room. I don't know what I expect to see. I don't know what answers I'm seeking but there's nothing there. It's just me in the pale morning light.

I know I didn't have sexy dreams. I know what I spent the night imagining was nothing short of the worst horrors imaginable so why does it feel like I'm aroused? What kind of fucked up shit am I into?

I get out of bed, force myself to take a shower. My clit feels like it's throbbing. I haven't touched myself, haven't made myself come in so long because I don't want to feel attractive. I don't want to feel sexy. I've had zero desire for anything, period.

And yet right now it's like my body is begging for something.

I drop my hand between my thighs, I tease myself but it doesn't feel enough, no matter what I do, how I touch myself, it feels like my body wants something else, that it craves a touch that isn't mine, as if I haven't had enough foreign hands on me.

What the fuck is going on?

My heart is hammering in my chest. I'm practically crying with a need I don't understand. I try to use the shower head to get some relief but even that does nothing. Is this how normal people react? How their bodies suddenly just wake up aroused and horny?

I give up, leaving myself even more unsatisfied and turn the shower off.

Downstairs the TV is on, just as I left it last night. But as I walk past the screen I freeze. My eyes dart back to the image, to the words flashing along the bottom.

And any thoughts about sex seem to die entirely.

This can't be real. It can't be happening.

I can feel my body shaking, can feel my heart thumping so loudly in my chest.

I flick from one news channel to another but it's the same image, the same words.

He's hanging there, crucified.

I never knew his name. No, we weren't exactly introduced in any civilised manner. I know the feel of his hands, the bruises his fists left, the way his teeth felt when he was biting into my skin. I know the sound of his grunt when he was getting what he wanted, taking what he wanted.

All that is seared into my memory. But his name, until today, that was a mystery.

Christian Moran.

He sounds human. He sounds like an actual person and not a monster.

I bite my tongue so hard I can taste my blood as I stare at that image. I should feel relieved that he's gone. Relieved that one more bastard is dead and will soon be rotting. And yet I don't, if anything it makes me even more on edge because who the fuck is doing this? Who the fuck is behind this? Is this another part of the mind games? Am I being set up for murder now?

I pour myself a glass of water, neck it back, then pour another. My hand shakes so violently I end up spiling half the contents all over the countertop and down myself.

If I was smarter, if I was more shrewd I'd be playing my own games but they didn't exactly turn out well the last time. I'm not stupid enough to believe it would end any differently a second time around.

My mind seems to race from one mad conclusion to another.

I don't want to do it, I hate that I am, but I pick up my phone and I call Roman.

He picks up after barely one full ring. "What's wrong?"

"Have you seen the news?" I croak. God, I can't even cover my fear, I can't even pretend.

There's a pause. A moment where it must dawn on Roman who this man is, who he really is.

"Do you want me to come over?" He asks quickly.

"No." I say back. That won't help. That won't do anything but stress me out more. And it'll prove everything Roman believes, that I'm not okay, that I'm not back to normal. That maybe they need to lock me back up again and this time potentially throw away the key.

"What…"

"What if it's them?" I ask cutting across him. "What if they're setting me up for murder now?"

"Sofia,"

I can't stop the tears, I can't stop the panic as it takes over. God, it would be a perfect plan wouldn't it? What a beautiful way to silence me. Making it look like I went mad, making it look like I'm an actual psycho.

"Sofia, I'm coming round."

"No," I hiss. I don't need that. I'm a damned adult, I can look after myself. I don't need my brother to protect me all the time. And I'm not going to get better until I start forcing myself to do it. To be brave. To be a damned adult.

He mumbles something but I don't listen. I just start rambling back about how I'm okay, how I have security, how I haven't done anything wrong anyway so there's nothing to worry about. And eventually he gives in. He relents the way he always does because Roman doesn't push me. I'm still his broken little sister, and I don't think I'll ever stop being that.

It's hard to ignore the bitterness in my stomach as that knowledge settles in.

I'll always be a victim, always be damaged.

I guess somethings don't change. Even with the passing of time, I'm still the black sheep of my family, still the embarrassment.

CHAPTER *Fifteen*

SOFIA

The clubhouse is buzzing. There's a group of mums in the corner, cooing over giggling babies, rocking their prams. There's a girl, with flamboyant hair and big noise cancelling headphones stuck-on over her ears as she stares at a laptop.

And then there's the in-crowd. The IT girls. All the beautiful, eligible twenty somethings, who in a different world might have been my friends if my father hadn't kept me isolated.

I glance in their direction then quickly drop my gaze. Oh, I know they see me. I know they're curious. But I'm not stupid enough to make contact. They don't want to be my friend now. They want information, gossip, stories they can pass around at polite dinner parties, behind covered mouths. *Silly Sofia Montague, did you see the bags under her eyes? Did you see how skinny she is? Did you notice her trembling when someone got too close?*

I grit my teeth, forcing those imagined conversations to the back of my mind because it's not helping. It's not helping at all. My hands feel sweaty, my heart is thumping erratically, and I can feel my chest tightening with all the tell-tale signs that I'm on the verge of a panic attack.

Christ, Sofia, pull yourself together.

I dig my nails into my skin, bite my tongue to give my brain something else to focus on and the pain works. The pain always works.

I used to come here all the time. I used to spend my days in the clubhouse, hiding out, flitting from the pool, gym, and here, feeling like it was a safe space, a retreat, somewhere my father would never be.

Almost every table is taken but I spot Rose immediately. I mean, it's hard not to notice her, even in a crowd, the woman stands out.

Her bodyguard stands behind her, his arms crossed in front like he already views most of the people here as a potential threat. My own trails behind me. I know he's meant to reassure me but he really doesn't. Having someone constantly watching you, constantly focused on you, is exhausting.

Rose waves me over and I'll admit I've never felt more grateful to see her than this moment.

It took us a long time to be at ease with one another. We'd started to build something akin to a friendship and then everything had gone to shit. She'd been forced to marry Darius and me, well, everyone knows what my life became. At least, they think they do.

"I got you your usual." She says handing me a large mug of the blackest looking coffee I've ever seen.

I can practically feel my body buzzing in anticipation for this caffeine hit.

I murmur my thanks, sitting down into the squishy chair and I ditch my wool coat.

"How are you doing?" I ask like we're not here to talk about me.

She was the one who reached out to me. I'm not sure if Roman asked her to but right now, I don't care. I feel like I've got cabin fever from hiding away and in truth it's not like I have all that many options.

"I'm good." She says. She's wearing a big, baggy jumper with a scarf strategically placed over the front. If you know what you're looking at you might guess her secret but she's still hiding it well. "And you?"

I give her a cheery smile, one she's no doubt given dozens of times before, when our roles were reversed, when she was married to Paris, when he was assaulting her and yet the whole of Verona saw them as the dream couple.

"You know you can trust me." She says quietly.

"I know." I sigh. It's not that I don't trust her. I just don't know where to begin, how to articulate what I'm feeling. I'm exhausted. It feels like I'm constantly firefighting. Like I'm constantly fighting a battle and all the while this entire city is just waiting for me to fuck up. Like they're expecting it and they've got the popcorn on standby.

I take a long sip of my drink. It's just as good as I imagined but, when I put it down, Rose has a very different look on her face.

"What…?" I begin but quickly fall silent as a figure moves right in front of us.

Valentina is stood, staring at me, making it damned obvious. Christ, why did she have to be here, of all places, right this minute?

Rose's bodyguard immediately goes to block her but I wave him off. Whatever this is, I'd rather deal with it now and then she can go on her evil way. He grunts, taking a step back, ensuring he's closer now, just in case.

Valentina acts like he's not even there, like he doesn't exist. She's got balls – I'll give her that.

"May I?" She says, taking one of the vacant seats before we can object and dumping her oversized Coach bag in the other.

"Actually, we were…" Rose begins but she cuts her off.

"I've been meaning to catch you, Sofia." She says, giving me a tight smile. "I think we need to have a little chat."

"Is that so?" I reply. I'm not sure if she was always this bitter or if Otto turned her that way. I guess being willingly married to him for seven years is bound to make you both twisted and resentful.

Her auburn hair is so crimped and styled it barely moves as she bops her head. Her face is smoother than mine, more youthful which is a feat in itself considering she's well over forty. But it's her eyes that show her age. They're watery, glassy even, like they're a window to her soul and there's nothing there, on the inside, beyond her vapid personality.

She opens her bag, pulls out a tin of tiny cigars and lights one up, even though there's a no smoking rule inside. When the waitress quickly comes over to tell her this, Valentina rolls her eyes and stubs it out on the actual table.

My eyes focus on the burn mark. On the blackened wood. My skin prickles, all those nasty little burns along my arms seems to react as if they can sense the heat, as if they anticipate it; that feeling of pain.

But Otto is dead. He is dead. I scream those words in my head, reminding myself that I'm no longer his walking ashtray. I'm no longer his punchbag.

"What do you want?" I snap, losing my patience.

"Well, aren't you just delightful these days?" She says sarcastically. "Maybe the press is right about you."

Yeah, I'll admit that gets my back up more. She knows as well as I that Verona thrives off fake news, fake stories. Half of what this city reads is made up bullshit.

"Get to the point." Rose growls.

Valentina casts her eyes over her like Rose is trash and I can't help the snigger. Valentina might be rich, filthy rich even, but she's new money. By Verona society standards she doesn't have the pedigree to look down upon anyone though judging by her snobbery she clearly thinks differently.

"I wish to talk to Sofia, alone." She states.

"You interrupted us." I retort. "If you want to talk, then talk, otherwise you can piss off."

I see Rose's lips quirk. I swear I can see a camera out of the corner of my eye recording this entire thing and I'll be honest, right now, I don't care. Let Verona see, let them watch, let them realise that I'm not a person they can all keep fucking with. Let them realise I do have a backbone, and if I'm pushed into a corner I sure as hell will come out punching.

"Fine." Valentina mutters. "I want to discuss this case."

"Excuse me?" I reply. My lawyers have been more than clear that I don't discuss it with anyone. That I keep my mouth shut. I doubt hers are offering differing advice.

"You heard me." She says folding her arms. "You were barely married to Otto for any significant time, do you really think you deserve a third of his wealth?"

I blink back and I swear my jaw hits the ground.

"He has a son." Valentina continues. "My son. He deserves that money far more than you do."

Her son. The memory comes flooding back. It hits me like a tidal wave and it's all I can do to keep breathing. Her son. I know of her son. Otto made sure of that. He's one of the few I can name, one of the few I can raise my hand and openly accuse, and yet, I don't dare admit it. I don't dare speak of what Otto told him to do. Of what he willingly participated in.

I reach out, taking a hold of my cup, needing to do something to distract myself as something inside me starts to grow, starts to stir, starts to rampage.

"…it's not like you need it." She continues. "Besides, we all know what you'd spend it on."

"What the fuck are you saying?" Rose snarls loudly and I swear half the room falls silent. That buzz of conversation around us dies.

"Oh, come on, you can all pretend as much as you want, but we can all see it." Valentina half laughs. "Your sister-in-law is an addict. All those millions will simply be spent on drink and drugs. At least if my son has it…"

"How fucking dare you." I snap.

I don't even mean to say it, but something seems to explode. Some sort of control that I didn't realise I had, just breaks.

I'm on my feet, though I don't remember standing up. I don't remember moving.

Valentina stays where she is, looking up at me the way a queen does from her throne, with all that smug superiority.

"Do you really think I want his money?" I hiss. "Do you really think I want anything of his?"

"You kept his house."

"I burnt it to the ground." I snarl, clenching my fists. "I burnt everything of his. And all that money, everything you so desperately want, if I get it, I'm going to donate it. To turn his disgusting legacy into something good."

"Bullshit." Valentina retorts. "No one would be stupid enough to…"

"I want nothing of his." I repeat. "You of all people should understand what it was like to be married to him. What he was like. You really think a few million would make up for it?"

"Oh don't play the sob story." Valentina says. "You married him…"

"Like I had a choice."

She scoffs more.

"I think you've said enough." Rose states. "Perhaps you should go."

Valentina narrows her eyes, glancing from Rose to me. "I haven't finished."

"Oh, I think you have." Rose says getting to her feet. Behind her, her bodyguard moves to 'assist' Valentina in leaving.

I don't know what makes her do it, I don't know where the audacity comes from but one minute she's facing Rose down and the next she's grabbed my cup, yanked it from my hand and tossed it right in Rose's face.

"You always were a whore." She cries. "Marrying your late husband's uncle, you should be ashamed."

I don't think. I don't hesitate, I raise my hand slapping her hard across the face.

She splutters, stumbling back and it's my bodyguard who's grabbing her, hauling her out of the door while a waitress quickly ushers us to a more private room.

They hand Rose some napkins. She thanks them, patting down her clothes which are now stained black.

"Are you burnt?" I ask.

"I'm fine." She says before she starts laughing.

The waitress who stayed with us glances at her and then me, and it's obvious she's as confused by Rose's reaction as I am.

"Why is it funny?" I ask.

Rose shakes her head. "After all this time I've realised I truly don't care what this city thinks of me. It's very liberating."

"I wish I could reach that point." I mutter.

"You did just slap Valentina for everyone to see."

"I was sticking up for you. After what she insinuated…"

"Oh, come on," Rose laughs. "Like you didn't want to punch her from the moment she sat down?"

Yeah, I'll admit I was considering it but I doubt it would have looked as good if I'd just launched right into her like some feral beast.

"It'll probably be all over social media within the hour." I state.

Rose smirks more. "Good. Now everyone will realise what a bitch she is."

The waitress makes us fresh coffee. Though they try to protest, we make a point of paying for it. Afterall, it wasn't like they were responsible for Valentina's bad manners.

When we go back to our table it feels like everyone is whispering. I guess I can't really blame them, I'd probably be discussing it if I'd just witnessed that little scene play out.

Rose orders cake, and she sits there, eating it like this whole thing is now a performance. Like she's making a point. I'll admit I admire the way she can still keep it all together, the way she has that perfect mask still in place despite everything she went through.

"How are you feeling about the case?" Rose asks.

I shrug. "It is what it is. I don't have a choice in being there but I'm not going to push anything either. And I meant what I said, if I do get any money then I'll donate it all. I want some good to have come from all of this. I want some positivity."

She smiles, nodding, and I know she gets it. I know she donated all of Paris's wealth after he died, and that it was pretty much for the same reasons. It felt like blood money. It felt tainted.

"Do you have any updates on the…?" I pause, glancing down to make a point of what I'm actually asking.

If Roman and Rose are trying to keep this pregnancy hush hush then me saying it in a packed room won't exactly help with the plan.

"It's good." She smiles. "We had a scan." She pauses, picking her phone up and types. Seconds later I get a message.

- *'The baby is good. I'm on some meds to control my blood pressure. Hopefully now everything will be smooth sailing'.*

I look up and grin at her. "That's great." I say.

She forks another mouthful of cake into her mouth grinning.

We've never spoken about that night, about the Cuckoo Club, about what she witnessed, about any of it. I guess somethings don't need to be discussed but I like the fact Rose has never treated me like a child, she's never tried to wrap me in cotton wool the way my brother and Ben have.

Maybe because she's been through hell too, she understands that sometimes gentle hands do not help.

Sometimes tiptoeing around doesn't benefit anyone.

CHAPTER

KOEN

I should stay away. I know I should.

But like an addict I just can't.

The way she felt, the sound of her gasp – it lingers in my head, it clings to me and I have to have more. I need more.

I creep in through the same window, only the house feels different. It feels empty.

I look around, search around, and to my utter surprise, Sofia is not here.

But the guards are on the door. My guards. If Sofia is MIA why the fuck do they know nothing about it?

Maybe my little devil is more mischievous than I first realised. Maybe she isn't quite so scared of her own shadow after all and I'll admit that makes me more curious.

A voice in my head tells me to leave, after all, if my quarry is not here there is little point in remaining. But the sound of a key in the lock makes me pause.

A door shuts, the side door. Her shadow appears in the kitchen. She grabs a glass, pours herself some water and necks it back like it's a shot.

If I was quick I could get out now, I could be gone before she noticed me. But where's the fun in that?

I race up the stairs. Thank god I took my boots off because they would have made far too much noise and then Sofia would have realised and gotten hysterical.

I dart into her closet, hiding amongst the fine dresses that I've never seen her wear.

When she walks in and turns on the light, the brightness almost blinds me. I fear for a moment she might stalk right over to where I am. Only she doesn't.

She crosses into the bathroom, goes for a wee, then brushes her teeth and removes what little makeup she had on. When she comes back out she's already ditching her clothes.

I should shut my eyes, look away, give her a bit of privacy but what would be the point? Sofia is mine, if I want to see her then I will. She unhooks her bra, turns her back to me and pulls on a t-shirt.

When she climbs into the bed, I pause.

That's new.

That's different.

When did Sofia ever sleep in a bed? Is that a sign that she's getting better, is that a sign that she's recovering? I hope to god it is. The sooner she recovers the sooner we can both stop playing these games.

It takes forever for her to fall asleep. At one point I need to cough and I almost give myself away as I'm forced to cover my mouth and try to ease the damn tickle in my throat with as little noise as possible.

Even once she is away in the land of nod, I stay still, waiting. I don't want to make any sudden moves and ruin this.

It feels like hours after I've climbed into her closet that I get out. She's laying there, eyes shut, on her back, with the covers up to her throat.

She looks angelic, but I know deep down this woman is anything but; she just hasn't realised it yet.

The other night she performed exactly the way we both needed. Will she do the same tonight? Will she lie there, letting me have my fill?

I can't deny I'm not dying to find out. Not itching to be fucking her with my fingers already.

It takes all my effort to slow this down, to slow myself down. If I fuck this up now there is no going back. I can't afford for her to wake. I can't afford for her to realise what is happening.

I lay down, savouring the sound of her breathing, the scent of her hair, the way she doesn't react, she just accepts my presence.

My hand traces her lips. God what would they feel like, wrapped around, sucking eagerly on my cock?

I slip a finger inside, meeting her teeth and as if she knows she opens her jaw, she relaxes.

I groan. I can't even help it. I twirl my hand, getting my finger covered in her saliva and then I slide it out, popping it into my own mouth, licking it off. She tastes of fresh mint, I wonder how she'd taste after her mouth was full of my come?

My right hand palms my cock. It's getting harder and hard not to touch myself. Not to pleasure myself as I pleasure her.

I carefully pull the covers off. She's wearing a cami this time. Just a cami and her panties. Another new development.

I can see the way her nipples harden as the cool air hits them. As lightly as I can I run my hand over her breasts. She's got great tits. She had greater ones, but with her weight loss these were the first to suffer. It's another thing I can't wait to fix. I want to bury my face in them, to suffocate between them.

A tiny gasp tells me that she wants that too.

"You'd like that, Sofia?" I whisper. "Me worshipping your breasts?"

She doesn't reply, she just lies still, like my perfect little plaything.

I slide my hand down. The panties she's got on are lace. Far sexier than the ones from the other day. It's like she knew I'd be returning and she wanted to dress up for me.

I slip my hand beneath the band. Fuck, she's so warm, so fucking welcoming. Once again her legs seem to spread. Maybe that is an instinct but I'd rather convince myself that it's her body's way of showing me approval.

"That's a good girl." I whisper. "I'm back to reward you again."

My hand spreads her lips wide. I took my time before and I want to do the same again, I want to tease both of us, to build this up. It's not just about the conclusion. Oh no, it's about both us enjoying this moment, about us enjoying the entire ride.

She's wet already. Another sign that she wants this.

I don't stop to think, I don't stop to consider how badly this might end. I've tasted her saliva, I've tasted her come but not directly, not straight from the source.

Like a man possessed I crawl between her legs.

I have to have this.

I need this.

If she is mine and I am hers then this one action will prove it. I take in a deep breath, Christ, she even smells like heaven.

I lower my mouth, running my tongue right up the middle of her and I swear my eyes roll back in my head. I swear that taste, that nectar, it's better than crack, better than heroin, better than any other substance on this earth.

She lets out a gasp. A loud one. One I *should* pay attention to.

Only I don't.

I can't.

I need another taste.

I fucking need it.

I lower my mouth, licking once more and then something makes me look up, something breaks the spell.

Our eyes connect. Mine are lost in the fucking incredibleness of this moment but hers, hers are wide, shocked, and obviously full of abject terror.

CHAPTER

SOFIA

I gulp, staring down, meeting his gaze.

He's between my thighs, he's literally fucking me with his mouth.

Oh, I had my suspicions. My gut told me that waking up repeatedly aroused wasn't just a thing. That there was more to it. That there had to be more.

And when I got home tonight and spotted his boots that kind of gave the game away didn't it? Turns out Koen Diaz isn't quite as slick as he thinks he is.

But I didn't expect this, I didn't expect him to be actually going this far.

My pussy throbs. As much as my heart is racing, as much as my head is panicking, my body wants this. I want this. And I don't give a fuck about the consequences. About what comes after. I've been so desperate, so on edge, searching for a reprieve that I can't grant myself. Why would I deny it now that I understand what it was I was craving?

"Why did you stop?" I ask.

He frowns, like he expected me to start screaming and freaking out.

"Don't you want to finish what you started?" I say.

That seems to have the effect I was after. His lips curl. His eyes drop from my face back to where they belong.

His hands move, grabbing my thighs. Now that I'm obviously awake he's less gentle in manoeuvring me, not that I'm complaining.

As he holds my legs apart, opening me up as wide as possible, he lowers his mouth and this time, this time he's not messing around. He goes to town, he starts eating me out like he's a starving man and I am a feast.

I arch my back, I cry out, gripping the sheets to tightly I think they might rip. Fuck, the things this man can do with his tongue. He's sliding it inside me, fucking me with it. I rock my hips as best I can. I want him to destroy me right now. I want him to do disgusting things, to use me, to get me off.

He's groaning, his hand reaches up and he slaps my breast. I gasp more from shock than pain. He's just so dominating. So fucking aggressive.

And more than that, I love the fact that he's not holding back. That he's taking what he wants, taking what we both want. He's not treating me like a victim, or a child. No, it feels like I'm his equal. It feels like he knows exactly what I can handle and he's more than willing to provide it.

His fingers thrust inside me, replacing his tongue.

He's not exactly a small man and even with two digits I feel stretched to the limit.

"Oh god," I gasp.

"You like that, Sofia?" He replies in that deep gravelly tone of his. He sounds just as high as I feel right now.

"More," I moan. "I need more."

He growls, fucking me harder, curling his fingers, making me see stars.

I claw at him, I don't even realise I'm doing it until I hear the rip of his t-shirt. How the fuck is he still dressed right now? Why is he still dressed?

I open my mouth to berate him. He's got to see my body, why the fuck can I not see his? Only words don't come out. Nothing comes out.

I arch my back, I jerk, suddenly coming so hard I think I might just snap my back in half.

Koen leans right over me, murmuring, praising me, telling me how beautiful I am, how fucking perfect I am, all the while still punishing me with those fingers. And the way he says it, he makes me almost believe that it's true.

I slump back, lying on what feels like soaking wet sheets.

Koen is sat back, on his haunches, watching me with a guarded look on his face. Does he think that was a mistake? Is he regretting it now?

"You weren't meant to wake." He says in a tone I can't figure out. Is he mad I woke up? Is that his kink? That he gets off only when the girl is asleep?

I chew my lip, unsure how to reply. There isn't exactly a rulebook for what we just did. You don't normally allow someone who's essentially assaulting you to continue when you catch them.

"I can lie back down." I hear myself saying. "I can pretend to be asleep."

His lips curl and I can't even explain the sense of relief that gives me. "It's too late for that. You've ruined it, Sofia. " He says.

Ruined. I've ruined it. Something inside me reacts to that.

"Will you, will you not come again?" I whisper. Christ, I sound pathetic.

He tilts his head, taking in deep breaths like he's trying to get himself under control. "Do you want me to?"

"You didn't get off." I reply, glancing down to where I know he's hard.

He lets out a low laugh that's so disarming. It feels like I'm bartering with the devil. I don't know how to manage this man, how to even hold a conversation with him. I'm so far out of my depth.

"It's not about me, sweetheart." He states, running his fingertips up my leg. "It's about you, I've been teaching your body, retraining it."

My eyes widen. "How, how many times have you…?" I can't even finish that sentence. I can feel my cheeks blushing but I don't know if it's shame at the fact I've been unaware or shame at the fact I'm not even angry at him.

He drops his gaze, staring at my breasts hungrily. "You want the truth?" He asks.

I nod quickly.

"Every night since you moved here. But I didn't touch you, not at first, but you're so hard to resist, Sofia. You're so hard to turn down."

The way he says it is like I've been seducing him. Like I'm some sort of temptress. That I've beguiled him, tricked him when I know I haven't done any such thing.

I can practically see the red flags flapping in front of me.

This man is dangerous.

Ben stated it.

My brother stated it.

Hell, the entirety of Verona knows it. But I don't care. I don't give a fuck. I'm tired of being this caged up little thing, I'm tired of being afraid of my own shadow. I want to be reckless, I want to be hedonistic. And besides, in the confines of this room, no one would even know, would they? Maybe this is my rebellious stage, maybe I'm a masochist. My father kept me virtually imprisoned for my teenage years, too ashamed to let me out in public. Surely it's natural to want to assert my own independence now that I have the chance?

I sink back into the pillows. Meeting that demanding gaze. "Then I guess we'll have to continue these lessons of yours."

He reacts like I've just granted him the world. His eyes darken like he really is the devil incarnate.

And then to my surprise he just gets up, walks out, like he's done the task he set out to achieve.

I grab a robe, though why I have no idea, and I race down the stairs, race after him. Only he's long gone. Will he come back tomorrow? Will be back every night from now on? Is this how we'll be, should I dress up? Order new underwear?

Fuck, my head feels so confused.

The orgasm he gave me is still making everything spin. I want another. I want him to keep doing that to me. And yet there's a voice already whispering in my head that I'm doing it again, being reckless, being stupid. I'm jumping without properly thinking through the consequences, and just like last time I'm going to get burnt.

CHAPTER Eighteen

SOFIA

The city is whizzing past us. I catch glimpses of it. Momentary flashes. I know I'm downtown, that my house is still a way off and my stomach knots, though it has no reason to.

Otto has been staring at his phone, furiously typing away as if something has happened but I don't want to ask what. It feels like he needs space. He feels like a damned bomb about to go off and I have no idea what to do about it. How to manage him.

And then he snarls, tosses the thing into the footwell, and turns his entire focus on me.

It's hard not to flinch. It's hard to stay still when I feel like a deer caught in the headlights.

Some days it takes everything I have to continue this charade, to tell myself that what we're doing is the right thing. If Otto realises what I'm really up to, I don't doubt he won't hesitate to snap my neck.

"You look stunning tonight." He says dropping his gaze and I don't need to look down to know he's staring at my chest.

I chose this dress carefully. I choose all my outfits very carefully. It's a fine line between showing him what he "could" have and not compromising myself. Tonight I'm wearing a Herve Leger dress. It's tight, really tight, to the point I wasn't actually able to eat all that much, which annoyed me because the food was incredible. The purple was bright enough to gain attention, but then, me being me, and Otto being Otto guaranteed all eyes would be on us.

He leans in, closing the distance that I've tried to maintain. I can smell the alcohol on his breath. Though we shared a bottle of wine with our meal, he seems far drunker than he should be.

His hand twists in my hair, he pulls my face down and I meet his lips for a sloppy kiss. I try to act like I'm enjoying it. I try to pretend that he's what I want – a man technically old enough to be my grandfather.

His other hand snakes under my dress. I jerk back, all but slamming into the car door.

"Just a taste." He says, moving once more, invading what little space I have left.

I shake my head. "I told you…"

"I know, I know. You don't believe in sex before marriage." He says dismissively. "But I'm not asking you to fuck me, what I'm asking for is just a taste."

"Otto," I begin but his hand smacks into the glass, silencing me. I flinch but there's nowhere to go.

"Don't be a fucking tease." He snarls.

I shouldn't do it. It's a stupid way to play this, a stupid thing to do. I should try to placate him, charm him, offer him something to keep him sweet.

Only I don't.

I raise my hand and I slap his face hard. His eyes seem to roll back. It feels like the car goes completely silent.

"You want it rough?" He says barely loud enough for me to hear but he's moving, pinning me down, shoving his knees between my thighs so I can't close them.

I cry out. My eyes dart to the front, to the driver, to the other person sitting metres from us. Our eyes meet in the rearview mirror. He can see exactly what is going on, he's more than aware, but he does nothing. Says nothing. He just keeps driving.

Otto's mouth is on me, on my neck, planting kisses that feel more like bites, and his hand is right at my core, he's ripped my dress, yanked my underwear aside and he's probing me, jabbing me. I shut my eyes, I whimper, while my arms try to push him away but there's no escaping this.

"Fuck, you feel so tight." He murmurs.

I don't reply. I swallow the bile that's rapidly rising and I pray this will be over, that any minute now he's going to be satisfied and then he'll stop this. He'll relent.

Only he doesn't, he keeps thrusting, stretching me like he's planning on actually taking this even further. I can't scream, I can't seem to make any noise. It's like my brain goes into paralysis, like I shut down.

When we pull up outside the house, I practically fall backwards out of the car. I don't remember grabbing my bag but it's in my hand when I slam the door shut behind me.

My heart is racing. Adrenaline is pumping so fast around my body. If this was a normal situation I know what I'd do, I'd go to the police, hell, I'd go to Roman and he'd make sure Otto paid.

But this isn't normal.

None of this is.

We need Otto. Roman needs him. He needs every bit of information I've passed on so far and every bit I will learn moving forward if we're going to get our revenge.

"Sofia?"

I gasp, jolting as Ben crosses the foyer.

"Why are you stood there all…?" He falls silent when he sees my face.

"It's just been a long night." I say, forcing a smile despite the fact that I'm now trembling uncontrollably.

He must know I'm lying, he must see what I'm trying to hide because he reaches out and grabs my arm to stop me.

"Don't touch me." I cry, pulling free, all but crashing into a priceless Ming vase that thankfully doesn't go flying.

"What's he done?" He asks.

"It's nothing."

"Don't lie to me."

"It's nothing." I repeat.

"Sofia," He sounds so caring, so concerned, the complete opposite of the bastard I've just spent the evening with.

"I can handle him." I state.

"You don't have to do this."

"Yes, I do." I cry back. I do have to. If Roman is going to win, if we are actually going to get the revenge we said we would, then this is just part of the plan.

Another thing I'll have to suck up for the good of my family.

My father's words ring out in my ears as I hurry off to my room. That I'm worthless. Useless. That it would be better if I'd died and my mother had lived.

Maybe, if I can do this, I can prove him wrong. I can prove that I have some worth after all.

Fuck you dad. Fuck you.

I STAY UP, WAITING. ONLY KOEN DOESN'T SHOW. NOT THE NEXT night. Nor the next. Maybe he's making some sort of point. Making me suffer now. Will he expect me to get on my knees and beg him when he next shows?

It feels like he's awakened some sort of beast inside me and as much as I try to get myself off, I can't do it.

When the third night rolls in, I decide to give him a taste of his own medicine. Apparently, we're both playing games.

I sneak out, wrapped up in that same thick coat, and I wander the streets like I have nothing better to do. Maybe I'm a masochist. Maybe I just don't care.

The city is quiet. Deserted.

Exactly as you'd expect it to be at this time of night.

I wrap my coat more firmly around me as the freezing wind whips through my air. It feels like even the weather is telling me to turn back. To head home.

As I leave the Old Town and enter the more lively district of the Bay I can hear music, laughter, all the sounds that other people are having a great night, even if I'm not.

I drop my gaze, making sure I'm not spotted and walk on.

My phone's in my pocket – any minute I'm expecting it to start going off, for my guards to realise I've got out and for Roman to be notified and for all hell to be let loose. Only it doesn't. It remains mercifully silent.

In my other hand, I'm gripping that knife so tightly. It feels like at every corner someone is going to jump out, someone is going to try and grab me.

But that's just the crazy talking. That's just the paranoia. I take in a deep breath, calming myself.

The whole point in being out is to prove that I'm safe, to prove that I'm in control. If I can manage an hour or two of this, if I can keep walking, keep being calm then it will feel like an achievement. It will feel like I'm taking some kind of stand.

My stomach grumbles. I can't remember the last proper meal I had. All around me is the smell of food emanating from the fancy restaurants, only I can't go inside, I can't risk it. But my mouth waters anyway.

And then I spot him.

Eric Turner-Black

I don't know how I know his name but I do. A wave of something hits me. A memory so strong I have to grab the lamppost to keep myself upright.

Hands, too many hands. Clawing at me. Grabbing me. Touching where they have no right.

"Are you alright, love?"

I jump at the voice, at the stranger's face full of concern, at the foreign hand on my shoulder.

"I'm fine." I say, smiling, stepping back, moving away from onlookers who think I've just had a funny turn.

Eric has crossed the road. He's on the other side of the street now, heading away from the crowd, away from the shop, away from everyone.

A voice tells me I can do it, that this is what I've needed, what will fix everything. That the taste of revenge will ease that awful pain inside me.

My hand clutches the knife. My heart races in my chest. Is this madness? Is this crazy? I'm not sure if I care either way.

I pick up my pace, darting between the cars and I stalk after him. I don't care if this blackens my soul, I don't care if this taints me forever, if it damns me.

I'm ruined anyway.

Otto destroyed my life so entirely there is no comeback from that.

No, there is nothing for me now, nothing but revenge. And seeing that it's so neatly presented itself, I'm not going to hold back, I'm not going to turn and run and be a coward.

I'm going to seize it, I'm going to claim it.

I'm going to have my vengeance no matter what the cost.

CHAPTER

KOEN

ric Turner-Black.

Oh I know what he's done. Witnessed every second of it on the footage we got off of Danny's phone.

But to look at him, to see him out and about you'd think he was the perfect gentleman. He holds the door, he smiles, he's polite. His parents clearly taught him manners. And he knows exactly where to demonstrate them and when they're not necessary.

He crosses the street, after politely seeing his date to her taxi. Of course it helps that she's worth a few bob so he's playing nice there.

And then he slinks down a dark road, disappearing into the shadows like he's on the hunt for something now that his appetite is up.

Reid walks slowly behind him. Marking his steps. Ensuring he doesn't slip through our grasp.

He's been clever in a different way to Christian. He doesn't have the funds for security, so he had to make do with being in public as often as possible. When the Blumenfeld's fell, so did the Turner-Blacks. They're entire fortune was wiped off the board. Sure, they still have their fancy houses, and their fine clothes but their up to their necks in debt.

It's another reason why he's being so respectful of his date. He needs someone to bail him out, and let's face it, marriage has worked for enough of his type in the past.

He ducks back onto a main street. One crammed with people. For a moment I think we lose him and then he pops out at the other end, where it's quieter.

I can't help the smile. It's like the universe knows our plan, like fate is on our side. There's a marker on Eric, an invisible timer that's about to blow. And it makes me feel like the very hand of God as I prowl closer.

"Boss…"

Colt's voice makes me turn. He's not one for theatrics. One for drama. It takes a lot to make him nervous but that's how he sounds right now. Nervous. Unsure.

"What…?" My own voice dies as I see what he's spotted.

The lone figure walking behind our prey.

It could be a mistake. It could be a coincidence. But I know that shape, I know that walk, I know everything about the woman ahead of us right down to the noise she makes when she comes on my tongue.

"What the fuck is she doing here?" I growl.

She's meant to be at home, with my guards around her, watching her, ensuring she's safe.

Only, she isn't is she? She's right here, stalking the streets like she's some sort of avenging angel. Is this where she was the other night? Is this where she goes?

I'll beat her arse when I get hold of her, I'll make her understand that such behaviour will not be allowed.

"What do you want to do?" Colt asks.

Our target is right there. Right within our grasp – but then, so is Sofia. We can't get to him without putting her in danger.

"We'll stay close." I reply, like we have any choice. Like we have any option.

Besides, if Sofia is stalking this man too then chances are we'll need to step in and clear up the mess. In my head, my thoughts are already spinning on how I can work this, how I can make this fall in my favour. If Sofia is bold enough to behave like this then she's ready for me. I narrow my eyes, staring at her back, I'm going to take her. Tonight. However this ends, whatever the conclusion is, Sofia Montague will no longer breathe free air.

My lips curl at that thought. At the beautiful cage I'll construct around her. It'll be so subtle she won't even realise it. No, she'll want it. She'll beg for it. I'll manipulate her just enough to realise that I am her future. I am everything she needs. I am the very oxygen in her lungs, the blood her heart is pumping through her veins.

It's her destiny to belong to me, and I'm going to do whatever it takes to make her realise that.

We cross a street, walk down another, then cross at a set of traffic lights. Sofia is ahead of us and Eric is ahead of her. We keep far enough back that neither of them are aware of our presence.

But as we move further away from the crowds, as the bustle of the nearby restaurants die I realise something else. That it's not just us following Sofia. No, there's a whole group of men behind her, stalking her.

Goosebumps erupt over my skin as I realise what this is.

This is a set up. This is an ambush.

Sofia clearly thinks she's got the upper hand when really she's about to be seriously fucked.

I curse her under my breath, curse her stupidity, her naiveté, did she really think she could just hunt them down and they wouldn't notice? Did she really think it would be this easy?

As Eric turns into an alleyway, I know it's game on. That this is the end point.

Whatever is going down, it's happening now.

I CAN HEAR THEIR TAUNTS.

Before I even get in the yard, I can hear the voices, the tone, the disgusting words.

When I lay eyes on them I freeze. She's surrounded. There's a pack of them, five in total, all taunting, prowling, like she's a piece of meat they're about to seriously fuck up. As my eyes focus on their faces I recognise them, I see their names flash, names we'd pinned to the board. Apparently fate really is on our side.

And then she snarls, she slashes out and I see that flash of metal.

Jesus Fucking Christ. She's armed?

Did she set this up? Did she come here, tonight with the intention of killing them? With the intention of getting revenge?

My dick comes to life at that thought. I knew she wasn't that fragile thing the world perceives her to be but to see her now, she's magnificent.

Only, that thought barely lasts a second before I realise she's in serious trouble.

She's got no control. She doesn't know how to actually protect herself. She's not registering half of what they're doing, how they're cornering her.

She might have rage, she might have fury, but her lack of skill is going to kick her in the arse.

I jerk my head, ordering my men to go in, to take over.

In my hand, my own knife feels heavy. Five are too many to take anyway. Five are too many to keep. I hate that some of my prey will get an easier end than they deserve.

Maybe I'll punish Sofia for that. Maybe.

I dive in, throwing myself right into the heat of this war. And that's what it feels like.

I slash, I lunge, fighting my way across the yard to where she is.

A man falls at her feet. I don't need to see the blood know covering her to know that she did it, she killed him.

But she stares at her hands, she gulps like she's suddenly in some death-spiral.

"Reid." I yell.

We need to get her out of here. We need to get her back home. But as that thought registers I see her knees buckle like everything is suddenly too much.

I rush forward, sweeping her up into my arms.

She whispers my name and it sounds like a prayer on her lips. It sounds like a hymn.

Her eyes are closed, she's passed out most probably from shock. I know if Reid takes her back, she'll wake up alone and confused in a place she doesn't know.

I don't want that. I don't want her to think I've abandoned her.

So I carry her out. And I leave my men to clear up the mess.

As I sweep her hair back of her face, I make a promise that I'm going to keep her.

I'm done with the games, I'm done playing nice.

Roman can shove it up his arse.

Sofia is mine.

And it's about time the world accepted that fact.

CHAPTER

Twenty

SOFIA

My phone keeps buzzing. It's been going off all day.

I don't need to look to know who it is.

Ben narrows his eyes and I can feel his judgement from way across the room. He doesn't know what happened but he understands enough. At least, he thinks he does. Because he sure as hell doesn't get the why.

Why I'm continuing this.

Why I haven't bailed.

In my head I can hear all those reasons, all those rational things I told myself. That I didn't help my father when he was alive. I didn't help my mother either. And when Roman left, when he was banished, I couldn't help him. I've done nothing, have contributed nothing to the Montague name. I haven't sacrificed a thing. I've lived in comfort, in luxury, while every one of my relatives have sacrificed. Isn't it time I put a little skin in the game? Isn't it time I proved myself?

My stomach twists at the memory, at the events of last night. I showered as soon as I got to my room. I scrubbed my skin raw. That bastard actually made me bleed from the way his fingers assaulted me and even now, I feel sore between my thighs.

My phone vibrates again.

"Sofia," Roman says. I can tell he's getting annoyed though he has no knowledge of what went down.

I curse under my breath, snatch the damned thing and storm out of the room. In the hallway I can see the notifications, the dozen of missed calls. The messages. The voicemails too.

I press the phone to my ear and I play them back one by one, trying to ignore the way my body reacts to just the sound of his voice.

He doesn't even sound contrite. He sounds irate, as if I'm the one in the wrong. He's ranting, going off about how no one understands him, no one gives him the respect he deserves. The call cuts out mid flow but he's quick to leave another that continues on the same vein.

Apparently Otto Blumenfeld doesn't have the word 'sorry' in his vocabulary.

I guess I should have expected that. I should have seen that reaction.

The next few are more placating. More desperate. Clearly he's getting the message from my silence that he crossed a line but still, he hasn't apologised. He's offering to take me out, to buy me jewellery, to essentially buy me.

I roll my eyes, silencing it. My brain hurts. I feel like I'm getting a tension headache from all of this.

"What did he do?"

I spin around and Ben is there, right behind me. God knows how long he's been there.

"It's nothing." I say.

"If he hurt you…"

"I can look after myself." I state cutting across him.

"Sofia,"

"No," I snap. I know what he's going to say. I know what words are going to come out of his mouth and I won't hear it. "I'm not doing it. You've all put yourself on the line."

"What you're doing is too risky."

"I think I'll be the judge of that."

He huffs, grabbing my shoulders. "Stop letting your pride override your judgement."

"I…"

"We've got enough, Sofia, you've given us enough. You don't have to see him again. You never have to even talk to him again."

I chew my lip. Is that even possible? Could I simply delete his number and that would be it? No, I'd bump into him, I'd come across him at the next ball, or the next political rally, or something. I can't escape him. Even if I cut off all contact I would still have to occupy the same spaces he did.

My heart sinks as that realisation hits me.

Maybe I was stupid. Naïve. Maybe I didn't think through the consequences thoroughly enough when I came up with this stupid scheme.

"I need to go." I state unable to look him in the eye.

"Sofia, please…" Ben begins.

But I don't listen to him. I know he's right. Deep down I know it. But I have to see this through. I have to see this right to the end. The only way I win now is if Roman is successful. If we are successful.

IT'S DARK. EVEN AS I OPEN MY EYES I CAN'T MAKE OUT ANYTHING IN the space I'm in but there's a soft light coming from the doorway beyond.

I shift and I can feel the fabric against my bare legs. As my breathing increases I can feel I'm braless. That I've essentially been stripped and all I have on is a t-shirt. Only, it's not mine.

And this bed, this bed is not mine.

The mattress is different. Not softer, not hard, just not mine. Besides, my sheets are silk. These sheets are brushed cotton.

I take a sharp inhale and that smell hits me. I know that smell. I've smelt it before but it's not one of danger, at least not to me. Maybe I've gone mad and become delusional? Maybe I smacked my head too hard and I'm actually unconscious, lying in a hospital somewhere.

No, this is real. This *is* real.

I move slowly, stretching out, just as a voice reaches my ears.

"Roman."

His voice is just as deep as before but he sounds less gentle than when he's speaking with me.

I can see him, shifting about beyond the room I'm in. His back is to me but I can see every muscle revealed by the tight top he has on as he holds the phone to his ear.

"No." He says. "She's here. She's safe. That's all that matters."

I can hear my brother. I can hear his mumbled words in reply.

Koen growls. "How the fuck do I know that?"

I scrunch my hands into the duvet, wishing I could hear the other part of this conversation. Wishing I understood what the hell was going on.

"No." Koen says. "What she needs is some space. I can give her that, I can…"

My brother cuts across him. He turns enough that I can see his face, I can see the scowl. Clearly whatever he's saying is not to Koen's liking.

"It's up to her." Koen says and then his eyes fix on me. I bite my lip, trying to keep some sort of composure but it's obvious I was listening. "She's awake." Koen says. "The decision is hers but either way, I'll let you know."

He hangs up before my brother can reply and I watch as he takes each slow, measured step towards me. God even the way he moves, he's like some sort of animal stalking his prey, except I'm not afraid, on the contrary, I want to be devoured. I want to be consumed by him. I want him to feast on me, to ravage my very soul.

"Little Devil." He murmurs in a tone that sounds so close to affection. He sits on the edge of the bed, slowly, as if he doesn't want to scare me. When anyone else acts like that it pisses me off, but Koen, with him it's disarming, like he's trying to lure me in, lull me into a false sense of security.

I gulp. Is that his pet name for me? I can't tell if I like it or not.

"Where am I?" I ask.

"My house but specifically, you're in my bed."

My cheeks heat. I don't even know why because I knew that fact already, but the way he says it, it shouldn't make me feel what I do.

"What happened to my clothes?" I continue.

"You were covered in blood." He states. "Your clothes were ruined."

"So you what, stripped me?" I half snarl. Though it's not like he hasn't already done far worse. He's touched me, technically assaulted me, not that I'd say that out loud. Is it assault if you give permission after the event?

He tilts his head, shaking it. "No, Sofia, I had the maid clean and dress you. I thought it was more respectful that way."

I don't know how to reply to that. My mind seems to short-circuit. He wants to act respectful now but the other day he was anything but.

I curl my legs up, pulling the covers more. This feels too intimate, it feels too dangerous to be here in this room. I don't know why but my bedroom felt safer, I felt more in control. Here, I feel like a captive again. I feel more like a prisoner. And the fact that I'm not panicking, yeah that scares me even more.

"I won't hurt you." He says watching me carefully. "But if you want to go home I can make that happen."

"No."

The word is out my mouth before I can think. I don't want to go home. I just need a moment to think, to collect myself. My eyes dart about the space, taking in the faint outline of objects, furniture, a chair in the corner, a picture frame. They all seem so mundane, so perfectly normal and yet out of place for *his* bedroom.

"What happened to those men?" I ask, forcing myself to look back at the man barely inches from me.

"They're dead." He states.

"All of them?"

He nods. And that one gesture seems to change everything.

It feels like some great weight is lifted. It feels like the pressure that's been wrapped around my heart is suddenly gone. They're dead? They're fucking dead?

I smile, letting out a half gasp of something akin to joy.

Koen frowns like he didn't expect that reaction. "You killed two of them." He says.

"Two?" I repeat. I killed two of the bastards? I meet his gaze and I harden mine because he's not smiling. He's not happy at all. "Do you want me to apologise, is that it? Because they deserved it. In fact they deserved a lot more than just a knife in their chest."

"Yes, they did." He says back. "But you put yourself at risk to achieve it."

I scoff like that's not the case when we both know, if he hadn't shown up, I'd no doubt be the one lying in a gutter right now.

"Sofia…"

The way he says my name makes me shiver to the point it's hard to ignore.

"What?" I half whisper shutting my eyes to hide the embarrassment. Thank god it's dark because I'm certain my cheeks are flushing.

"Promise me you won't do that again."

My eyes snap open. My awkwardness turns to anger. "I will do no such thing."

He shakes his head, moving closer. "Do you not get it? How close you were to danger?"

"Oh, I knew." I retort. "But it was worth it, after what they did I had to do something, I had to…"

"Stop." He murmurs placing his hand on mine and I stare at where we're suddenly making contact. Skin on skin. Sure, he's touched me before but this feels so different. Right now I'm not in the middle of some pre-orgasm haze. I'm not begging him to make me come. Nor am I clinging to him for dear life.

"Sofia, I won't have you putting yourself in danger."

"Like you can stop me."

He narrows his eyes and for the first time I see it, that ruthless man that everyone else in this city is so petrified of. Maybe I should consider my words better. Just because he enjoys playing with me doesn't mean he's going to always be kind.

"Why do you care?" I ask.

He blinks, looking as though he's weighing up the wisdom of his next words. "I know what it is to want revenge, I know how it feels to be wronged, to need to do something…"

"You have no idea what it feels like to be me." I hiss. Christ, does he see me as just a victim too? Is that it? Besides, whatever this man has experienced, I know it doesn't come close to the horror of what Otto put me through.

"Perhaps not. But I do know what happened to you."

My heart suddenly thumps so loudly. I jerk away, as though I've been shocked. "Whatever you think you know…" I begin but he cuts across me.

"Who do you think is responsible for Christian Moran's death? For Danny Campball's too?"

My breath catches. I hate the fear that rushes through me at the sound of just their names.

"I killed them." He states. "I killed your husband too. I strung him up like the pig he was and I have hunted every man I can find who touched you."

My eyes widen. I know I must look afraid of him but I'm not. I just don't understand why he would feel compelled to do such a thing when he doesn't even know me.

And yet that answers it, I'm not being set up for murder. Apparently this was some sort of justice I was being delivered instead.

"I killed them for you, Little Devil. That's why I can't have you risking your life, because if you're gone, there's no point to any of it."

"What *is* the point?" I whisper.

He frowns confused and part of me wants to smile at the way he looks. He doesn't seem the kind of man that would ever feel something as human as confusion.

"The point," He says, "Is that you get justice."

"Why?"

"Why are you questioning it?"

"I'm not questioning why I deserve it, I'm questioning why you feel so compelled to give me it?" I state.

I expect him to deflect. I expect him to give some half-assed answer about how it's the right thing. Instead his lips curl. "You know why, Sofia. Deep down, you know exactly why."

I stare back at him, waiting for the fear to hit. Waiting for the panic because it's obvious what this is. What he wants. What, in so many ways, he's already taken.

"I'm…" I trail off, dropping my gaze. I don't know how to answer. I don't know how to respond in a way that doesn't make me sound like a child, or worse, a victim.

He puts his hand back on mine. "Let me give you the justice you deserve. Let me do this for you."

"While I what?" I reply, "Just stay here in your bed?"

His lips curl while my face heats worse than ever. "In my bed if that's where you choose to be. But I will not keep you here. If you stay it's because you want to, not because you feel like you have some obligation to me."

"I don't feel obligated."

"No?" He muses.

"No." I reply jerking my chin up. Christ, who am I kidding right now? This is Koen, and I'm here in his bed. I don't know how many times he's made me come in my own bed, how many times he's touched me while I was sleeping. Is that what he plans, me to just stay here, waiting for him while he avenges me?

Only, I've already done pretty much that, dressed up, waited for his arrival night after night once I knew what he was up to. Is it really any different to be in his space and not mine?

"Why, why would you want me?" I whisper, looking away, my head telling me how in so many ways I must be disgusting, repulsive even. Nobody wants a woman who's been used as much as I have, who's as damaged as much as I am.

He takes a sharp breath. "No." He growls. "I will not have that. I will not stand for that."

"What?"

"You, thinking you're not beautiful. Thinking that you're not the most incredible creature to grace this planet."

My eyes widen but I'm crying all the same.

His arms wrap around me, the covers are between us but the feel of his body, the strength of his arms, it's both so comforting and completely shattering to the resolve I've managed to hold for so long.

I sob as he soothes me, as his hands cradle me. I don't care that I'm clinging to him, I don't stop to think about how pathetic I am. I just seek the comfort of him and the reprieve that this moment is giving me.

"You're okay." He says softly. "You're safe. I will never let anyone touch you again."

I nod, taking a deep breath and my lungs fill with the same scent I've been dreaming about, the same scent my head has been fixated on for so long.

He cups my cheek, lifting my head gently to look at him. "Do you want to stay or go home?"

I bite my lip, the coward in me wants to retreat, to hide, to run and not look back. But I'm sick of living in the dark. Sick of hiding myself away. Sick of just existing. I want to be free. I want to laugh, to feel the sun on my skin and not flinch from the glare. The only time I've felt alive in the last year was when I woke to find him between my thighs. Surely that says something? Surely that means something?

"Stay." I say more aggressively than I mean, but I can feel my body trembling.

He seems to relax at those words. As if my acquiescence allows his own unease to settle. Maybe he was feeling guilty after all, maybe that's why he stayed away from me. I guess I'll have to show him that he has nothing to be guilty for.

I stare at him, trying to take in all the finer details of his face that I've not dared to notice until now.

He stays still letting me look as long as I want.

"I remember," I say quietly. "When my brother rescued me. I remember being in your arms. That you carried me."

He smiles a sad smile like that memory hurts him in some way. "You were so broken." He states. "I couldn't believe I held something so precious in my arms."

I gulp unsure what to say back and I drop my gaze as shame heats my cheeks.

"It's late." He says after a moment. "Get some sleep, Sofia. In the morning we will talk more."

I feel his arms loosen, I feel his body move away and though I so desperately don't want to be alone right now I can't find the words to ask him to stay.

So instead I sink back into his bed, pulling the covers up and try my best for once to just stop thinking and sleep.

CHAPTER
Twenty-One

KOEN

I open the door, already knowing exactly who is on the other side.

Roman tries to push past, to walk right in, like he owns the place and I put my hand out blocking him. He's lucky he's her brother or I would have squished him as easily as an ant.

"Where is she?" He growls. "Where is my sister?"

"She's in bed, sleeping." I reply.

He narrows his eyes. "I told you to stay away from her."

"And I told you that the decision was hers to make." I retort.

He looks like he's going to punch me. I guess I can't blame him for that.

"Come in, have a drink, you can see for yourself that she's okay when she wakes up."

He grunts, following me inside, strutting along. Though he's only been here a number of times, it's clear he remembers the way through to the kitchen.

I follow after him as if this is his house and not mine, and I tell the maids to shove it. Whatever this conversation is, we don't need witnesses and I don't want them to gossip, for Sofia to overhear anything she shouldn't and all my carefully laid plans be ruined.

While I put some coffee and toast on he surveys the room like he's expecting it to be littered in torn underwear, as if I brought Sofia back here and spent the entire night fucking her on every surface.

Does it ease his conscience when he finds no such evidence? I don't think I care either way.

I played a careful game last night, letting Sofia believe she had a choice, easing her in, ensuring she picked me. If she'd said she wanted to go home then I would have taken her. But I wouldn't have left. No, our souls are intwined, twisted. From now on, she is mine, I just have to be careful with ensuring she comes to understand that fact. She's flighty, scared, understandably so considering what Otto did to her, but I won't let her past come between us. No, instead I plan on using it, on manipulating her trauma so that she chooses me, so that she always chooses me.

I place a mug in front of him and we both lean against opposite counters, facing off.

I can see the anger in his face but underneath I can see the concern too and part of me gets it. It's his little sister, if he wasn't overprotective of her, he'd have to be some sort of psychopath.

He sips his coffee, frowning, clearly trying to formulate some sort of plan to navigate this.

The toast pops behind me and, though neither of us jump, the noise seems to enhance the silence hanging between us. I grab the slices, sticking them on a plate and put them on the breakfast bar.

I've no idea how long we might be sat here, glaring at one another but I sure as shit am not going to stay hungry.

"I told you to stay away." Roman states, like he's a broken record.

I narrow my eyes, putting my own cup of coffee down. "Sofia is her own person. And I said before, you can't stop me from protecting her."

He grunts back and though I shouldn't say it, shouldn't twist the knife, my give-a-shit level is too low to care. "It's not like you haven't needed that protection, Roman."

"What did you say?" He half-snarls.

"You heard. Whatever you say, you know you can trust me, you know she's safe with me. That's why I'm the one you call when the shit hits the fan."

"You have men." He replies dismissively. "Don't overthink it."

"And here I was, thinking we were partners." I mutter.

He narrows his eyes and I see that flash of anger. "In business maybe, but my sister is not a part of that. Sofia is separate."

"Yes, she is." I snap. "She's her own person, she makes her own decisions, and you should respect that."

"She's not in a good state of mind right now. If anything, last night proves it."

"Why?"

He frowns at my question like it makes no sense.

"Why does it prove it?" I repeat.

"She's not thinking straight, she's not thinking logically." He argues.

"Because she decided to do something rather than simply remain a recluse?"

His eyes widen. "Don't twist this, don't…"

"What?" I snap. "You got your revenge, Roman. You took your time ensuring everyone that screwed you and your wife over paid very dearly for it."

"You think I don't care about my sister, is that it? You think I don't think she deserves justice?"

"She does deserve justice." I snarl. She deserves a damned sight more than just that.

"She's vulnerable." Roman states. "Don't take advantage of her, don't create a situation that she might regret."

"You think me capable of that? You think I would hurt her?" My fists curl and I'm itching to slam them into him, to silence the bullshit coming out of his mouth, but I doubt Sofia will thank me for it. I doubt she'll think too kindly if she realises I've beaten the shit out of her brother and it certainly won't endear her to me if I do. "It's her decision." I say. "Whatever she wants, whatever she chooses, I'll abide by that. And I expect you to do the same."

Oh I know she'll choose me. I know it in my soul. And the way he looks right now, yeah he knows it too.

He opens his mouth like he wants to argue more but the sound of footsteps makes us both fall silent.

I look across to the doorway and she's stood there, dressed in the same t-shirt the maid put her in. My t-shirt. Her dark hair is ruffled, she looks sleepy and yet so beautiful. Her cheeks are pink, she blinks, looking back at me, holding my gaze as she bites her lip and then Roman clears his throat. Loudly.

Her eyes widen as she realises he's watching us. "What, what are you doing here?" She half-whispers.

"I had to check on you." He replies. "After last night, I had to make sure you were okay."

She lets out a sigh, walking over to where the bar stools are and she perches on the end as if this place is already her home. "I'm fine."

"You killed a man." Roman states.

"Two." I correct him.

Roman looks at me then back at his sister. "Two?" He repeats.

Sofia huffs, leaning over to snag a piece of toast like we're simply discussing the weather. I'll admit I like her like this, relaxed, comfortable, at ease. My eyes drift to her exposed legs, to how fucking gorgeous she is. And then I notice the scars, the cigarette burns all up her arms. It's hard not to react, not to show anything on my face.

"Sofia…" Roman begins like he's about to lecture her.

"Come on." She mutters. "You can hardly talk, not after the list of people you've done in."

"That's different." Roman snaps.

"Is it?" She says tilting her head. "They all fucked you over. They all fucked our family over. How is this any different?"

"You know it is." Roman says.

I shake my head, pouring out a third coffee. I don't even know how she takes it. If she likes it milky, if she likes it sweetened. I put the mug in front of her and she smiles at me, sipping it, before I can grab the milk.

So she drinks it black, huh? Good to know.

Once she's taken another mouthful she puts it down, fixing Roman with a determined look. "It's only different because I was the one wielding the blade." She states. "If it'd been you, if it'd been Ben, or Holden…"

"That's not the issue."

Sofia rolls her eyes. "You're so concerned with Hastings, aren't you?"

"He won't turn a blind eye…"

"Relax." I say. "We've sorted it. There's no evidence. No witnesses. Hastings won't even be aware anything went down."

Roman narrows his eyes, staring at me, but I can feel Sofia's look more. Like my body is tuned into every move she makes.

"You mean you won't make an example?" Roman asks.

I shake my head, "Not this time."

"Why not?"

"Because…" I pause, not sure if I want to admit it. Not sure how she would feel about me saying it.

"Because Sofia is involved?" Roman guesses.

"Yes."

I hear the sharp intake of breath. I see the way Sofia tenses.

"Why not? How is it any different if I'm involved?" She asks.

I fix my eyes on her, noticing the way she doesn't blink all that much, the way she tilts her head, the way she hides her fear and her nerves behind a hard mask that right now is firmly in place. But I also notice the way a pulse on her neck is giving her away. The way her heartrate is steadily picking up.

"I wouldn't do anything that risks fingers being pointed at you." I state. "The fact you were there last night makes it too high risk."

"But you were there." She says with a hint of concern that makes my lips curl.

"I can handle anything that comes my way." I reply.

"And you think I can't?" She asks, narrowing her eyes, showing that petulant streak she keeps mostly underwraps.

"I know you can. Last night more than proved it. But this is about your future, this is about ensuring the sins of the past don't sully your hands."

I hear her mutter, I don't catch the words but I know it's along the lines of her already being sullied enough for it to make little difference now.

Roman looks between us with an expression I can't quite read. Is it anger? Frustration? Fear, even?

"Sofia," He says quietly, "Perhaps it would be best for you to stay with me for a bit. Take a little time out."

"No," Sofia says back. "I'm happy where I am."

"Then I want more guards, I'm not sure how safe your house is considering…."

"I didn't mean my house." She replies and her cheeks heat just a little.

Both of them look at me - Sofia with obvious hope, and Roman, as if I will back him up and send her packing.

As if I would. I'm not going to deny her. It's not like she has a choice but I need her to believe she has options. I need her to not see this as a new prison. A new cage.

"Sofia decides." I state. "If she wants to stay then she is welcome to."

The way she reacts tells me she takes the bait, that those words are exactly what she wanted to hear. But then she asks, "Do you want me to?"

Her question catches me off guard, not because of the reasons it should. Not because her brother is watching this play out right in front of him. It's because she's such a damn people pleaser, she never puts herself first. She never does what she wants without making sure everyone else is happy. I'll admit it pisses me off. She should be her own priority and I'm going to make sure she learns that fact.

"Of course I do." I say, ignoring Roman completely. "But this isn't about me. This is about you. You need to start taking control, start making decisions for yourself."

Her eyes widen, she looks at Roman then back at me, drawing herself up like she's actually pissed. "I want to stay." She says more determinedly. But of course she does, I've just presented myself as her champion. Her perfect knight.

"Then you stay." I reply and she smiles like I've just taken the weight of the world from her shoulders.

"I want to speak to my sister alone." Roman states.

Sofia scowls in response.

Of course Roman will try to persuade her, to try to prove the folly of the path she's choosing. Perhaps this is a good test to see how determined Sofia can be. If she has the strength to stand up to her brother.

And if she doesn't, it won't matter all that much. I might have to turn to more forceful means, I might have to manipulate her further, but Sofia won't be leaving here.

She won't be going anywhere from now on unless I allow it.

CHAPTER

Twenty-Two

SOFIA

I watch as he walks away. As he leaves us to it.

Even from behind, you can see every single muscle and it's hard not to drawl.

And then I realise Roman is watching me, studying me. I mentally slap myself, and fix him with a look that I hope shows I'm not taking his shit.

He sighs, running a hand through his hair. "I'm trying to help." He says quietly.

"Really? That's what you think you're doing?" I retort.

"Sofia, I only ever want the best for you" He states. "I only ever want your happiness."

"Like I've had a lot of that lately."

He winces, "If I could go back, if I could undo everything…"

"But you can't." I say. "Neither of us can."

He narrows his eyes, scrutinising my face. "I know I fucked up, I just want to make this right. To protect you now, because I wasn't there for you when I should have been."

"I don't need that." I gasp. "I don't need you to play the big brother anymore. That's half the problem, all of you tiptoeing around me, trying to fix me like I can be fixed."

"But you can."

"I know I can." I reply tersely. "But on my terms, in my way."

He glances to the open doorway, to where Koen disappeared. I don't think he's eavesdropping, I certainly hope he isn't but I've also not said anything I wouldn't say in front of him.

"You really want to stay here?" He asks.

"Yes."

"And you think he can keep you safe?" He says like I don't know it's been Koen's men helping to guard us from the moment we left the Tunnels.

"It's not about safety." I say, because it isn't, at least, not in the way he's insinuating. I didn't run to Koen because of who he is, because the entirety of Verona shits themselves when he looks their way.

No, I'm here because he makes me feel *something*. He makes my soul feel for the first time like I'm not caught up in some battle for my very existence. When I look at him, I feel the kind of safety you get from being at peace. Only, I don't know how to articulate that, how to explain that. It sounds preposterous considering everything that he's done.

"You know I would give you the world if I could."

My lips curl. "I thought you already promised that to Rose."

He chuckles slightly. "Alright, you got me there." He mutters. "But I would do anything for you. Anything that would make you happy."

"Then let me have this, let me have your trust."

He gets to his feet, closing the distance and, though I know he wants to reach out, to touch me, he doesn't, he keeps his hands by his side. "I trust you, Sofia. I will always trust you. And if I've ever made you think otherwise then I am deeply sorry for it."

I nod, feeling my eyes prick with tears. This last year we've argued so much. More than the rest of our lives put together. I know a lot of that is my fault, that the way I've been handling everything has caused a rift between us. My anger, my pain, all of it has made me lash out, has made me want to hurt those around me only because that's all it felt they fixated on. All they saw when they looked at me.

But now it feels like we might be able to move on. That Roman might finally stop seeing me as his broken, traumatised little sister, and start seeing me as more than that.

"This doesn't affect you and Koen, does it? It doesn't change anything with your business?" I ask.

Roman shakes his head. "No, business is business."

"Good."

We stand, staring at each other awkwardly for a moment and then he mumbles about leaving me to it. I don't even know which way is the front of the house but clearly Roman does so apparently he's been here before. I follow after him, saying my goodbyes and once the door shuts I stand there, listening to the roar of his engine, to the sound of his tyres on the drive, to the confirmation that he has truly done as I asked.

And then I don't know what to do.

Suddenly I feel nervous, so nervous, like a little girl so far out of her depth. I talked a good game but reality is really starting to bite.

"He's gone?"

I spin around, facing Koen, seeing him stood close enough to touch. The air seems to bristle with tension, but maybe that's just my head imagining it.

"Yes." I say.

He draws in a long breath, running his eyes over me, still in his t-shirt, still barefoot.

"Do you want a shower?"

"I have nothing to wear." I say back. It's not exactly an answer but if I do shower, what then? I can't walk around in a towel all day. And I can hardly wear Koen's clothes, he's got to be twice my size.

"The maids got you some clothes. If you want we can get your stuff later."

Like I'm properly moving in? I guess it makes sense. I did just declare that I wanted to stay here, but now my head is starting to whirl with the reality of what I've done.

He tilts his head, scrutinising me more. "We should talk."

Talk. Right. That would make sense. That's the logical thing to do.

I follow him back into the kitchen, sit back on that same barstool and watch as he pours out two more cups of coffee.

"How does this work?" I ask, trying to steer the conversation, trying to take some form of control.

"How does what work?"

"You. And me." I reply. And my damned face burns up like an oven.

He leans back against the counter, obviously considering what his next words are. "What do you want, Sofia? You asked to stay here, how did you imagine that to be?"

I drop my gaze, staring at the black liquid in my hands. "I, I didn't think beyond…"

"Last night you seemed happy enough to be in my bed."

I gulp feeling like I've set myself up for this, once more I've created a situation I can't get out of. He shakes his head, his eyes flitting to something akin to sympathy and for a second I hate it. I hate that softness, that kindness. Koen is meant to be an arsehole, a man so ruthless he doesn't feel any other emotions beyond hate and revenge. I hate that even he looks at me like that.

Maybe that's why I do it. Maybe it's my pride that that makes me act.

"I'll make you a deal." I say quickly, fixing him with a look I hope makes him realise how serious I am. "You're hunting them. You're killing the men who hurt me. I want in. I want to be a part of it."

"No."

"Koen,"

He tilts his head, his face so close to mine that I'd only have to lean forward a little and.... Stop it.

"I want in." I state.

"I'm not putting you in danger."

"I won't be in danger if I'm with you."

His lips curl in amusement. "You trust me that much, Little Devil?"

Yeah, my heart seems to flip at that name again. "How can I be a devil if you won't let me use my claws?"

He grins more, that gold tooth of his glints. He picks up my hand and starts examining it like he actually expects to see talons. "They're not sharp enough."

"Not yet."

He laughs, a deep rumble that makes my body react in a way that is not okay. Despite our proximity, despite the fact he's touching me right now and I should be running for the hills, only my heart seems to beat louder, something akin to pride settles there at the fact it was me that made him laugh.

God, I'm pathetic.

"And what do I get in this deal?" He asks like it isn't obvious.

"Me."

His eyes darken, his gaze drops and I know he's staring at my body, probably trying to decide if I'm worth it. God, what if I'm not? What if he's already decided I'm too disgusting after all, that he's had his fun already and he's simply going to toss me out into the street like I really am trash?

"You'd sell yourself to me?" He murmurs.

"If that's the price." I say, sounding more confident than I feel. Yes, he's attractive, yes, he's god damn gorgeous to look at, but if he decides he wants to fuck me right this minute, I'm not so certain I won't completely fall apart with fear.

Only I can't do that.

I refuse to do that.

I want my vengeance. I want my revenge. Koen can give me all that and more.

And I've fucked enough men, been fucked enough times, for one more not to matter.

He puts his hands on my thighs, it's a test I know it is, but I can't hide the flinch, the way my body reacts to the sudden contact.

"If I fucked you now, I'd break you." He states so coldly, so matter of fact.

"You think you're that strong?" I sneer, trying to cover my panic and hurt with false bravado.

He growls, moving to pin me in place, pushing me flat against the counter and suddenly adrenaline is pumping through my veins, my heart is slamming into my chest.

"Spread your legs." He orders, but he's the one doing it, pushing them apart, forcing me wide open for him. The t-shirt I'm in rides right up, baring my panties. The cold marble worktop makes my skin erupt into goosebumps. I shut my eyes, clench my fists, trying not to hyperventilate.

This is what I offered, this was the price. He has every right to claim it.

As his hand brushes against the fabric covering my core I'm not sure if it's fear or desperation that's taking over. This feels so different to the other night. The other night it felt caring, loving, now it's possessive, dominating, like I'm a thing to be owned.

"New deal," Koen says, pulling his eyes from my chest and meeting my gaze. "You'll get your vengeance, and I get you, but on my terms."

His hand is still on my thigh, still pinning me down and I force myself to stop trembling, to stop giving myself away.

"What, what does that mean?" I stammer. Have I misunderstood this man? Is he going to whore me out, just like Otto did?

"You're going to work on fixing yourself. You're going to eat properly, get stronger, and you're going to stop hiding away. Right now you hate yourself because you still feel weak. You still feel powerless. If you are physically stronger, if you can fight, if you can protect yourself without having to depend on anyone else, then mentally you'll be all the better."

I blink, I gulp. His face is so close to mine and though I hear the truth in his words, the logic in them, it feels like he's asking me to scale a mountain.

"That's the deal?" I whisper feeling like it would be easier if he just fucked me after all. Why doesn't he want to? Surely most men don't care beyond getting their dicks wet? It makes me wonder what his motives are. He's been sneaking into my house, into my room, essentially assaulting me for god knows how long, and now when I'm laying myself out on a platter he suddenly seems to have grown a conscious? It doesn't make any sense.

His lips curl, "That's the deal. I'll bring you your enemies and in exchange," His hand strokes my cheek so gently I almost melt.

"In exchange I'm going to show your body what pleasure is, I'm going to mould you, Sofia, I'm going to teach you, but at my pace."

"I thought we already agreed to that the other night?" I say.

He lowers his mouth, capturing mine and my mind turns to mush. His tongue swirls against mine, his hand moves to grip the back of my head. I gasp, arching my back, rubbing myself against him. All that fear, all that confusion is gone. If he started stripping me now I don't think I'd fight him. I don't think I'd do anything but just lie here and let him do as he wished.

When he breaks it off, I'm panting. I'm a needy mess. He smirks like he knows it, releasing his grip and I all but slide off the counter, landing at his feet like he's some sort of god.

"Get dressed." He says. "We'll get your things and later tonight, I'll hold up my end of the deal."

"Tonight?" I repeat. So quickly?

"We always like to keep one alive." Koen explains. "To extract information."

"You told me they were all dead." I say folding my arms.

"They are dead. Eric Turner-Black is a dead man walking. Or, hanging technically."

"You're going to torture him? To kill him?" I splutter.

"For you." He says and those black eyes seem to sparkle.

Any words I have, any reply is forgotten. I just stare back at him, blinking.

CHAPTER Twenty-Three

KOEN

She seems unsettled. I guess I can't blame her for that.

After she's showered and dressed we take the G-Wagon and head to her house and all the while she's staring out the window, watching the city streets whizz by like she's trying to sear the memories of freedom into her mind.

Is it because she's still trying to convince herself she's escaped her husband or is it because, deep down, she's already sensing the cage I'm constructing around her as we speak?

Silence hangs between us but it doesn't feel exactly uneasy.

I can tell she just needs a little thinking time, a little processing.

I don't doubt she's coming to terms with the fact she's now my plaything. I wonder if her pussy is wet with the idea of it. Should

I slide my hand and check? No, I can't, not yet. I need to tread carefully. She might have ridden my face once but that doesn't mean she's ready for all of me.

Besides, tonight she'll come face to face with one of her abusers; again. I know she's mentally preparing herself for it.

Her house isn't in the Bay District, where so many of the mega rich reside. Instead, she's in the Old Town, the other side of the city from where I live. I keep my expression locked down as we pull in through the gates, past the guards who are technically my men and come to a stop outside a bland, characterless building.

I know I've already seen it, been inside it, but in my head I imagined it to look so much different in the daylight.

"This is it?" I say surprised.

Sofia nods, pulling out the keys from her pocket. One of my men picked them up from the alley, after I'd carried her away and we had to wash the blood off them before we gave them back.

She mutters something about it being a nice change for me to use the actual front door and that makes me laugh. She's a bratty, sarcastic thing, under that petrified demeanour. I'm going to enjoy bringing that side out and then punishing her for it.

Inside, it's the same story; all blacks and whites and monochrome, which when done well can be dramatic, but here, here it just highlights that this place isn't really a home at all.

I know this is technically a rental, I know Sofia has technically only just moved in, but it feels so soulless.

She mumbles about being quick, then disappears up the stairs as if she's anxious to be out of here too.

I'm half tempted to follow her, to pin her down on the bed and continue our playtime from the other night but she feels flighty. She feels off. And with what I have planned tonight, I want her to be at her best. I don't want her half-exhausted from coming too many times. I want her to have enough energy to enjoy the sacrifice I'm providing.

So I stay downstairs, examining the space now that I can see it in a good light.

There's a huge sitting room with two long, leather corner couches. Someone's strewn a few fluffy cushions, brightly coloured ones, and though I have no evidence to back it up, I suspect even those weren't chosen by Sofia.

In the kitchen there are no appliances on the side, nothing much in the cupboards beyond one set of bowls and plates.

It all feels lifeless.

I open the fridge and there's nothing. Not even a carton of milk. What the hell is this girl eating? She can't be living off takeaways, surely?

When I open the freezer my eyes widen. It's packed. Rammed. Full to the brim of frozen ready meals. Lasagne, curries, even a mini roast. As I pick a box up and examine it, Sofia walks in.

"This is what you eat?" I ask her.

Her face goes pale, the way one does when you've discovered a horrid secret.

"I can't cook." She says. "And I, I didn't trust deliveries."

I frown. "Trust them?" I repeat confused.

She sighs, dumping the bag in her hand. "When I was back at the hotel they spiked my food. Now I can't eat anything because I know it's an easy way to get to me."

"But microwave meals are okay?" How does that make any sense?

"They're sealed." She states. "They come in a big order from online. I made sure they couldn't be contaminated."

Fuck, is this how she's living? Fearful of even eating? No wonder she's a mess.

My eyes scan the room again. Perhaps that's why it all feels so lifeless, because she's not living in this space, she hasn't made it her home, she's just existing here the way she does everywhere else.

"I'm all packed." She says.

I raise an eyebrow, staring at the one bag at her feet. It's not small but it's certainly not big either. Most girls I know travel with a whole city's worth of shit. How has she managed to fit everything she needs into the one holdall?

I grunt in reply, crossing the kitchen, noticing more, seeing blank walls, empty shelves where there should be books, trinkets, picture frames. "Where is everything?" I ask.

She blinks back at me in confusion. "What do you mean?"

"Your stuff? Where is all your stuff?" I'd put money on all this furniture coming with the house because none of it *feels* like items Sofia would choose. It's all too generic, too safe. It feels like a safehouse. Like she's in witness protection.

"I, I don't have anything."

I turn back, staring at her expression that seems locked down like Fort Knox. "Why not?"

"They destroyed my things when they burnt the Montague House down." She says quietly.

"All of it?"

"Everything."

My eyes fix on the wall behind her. Where someone has scrawled in a thick black ink *'You're letting them win.'*

Apparently I'm not the only one thinking it.

She sighs, eyeing the writing in a way that makes me wonder if she was the one that wrote it.

"Let's get out of here." I say.

We'll keep the guards in place, more as a precaution than anything, Besides, it'll be interesting to see if anyone attempts to break in now that Sofia is no longer staying here.

I LET HER UNPACK, AFTER INSISTING SHE TAKE MY ROOM. THERE'S A saferoom built off the walk-in wardrobe so logically it makes most sense. But I'll admit there's a deeper, more primal want for her to be there, in my space, in my bed. In time it will become our room - I just have to play the long game for the moment. If I move too quickly I'll be fucking her before she's ready and I'll do far too much damage.

I want her to come to me. I want her to be the instigator. She doesn't realise it but she's going to lock herself inside my trap, willingly step inside, and then let me devour her.

When she comes back down, she's wearing her own clothes, a pair of jeans and a thick woolly jumper. Her hair is scraped back into a bun and she's obviously put some concealer on to hide the bags under her eyes.

She searches my face as if trying to read my thoughts.

"We need to establish a few rules." I say.

"I thought we already did that."

My lips curl. She *is* a brat, at least some part of her is. God, how I'd love to put her on my knee and spank her. All in good time.

"House rules." I reply forcing myself not to react. "You can go anywhere in the main house, but the basement is off-limits unless I'm with you."

She folds her arms, her lips pouting. "Is that where you keep your skeletons?"

"No," I answer. "It's where the house connects to the tunnels."

She blinks, registering exactly what I'm saying. "It all connects?" She half-whispers.

I nod. "I've built a fortress, an entire underworld beneath Verona."

"And you don't want me to see this?"

I don't have any exact reason why she can't go down there alone. I know my men won't cross any lines, but still, I want to keep her here, upstairs, where I can watch her.

"Fine," She says quietly sinking onto a bar stool.

I place a glass of water in front of her and she eyes it suspiciously before she takes a sip.

She doesn't speak when I get all the veggies out, when I get the meat out, when I start prepping. But she watches me like a hawk. Perhaps she's trying to ensure that this food isn't contaminated the way she's convinced herself every other meal is.

As the meat starts frying, I turn down the heat, leaving it to cook slowly.

She arches a brow, her lips quirking. "The great Koen Diaz can cook?" She teases.

"I'll let you be the judge of it when it's in front of you." I reply.

She frowns, dropping her gaze, like I've made some indecent comment. "I don't," She chews her lip like she doesn't want to get the last of the sentence out. "I don't like eating in front of other people." She murmurs.

Does she have an eating disorder? Is that it? As my eyes drop, I disregard that notion. It doesn't feel like she's intentionally starving herself, it feels like there's something else going on, some trigger when it comes to her food.

"What did he do?" I ask.

She gulps, crossing her arms, and refuses to look at me.

"Sofia?"

"I don't want to talk about it."

"You can tell me anything…" I begin but that seems to turn her from some broken thing into a rageful beast.

She's off her chair, all but snarling. "Sure I can," She snaps. "I'll just cut open more bits of myself, lay them out for you to pick over. You can feast on it all, feast on the worst moments of my life."

I hold my hand out, silently ordering my men who're on the peripheries, to get the fuck out. They exchange looks, glances, no one would dare speak to me like this. No one raises their voice to me if they know what's good for them. The only reason I've let Roman get away with as much as he has is because he's *her* brother.

But this girl in front of me, she's not angry at me, she's angry at the world, she's fucking raging and I get that, I understand that. I want to nurture that the right way.

"Sometimes it helps to get it off your chest, to get it out of your head." I state.

She scoffs, rolling her eyes and she clenches her fists. "That's what he said too. What he kept saying and you know what, it never helped." She screams the last before deflating like a balloon that's lost all its air. "It never helps."

I walk up to her, putting my hands on her shoulders. Maybe I shouldn't touch her, maybe that's a step too far but she doesn't flinch, if anything she seems to lean into my body like she needs the support.

"Who said that?" I ask calmly. Even now I've not raised my voice. If she wants to scream, if she wants to fight, if she needs to sate her anger on me, then fine, I'll be that person, I'll let her vent, I'll let her purge. It'll only make her depend upon me more.

"The therapist they make me see." She spits the words. "He delighted in going through it all, wanting to know how I felt, wanting to psychoanalyse me like I'm a bloody lab rat."

"Yeah?" I reply. "And you didn't put him in his place?" Oh I see the need for a therapist, the need for a counsellor, for some people they work wonders, but for me talking was not going to fix my trauma, fighting was far effective than talking ever was. And by the looks of it it's not helping Sofia all that much.

She jerks her chin, looking up at me and those beautiful dark eyes flash. "Maybe I did a few times."

I can't help the chuckle. She's like a raging animal that doesn't know how to control all the anger inside her and that's why she keeps exploding. Maybe after tonight she'll have a better outlet, one that truly eases her soul.

I turn back to the food, giving her a moment to recollect herself and she slips back onto that same barstool.

When I put the plate in front of her, I expect her to react, to visually respond but she just stares at it before picking up her fork and begins to poke.

I pick my own up, scooping up some grilled peppers and make a point of focusing on that.

"He…" She gulps, stabbing a bit of chicken. "He used to keep me chained up." She says so quietly. "He didn't feed me much but when he did it was in a bowl. A dog bowl. Half the time I think it was actual dog food he gave me and they'd all be there, laughing…"

She stammers most of it out, like she's confessing her sins and not someone else's. My eyes snap to her, seeing the way her eyes are down, the way her hand trembles. She looks like she's on the verge of a panic attack.

"…I used to only eat when I absolutely had to and then, after the drugs, I stopped caring."

"That's why you don't eat around others?" I reply softly.

She shrugs. "It feels too intimate, it feels too personal. Maybe he fucked with my head too much and I can't separate it."

I reach across, taking her hand and squeeze it. "Your head just needs a little time."

She bites her lip, "Maybe," She shrugs. "But them spiking my food hasn't helped either."

"That won't happen anymore." I state. "No one can get near you now. Everything is checked, everything is tested."

Her eyes widen. "Seriously?"

I give her a grim smile. "I learnt from Darius. I won't make any mistakes, have any weak points that allow our enemies to strike."

She stares at me for a moment, as if she's trying to see the lie in my words and then she turns her head, focuses on the chicken still impaled on her fork and slowly, almost delicately she takes a bite.

CHAPTER
Twenty- Four

KOEN

I gave her some space after we ate. Maybe she's unpacking her things, maybe she's just clearing her headspace.

But I wanted her to have that, a few hours, some time before I took her down.

When I tap on her door, technically my door, she's quick to open it. She's got a bright, fake smile, like she hasn't just been crying her eyes out or something and is trying to cover it.

"Are you ready?" I ask.

She nods, folding her arms, clearly trying to put on some show of bravado. I know I could call this off, give her a few more days, weeks even but what good would that do? No, I promised her this, I'm going to deliver.

She follows silently after me. The house is empty apart from a few guards and they're smart enough to keep their eyes forward as we pass by.

I open the heavy set door and Sofia's gasp echoes down the stark, unlit stairwell.

"It's a good few stories." I murmur, hoping this doesn't freak her out.

"You could have sorted the lighting." She replies.

My lips turn into a smirk as I flick the switch and bright, fluorescent strips illuminate the space. "Good enough for you, princess?"

She lets out a laugh that sounds far less strained than I thought it would.

"Your sacrifice awaits." I state, leading her down.

I'm not sure what she's expecting, I'm not sure if she even has memories of what the tunnels used to look like but as we open the doors and I reveal them to her, her eyes widen.

"It's, it's civilised." She says.

Yeah, it's more than that. We painted the walls, put proper flooring down, everything is state of the art. If the entire city above us turns to chaos we could hunker down here, surviving for decades.

Tia meets us on the second level. Technically this place has five floors and then the basement. Some of it are sleeping and living quarters but most is for work, for training, surveillance, storage of our armoury and the basement, well let's just say it wouldn't be a true underworld if we didn't have space for our very own version of hell.

Tia's hair is up, in a high bun. She's got her thick black glasses perched on nose. In the cute little pinafore dress you'd think she was more than a little out of place for her surroundings but I know she's a wolf in sheep's clothing. She likes to be underestimated, she likes to be written off as not being a threat.

"It's all ready." She says before glancing at Sofia.

Sofia eyes her warily, like she understands exactly the game Tia is playing.

"It's good to properly meet you." Tia says. "I mean, we met before, but it doesn't really count."

Sofia nods quickly.

"Shall we get this started?" I ask. Though she's putting a good show on I can feel her nerves starting to take over.

The three of us head down together. I had the man strung up in the nearest room I could, not wanting Sofia to have to walk past every other fucker we have down there.

As we reach the door I pause, "At any time you can walk out." I say.

She nods.

"You're in control here, Sofia, this is your court, however you want this to go down, that's how it will be."

She murmurs her thanks, but I can see how tightly she's clenching her fists. Maybe I've misread her, maybe she's got this and I'm the one overthinking this.

I open the door and that stench hits me like a train. Eric's been hanging all night and all day so I'm not surprised the bastard has shit himself.

He's in the middle of the room, suspended from a steel beam. There are eight men, my men, stood around, having made sure the bastard got no sleep. Afterall, they fucked up Sofia's dreams, they've haunted her enough that she's taken to stalking the streets, the least we can do is return the favour.

On the right wall we've had a variety of what I'll call instruments prepared. They all hang neatly, like this is some sort of hardware store and not a torture chamber.

I glance at Sofia, seeing how pale she looks.

"You want to…"

"You first." She says already guessing what I'm going to say.

My lips curl into a grin. I'm more than happy to break this man in, to give my Little Devil a performance on how it's done.

I pick up the bat, not my weapon of choice, but I don't want to maim him too badly – at least not in any way that will shorten Sofia's play time.

I swing wide, putting my entire upper body into it and the crack as it hits his leg is pure perfection. He screams out, he jerks, the chains that are stringing him up make a merry little tune as they dance against the beam.

"Did they break your bones?" I ask Sofia over my shoulder.

She nods, rubbing her hand and I stare at the finger that never seems to straighten. I guess that answers that, doesn't it?

I break his other leg, relishing in the pain he's now in and then I toss the wood. He's already a blubbering mess but if I have my way we've got hours left of this.

As he's hanging by his hands, I sadly have to let him down and he falls in a heap, landing right on those broken legs of his. He screams out more, trying to move, but my men are quick to surround him and ensure he's going nowhere.

I grab his left hand, raising it up and one by one I snap each digit, rendering them useless.

When I've done all ten, I place each hand flat on the ground and stamp on it hard enough to break his wrists. It's not just that they broke her finger, but these hands, they caused her pain, they inflicted that on her, so they'll pay the price.

He howls, curling up as best he can.

"You touched what wasn't yours." I state.

He mumbles something incoherent, nonsense words. I've a good mind to cut out his tongue but I think that might be a step to far for Sofia to witness just yet.

"Little Devil," I murmur, turning to look at her. She's still stood, staring at the scene in front of her and then it's like she forces herself to move.

She crosses the room, grabs a knife, and clutches it like it'll give her deliverance.

I can feel the way the room reacts, the way all the men seem to back off just a little. Maybe they can sense how on edge she is.

She draws in a deep breath then winces as that stench no doubt fills her lungs.

"You got this." I say quietly. I want her to make this move, to take the step that an ignorant man would argue will blacken her soul, but to me, I know it'll set her free.

She takes a step. Then another.

I tilt my head, see that firm mask on her face, wondering where she's going to strike. Will she take his eyes? Will she cut his flesh the way they cut hers? Or will she choose to stab?

Her jaw tenses, she's barely a metre from him and he looks up, whimpering like he deserves mercy.

She blinks, staring down like he's a ghost, like none of this is real. Her hand is shaking. The knife is sending flashes of light around the room.

She gasps, takes a step back, then another and she crumbles, before I can move to grab her.

CHAPTER
Twenty- Five

SOFIA

This wasn't supposed to be like this, I wasn't supposed to react like this.

Something latches onto my heart, clamping around it so tightly I can't think. My throat closes up. My body seizes as one memory after another hits me.

I try to speak. I try to fight it. To be strong, to be what Koen and everyone else here expects of me. Afterall, didn't he say this was a gift? That this man here was a sacrifice?

Only, it doesn't feel like he's the one on the verge of death.

I blink and I see those eyes, his eyes, except we're not here, in this room. He's not the one restrained, he's not the one covered in blood, covered in bruises.

A noise escapes me. Something broken. Something animalistic.

And then hands scoop me up, they carry me away, even though I wasn't aware I'd collapsed.

I shut my eyes, I bury myself into his chest, knowing that it's Koen, he's the one who has me right now, that once more he's become my saviour. Only I don't want to be saved. I don't want to be rescued. I want to do it myself. Why can't I do this? Why, even now, can I not just take my revenge when I so desperately need it?

"You're okay." He murmurs softly. "I've got you."

I don't reply beyond another pathetic, broken wail. What his men must think I don't know but those words still whisper in my head. That I'm weak. Pathetic. Just as broken as the day Otto forced me to marry him, and every horrific day after.

Koen puts me down. Sits me down. My breath is still coming too fast. My hands are still clinging to his t-shirt. He's knelt, staring up at me but when I force myself to meet his gaze I don't see disappointment, I don't see derision.

"This is my fault." He says quietly. "This was too soon."

"No," I whisper. "I wanted to, I needed to." I shake my head, trying to clear my muddled thoughts but it makes no difference. The panic is still there. My fear has me in a chokehold.

"Breathe with me, in and out."

I shut my eyes, focusing on his voice, on the gentle feel of his hands as they cup my face.

And slowly, so slowly, I come back to myself. I master myself.

"I'm sorry." I whisper. "I should have been better. I should have controlled myself…"

"Don't you dare apologise." He growls.

I can't quite look at him. It feels like my shame is erupting all over my skin. I shudder, wrapping my arms around myself as if it's simply the cold that's affecting me and not something far more nefarious.

"Tell me, Sofia, was Otto your first?"

I gulp, shaking my head. I guess now that I'm technically 'his' he has a right to know. A right to all my past, all my nasty little secrets. "No." I whisper. "But he thought I was a virgin. That's why he did what he did, he said it was to punish me, because I'd pretended to be pure when really I was nothing but a whore."

My words turn to sobs at that admittance. Maybe if I hadn't have played him the way I did he wouldn't have abused me so much.

"You being a virgin had nothing to do with it." Koen states. "He wanted to shame you because you were a Montague and because he's a sick, sadistic fuck. Add the fact that if you died he'd inherit all your money and that sealed the deal."

I frown at his words. Was that really it? All this time I'd convinced myself that I was responsible -what's the phrase he kept saying, play with fire and you get burnt? Well, I'd certainly done that. I led him on, I tricked him and played a part because that was what Roman needed. And yet Koen is saying something else entirely.

He watches me as if he can understand my thoughts and then something else strikes me, something I've been more than aware of but have been too cowardly to face.

"You held up your end." I say. "Aren't you going to take your fee?"

His eyes narrow but he doesn't move. He just stares at me.

But I need him to do this. I need to cross this line now, to rip the band-aid off and turn this fear into something that feels good. I grab my top, slowly pulling it up, only he yanks it back down quickly.

"What the fuck are you doing?" He snaps.

"This was our agreement." I whisper. "You get to fuck me."

"Not like this." He growls. "I said it would be at my pace."

I blink in confusion? Am I that disgusting that he needs to mentally prepare for it? Why would he then have agreed in the first place?

"Sofia," He murmurs, "You're mine now, and I'm going to take my time stripping you back, enjoying you, but most importantly, I want you to enjoy it to."

"Why?"

He lets out a huff like he's about to divulge some great secret. "I get my pleasure from other people's pleasure." He states.

My eyes widen, I shift, not sure if I'm trying to get away or just that I need to see his face. "What?"

"The term for it is a 'Pleasure Dom'."

I try not to squirm at the image that pops into my head. "What does that mean?"

"You want specifics?"

"Yes." I reply, though I'm not sure I'm ready to hear the words he speaks.

"It's about control. I enjoy making my partner come when I want. I enjoy forcing them to come, over and over, to teasing them, edging them until they're begging me for release."

My heart thumps so loudly in my chest. "Forcing?" I whisper.

"It's consensual." He says quickly. "There are safe words, hard limits. I don't do anything my partner doesn't want."

"But you force orgasms?" I state. How the fuck does that even work?

His lips curl. "When it's done right, it's incredible for the receiver."

I blush so much I think you really can fry an entire breakfast on my face. But I need to know, I have to know, "Is that what that was the other night then? Back at my house?"

His eyes seem to darken even more. "No, that, that was different."

"How?"

He shakes his head, "I crossed a line. I couldn't resist. Sofia, you don't understand how fucking desperate I am for you, how hungry I am."

My breath hitches. All that fear that had me clasped so tightly seems to vanish. "Why don't you just take me then?" I whisper.

His hand slams into the bed. I flinch more on instinct than anything else. "You think I don't want to? You think I'm not dying to spread your legs wide and fuck your sweet little pussy until she's weeping?"

I don't know what to say, how to reply. He seems angry now. Really angry. And some crazy part of me wants to do everything I can to change that.

I grab his hand, forcing it down below my trousers. "We made a deal, Koen," I state. "I'm yours to do as you like. And clearly you want this, so why are you holding back?"

He growls, one hand wraps around my throat and the other spears deep inside me. I barely have time to adjust before he slides a second in to join it.

"You want to simply be my plaything, is that it?" He taunts. "You want me to use you, to toy with you, to turn you into my own personal whore?"

I'm torn between my lust and my fear. On some level I do want that. I really do. But my body seems to revolt. I jerk, I struggle. Koen holds me down, keeping me in place.

"You can take this, Sofia," He groans as he starts thrusting inside me. "I know you can. You offered yourself to me, you want this as much as I do."

I shut my eyes, then have to force them open because the face I see when they're closed is not Koen's and I can't deal with that.

My hands grab at the one gripping my throat. He's fucking me so hard my whole body is rocking up and down.

"Such a tight little pussy." He states. "So wet, so needy, you asked for this, Sofia, you asked for me to use you."

I nod, moving my head only as much as he'll allow. I can hear how much I'm squelching, I can hear how wet I am. Christ, am I this fucked up now? Do I have some sort of rape kink, is that it? I should feel ashamed, I want to be ashamed. The way he's dominating me is making my adrenaline spike more and more. I can barely breathe from the hand compressing my throat.

But I'm moaning all the same, and I'm riding his hand, desperate for more. Desperate for whatever he'll give me.

"There's my good girl." He praises. "You want this as much as me, you're just too scared to admit it."

"Koen," I gasp. I'm so close now. But a voice in my head is telling me if I come, if I do this I'll only prove how broken I am. I'll only prove all those hateful things Otto used to say. The names they carved into my skin.

Maybe he sees that.

Maybe he feels the way I'm pulling back.

He shifts, moving his weight and then his mouth is on me, he's sucking my clit, forcing me to perform the way he expects.

I lock my legs around his head, I need more. I need all of this.

His teeth scrape against me. He bites me, enough for it to hurt, enough for it to feel like he's drawn blood and then I am coming. I'm screaming. I lose control, and it's only his hand against my throat that holds me in place as it feels like my entire world shatters into delightful pieces.

As I lay panting he stares up at me. And I see that hunger, that need, all that emotion inside me reflected in that gaze.

"I can't control myself around you." He murmurs, like he's confessing his sins.

"Then don't."

He narrows his eyes, shaking his head. "Don't say things you'll regret."

"You think I regret this?" I snap back. "You think I don't want this too?"

He smirks, dropping his gaze, staring at where I'm still spread wide open for him. "Oh, I know you want it, I can feel how much you want it, I'm just not sure you can handle everything I plan to do to you."

I can't find any words to say but as he prowls up my body and claims my mouth, I pucker my lips and I let him kiss me. No, I kiss him back, I welcome it, I let his tongue slip into my mouth and I don't feel fear, I feel panic, I just focus on the now, on this moment.

On the fact Koen Diaz is kissing me like I'm something somebody would want.

Like I'm someone he wants.

CHAPTER

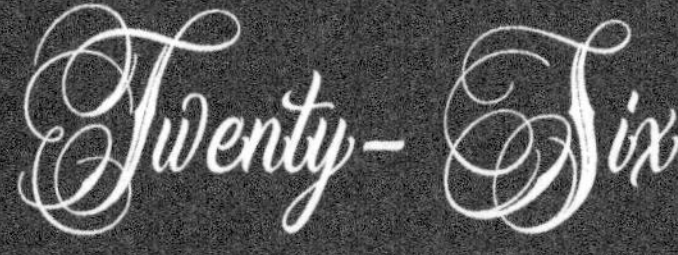

Twenty-Six

KOEN

I leave her to sleep. Or at least try to.

When I return back to the basement, Eric has already been dealt with. Apparently he didn't have any new information and my men hauled him out, still bleeding, still protesting his innocence, before throwing him into the incinerator alive.

It's a brutal ending.

But one that bastard deserved.

As I cross the room, Reid fixes me with a look.

"What is it?" I ask.

"Nothing." He mutters but we both know that's bullshit. Clearly he has something he wants to say. And playing coy was never his style.

"Spit it out."

"You sure you know what you're doing?" He asks.

"About what?" I reply.

"Those men, that girl in your bed. She might be rich but…"

"But what?" I snarl. Like her money is even a footnote in any of this. I have my own wealth. I have more than enough for all our present needs, and with Roman and my business plans, we'll be two of the richest fucks in this city.

No, I made that deal because why wouldn't I? I was going to kill these men anyway but when Sofia offered herself to me, when she all but laid herself out, I wasn't going to be noble enough to turn her down.

I wanted her here, I wanted her trapped but by her own hand.

I can still taste her on my tongue. I can feel the way her body seemed to melt as I kissed her. Fuck, what will she feel like when I'm inside her, when I'm there, worshipping her curves, when I'm teasing her until she's begging me for release?

"Those men we're killing, they're not nobodies. They're not insignificant. Someone is going to put this all together."

I grin back at him. "Let them. They can't come for us. I've made sure of that."

He narrows his eyes, muttering but I don't catch the words as he starts to walk away.

"And for your information," I call after him. "That girl might be in my bed but the only thing she's doing is sleeping in it."

I don't know why it matters. I don't know why I give a fuck what my men think but I also don't want Sofia to hear whispers, to think that I've let everyone believe we're fucking already.

No, I need to play this carefully.

I need to win her trust, prove that it's not just about getting in her pants.

She needs to know that this is more than that.

So much more.

Over the next week we find a routine of my choosing. Sofia eats breakfast under my watchful gaze and then, while I'm out seeing to business she works out, she swims, she makes herself at home.

She's still flighty, jittery, uncomfortable under the gaze of my men but they're under strict orders not to touch, not even to be in the same room unless they absolutely have to.

I know some of them are muttering, I know there are whispers about me becoming pussy-whipped but none of them dare say it to my face because they know I'd cut out their god damn tongues.

At night we sleep in separate beds. I don't know why I put that restriction in place but it seems necessary. Maybe I'm a masochist after all, maybe I get off on torturing myself, but it plays into my plan. I know it'll put her more on edge, confuse her as to my motives, and soon enough she'll seek me out, she'll come begging for me to get her off again.

Will she crawl on her hands and knees? God, I hope she does. She'd look magnificent, resplendent. And then I'd take that bratty mouth of hers and force my cock so far down her throat she'll be choking on it.

I just have to play this my way, I have to make the beauty come to me. To let her believe she has some control when really I'm stripping her entirely of it.

The next free day I get I take her out. Out of the city. Out of Verona.

She clambers onto the front of my bike, in borrowed leathers that fit her arse almost to perfection. The helmet she's wearing has a microphone and headpiece so we can talk while we ride. When I get on behind her, her body tenses just enough to tell me our proximity is making her heartrate spike.

I don't comment. I don't act like I've noticed but Christ does my cock harden anyway.

"It's a good hours ride." I say.

She nods, keeping her eyes forward.

The engine roars as it comes to life. Two of the guards open the gates and around us, the other motorbikes begin to move.

It would be a far more intimate thing for it to just be us. I know Sofia would probably be less on edge without so many men around her but I won't take the risk that such vulnerability would present. Besides, it's not like it's the entire gang, there are only ten other bikes beside our own. Ten other men, all armed, all ready to defend us should the necessity arise.

We make it to the beach in record time. As it's close to winter it's deserted.

"Why did you bring me here?" She asks.

I shrug. "I grew up not far from here. I spent a lot of my childhood playing on this beach."

"Oh so this is for nostalgia?" She teases.

I smirk. "Perhaps. I also thought you could do with a little fresh air."

She bristles. "I've been out." She states.

She has technically. She's wandered around the gardens. But we both know that's not what I was getting at.

"I thought being away from Verona might help."

Clearly she chooses not to reply, and instead bends down and picks up a rock. As hard as she can she tosses it into the sea and we both watch as it slips beneath the surface with a splash.

"How are you feeling?" I ask.

"About what?"

"It's been a week since you moved in. I wanted to check in, to make sure you're comfortable. That none of my men have crossed any boundaries."

She pulls a face. “It’s fine. Although I don’t think Reid likes me that much.”

I chuckle at that. “Reid doesn’t like anyone.” I state. “But has he done anything? Said anything?” If he has, I’ll have his fucking balls.

“No,” She says, “It’s just the looks. Maybe he thinks I really am a devil of sorts.”

I don’t think about the consequences, I don’t consider them, as though it’s instinct I run my eyes over her, taking in the way the leather highlights every delicious curve. Maybe I’m imagining it but it looks like she’s put on weight, though I doubt one weeks’ worth of proper eating has made that much difference.

She clears her throat, her cheeks heating, and she looks in the direction of where we left everyone else. “I’ve never ridden a motorbike before.” She says, deliberately changing the subject like she knows I’m imagining throwing her into the sand and fucking her right here, in front of the dozen or so eyes watching us.

“No? Prefer your supercars?” I reply.

She pulls as face. “I don’t like cars, at least, not driving them.”

My mind flickers to that incident, to her apparently being intoxicated and crashing a brand new Ferrari. Of course, we know it was a set up but the rest of Verona doesn’t.

“Why don’t you like driving?” I ask.

Her eyes meet mine. I see the twinkle in them as she bites her lip. “You’ll mock me if I tell you.”

“No, I won’t.”

“Promise?”

“I promise, Sofia.”

She stares at me, blinks, then shakes her head like she knows she’s going to regret this. “Why would I when I’ve always had people to drive me around? It always seemed like a waste of my time to get behind the wheel.”

I laugh before I can stop myself. "What a pampered little princess you are?" I tease.

She pouts, raising her hand and smacks me across my chest, not hard, teasingly. "You said you wouldn't laugh."

"I said I wouldn't mock you." I correct her.

"You promised, and now you've broken that promise."

"Forgive me, princess." I say, and she huffs more, folding her arms, but I can see from the expression on her face she's not really mad.

"You broke your word. Now you owe me." She states.

"Owe you what?" I ask.

"A favour. No questions asked."

My eyebrow raises. "What are you thinking, Sofia?"

"Nothing to concern yourself with yet." She steps away, and Christ, that haughty tone, one day soon I will beat her arse for it.

"No? It sounds like you want me to sell *my* soul now." I reply, ignoring the way my cock stirs.

"Does Koen Diaz even have a soul?" She murmurs glancing over her shoulder back at me.

I grab her, my hands wrapping around her throat and pull her close enough that our bodies connect. "I have a soul." I growl. Right now it's the only thing stopping me from taking what I want and damning the consequences.

She shivers in my arms but I can't tell if it's from fear or something else. Her pupils are dilated, her pulse is racing but both of those could be indicators of panic *or* arousal, and I'm so damn tempted to rip the bandage off and find out.

But I don't. To do that would ruin everything I've done to date. To do that would make her think that all I'm after is her cunt. When in reality, I want it all, everything. Every breath she takes, every glance, every second of her life. I want it all. And I will damn well have it.

I'm not a patient man. I never have been. But this *is* working. I'm luring her in, like some monster whispering to an angel, slowly seducing her, until she's falling right over the edge and toppling into my unbreakable trap.

I let her go, step back, giving her space.

"I didn't mean to offend…" She begins.

"You didn't." I reply before my mind fixes on something. If she doesn't like driving, that means she won't be very good at it. It's another weak point. Another vulnerability.

When I state that fact, she huffs.

"If you needed to escape, if someone was tailing you then it would be prudent for you to get better."

"I can't drive, can I?" She says. "They banned me."

I roll my eyes, like I give a fuck what the Governor or the Police have to say about it.

"You could always teach me to ride." She half-whispers.

"What?"

"You could. Surely, in a pursuit, a motorbike is better? And it definitely was more fun than a car."

My lips curl. "Maybe that was just being on my bike."

She blushes, shaking her head at the blatant innuendo. "You could teach me, though."

"You really want to learn?"

She nods before casting her eyes back to where I know my men are all watching. "Would they have a problem with it? A woman learning?"

"No." I mutter. "They'd probably respect you more."

Her face lights up. "Well, now you have to teach me."

I'm curious as to why she thinks she needs to earn their respect, but I admire it to. She doesn't seem to want to just swanny around the entire time, acting like my men are her subordinates. No, she might be a society princess but from what I can tell she's as down to earth as the rest of us. She might speak with a fancy arse accent but she's not stuck up, she's not pretentious, as far as I can tell.

I jerk my head, signalling for her to follow.

"Is this the part where you tie me up and throw me in the sea because I'm too high maintenance?" She teases.

Again, I run my eyes over her before I think. "If I'm tying you up, Sofia, it won't be because I'm going to chuck you in the sea."

She gulps, her cheeks flush and I'll admit I like the way she seems almost shy, bashful even around me. Perhaps that's what I need to do then, to tease that part out of her, to get her all hot and bothered and maybe she'll act from a place of desire, not a place of fear.

I hold my bike out, tell her to clamber on. She eyes it warily, like she hasn't already had her legs straddling it. It's far too big, I doubt she'd have the strength to control it by herself but I'm not stupid enough to try that.

I clamber on behind, scooting close enough that my groin makes contact with that perfect fucking arse.

She tenses, and if anything that makes my dick harden more. She's so flighty, and though I know the reasons why, it's taking every ounce of control I have not to just hold her down and show her exactly why she should be scared around me.

"Grab the handles." I instruct.

She bends forward, gripping them so tightly her knuckles turn white.

Slowly I tell her what to do, how to accelerate, where to put her foot for the brakes. My hands are right next to hers, holding the bike steady and as we start to move I can feel her excitement. The bike vibrates beneath us. Her body seems to shift, like she's noticing it more.

I'm half tempted to place my hand on her hip, to pull her back enough so that she can 'truly' feel the engine beneath her but perhaps that's a step to far.

Besides, I think it's better to edge her, to tease her, to build this up like a frog in a hot pan.

I'll heat the water, I'll watch as she slowly starts to sweat and when she does break, I'll be the one to witness it, I'll be the one to savour it. I'll be the one to enjoy it.

CHAPTER

Twenty-Seven

SOFIA

The house is quiet. Rose left after breakfast for a meeting with her lawyer and Roman and Ben disappeared off, no doubt to cause more havoc before we finally pull the rug right out from under Darius.

I let Lara play in her room with her new toys, and I'm sat in the parlour, book in hand, feeling restless though I can't put my finger on why.

We're almost at the finish line.

We're so close to ending this that I can practically see our victory - I can taste it.

And the best thing? I broke it off with Otto. I blocked his number. Blocked him on everything. As I shut my eyes I feel that wave of relief, that I'll never have to laugh at his unfunny jokes, never have to smile at his misogynistic comments as if they're okay. I'll never have to pretend again.

And I make a vow, from now on I'm done playing nice, playing polite. I'm never going to sit in a room, never going to smile when I don't want to, never going to put up with people I don't like. If that's the one positive I've taken from this entire situation, it's that I'm no longer a people pleaser. Life is too short for me to be constantly sacrificing my own peace for the sake of others.

No, from now on I'm going to speak my mind, I'm going to act without caring what arsehole I offend.

I'm done playing the sweet, simpering, naïve idiot that society expects.

I'm so fucking done.

I take a swig of my coffee. I even pretended with that – drinking sweetened frappucino god knows what instead of the pure black delight I love.

From now on I can return to being the recluse. To being the quiet, introverted, book loving geek that spent her time avoiding crowds, avoiding gossip, avoiding everything I've pretended to be over the last few months.

Beside me, my phone buzzes. Now that Otto's presence has been purged the only people who have my number is my brother, Ben of course, Holden, and Rose – not that she's ever used it.

But it's not a message. It's an alert. Our security system is down. I frown, sitting up, and place the book on the side as a sinking feeling rapidly spreads through my body. Why the fuck is our system down?

Before I can get up, before I can move, it feels like an explosion goes off. Glass shatters behind me and I'm thrown from my chair onto the thick Turkish rug.

"What the…?"

Footsteps. Dozens of footsteps echo from what feels like every room beyond the one I'm in.

I scramble to my feet. My heart is racing. Fear is threatening to engulf me but I swallow that down. Whatever the fuck this is, I'm not just going to crumple, I'm going to fight back.

There's a gun room across the hall, if I can make it there I at least have a chance of beating this.

My feet scream in protest as the glass bites into them but I force myself onwards, darting from one door to the next, with what feels like World War Three being raged around me.

As I grab the nearest rifle, my mind registers what I've forgotten. Who I've forgotten.

Lara.

Lara is here. Upstairs.

Fuck.

I click the safety off, darting once more down that same corridor but I head for what was once, centuries ago, the servants stairs, figuring they'll be a damned sight less conspicuous than the main one.

Around me gunshots echo. Apparently our system might have failed but the men Roman left behind are at least doing their job.

When I get to Lara's room it's empty. Deserted.

I call out her name, I scream it. God, if I can grab her, if we can get to the gardens and hide there until Roman gets back…

My thoughts die as someone struts in behind me.

"So this is where you're hiding…"

My throat constricts at that voice. When I turn, Otto's Head of Security, Marsden, is smirking, like he's caught a prize fish.

"What are you doing?" I gasp. "You can't just attack my home…"

"The game is up." Marsden says, folding his arms, not even caring about the rifle that I have pointed at his chest. He's wearing a bulletproof vest. But of course he is.

"What are you talking about?" I snap back.

"You, and your brother." He states, taking a step closer. "You think Otto didn't know? You think he really believed you were actually dating?"

"I was,"

His laugh cuts through the air.

I scowl, firming my grip. If I have to shoot him a hundred times I will. If I have to empty the entire magazine, then I'll do it.

"Your brother is dead." Marsden says with more than a hint of glee. "His buddies are all dead. You thought you could play a stupid game like we wouldn't realise. This is the consequence, Sofia."

I gulp, trying to stop the way my body is trembling. It won't help me shoot straight will it?

But Roman isn't dead.

I know it. They couldn't kill him that easily. They just couldn't.

But then, how else did they breach our security? How else are they standing here? Attacking us?

"Are you here to kill me too?" I ask.

It feels almost poetic if that's the case. All the Montagues killed in one final sweep. Maybe they'll turn our house into some sort of mausoleum. Afterall, they'll have to come up with a good story as to why we've all been wiped out the way we have. A vision flashes in my head; this house, blackened, burnt, like a permanent memorial.

He laughs again. "Kill you? Why would we do that?" He replies. "You're the sole heiress, Sofia. You're worth a fortune now. No, we won't kill, at least, not yet. You've got your sins to atone for first."

I don't think. I don't hesitate. I pull the trigger, aiming right for the bastard's chest. He groans as the bullet hits him but it does little beyond that. He pulls it out, holds it up and drops it with a look of contempt. "Gotta do better than that." He sneers.

And then a scream echoes. A scream that makes me freeze.

Lara. They have Lara.

"I'll do you a deal." I say quickly. "I'll go with you. I won't fight."

He narrows his eyes. I doubt he got orders not to hurt me but by the sounds of it he definitely won't be rewarded if I end up dead ahead of schedule. It's all I have to barter with. All I have to offer. My stomach twists in disgust and a cowardly part of me is already protesting.

But I can't not try.

I can't not attempt to spare Lara from whatever fate is awaiting me.

"In exchange for what?" He asks.

"The girl. Let the girl go."

He frowns, just as his men strut up behind him, just as they drag Lara into view.

She's sobbing uncontrollably. Her face has a handprint where someone has obviously slapped her. She looks so small, so fragile in the grip of a man three times her size. His hand is wrapped around her neck like he's about to tighten his grip and snap it in half.

Maybe this is all over.

Maybe the Montagues are fucked, I am fucked, but if I can get her out, if I can save her, it will be worth it. It has to be worth it. I can't just give in, roll over, let them do whatever it is they plan, knowing that I've failed.

No, if I can save Lara at least that will take away some of the bitterness at my own failure. At least it will make the pain that tiny bit more bearable.

"Let her go." I repeat. "She's a nobody. A nothing. Let her go and I will walk out this door and get in that car and do whatever you want."

His lips curl like I've just propositioned him. His eyes sparkle with amusement. "Who is she?"

"Like I said, she's a nobody." I repeat.

"If she's so insignificant why do you care so much?" He replies.

For a second I panic. For a second my mind goes blank. Fear takes over and I can't think. But I have to have an answer, something that explains who Lara is without putting a target on her back.

"She's just a girl, a child. That's why I care…"

He snorts, clearly not buying it and, as he jerks his head, as Lara is yanked back, she screams out the words that seal her fate. That seal mine too.

"Aunty Sofia, Aunty Sofia…"

Marsden gives me a shit eating grin that makes me want to punch him so badly.

"You're so full of shit." He says crossing the room, coming right at me.

I take aim, I shoot again, and again. Aiming right for his damned head. Only the damned rifle seems to jam. I try to uncock it, to clear the chamber, but there isn't time.

He grabs me, grabs the rifle and tosses it. "You better pray Otto's in a good mood." He says as he starts to bundle me out.

I kick, I scream, I give up all pretence at being rational. Otto's not going to be in a good mood, at least not in any mood that will help me.

If my brother is truly dead, if my entire family is gone then I am so utterly fucked. They'll be nothing to stop Otto, nothing to stop Darius. They're going to hurt me, they're going to make me pay. Marsden spoke about atonement – I know that the kind the Blumenfeld's are looking for will be paid with blood. My blood.

As I'm bundled into the car, as the door is slammed shut it feels like I'm already locked away in a dungeon.

It feels like I'll never see daylight again.

It's reckless. Stupid. But once Koen shows me the basics he gets me my own bike. One not nearly as powerful, or as big, or as heavy. And I spend hours riding it around, trying to get some sort of balance and control.

More often than not I end up losing my balance and crashing it and I have some damned impressive bruises.

A few of Koen's men give me pointers, setting up a little course for me to complete. A few try to hide their sniggers at how bad I am but it doesn't put me off. I mean, it's not like I haven't been laughed at for worse things, is it?

Whatever Koen is up to during the days, wherever he goes, he doesn't share that with me. A few times he doesn't come back at night either. I keep my mouth shut, deciding it's better not to know.

But the house feels strange without him, it feels empty, and in truth, I feel a little lost.

I wake most mornings wondering why he hasn't visited, why he seems to be losing interest. Did he have his fun and that's it, he's bored now? Maybe it's the fact that I'm readily available. There's no sneaking around, no chance of getting caught. I've ruined the fun. I've made myself boring.

No, if that was the case he'd have kicked me out already, would have sent me away.

Koen is up to something, he's playing games. Only I don't understand why. He obviously wants to fuck me, why doesn't he just get on with it?

After one particularly disastrous bike ride I walk in through the back of the house and come face to face with Reid. As usual, he's scowling at me.

Normally I'd walk away, scurry away. But today, with the bruises fresh and my adrenaline still pumping, I decide that I've had enough.

"What exactly is your problem?" I ask.

He narrows his eyes, stepping closer in an obviously threatening manner. "You don't belong here."

"No?" I reply, clenching my fists, refusing to back down, despite the voices telling me I'm picking another fight I can't win.

Stupid Sofia never learns her lessons, does she?

"No. It would be better for everyone if you left. If you walked away and returned to your flashy little life of cocaine and champagne."

My eyebrows raise. Cocaine and champagne? As if that was ever my life.

"Koen wants me here." I state, burying the doubt at those words.

He sneers. "You don't get it, do you? You don't get that you're putting all of us in danger."

"How am I?" I haven't done anything. I stuck to the rules Koen gave me. I haven't left without his men following me. Beyond learning to ride a motorbike I haven't done anything reckless at all.

"You're cursed." He says.

I blink, wondering if I've misheard him, or that maybe this is some sort of a joke, but the look on his face tells me it isn't.

"Cursed?" I repeat, unable to keep the scorn from my voice.

"You're unlucky." He states. "You're whole family is. You bring death and destruction wherever you go and you're going to get us all killed."

What the fuck is he talking about?

"That's enough." Someone says behind us.

I turn and see Colt eyeing us both warily like he's not sure how to defuse this situation.

My anger spikes and I cross my arms, glaring at him as if he's the one who just insulted me. "Do you think I'm cursed?" I ask.

His face hardens but he drops his gaze. "It's not for me to say."

I gulp, taking a step back. Is he serious? Are they both serious? They're grown men, what the fuck is this? "I'm not cursed." I state feeling like this is ridiculous.

"Yes, you are. You think I didn't check, you think I didn't look up it up?" Reid says. "We know what your father had…"

I screw my face up even more confused. What the fuck is he talking about?

"Reid." Colt growls only I don't stay to hear it. I storm off, needing to get some space.

REID'S WORDS KEEP ECHOING IN MY HEAD.

That I'm cursed.

That I'm unlucky.

Perhaps he's right; my own mother was found dead beside my cradle, my whole life has seen me flit from one disastrous situation to another.

As I make my way down to the pool, I wonder if everyone else here thinks the same. If that's what they see when they look at me. Something dangerous. Some sort of harbinger of death.

I toss off my robe, fling it in frustration onto one of the loungers. I didn't feel like a gym workout would suffice and besides, I used to love swimming, I used to be damned good at it.

Koen's pool is in the basement. A different basement from the one where he likes to keep his prey. It feels like there's an entire underground network beneath the hills that his house sits on. That he's got an army stationed here. I know they have sleeping quarters, living quarters, but Koen was more than clear that certain doors, certain areas were off-limits and I've made sure I respected that despite my curiosity.

Though there's no natural sunlight, there's a huge glass light above the pool, giving the illusion that we're in the Bahamas or somewhere equally as luxurious. Around the pool are tropical plants, with giant leaves, in pots so big they could fit a human easily.

There's a separate jacuzzi. And a plunge pool. There's even a sauna at the very end, though I don't like the heat of it, so I don't indulge.

I dive in and it takes a few lengths before I manage to find that mental calm that turns this from a conscious effort of coordination into something streamlined. Something effortless. I channel my anger, my frustration, even my fear into every stroke of my arms, every kick of my feet. I don't know how long I swim for. I don't really care. I just know that when I come to a stop I feel calm, I feel okay.

I ease myself out of the pool, grab the towel and dry my face.

It's the sound of hurried footsteps, the sound of someone all but smashing into the room that makes me turn.

Koen comes to a stop. His eyes seem to bore into me like he's never seen a girl in a bikini before. A part of me wants to squirm, to cover myself, but it's the heat in his gaze that holds me captive.

It feels like time stops.

It feels like everything stops.

I can see it, that look in his eyes, the want, the need, and then his eyes drop, his face turns from pure hunger to utter fury.

"What the fuck is that?" He growls.

I don't need to look. I don't need to see where his eyes are staring because I already know. I've kept my body hidden, have been careful to ensure no one sees even a hint of anything beneath my thick jumpers. But right now, I feel like I'm naked. Like I'm stood before him and he can see every awful scar. Every awful mark on my body.

I'm trembling, I'm shaking, I'm reduced back to that fearful creature I was, as a memory latches onto my mind.

…pinned down, held down, and, while they laugh, while they taunt, they take turns cutting into my skin, carving it up, before they're raping me again.

"Sofia?"

I blink but my eyes don't seem to focus.

My legs feel like they're barely holding me up.

I can feel something being wrapped around me - a robe. I know on some level Koen is covering me but I'm still trapped, like a prisoner, caught up in my own head, caged within it.

And I can't get out.

I can't get free.

CHAPTER

Twenty-Eight

SOFIA

We're in my room. Koen's room technically.

I'm sat on the bed. Again. And Koen is beside me, his arm wrapped around my shoulders to keep me upright.

Neither of us has spoken. Neither of us has said a word.

I can hear the clock ticking away what feels like hours.

Does he find me repulsive now that he knows there's physical evidence of my abuse? Evidence that can never be erased. Can never be removed.

"Who did that to you?" He asks quietly, gently.

"I, I don't remember." I say. My voice sounds so meek. So pathetic.

"None of it?"

"Not their faces. I remember hands, I remember smells, the stench of their sweat as they…" My chest heaves at that admission and I think for second that I might just puke.

"You knew it was those men the other week." He states.

"Yes, some faces I recognise. But most of it's a blur."

He frowns and I wait for him to repeat what the damned therapist said, that it's better I don't remember, better I try to forget. As if it's that easy.

Only he doesn't.

He just sits there, as if he wants to give me this moment to gather my thoughts.

"Do I disgust you?" Though I force them out, they sound like a whisper and I'm so fearful of what he'll say, if he'll say yes, if he'll tell me that I'm everything I believe myself to be. Tainted. Degraded. Unhuman.

"Why would you?" He growls.

"Because of my body, because of what they did to me."

He pulls me back, lies me flat on the bed and undoes the robe, baring me to him. I flinch but, before my terror can truly takeover again, he leans over and plants a kiss. It's soft. Delicate. So light I barely feel it but I know he's done it.

He plants another.

And another.

He's *kissing* my scars. Kissing all those awful reminders. All those words they carved into my flesh.

"What, what are you doing?" I stammer.

"You have the body of a warrior. You bear the scars of so many battles." He says meeting my gaze. "Someone should give your body the honour it deserves."

My tears erupt out of me. I wipe one away but another takes its place. "I'm not a warrior." I whisper. Warriors are brave. Warriors are courageous. I'm a coward. A pathetic, weak, useless person who couldn't even save themselves.

He soothes me, he brushes away my tears with his thumb as my sobs grow louder.

"It's over." He murmurs. "They can never hurt you again."

"It's not." I reply. "It's not over. As long as my body carries these scars, as long as my head remembers, I will always be there, in that room, trapped."

He growls, "That's not true. You might not forget but you can move past this. You can reclaim everything they stole from you."

I shake my head because that sounds as possible as me sprouting wings and flying to the moon.

"Sofia, it just takes time."

"It has been time." I snap. "It's been over a year."

"And maybe it will take longer, maybe it will take five years, ten even. But one day you will wake and you will realise that you are free, that they hold no power over you."

God, how I wish that was true.

"What if I don't?" I murmur. "What if I can't ever…" I trail off, dropping my gaze, shame erupting in my cheeks as I ask the question I've been so afraid of.

"Can't what?"

I don't answer. I don't say it. But he knows, I can tell he knows. Will he renegade on our deal now that he has confirmation the goods are faulty?

"Otto wasn't your first." He says. "But you didn't have much experience before that, did you?"

I shake my head. By the time I was interested in sex, Verona was a snake pit. I didn't trust anyone. I slept with one boy, one person who pretended to like me then ditched me soon after he got in my pants. It was a brutal lesson at the time but one I needed to learn.

Koen leans me back, stroking my hair. "I should be more gentle with you." He murmurs.

"No," I almost shout the word. "I don't want that, I don't…" I clench my fists, pushing him away. "I'm not a victim. I'm not that girl anymore. I don't want you to treat me like I'm broken. I want to be normal. Please, even if you have to force me, please..." My words die as my cheeks burn. I don't even know how to explain what I want. I just know I want this, whatever Koen is offering, I want his touch, his hunger, I want him to claim me without second-guessing my reactions, without constantly holding back.

Christ, I really do have something wrong with me, don't I?

He frowns, his eyes turning from sympathy to something else I can't quite read. "Fine," He says, pulling me around, yanking on the straps of my bikini so that it pings loose.

I know I should cover myself. My head is telling me that. That I'm a slut. And a whore, and everything my dear dead husband called me. But I don't. I sit there, topless, letting him look his fill.

His hand cups my breast. I jolt a little but I keep myself upright.

"We're going to fatten you up a bit." He states. "Get these back to their full fat goodness."

I blink, biting my tongue. Am I too skinny for his tastes then, is that it?

He pinches my nipple, not hard, but enough. "Do you like pain?" He asks.

I should say no. After everything I've been through I should really say no. "Sometimes." I whisper.

His lips curl like I've just rewarded him with some sort of prize. "Do you know how long I've wanted to feast on these?" He asks, circling them, teasing them, slapping them lightly.

"Did you touch them when I was asleep?" I ask.

God, I sound breathless. I don't even sound like me right now.

"I did." He says looking me right in the eyes without a hint of shame. "But not nearly enough."

He cups my other breast, squeezes them together. I can't tell if I like it or not. I'm not overly sensitive when it comes to my nipples, maybe that's why I like the idea of pain, it's not like pleasure is doing anything.

He leans down then takes a bite.

I cry out. I jerk, twisting, only my nipple takes the full brunt of my movement.

Koen groans, pushing me onto my back. "I've dreamed of that." He says. "I've dreamed of biting you so hard I leave teeth marks."

Yeah, that should send me running to the hills.

That should have me freaking out.

My adrenaline is spiking, my heartrate feels through the roof, but if anything it's turning me on. Apparently I'm a full on junkie now when it comes to Koen.

He gets up, stalks across the room, then comes back with something in his hands. I'm not sure it's even safe to look but when I do my jaw drops.

He kneels down, leaning right over me and fixes the clamps, one after another. They're tight, painful, but it's definitely bearable.

"Sofia," He growls. "You look so damn good right now."

I can't take deep breaths. When I try it sends a shooting pain right through each breast. But I want to please him, I want him to enjoy whatever this is. If I refuse him now he might just walk out and never touch me again.

My nipples look engorged. They've gone so dark red, as if all the blood is pooling where the circulation is being restricted.

He slides my bikini bottoms off, places his hands on my knees, pushes them apart and stares at my pussy. I know he can see all of me. That I'm entirely bared for him and I can't help the squirm, nor the way my insides clench.

"I'd put a clamp on this pretty clit of yours." He says, "But I don't think you can handle it yet."

"I can." I whisper.

He lets out a laugh. "No, Sofia, you can't." His hand slaps me. He literally slaps my pussy and I yelp. Only the movement sends a jolt right through my breasts and my eyes well with tears.

He looks up, stares at my face and I know he can see it.

Then he raises his hand, and he slaps me again. Right on my clit.

Once more I jump, once more that pain hits me but this time he's already soothing it, soothing with his fingers.

"You're being such a good girl." He states. "You're taking this so well."

I don't know how to respond. His words sound so calm, so gentle, but his actions are anything but.

He slips one finger into me. I grit my teeth, trying to hold still, to spare my breasts. If he starts actually thrusting then I don't stand a chance.

"You're so wet, Sofia." He says. "I think you like having your pussy slapped, don't you? I think you like me using you like this."

I nod, as shame radiates on my cheeks. I do like it. I can't deny that. It hurts, it's humiliating but in my fucked up head I've already been trained for this, I've spent an entire year being conditioned into enjoying whatever shit is thrown my way.

"Such a good girl." Koen groans, curling his fingers, teasing a spot deep inside me that makes me arch my back despite myself. White hot pain shoots down my chest but I don't care. I don't give a shit. The pleasure far outweighs it. What Koen is doing, how he's manipulating my body right now is better than anything I could ever imagine.

My legs open wider, I beg him with my body to continue this, to use me.

His hand once more wraps around my throat and he starts thrusting, pumping, fucking away relentlessly with his hand.

I whimper. I cry. Actual tears are streaming down my face but I don't ask him to stop. I don't want him to.

"That's it." Koen growls. "Take it, let your pussy enjoy every second of this. Clench around me, show me how much you're enjoying this."

"Fuck," I don't know if it's from pain or pleasure but the word slips out.

Koen looks at my face, he stares into my eyes, and then he lowers his mouth planting his teeth onto my right thigh and he bites.

The effect is instantaneous. I explode. I combust. I lose myself in what I know is merely an orgasm but it feels so much more than it, it feels so much more intense. It's earth shattering.

I scream, I writhe, I don't care how the clamps rip my flesh, I don't care how Koen's teeth tear my skin. I become something else, I rock my hips, fucking his fingers so desperately as I ride out every second of this euphoria.

And when I do finally come down, I can't even speak. I can't even think. I just lie there, like I'm mute, seeing how Koen cleans me up, how he undoes the clamps and places ice on both my nipples, circling them until it's all melted.

He carries me into the shower. I don't really understand why he's washing me off, it's not like I'm dirty, but I don't complain, I don't have the energy too. I just hang limply in his arms until he's finished. And then he's drying me off, tucking me back into his bed and turning off the light.

The last thing I see before I drift off is him sat there, watching me, like he's some sort of guardian angel, only I've come to realise he's not that.

He's the devil. The actual devil.

And I'm a sinner happily caught in his particular version of hell.

Maybe I'll rot here.

Maybe this is my ultimate punishment.

My true life sentence for all the sins I've committed. All the mistakes I've made.

I've stepped into this trap of his, and it feels like he's slowly turning the screws, locking me up, but I'm okay with it. I'm content with it.

As long as he keeps playing with me, as long as he keeps touching me, torturing me so deliciously, he can imprison me forever.

I just want him.

All of him.

Every last piece.

CHAPTER Twenty- Nine

KOEN

I stay with her, waiting until she falls asleep and then I tuck her up into the covers.

Once more I've gone too far, taken things way beyond what I wanted. And yet I have no regrets. She was beautiful. Magnificent. The way her nipples swelled, the way her cunt turned dripping wet after I'd spanked her.

Yeah, she is into pain – she clearly wasn't lying about that.

I couldn't resist biting her, I couldn't resist leaving a memento that will last, that will linger.

Tomorrow she'll wake and her breasts will hurt and her leg will be bruised. I'll admit I like the idea of that, that she'll be walking around, carrying the evidence of what we did tonight for days.

My cock is desperate for attention. There are enough whores down in the basement for me to know I could get myself sorted there, but it feels a betrayal. We may not be a couple in the normal sense of the word but while I'm with Sofia I have no interest in any other woman. I doubt if I tried I'd even be able to fuck another. I've wanted Sofia for more than a year and now that I finally have her I know I won't be satisfied with any cheap imitation.

Once it's clear she's not waking up, I stalk back through the house and down to the basement, the side where my men have an entire fortress worth of space.

There's a group of them playing cards, drinking, relaxing. On any ordinary night I wouldn't give a shit but when I see Reid amongst them my fury explodes.

I grab the table flipping it one handed and whatever is on top, all the chips, go flying.

Half the guys sat around fall off their chairs. A few pull out their guns but when they see it's me, they quickly re-holster them.

"You fucking piece of shit." I snarl, grabbing Reid by the throat and haul him off his feet.

He jerks, kicking out wildly, and I toss him hard enough that he slams back into the wall.

"The fuck did you say to her?" I shout.

"Nothing I haven't said before." He shouts back.

"I told you to stay away."

"And I told you that she's cursed."

A murmur goes through the men watching us and a few of the idiots cross themselves as if they're religious.

"That is complete bullshit and you know it." I snap.

"Is it?" He replies. "Her mother's dead. Her father's dead. Everyone she's ever come into contact with has met with a bad ending."

"Yeah?" I snarl. "The same could be said for me."

"Her father had the diamond." He snarls. "We all know it."

It's hard not to snort. Not to scoff. Oh, I've heard the rumours. We all have. A jewel worth more than an entire country? A diamond so black and tainted, they claim it's the actual devil's heart. But it's bullshit. Even if Horace Montague did possess it, it's long gone. Darius probably smuggled it out after he burnt their house down, then he squirrelled it away somewhere and now it's lost forever.

Reid shakes his head. "She'll be the death of you. The death of all of us."

I slam my fist into his face. If I have to beat those words out of him I will. He groans, collapsing on the floor.

"Stay away from her." I growl. "You don't look at her, you don't speak to her, you don't even be in the same room as her, you hear me?"

I can see the look of fear, I can see the way all my men are reacting.

Good, I want them afraid, I want them to understand the consequences.

Sofia is here to stay, this is her domain now and I won't have them fucking it all up, I won't have them making her doubt herself, I won't have her recovery set back because they're a bunch of morons.

I need her to choose this. To want this. She'll hardly feel content in her new prison if she's constantly surrounded by people who are making it more than clear they don't want her here.

CHAPTER

KOEN

The next day we're up early. Sofia looks like she's had as shit a night despite our playtime and she's definitely grumpy.

Though I try not to, my eyes drop to stare at her clothes, at her stomach, at where beneath, I know those scars are. What if she *is* too broken? What if she *isn't* capable of truly healing?

No, I refuse to accept that.

I refuse to believe that she can't move on.

She just needs to believe in herself. She just needs to get out of this death spiral she's caught up in.

"We're gonna work some of this out." I murmur. If it have to, I'll drag her through it, I'll carry her from the very gates of hell with her hissing and clawing me the entire time.

"What?"

"Your trauma, your pain, your anger too." I say.

She shakes her head. "If it was that easy I would have done it before."

"It's not a miracle cure." I reply. "It takes time. You can't keep expecting to just wake up and it all be fixed."

She scowls back at me but whatever curse she wants to say, she keeps it to herself, following behind me as we head to the gym.

She's wearing a baggy jumper. It's not really ideal for what I have in mind but it's just tough. I jerk my head, motioning for her to follow me over to the ring. She's used the equipment a number of times, mostly just the running machine and a few free weights, but today I want to try something different.

I pick up a set of gloves and toss them at her. They almost smack her in the face because her reflexes are shit – that's another thing I want to work on.

"I've never boxed before." She says.

"Today you're going to learn." I state.

She lets out a huff, pulls her gloves on and secures them.

I start off with the basics, showing her how to stand correctly, how to angle her punches for maximum impact.

It's slow, methodical. I can tell she doesn't have the patience, but she bites her tongue and she continues on, pushing herself.

It doesn't take long before she's sweating. She wipes her brow but, with that jumper on, it doesn't make much difference.

"You could take it off." I say.

She turns her head and narrows her eyes. "You'd like that, wouldn't you?"

I smirk. Yeah, I like her being a brat. Perhaps that's how she was before all her trauma fucked her up. I'll happily tease that side out of her more.

"You're hot." I state. "And not just to look at. Take your jumper off, maybe you'll be able to hit better when you're not constantly overheating."

She glares at me, lifts her arm and delivers a perfect punch to the pad. "I'm not bad thank you very much."

"You can be better."

Clearly she ignores that comment, landing another punch, and then another before she stops, muttering under her breath.

"You can't hide forever." I say.

"Excuse me?"

"Those jumpers, all that material you wrap your body in." I reply.

She snarls, pulling the gloves off and tosses one after another onto the ground. "You know why I'm wearing this." She says, getting right up into my face, yanking on the collar as she does. "You saw."

"I saw." I confirm. "And like I said, what I see and what you see are two very different things."

"I'm not a warrior." She states. "I'm not."

"You are, you just need to realise it."

"Maybe you need to realise that somethings can't be fixed. That *I* can't be fixed."

"Is that what you tell yourself?" I reply. "No wonder you spend your time wallowing."

I know I'm being a dickhead. I know I'm pushing her, probably beyond what she can take right now but I want her to snap out of this, to take that snarky little attitude and that fire inside herself and put it to something worthwhile.

"I don't wallow."

"No?"

"I was doing fine, I was…" She draws in a deep breath. "Can't you just fuck off and leave me alone? Use me just for orgasms and pretend I don't exist beyond that."

"We had an agreement, Sofia, this is part of it." I state.

"Maybe I should have agreed to just fuck you."

"Yeah?" I murmur. "Go right ahead. Show me that pretty pussy I own."

Her eyes widen, like she's let her mouth run and only just realised what she's said. "You want me to strip, then fine."

She yanks her jumper, practically ripping it up and over her head and then she flings it as hard as she can. Underneath she's just wearing a tank top. It covers her but it clings. Her arms are bare, her collarbones, her neck, all that skin she seems to cover like she's a leper, it's glistening with sweat.

"Does it feel better?" I ask.

She scowls. "No."

My lips curl. "Little liar." I say loud enough for her to hear before I bend down and pick up the gloves. "Put these back on. We're not done with this lesson."

CHAPTER

Thirty-One

SOFIA

The room is dark. I'm curled up, huddled up, pressed into the corner between the wall and the bedside table. It's where I've been all day. Where I've stayed after Marsden brought me here and locked the door.

I don't know where Lara is.

I don't know what the fuck is going on.

But when I hear footsteps I freeze. They're getting closer. Too close.

I already tried the window but it's barred. I know there's no way out, no other exit but the door across from me. The one someone is about to walk right through.

When it opens, light pours in and for a second I'm completely blinded.

"Where is the slut?"

Otto's voice carries to where I am and when his eyes find mine, I can't help the shudder. I know I'll find no mercy there, no matter how nice I play. No matter how much I plead.

"Get up." He spits.

"What's going on?" I ask.

His lips curl. He glances across at the person blocking the door. At his brother. Darius.

"Still playing the game, Sofia?" Darius sneers.

"What game?"

Otto crosses the room and yanks me to my feet. His fingers dig into my arm enough to make my eyes water and a yelp escapes my lips.

"It's over, Sofia." Otto states. "All of it is over. Your family are gone. Congratulations on being the last of them."

I blink, trying to register those words but they don't sink in. Nothing sinks in.

"Look, I don't understand…" Otto's hand silences me. He grasps my face, pushing me back by it and I land haphazardly on the bed. When I try to get up he pins me down and my fear multiplies because he's already made it abundantly clear what he's capable of, hasn't he?

"You're full of shit, Sofia." Otto spits. "But it's over now." He glances at his brother.

Darius has moved closer now. It feels like the pair of them have me cornered. It feels like I'm their prey and they're about to do something abominable.

"Let me explain a few things." Darius says, unbuttoning the cuffs on his shirt like he doesn't want to get it dirty from what's about to go down. "Your brother is dead. Whatever shit you two have been trying to pull is over. Rose Capulet is mine and you…" He grins, "You belong to my brother to do with as he likes."

I blink, staring between them. "I won't…"

A hand strikes me. I don't know who it belongs to, but for a second I lay dazed. It's the sound of a zipper, the sound of clothes being removed that makes me focus. That forces me to act.

I try to sit up and realise that Darius is there now, at my head, holding me in place with an arm wrapped around my neck.

"My brother deserves a reward, don't you think?" He murmurs into my ear. "After all the games you've played, after all those evenings of leading him on, of not putting out."

"Please," I gasp. He's pressing on my throat, restricting my airway just enough to force compliance and I hate that it's working.

Otto stares at me, not my face, he doesn't give a shit about my face. No, he's staring at my body. He starts ripping my jumper, shredding the cashmere right down the middle as I shriek. He undoes my jeans, yanking them off before he's tearing at my underwear like this is some sort of race.

"I bet you're not even a virgin, are you?" Otto spits. "I bet that's another lie."

"Fuck you." I cry.

He clambers on top of me. That stench, that disgusting mix of body odour and whiskey covers me. "I told my brother I get first dibs." He states. "But you know, Darius deserves a reward too. You Montagues have caused enough of a headache. Why don't you be a good girl and make it up to us both?"

I scream. I kick. I do everything I can to try to throw him off but he's too strong. Darius tightens his grip around my neck and for a second I think I must pass out. Only, when I come back around I wish I was still unconscious. I wish I could shut my eyes and never wake up.

I'm now completely naked. All my clothes have been removed. Otto is grunting, groaning, clearly enjoying every second as he's violating my body. I feel like I'm on fire, like every thrust he makes is a dagger tearing me apart.

His hands pin my legs wide open, while his brother continues to hold me in place by my head.

I can't stop this. I can't do anything and that realisation makes it so much worse.

As my tears stream down my face, he licks them off, one by one, like they're a delicacy he has to savour.

And when he's done, when he's finished, Darius releases his grip, he moves on top of me, and he grabs my legs, no doubt angling me better, before he pushes himself inside me, tearing me even more.

I scream, I cry out, I try to fight but it makes no difference.

And all the while, the pair of them are laughing. Like this is some kind of joke. Like any of this is funny.

ANOTHER WEEK PASSES. ANOTHER WEEK WHERE ALL I DO IS SPIN MY wheels, metaphorically speaking that is.

Only, that's not exactly true.

I feel like I'm making progress. Slow progress. Baby steps, as Koen keeps calling it.

He makes me train with him every morning, before he disappears off to god knows where.

He's calm, patient even. He doesn't criticise when I fuck up. He just quietly corrects my posture, corrects my aim. Some days I have to fight to keep my body from reacting, from flinching at his proximity.

But some days it's like I'm not really me. Like some mad woman has possessed me.

He stands so close I can feel his breath hitting my skin. When he has to touch me, he's careful, only doing enough to correct my mistakes and then he instantly lets go. Maybe he's doing it on purpose, maybe he's trying to wind me up, make me desperate.

Either way it's working and I hate it.

I'm not wearing jumpers, I guess I learnt from that mistake the first day. But the tops I am wearing are still covering enough so that none of the horror of my skin is on show except for my arms.

A few times his men are there, working out, training. They keep to themselves, they avoid looking in our direction. Maybe that's an order Koen gave them. Maybe they also think I'm cursed.

As I land one punch and then another, I feel that anger, that spark of fury. I'm not fucking cursed. I might be unlucky. I might have had a string of bad luck but that doesn't mean everyone around me is destined to die a grisly death. I mean, this is real life. Curses don't exist. Bad mojo or whatever you want to call it isn't actually a thing.

Roman calls me a few times. He checks-in enough to make sure I'm okay but not enough for me to feel like he's stalking me. Apparently he's done some sort of deal with Hastings in regards to my therapy sessions. Apparently they're turning a blind eye to my 'non-attendance' to date. I don't think I give that much of a fuck really.

They never helped. They never eased my trauma. If anything, talking about it, discussing it made it worse.

But today all that changes. Today I *have* to see Martin again.

He struts into Koen's house with a judgemental look in his eyes.

I refused to go to his office, refused to be anywhere near it. I know we could have met somewhere else but this felt safer. Being in my space felt safer.

My lips quirk as I realise I know consider Koen's home as mine. Would Koen enjoy that fact? I guess it doesn't really matter either way. I belong to him now, that's the deal I made and I won't go back on it. I won't change my mind. I made my bed, and I'm more than willingly to let Koen fuck me in it.

"So this is where he lives?" Martin says like he's more interested in Koen than me.

"There's a study we can use." I state ignoring his comment entirely as I lead him through the hallway. I've already shut off the main doors, hidden as much as I can. I don't know why but this feels like an invasion of privacy. It feels like an insult to have him here.

He takes a seat, crossing his legs, fixing me with a judgy look that I try to ignore as I shut the door and force myself to not flip out.

When I sit down he makes a point of just watching me. Like he can read my thoughts. Like he knows every sordid little detail of my life.

"How have you been?" He asks.

"Fine." I say quickly.

His eyebrow raises, he pulls something out of his battered leather satchel and he flicks through the papers like he's some sort of tv cop and this is an interview. "You got drunk and crashed a car." He comments. "And now you appear to be hiding out with a known criminal."

"I'm not hiding out." I snap.

His eyes seem to sparkle like my annoyance is amusing to him.

"Are you fucking him?"

"Excuse me?" I gasp.

He sits back in his chair, assessing me for a second. "If you're having a sexual relationship…"

"It's none of your damn business." I reply.

"Sofia, after everything you've been through now is not the time to be shacking up…"

I'm on my feet in an instant. "Whatever is going on between me and Koen is no concern of yours." I repeat. "Surely you didn't come here simply to discuss my love life?"

He lets out a low breath, gesturing to the chair I just got up from. "Of course not. We're here to talk about your feelings, your trauma, to help you work through your severe PTSD."

He sounds so smug. So damn condescending. I don't think I've ever wanted to punch him more than in this moment.

But a voice in my head is whispering that I don't have a choice, it's a hoop I have to jump through. Hastings won't keep giving me an entirely free pass. I have to play my part to, and this is sadly part of it.

I sit back down, folding my arms, glaring at him.

He starts flicking through the papers again and I realise it's my file. Everything he's ever written about me. He's never had this out before, he's normally kept this hidden away. I'm so curious to know what he's written about me that it takes everything I have not to rip it out of his hands and make a runner.

"Last time we met we were discussing the videos. How they made you feel." He comments.

I huff, that's not how it went but fine.

"He took you to the Cuckoo Club, didn't he? What did those nights involve?"

I gulp, shutting my eyes, trying to bury the emotion that rises up and threatens to drown me.

What did they involve? I was dressed up, drugged, and laid out like a five course buffet for Otto and his friends to feast on. Of course, once Otto started turning to more hardcore drugs everything gets hazy. Perhaps I should be grateful to my husband for that. The heroin spared me some of the worst parts at the end, but then, not knowing is just as bad.

My memory of those last few months is patchy at best and I think that's partly why my mind keeps getting stuck. It's like I can't move on because my brain can't process it. I can't fully deal with what I went through because I don't understand everything I went through.

But I understand enough.

I remember enough.

"Sofia?"

I blink, looking back at his bland, boring face. I have no idea how long I just zoned out for.

"What about your father, I know there's some history there…"

I scowl, folding my arms, muttering that we're not here to discuss him. We're not here to talk about my family, about my parents, about Roman. We're here to talk about my dear dead husband. About what he put me through. That's it. Nothing more.

He shakes his head like he wants to actually snap back but clearly thinks better of it. Apparently, I really am pissing him off today and I'll admit I kind of like it.

"How are you sleeping?" He asks. It's one of his favourite questions. One he seems fixated on.

"I sleep fine." I lie.

And he knows I'm lying. Of course he does but like always he doesn't probe me.

"I want you to try some new exercises. When you're alone, when you're in bed, I want you to shut your eyes, I want you to think back to one moment, one memory, visualise it in your head, visualise what your husband is doing, what his friends are doing, and then I want you to imagine that you can walk away. That you can simply leave."

Is he for real? He wants me to actually try that? It's bad enough dreaming about it. There's no way in hell I'm going to consciously try to bring up those memories.

"It'll retrain your brain. It'll make you think that you had control in those moments."

"But I didn't." I say before I can stop myself. "I had no control."

"Exactly." He replies with a smile that feels so out of place. "Your husband took that from you. He stripped it from you."

My heart is thumping, I feel like I'm on the verge of a panic attack at just the thought of what he's suggesting.

"I also think we should try the meds again." He adds so casually.

I almost let out a laugh. Thankfully my fury seems to override my panic and I flit back from fear to anger. "No."

He tuts, pulling the bottle and he places it down on the side table beside him. "It will help, Sofia. You're clearly not making any progress without them."

I narrow my eyes, half tempted to tell him to shove them up his arse but thankfully he's getting to his feet. "Let's call it a day."

"Fine." I reply through gritted teeth.

He all but sees himself to the door, like he's got some sort of eidetic memory and has already has the entire floor plan memorised.

"I'll see you again next week." He says cheerfully and I grunt back before slamming the door in his face.

I'm trembling, shaking, like I'm on the verge of a breakdown and it takes everything I have not to curl up into a ball.

When I get back to the study I grab the bottle and toss it into the bin. I won't do it. I won't willingly drug myself. He may think I'm not getting any better but I *feel* better. At least, I did until he walked through the door.

CHAPTER Thirty-Two

SOFIA

The door opens. A torch is shone right in my face. Before I can do anything beyond shield my eyes, someone yanks on the chain secured around my neck.

I gasp, grabbing hold of it but it makes no difference and I'm dragged out of the solitary room he keeps me in. My knees protests, my feet try to get some sort of anchorage but I'm moving too fast to get any grip.

Every step bashes into my already battered body and whoever is doing this just laughs as I cry out.

The metal around my throat digs into my skin and I desperately try to get some leverage.

Above me, the semi-darkness turns to light, I know I'm no longer in the cellar, that I'm being taken to where my so-called husband is waiting for me.

Normally they hose me down first, normally they wash me and then dress me up to make me more appealing, so I guess I'm not going to the club, though that thought doesn't give me any comfort. Otto's already proven he can do whatever he likes and here, in the confines of his house, he morphs into something far more sadistic.

"Jesus." Someone mutters when I'm finally dumped on a rug. My nails clench the soft fabric. I'm face down, my body curled up, pressed against it but I'm not wearing anything so I'm completely exposed and the cool air makes my skin erupt into goosebumps.

"She stinks." Another voice says.

I hear Otto's deep, throaty laugh and though I know I shouldn't do it; I look up, I glare at him.

He's leant against a sideboard, arms crossed, that arsehole grin across his face.

"Hello, wife," He says in that tone that always puts the fear of god into me.

I don't know what's about to happen, I don't know what he has planned for today but I know I'm going to have to endure every awful minute. I grit my teeth, telling myself that I can do this, that I can beat him, that I can endure, but what's the point?

Roman is dead.

No one is coming to save me.

Darius won. He outplayed us.

My only salvation will be when my body finally gives out and I'm dead. Though that feels a long way off.

No, Otto will make sure I don't receive a speedy one, he'll ensure I live for years, that I suffer like this for decades.

A man squats down beside me. My breath goes more shaky and I can't help the tremble as he runs one long finger right down my spine. "Is all of this necessary?" He asks.

"She's mine to do as I like." Otto replies.

Another man snorts.

I turn my head, counting, there's four here, four men including my husband. Will they all rape me? Is that what this will be? Another night of the worst kind of degradation and abuse?

A pair of shiny oxfords appear by my head. They're so shiny I can almost see my reflection. As the man leans down, I whimper.

"Ssssh," He says, stroking my hair like I'm not disgusting. "If you're a good girl you'll have nothing to fear."

It's a lie. I know it is. Whatever they have planned is about them, not me.

He grips my chin, forcing me to look at him and my heart slams into my chest as I take in that hard face and those ice-cold eyes I'd recognise anywhere.

"You." I gasp.

His lips quirk.

I might not have seen him in well over a decade but I know who he is. That moment in my father's study was seared into my brain. And the man in front of me haunted my dreams for years afterwards.

"It's been a while, Sofia." He replies. "I must say, I expected to find you in a better state than you are."

Otto huffs and I can't make out the comment he makes.

"You said you didn't hurt girls." I stammer, not that I think this man is going to be my saviour, far from it.

The man laughs. "You do remember." He sounds impressed, he sounds like he wants to give me some sort of prize. "Only, you're not quite right, I said I don't hurt little girls. You're not little anymore, Sofia."

Fear clutches at me, I don't know why this man terrifies me as much as he does but I have to get away, I have to…

That chain around my neck is yanked and whatever futile attempts I make are just that; futile. I slam back onto the rug with a groan.

The man is standing now, tutting, looking just as annoyed as my husband.

"Bring the bag over." He orders.

My eyes dart across the room, someone dumps what looks like a leather holdall right in front of me. Are they going to murder me? Cut me up and dispose of my body in that? No, Otto doesn't need to hide the evidence, he doesn't need to go to such lengths, he and his brother own this city now, they have no need for subversion.

I'm pulled to my feet. Held firm by two pairs of hands from behind.

That same blue eyed man steps up, staring at my naked body and I squirm, hating that I can't even cover myself. You'd think I'd be used to it by now, you think after everything they've done that I wouldn't still feel shame at being so exposed, but no, every second I'm forced to stand like this feels like an eternity.

He makes a point of studying me, of cupping my breasts, of groping my arse as I screw my face up in disgust.

"You've grown into a fine woman." He comments. "I always knew you'd be pretty but my, Sofia, these breasts…" He pinches a nipple, twisting it to the point that I'm screaming in pain.

Behind him, Otto laughs and that sound seems to draw his attention away from me.

Blue Eyes face darkens, he turns bearing down on my husband. "You're lucky we let you keep her."

"Like you have any say." Otto snaps back.

Blue Eyes smirks. "You and your brother might run Verona but you don't have the man-power to take us on."

Otto's face tells me the truth of those words. That this man is so much more dangerous, more powerful than even the Blumenfelds. Who the hell is he?

"Get her on her knees." Blue Eyes orders. "It'll be easier."

I struggle, I fight but someone kicks out my legs and I slam onto the rug. I expect him to undo his trousers, to force me to suck him off, after all, isn't that what I'm here for? I'm a sex slave for my husband, a piece of meat for them all to use and degrade.

Only, instead he grabs something out of the bag, it's long, shiny, as my eyes register what it is I tremble more because I have no idea what he could possible need a wrench for.

"This can go one of two ways." Blue Eyes states. "You tell us where your father hid the jewel or we beat the answer out of you…"

I can't find any words. I shake my head, trying to get my head to work. Hid what jewel? Anything of worth was taken before they burnt our house down. My eyes dart to Otto and he stares back at me with that awful blank look. Apparently he doesn't have a clue either.

"What are you talking about?" I reply.

Blue Eyes tuts. "Don't play dumb, it doesn't suit you."

"I don't know anything." I gasp, staring at what I now know is a weapon meant to be used on me.

"Sofia, you were there, do you really expect us to believe your father didn't divulge…"

"He hated me." I scream, cutting across him as my fear takes over all rational thought. "Why would he tell me anything?"

His lips curl, he bends down, getting right in my face. "Shall we see about that then?"

Someone grips my hair, holding me in place. Someone binds my hands behind my back so I can't even defend myself. I jerk, trying to get free but there's no chance.

As the wrench comes down I scream and my body takes the full impact. My ribs shatter. They let me fall before they yank me back up again and white hot pain shoots through my right side and I can't breathe. I can only sob and gasp as that pain radiates through me.

"Tell us, Sofia." Blue Eyes says in that cold, emotionless tone.

Only I can't tell him. I have nothing to tell.

He strikes me again, this time going for my forearm. From the angle he hits at, I feel my shoulder dislocate. I collapse once more and this time they leave me there, on the rug, broken and pathetic.

"You're making this far harder than it needs to be." Someone says.

I don't reply. I don't do anything but just turn my head, sobbing into the rug. It doesn't matter how much they hurt me, how much pain they put my body through. I don't know what it is they're looking for. I don't have a clue.

Maybe they realise that.

Maybe that's what makes them eventually stop. Only they break my leg first, they shatter a few more ribs too.

As Blue Eyes snarls in disappointment.

Otto steps up to him. "Guess she doesn't know." He says, like it's not obvious.

"Guess not." Blue Eyes says, spitting onto the rug, right by my face. "What a waste of my time." He pauses, staring at me. "Unless…"

Otto turns his gaze on me, on where I'm lying half-conscious, with my arms still behind my back and I can see that glint in his eyes, I can see that thought already forming.

I shake my head, not him, please god, not him.

As his lips curl, I already know that I won't be granted any mercy, that I'll never be granted that. "If you want to fuck her, you only have to say."

Blue Eyes stares at me. "You share her so easily?" He replies.

Otto shrugs back with a smirk. "She's a whore, I'm just making sure she understands her place. Besides, what other use do I have for her?"

"You could breed her."

My stomach twists. The thought of being pregnant with Otto's child makes me want to vomit, but then that thankfully is not an option. That'll never be an option.

Otto's smirk turns into a sneer. "Useless bitch can't do it." He says kicking me in my ribs, sending a white hot searing bolt of agony back through my body.

Blue eyes grunts. "Then why not just kill her and be done with it?"

My eyes connect with Otto's. I think I'm so broken now that I would beg for that, I'd thank him for it. If my husband produced a knife and ran it slowly across my throat, I'd smile and wish him well and finally, I'd know peace. Finally it would all end.

"And why would I do that?" Otto retorts. "It took me long enough to get my hands on her, why would I simply waste the opportunity now?"

"She's worth more to you dead than alive." Blue Eyes states like we don't all know that's true. I'm worth a fortune now that I'm the last Montague still breathing.

Otto chuckles like that's some sort of joke. "She is precious to me." He mutters. "Too precious to cast aside just yet."

My heart sinks. He's said the same before. Like he's got some timeframe for all of this. That one day he'll decide he's had enough and he will kill me, but it's not today. It's never today.

"Guess this is all she's good for then." Blue Eyes says as he crouches down, running a finger down my body. "But I prefer to play alone." He adds.

"Of course." Otto smiles before ordering everyone to leave.

I'm too broken to move. To terrified too.

As the door shuts, he tilts his head, slowly undoing his tie and then removing his jacket. The way he undresses feels like a whole different level of torture. I don't want to look. I don't want to see him but I know only too soon he's going to be on me, in me, he's going to be violating me.

"Please," I gasp. It hurts to move, it hurts to even breathe, I'm in agony and the thought of what's about to happen, I don't think I can endure it, I don't think physically I'll be able to.

He shakes his head, crouching over me, manoeuvring my broken body as I flinch. "You know I heard how your husband was treating you." He says, "I didn't quite believe it but now…"

His hands grab at me, his body weight presses on me and with so many injuries it's absolute agony. I start screaming and he's quick to muffle it, like anyone outside gives a shit.

"Ssssh," He murmurs, wiping my tears away. "Don't spoil this moment for me."

"You're a sick bastard." I spit.

"That I am." He groans as he pushes himself into me. "Do you know how long I've imagined this, Sofia Montague, naked beneath me?"

"Fuck you."

He lets out a laugh, one hand wrapping around my throat. "I believe I'm the one fucking you."

I WAKE, SWEATING, SCREAMING, THOUGH NO DISCERNIBLE SOUND seems to have left my lips. The covers are wrapped around me and it takes all my effort to figure out how to get them off.

I get up, forcing myself to move, to wake properly.

With every blink of my eyes, I see flashes, moments, horrific memories I don't want to acknowledge. I didn't do Martin's exercise, I knew better than to try it, but apparently my brain fixated on it anyway and the nightmare I had was worse, so much worse than they've been in a long time.

It's reckless to do it. Stupid. Completely insane but I don't care.

I creep out of my room, out into the silent hallway beyond.

I know exactly where Koen's room is. He might not have pointed it out but I've spotted him leaving it enough times to remember. I still haven't figured out why he insists on this separation. Why he's being so damn chivalrous about it.

When I step inside all I can hear is the soft sound of someone breathing. I pause, realising that he's asleep and suddenly my nerves get the better of me. My fear takes over.

Maybe this is a mistake.

Maybe this really is stupid.

As I turn to go, something grabs me. I'm thrown back and I land, smacking my head in the process.

A gun is rammed under my chin, forcing me to stop fighting, to stop moving. I whimper but strong arms hold me in place. I can't move an inch. I try to shift but it feels like my body won't respond. Like I'm suddenly trapped.

"Sofia? What are you doing in here?" He growls.

"I, I couldn't sleep." I stammer.

Koen lets out a low breath and I realise he's on top of me. That it's his weight is holding me down, stopping me from going anywhere.

He takes the gun away, tosses it aside, and then scoops me up in his arms.

"You shouldn't be sneaking about after dark." He states as he starts moving. "Especially not into my room. It's not safe."

"I thought you were safe." I murmur back.

He pauses, looking down at me and even in the semi-darkness I can see that frown on his face. "Why did you come?" He asks.

I gulp, unsure if I can even explain it. "I, I had a nightmare," I begin. "It was dark, and I just, I needed you."

"You needed me?" He repeats.

I nod, slowly, worried how he might react. "I needed you to make me feel safe." I clarify, just as I realise he's carried me back to my room.

He lays me down gently on the bed, then tries to pull the covers, only they're not there, are they?

I see him frown, I see him scanning the room, trying to locate them, and his whole body seems to change as he sees the pile, too far from the bed to have simply fallen off in my haste to go find him.

"I don't, I can't sleep in a bed." I murmur as a wave of shame flushes over me.

"Why not?" He asks in that deep, protective voice.

"The floor is safer." I reply. I know logically that's not true. Anyone can get me just as easily on the floor as they can from the bed, but still. A bed holds too many memories. A bed feels too dangerous.

He gets up, stalks over to where the covers are and grabs them. When he returns he throws them over me.

"You're not sleeping on the floor anymore." He states. "Dogs sleep on floors. People do not."

I want to argue, to snap back that most people don't experience what I have, that even dogs don't go through the level of trauma and abuse I've endured but my words die when I realise he's lying down. He's getting in beside me.

"Is this not what you wanted?" He asks, scanning my face. "Me to make you feel safe?"

I blink, feeling my heart race with an entirely different emotion than fear.

"I was actually just looking for a guard." I reply with a tease.

His lips curl, he reaches out, tucks a strand of my hair behind my ear and murmurs softly. "I can guard you much better if I'm in your bed."

I can't think of anything smart to say back.

I can't think of anything at all.

My mind seems to fixate on something I really shouldn't want. I really shouldn't crave.

So I just lie there, waiting for my sleep to take me and when it does, I don't dream, I don't suffer any flashbacks. I see nothing at all.

I WAKE, HYPER AWARE THAT KOEN IS BESIDE ME.

I've moved in my sleep, shifted, and now my body is pressed right up into his.

As I try to create distance his arm holds me in place. Apparently he's spooning me. One arm is under my body and around my waist and the other, it's on my thigh, with his massive hand gripping me in a way that feels tight but not claustrophobic.

I want to savour this moment. To try to make it last for as long as possible. I turn as much as I can, rolling so that I'm on my back and he's on his side, staring down at me.

He lifts his hand, the one that was on my thigh, and he strokes my cheek lightly. I bite my lip, trying to hold still, but I'm not afraid. I'm still not panicking.

And then I register what's been poking into me this entire time. He's hard. And I'm not talking about his muscles.

"Do you fuck other women?" I ask, though that's not exactly what I'm trying to get at. It's just he spends all his time either with me, or with his men. When does he get his 'needs' seen to? Or is there someone else in this house, someone I haven't met because half the rooms are out of bounds. I doubt it's Tia, though my mind flickers to her, no doubt because she's the only girl I've met. Surely he's not fucking her?

He tenses and the hand that was touching me stills. "Would it make you jealous if I did?"

Yes. Yes it would.

I know that's irrational. I know I have no right to ask him not to. We're not even a couple. We're not together in any meaningful way, and yet it feels like we have something, like we're more than just two friends.

Besides, didn't he allude to that? Didn't he say as much, the night I came here? God, I feel so confused.

"I don't want you fucking anyone else." I state, sounding far more confident, far more brave than I feel. Koen could have anyone he wanted, he practically rules the entire underworld of this city, I feel like I'm pushing it, that any minute he's going to tell me to get stuffed.

"I see." He says. "So what, you want me to relieve myself from now on?"

My cheeks flush. I hear the words he's not saying. That I'm not putting out. That I'm not doing anything to warrant such a request.

"You can use me." I say though it comes out practically as a whisper.

He groans, running his fingers over my lips. "Is that what you want?" He asks. "Me to use you?" The way he says it sounds so much worse. Like I'm just a thing to fuck, and yet I don't feel ashamed, I don't feel disgusted.

I nod. I'd much rather that, no I want that. Besides, it's not like I've not gotten something out of this. He's made me come countless times while I haven't even seen his dick once.

He slides two of his fingers into my mouth, pushing them as far back as he can. I loosen my jaw, trying not to gag, being as compliant as I can be.

"Would you swallow my come?" He asks. "If I fill up this dirty little mouth of yours, would you swallow it all down?"

I nod but that only makes me gag more as his fingers hit the back of my throat.

"Relax." He says waiting until he can feel I have and then he pushes them down till I feel like I'm choking.

He groans, pumping back and forth as though it's his dick. "You're so eager for it?" He murmurs. "If I get my cock out now will you get on your knees and suck me like a good girl?"

My response comes out as a gargle. A confused mix of sounds not words.

He grabs my hair, twisting his fingers through it so he can pull my head back and he pushes me down. I know where I'm headed, what he wants.

He was wearing boxers when I woke him up but evidently at some point in the night he decided to get rid. I come face to face with his dick, not that I'm complaining.

"Lick me, Sofia, show me what that delicious tongue of yours can do."

I stretch my tongue out running it up his shaft. He's still holding my hair, controlling my movements. Controlling me. His cock feels veiny, thick, the skin is velvety smooth and I'm dying to get a proper look at it but I'm under the covers, in darkness.

He groans as I work my way up and down, tracing a pattern.

As I come to the very top, my tongue connects with something metal. My eyes widen as I realise what it is, what it means. He's pierced? Of course he is.

He suddenly springs up, dragging me with him. The bedside light goes on. I'm shoved off the bed and I'm there, kneeling with his hand around my throat.

"If you're going to suck me off I want to watch every second." He growls. "I want to watch as my cock slides down your throat,

I want to watch as you pleasure me, and most of all I want to see how my come drips from those pouty lips of yours."

I blink, gawping back at him and he takes the chance to push himself right into my mouth. His hand controls my movements. He's not letting me have any control over this whatsoever. He's using me, just like I asked.

His dick is so girthy it hurts my jaw. He's not even fully in my mouth before I'm forced to take him down my throat. I guess I should have known a man as big as Koen would have a dick to match. If he ever does fuck me he might well break me in half.

My nose hits his stomach. I can smell that dark, heady scent of him. He smells musky. He smells of danger.

"Fuck, Sofia," He growls. "You're doing so good."

I moan back, hoping the way my voice box vibrates will give him pleasure. And it clearly does from the way he grips my scalp tighter.

"That's it." He murmurs as I suck harder, as I focus on getting him off. His pace is relentless. He clearly knows how he likes this and he's determined to have this his way.

My eyes are streaming. Drool is dripping down my chin. I lift my hand to cup his balls and that seems to send his feral. He growls, slamming into me even harder, so hard I'm afraid he might just break my jaw.

I start choking. I don't mean to but then I can't stop.

He eases off but only a little. Telling me to relax, telling me to breathe through my nose, like I can do anything else. That piercing traces up and down the top of my mouth, like it's teasing me and not the other way around.

"You can take this, Sofia," He states. "I know you can. Your mouth was created for my cock, you just need to learn."

I mutter back that I'm trying, and anyway, it's not like I want him to stop. Even if I do choke I'm okay with that.

He picks up pace again, fucking me once more. My drool drips from my chin onto my chest and I try not to grimace.

He tightens his grip on my neck, growling, and that's the only sign I get before he slams into me one more time.

Hot, salty come pours down my throat. I swallow it down, wishing I had more of a chance to taste it. When he drags his cock out he does it really slowly, spreading the last of himself over my tongue, over my lips.

I shudder, taking in a deep breath of oxygen.

"Fuck," Koen gasps.

I look up, and I can't help the grin. He's breathless. Speechless - I did that. I made Koen Diaz come so hard he's lost for words.

"You are something else." He states, helping me to my feet, holding the duvet so I can crawl back in bed beside him.

"You taste good." I say as he wipes my lips almost lovingly with his thumb.

"Yeah?"

I nod. "So I guess we have an agreement then."

"And what's that?"

"That you can't fuck anyone else. If you want to get off you have to use me." Christ I sound bold. I sound so confident.

He lets out a low laugh that rumbles from his chest. "Oh, I'll use you alright, Sofia. But you may live to regret those words."

CHAPTER
Thirty-Three

KOEN

It's late morning. We're both still in bed and though neither of us is asleep, we're not making any moves to get up.

My cock is so hard it hurts. I can practically feel it weeping with the need to be shoved down her throat again.

My hands are tracing up her body, feeling the way her skin turns to goosebumps, the way she squirms just a little, the way she's rocking her hips, trying to build enough friction to ease that tension between her thighs.

"You're feeling needy?" I whisper in her ear.

She nods, rocking that arse against me.

"Tell me what you want." I ask.

She huffs like she doesn't want to admit it. Like she just wants me to take over, only as much as I enjoy that, I want her to be present, to be actively choosing this. This isn't just about me fucking her, this is about me giving her everything she needs.

"You want to come, right?" I state. "How do you want that to happen?"

"With your cock." She says almost petulantly.

I pause, narrowing my eyes. There's no way she's mentally ready for that. But I'm not going to refuse her if that's what she truly wants. Nor am I going to deny myself.

I slide her panties to one side, probing her entrance. "You want me to fuck you?" I ask.

She nods back, burying her face into the pillow like she's ashamed to admit it.

I snarl, pulling her back, forcing her to look at me. "If you want my cock inside you then you'll look me in the eyes." I state.

She gasps, her own go wide as saucers and I see the way that vein at her neck starts pumping more rapidly. Does she get off on the fear, is that it? Is that what her kink is?

I rip her underwear off, tossing it, then place myself so that I'm right on top of her. It's dominating. Possessive. And that's the point. She needs to understand who I am, what I am, that I can be gentle but if she pushes me, this is what she gets.

At my core, I'm little more than a monster, a wolf in sheep's clothing, and every time she goads me, she chips away a little more at my carefully constructed façade.

She gulps and I can feel from the way her body is trembling that she's already struggling.

Only it's too late now, she asked for this. This is what she's going to get.

I've waited too long, have forced myself to do nothing. She wants to taunt and tease, she wants to offer herself up then she can't blame me for the consequences.

I lean over, grabbing the lube from the bedside table. She's tight, unprepped. If I fuck her right now I'll rip her in half and she won't thank me for it.

I pour enough liquid over her cunt to fill a jar.

She gasps squirming as I run my fingers down, spreading it all over her. I slide two fingers in. Both at the same time. I know I should be gentler but this will be nothing compared to my cock.

She clenches around me. Christ, she's too tight.

Even after I start thrusting, stretching, she's still too damn tight.

I snarl, trying to calm myself down. Except, I want her too much. I want to bury myself inside her and not give a damn if she's crying and begging me to stop.

I shake my head, grabbing the bottle of lube. I don't know what makes me do it, I don't know why I think it might help but I shove that into her.

Her eyes widen. She freezes as I start fucking her with it.

But her body seems to melt around it. I can feel the way she's suctioned against it as I thrust in and out.

"Fuck, Sofia," I growl. "Look at your greedy cunt, look how much you're enjoying this."

She nods, widening her legs more. "Fuck me, Koen, please. I don't care if it hurts. I want it to hurt."

That should be the warning.

The red flag.

It should make me stop. It should make all this stop.

Only it doesn't. How the hell can I stop? I'm too desperate for this, too fucking incensed to stop now. I pick up my pace, I fuck her harder, slamming the plastic inside her. She's crying, full on sobbing but I can't stop now, I want her to come, I want her to be stretched enough that I can actually sink my cock inside her and finally enjoy her like I damn well deserve.

She's still wearing that damned t-shirt she was sleeping in and I reach up and rip it off. I won't have anything obscuring my view. Her tits are bouncing. Her nipples are so hard. I reach up and slap the side of her breast leaving a bright red handprint.

She hisses, but she doesn't do anything other than take it.

"You like this?" I growl. "You like to be degraded?"

She's got her eyes shut, she's biting her lip so hard I think it might bleed. I pull the bottle out, tossing it and then line myself up.

"I'm going to fuck you now, Sofia." I say before forcing myself inside her. And that's what it feels like. Force.

She screams, she fights. Her nails dig into me and I have to hold her down.

But she doesn't tell me to stop. At no point does she say those words.

God, she feels so good, so warm, so fucking wet. I guess part of that is from the amount of lube I used but it's incredible. She is incredible.

"You're cunt feels like heaven." I groan. "Now that I've claimed it, I won't stop. I'm going to keep doing it. Keep using you."

She doesn't reply. She's got her head turned to the side, buried into the pillow like it's all too much.

I grab her thighs, pushing them further apart and I use them as an anchor, slamming myself as deep as I can go. I want to feel what it's like when she comes. I want to feel exactly how tight her muscles will grip me.

I start groaning, heaving, and she's lying there, taking it all.

"Such a good girl." I praise. "You're doing so good."

A wail escapes her lips but I'm already leaning down, claiming them. She opens her mouth, lets my tongue slip inside and I devour her mouth while my cock is devouring her cunt.

My hand finds her clit, I pinch it, knowing how much she enjoyed pain the last time. My Little Devil has a dark side, and

I'm willing to taint both our souls if that's what it takes to give her what she needs.

She jerks, she gasps. Her tits bounce again I take the chance to bite them, biting one breast and then the other.

She screams. Her hands dig into my hair but she's not pulling me off. She's not giving any indication that she needs me to stop. Though in truth, I'm not sure if I could. Madness seems to have taken me.

"You feel so good." I growl. "You feel so damn perfect."

I thrust harder, I slam into her. My thumb circles her clit over and over and I can feel the way her resistance is melting, I can feel the way she's giving in.

"That's it." I praise. "Come for me, Sofia, come all over my cock."

She shudders. She whimpers. And then she does it, she arches her back, she kicks out, screaming, crying too, coming so hard I swear she almost breaks me.

I growl, pushing myself deep inside her. I know I can't claim her the way I truly want, at least not yet, so I pull out, only just making it in time before I'm coming all over her breasts, all over her stomach, marking her skin with my DNA.

For a few seconds, I just lay there, slumped, in complete and utter euphoria. And then I drag myself up, force myself to leave her side and grab a wet cloth to clean her up.

She's still got her face buried in the pillow when I return.

I kneel down beside the bed, wiping away the remnants of me. Washing her clean.

"You did so good." I praise.

She lets out another sob.

"Sofia?"

Still she doesn't reply. I grab the pillow yanking it away. Her face is red, flushed though I'm not so sure now it's from arousal.

Everything seems to change. All that lingering lust inside me dies.

"Sofia?" I growl.

"Please don't." She whispers.

"Don't what?"

"I just, I need a minute."

"Was that too much?" Fuck, she didn't ask me to stop, and I was enjoying it too much to realise she wasn't.

"I…" She shakes her head, curling up, whimpering.

A better man would give her some space, a better man would let her have a moment alone, but I'm not that. I've never pretended to be that. I grab her, yanking her around by her jaw to face me. "What the fuck is going on?"

"I shouldn't…" She starts sobbing, ducking her eyes like she's ashamed. "I shouldn't like that. Not after what they…"

The penny drops. As I stare at her I realise what this is. Not buyers regret but self-loathing, judgement, all those nasty little voices in her head that have been tormenting her for so long.

"You think enjoying sex is shameful?" I ask.

"Enjoying pain is." She replies. "Enjoying you forcing me, enjoying that bottle."

I pick her up, cradle her in my arms, and hold her trembling body to mine. "You never have to be ashamed for what you like."

"I shouldn't like that. I shouldn't enjoy feeling overpowered…"

"Sofia, if that's what your kink is..."

"I'm fucked up." She cries cutting across me. "They fucked me up. The things I want, the things I dream about. Why the hell would anyone like me ever desire that?"

"What do you dream about?" I ask. I thought all her dreams were flashbacks, nightmares, awful moments from her past but apparently that's not it.

She shakes her head refusing to answer.

"Tell me, Sofia."

"You'll judge me if I do." She whispers back.

"I'm judging you anyway." I state before I can stop myself. "And from what I see, there is nothing to be ashamed of."

"I want," She gulps and if it's possible her cheeks turn ever redder. "I want to be held down, I like being held down. I like you forcing me, dominating me. It's not that I want anyone to do it. It's you, I like the idea of you doing it."

"Doing what?" I ask, though I already know, it's damned obvious isn't it? It's why she let me fuck her with my mouth all that time ago in her house. It's why she keeps pushing me, getting me riled up, getting me angry enough that I act without thinking.

"Doing what they did." She replies, clearly unable to say the 'r' word right now.

"You want me to rape you?"

Her eyes widen and she gulps before answering. "No," She splutters. "Yes. No, it wouldn't be rape. I want it, I want you, I just…" She crumples again, burying her face in my chest. "I'm disgusting. I'm so fucked up."

"No, you're not." I reply, stroking her hair, letting her lean further into me.

She sniffs, lying still, staring at my chest as those tears continue to fall. "I want you to use me. I want you to take me, whenever you want. I don't care if it feels like rape. I just…I need that."

My cock stirs. I'm a fucking monster for the way I react, the way I feel at those words. She wants to be my whore? She's giving me fair use? Permission to fuck her however and whenever I want? It feels like all my dreams are answered, it feels like this woman has just granted me the very keys to heaven.

I can practically see the trap slamming shut. My angel has caged herself so perfectly. She's walked right into the devil's snare and now I can devour her whenever and however I want.

"Okay," I murmur, cradling her tighter. "If that's what you want, from now on you don't have to worry. I'll take care of you, I'll see to it that both our needs are met."

My words sound so soothing and yet, already I'm imagining all the depraved ways I can fuck her, how much I'm going to brutalise her cunt and make her cry and plead.

She might not realise it but she's opened the floodgates.

She's unleashed a monster.

And I can't wait to show her exactly what that means.

CHAPTER *Thirty-Four*

KOEN

"It's my fault." She whispers.

We're still lying in bed, still curled up, having not moved in what feels like hours. She's been staring off into space while I've been savouring this, savouring her body pressed into mine, trying to decide how soon I can fuck her again and in what way.

"What is?" I ask.

"Everything that went down."

I let out a growl, gripping her jaw, forcing her to look at me. "That's bullshit."

"No, it's not." She says. "I'm responsible. For all of it."

The look on her face makes me pause. "What are you saying?" I ask carefully.

She sniffles, wiping her cheeks. "It was my idea. I came up with it and convinced Roman to let me do it."

"Came up with what?" God, I'm trying so hard not to snap right now, not to lose my temper.

"We needed someone on the inside, we needed information." She says no longer meeting my gaze. "I knew Otto was after me, he was sniffing around, even before my father's funeral. I thought…" She trails off, biting her lip, "I thought I could control him, I never thought he was capable of…"

Suddenly, she's sobbing, covering her face with her arms as if she's trying to hide her shame.

"You didn't cause this." I state. "Otto was a grown man."

"I led him on, I made him think I was a virgin."

I stroke her hair, fighting every cell in my body that's threatening to go on a fucking rampage.

It never made sense to me, her and Otto. Sure, he had money, but so did she. What could she possibly see in a man old enough to be her grandfather? I guess this is the answer isn't it, it was all a game, an act, a ploy that she and Roman came up with, only it backfired spectacularly.

Though they're equally as culpable, I can't bring myself to blame her. She's twenty one. Barely old enough to understand what she was getting into. But Roman, Roman must have known. He wasn't stupid. He would have understood the risks and yet he let her do it anyway. He sent her off, like a sacrificial lamb all in pursuit of his so-called revenge.

My anger stirs and I can't lay here, I can't let this go.

I get up, out of the bed, making some excuse about needing to get work done, and though it's not a lie, we both know that's not where I'm going.

She gives me a look full of hurt. Like she thinks I'm running from her. Like she thinks I'm disgusted by her. Part of me wants to reassure her but I'm too riled up, too fucking furious. I yank on my clothes, storm out of the house letting the door slam behind me.

The ride over does nothing to calm that rage. If anything it festers. It grows.

As I pull up to the great white house, I don't give a shit that I'm churning up the gravel, that I'm making one hell of a mess. I only just manage to kick the stand down on the bike in my haste to find the man.

The front door slams open as I barge my way in. A maid comes rushing and she shrieks when she lays eyes on me. I guess, with my helmet on, I must look like a murderer here to finish the job Darius started more than a year ago.

When I get to his office I don't stop to register that there are voices, that he's not alone, I just smash my way in, cross the room, and grab him by the throat, hurling him out of his fancy chair and I slam him into the wall.

"What the fuck?" Roman gasps.

I slam my fists into him, one after another, turning his pretty face into a purple mess.

From behind someone grabs me yanking me back and I swing wildly before I register who it is. That it's the Governor.

"Calm down." Someone else says behind me. Like those words have ever, in the history of the world, ever actually calmed somebody down.

"What the fuck is going on?" Roman gasps, grabbing his nose that is bleeding profusely.

I pull of my helmet, tossing it onto the fancy arse couch. "You piece of shit." I snarl. "You knew what he was, you knew what he was like and you let her do it anyway."

He stills, meeting my gaze but it's not him who speaks.

"She wouldn't listen." Ben says. "I tried to warn her, even after…" He falls silent glancing at Roman with a look that says it all.

"After what?" Roman asks before I can.

Ben slumps, sinking back into the chair that he was no doubt sat in moments ago before I burst in. "Otto did something, he assaulted her, before Darius made his move and staged our deaths."

"What?" Roman snarls.

I clench my fists, taking a step closer to him. So Ben knew, he fucking knew and he just let her continue?

"She'd been on a date." Ben explains. "I could see it from the look on her face. But she wouldn't listen. She just kept saying that it was necessary. And then you and Rose sorted everything, we found out about Lara and I figured she'd never have to see him again, that we'd make him pay and then that would be that."

"Fuck." Roman growls, burying his face in his hands.

I stare between the pair of them, ignoring the man stood the other side of the desk from me, the man witnessing all of this.

"She did it for you." I state fixing my gaze on Roman. "She sacrificed herself for you."

He shakes his head, "I never wanted her to do it, I tried to stop her."

"Clearly not hard enough." I snap back.

"She wasn't sleeping with him." Ben says. "At least…"

"Not until he was raping her." I finish that sentence and see how much he winces. How much all of them do, even the Governor, who still hasn't spoken a god damn word.

"How is she?" Roman asks. His right eye has swollen up, his jaw's got a nasty bruise and yet still it doesn't feel like I've hurt him enough.

"She's been better." I state.

"Maybe she should…" Ben begins but as I turn on him he clearly realises he needs to keep his mouth shut.

"She's a fucking cannonball." I snap. "She's so wound up by her trauma, and her anger and her self-hate that she can't see past it, but I'm working on it, I'm helping her to channel it the right way."

"We'll need a drug test." Hastings says. "It's part of her DUI conviction."

I grunt back. We all know that was bullshit. If Hastings had any balls he'd tell the courts and the press to shove it.

"And we need to discuss next moves." Roman says glancing at the Governor.

"Meaning?" I ask. What the fuck is going on, what don't I know about?

"We think there's a purge." Hastings says. "Suspects, individuals we believe to have been involved with Otto have been disappearing. It's likely it's an inside job."

I grunt, hiding the smirk. Yeah, they've been disappearing alright. I've made damn sure of that.

If Hastings sees something in my face he doesn't say it but he narrows his eyes at me and he pulls out a piece of paper, bagged up like evidence from a crime scene, and he lays it down for us all to see.

"This goes no further." He murmurs.

Roman nods. Ben quickly agrees.

I snatch the thing up, staring at it before anyone can stop me.

"Where the fuck did you find this?" I growl, barely believing my eyes.

Hastings stares back at me. "That's need to know."

"Is Sofia in danger?" It's a stupid question, because of course she is. She's got to be number one on their target list.

Oh, I know about the Brethren. I know how much influence they have. How much power. They make the likes of me look like amateurs in comparison. They say the President himself is a member. That most of the political elite are. For a while I believed

Darius was but his downfall proved that wasn't the case. That or he caused too much shit for them to protect him anymore.

But them being after Sofia makes no sense. What the fuck has she done to gain their attention?

My skin prickles, my fists clench and it's taking everything I've got to not run and get back on my bike, to race across the city and see for myself that she's okay.

"What do we do?" Ben asks.

"You do nothing." Hastings states. "Leave it to me."

I don't listen to anymore. I don't care what bullshit resources he has, I don't care that the President himself placed Hastings here and that that should grant her some protection.

Sofia is my responsibility. Mine to protect.

Roman calls out to me as I leave and I don't look back. I don't pause. I just snatch up my helmet and head right back out the door I came through.

She's in the kitchen with Tia. Apparently Tia is teaching her how to make cakes. Apparently the two of them are becoming friends, though I'm not sure when exactly that happened.

She smiles at me in a way that tells me she's uncomfortable and embarrassed about our earlier conversation, about how it ended, about what she admitted as though she has a reason to be ashamed.

I'm still so riled up that I don't think of the consequences, I don't think about the fact that Tia is right there. I grab Sofia, yanking her from the room, all but dragging her down the hall.

She screams, fighting me but it doesn't make me stop.

I shove her into the study, shove her face first onto the desk.

She said I can have her whenever I want, didn't she? Well, that starts right now. I'll show her she has no need for embarrassment or shame, I'll make it clear that from now on, I'm giving her everything she's ever dreamt of. Every sordid, dark twisted moment.

My cock practically jumps out of my jeans. She's wearing a tight pair of leggings that cling to her arse and I rip them right down the middle in my haste to get inside her.

There's no lube. Nothing to make this more gentle, but then she said she likes pain, she said she wants me to fuck her like I'm raping her, and what rapist would take the time to lube her up?

I groan as I force myself into her. She struggles. She fights. Her hands dig into the desk and if anything, it makes me more aroused.

"Christ," I growl. She's just so damn tight. It takes me a good few seconds to work my entire cock in.

She's gasping, crying, clearly struggling but I can't stop. I won't stop. I need this too much. I need her.

And I know she wants it.

"You can take this, Sofia." I state. "You know you can."

"Koen," She sobs and that moment there, her saying my name, it spurs me on.

I grunt, thrusting my hips, fucking her mercilessly. I need to get rid of this anger. I need to purge myself, and I know the kind of redemption I'm seeking can only be achieved with her cunt.

"It's too damn good." I growl, "You feel too damn good." I don't want to blow my load too quickly and yet I'm already there, so close to coming.

I pull out only just in time and then I'm covering her back, covering her arse, growling as I pour out over her soft, delicate skin.

She pants, staying still like the good girl she is.

I force myself to take a step back but this image, this vision of her, she's resplendent, she's so beautiful.

She's sniffing, trembling, her whole body is heaving.

I grab her hair, yank her head back so that she's forced to meet my eyes.

"I'm going to ruin you, Sofia." I growl. "I'm going to claim your body in so many depraved ways you won't be able to move without leaking out my come. But you want that, don't you? You'd like that?"

She whimpers, nodding her head, moving just as much as I'll allow her.

I should comfort her. I should soothe her but, now that my bloodlust is gone, I know I have to see Colt. I have to ensure we take action. If this is what Hastings thinks, if this is some deep state shit, I need to make my own plans, I need to ensure we're fully prepared for every and all eventualities.

So I leave her there, in torn clothes, used and in pain, and I storm down to the Ops room.

COLT IS READY THERE, AS IS REID AND A FEW OTHERS I TRUST. IT'S like I'm the devil himself and we're about to wage a fucking war, we're about to rise up from the depths of hell and wrought destruction on the realms of mankind. But then, I guess that's exactly what's happening.

I will destroy this city if I have to. I will destroy this damned country if that's what it comes to. I'll take on the entire Brethren if that ensures Sofia remains mine.

"We're increasing all security." I state. "No visitors. No one is allowed in without my express approval."

Colt nods before wincing.

"What?" I snap.

"The guys won't like it." He states.

"Excuse me?"

"You know how they are, Friday nights they like to let loose."

He means they like to fuck. They pretty much have a damn orgy most weeks. Do I care? Not if it doesn't affect my business, they're free to do as they please with their downtime. At least, they were.

"No more." I growl.

"Boss?" One of the other men gasp, like I've just cancelled his entire social life.

"You think getting your dick wet is worth risking all our lives?" I growl.

He narrows his gaze, muttering under his breath but we all hear it. "If you weren't getting yours sucked we wouldn't be in this mess."

I don't hesitate. I don't give a shit what the consequences are, I pull my gun and I blow his fucking head off. His lifeless body slams into the concrete and a pool of blood rapidly spreads from the gaping wound in his skull.

"Anyone else want to insult her?" I growl.

No one says a word. The few men who dare to look me in the eye keep their expressions locked down.

I raise my hand, pointing to the pictures of the men we haven't yet located. "We have bigger things to focus on." I state. As long as those men are out there, as long as they're still breathing the same air as us, they're a threat too.

"We've identified another one." Colt says quickly.

"Who?"

He moves pointing to the picture on the right. The one where a man is leant down, knife in hand, obviously about to use it to cut up Sofia's skin.

"Have you located him?" I ask.

"We wanted to wait for your go-ahead to bring him in."

I grunt. We'd discussed that. Being smoother with our captures. Not playing with our toys in public. Simple smash and grabs from now on. Reid was right in some ways, these men are too well-known for someone not to spot something sooner rather than later.

"Make the grab." I say before walking back out.

CHAPTER

Thirty- Five

KOEN

I don't feel guilty. I don't feel an ounce of remorse.

She may have been fighting me, she may have been crying but I knew deep down that's the way she wanted it.

Besides her cunt was gripping me hard enough, was wet enough to prove that she liked it.

After spending the rest of the day and most of the evening focused of shoring up our defences I creep into her bedroom - my bedroom if I'm being particular about it.

She's lying in the bed, covers up over her, with a lamp on in the corner.

I know she likes to sleep on the floor so I'm guessing her being in bed is because she's waiting for me. Well, she doesn't need to wait any longer.

I ease my t-shirt off, drop it silently onto the floor, then remove my jeans and boxers. Once more I'm hard, my cock knows what's coming, what pleasure we'll both have in a few moments and I can feel it drooling with anticipation.

Sofia's soft breathing tells me she's asleep.

I clamber onto the bed, easing the covers off, anxious not to wake her.

I was cruel with her earlier, aggressive, right now I want to show her body the other side, the side that's caring, loving.

My eyes widen as I see the sexy underwear she's got on. Apparently she *was* waiting for me.

Scarlet lace covers her. An underwire bra pushes her tits up but as she's twisted onto her side her left breast is practically tumbling out.

She looks like a fallen angel. She looks like temptation itself.

I lick my lips, carefully manoeuvring her legs so that I can better get her thong off. It slithers down her thighs, catching on her knees and for a second I think that might just wake her.

I pause, watching her face and realise with relief that she's still asleep.

I pick her left leg up, placing it so that she's opened up enough for me.

As carefully as I can I pour the lube onto my cock, rubbing it over myself and then run my fingers down her cunt, making sure she's nice and wet too.

My fingers slide inside, I tease only enough to ensure she's ready and then I'm pushing myself in but I'm slow this time. I savour every second, every inch that I claim.

She gasps out, shifting slightly, and I pause, waiting to see if she'll wake. It feels like we've been building to this, me training her body so that now she's so comfortable with me she just accepts me however I choose to take her.

"There's a good girl." I praise when I see she's still asleep.

I place my hands on her hips, leaning close enough that I can smell her but not in a way that places too much weight on her body.

And then I pick up my pace, rocking her body, thrusting into her over and over and over.

She's so damn soft, so damn good. Her muscles clench around me, welcoming me like I'm a sinner entering through the doors of hell.

I shut my eyes, growling out, forcing down that pleasure because unlike before when I couldn't control myself this time is measured, this time is more sacred. I want her to come. I want us both to enjoy this.

I tilt my pelvis, angling my cock deeper, and with my thumb I push down on her clit. A moan escapes her lips.

"That's it." I say. "Take what I give you, let me show your body how good it can feel."

She doesn't respond, she just lays there.

I press my lips to her belly, kissing those scars. If I had my way I'd cover her skin in tattoos, I'd replace every inch of that trauma with something delicate, something that reflects her beauty. I'd turn her into more of a work of art than she already is, instead of the current cenotaph to the horrors she survived.

But it's not my body, not my decision. It's hers. She gets to decide how and if she wants to take that step.

The sound of our bare skin slapping fills the air. The sound of her cunt squelching as I fill it over and over is like a herald of angels cheering me on.

I'm so close now. My blood is ringing in my ears. My thumb is twisting, flicking, teasing her. I need her to come. I want her to come. I'm not going to stop until she performs for me. Until she gives me this.

She jerks, she tenses, and then just as I feel myself topple over she does it, she climaxes right on my cock, covering me as I pour myself deep inside her.

I slump over, only just managing to keep my bodyweight from crushing her.

A voice in my head tells me I should have been smarter, should have worn a condom. We've not discussed birth control. Now that's another thing on my list, but it's a problem for the future. A problem for tomorrow.

I'm too tired, too content, in truth, too fucking entranced by the sleeping beauty beside me to give a fuck about the consequences of my actions now.

I pull the covers up, I tuck her back in, not bothering to put her underwear back in place and I lie there, feeling as my come slowly leaks back out of her.

Yeah, I'll admit that makes it all the better. That soothes the concerns about getting her pregnant. I've wanted to fill her up, to mark her insides from the moment I laid eyes on her and now, finally that's another thing I've achieved.

I drag one slow finger down her arm, when she wakes I'm going to have her again, I'm going to make her come more times than she can count, I'm going to reward her for being such a good girl tonight.

CHAPTER Thirty-Six

SOFIA

I wake, slowly open my eyes, realising that Koen is here, that his arms are around me, that I can't move because of how he's holding me.

But as I try to shift I realise my underwear is gone; I'm not wearing my thong. My pussy is throbbing, it's sore, really sore, and I feel wet.

Did he fuck me last night? How on earth did I sleep through that?

I take a long slow breath, turning to look at him.

He meets my gaze, grinning back.

"How are you feeling, princess?" He asks.

My eyes widen. If that's not an admission then I don't know what is.

"You fucked me while I was sleeping." I state.

He nods. "I wanted to give you the attention you deserved after using you yesterday the way I did."

I gulp. My mind starts to race at what feels like a hundred miles an hour.

Yesterday, when he dragged me into the study, I had no idea what was going on. I went into full panic mode but all that adrenaline, all that fear made me enjoy it more. Not in the moment though. No, in the moment I was truly fighting for what felt like my life, but after, when he left me there, in torn clothes, covered in his come, Christ did I like it then.

I didn't realise he would take the 'fair use' so literally.

I didn't realise he was that eager to fuck me that he'd get right on it.

I bite my lip, clenching my muscles, feeling a flash of pain. He tore me, he ripped me down there and yet if he pinned me down right now and did it again, I know I'd love every minute of it.

"What are you thinking?" He asks. "Are you having regrets now?"

"No," I say quickly. I don't want him to get the wrong idea. I don't want him to start thinking that I need him to stop whatever this is.

He leans down, claiming my lips and I wrap my hands into his long hair, deepening it.

His hand snakes around my body, finding my nipple and he twirls it, fondles my breast, starts clearly enjoying just playing with me.

I can hear my breath picking up. I can feel that wetness between my legs increasing.

I don't care if it hurts, I don't care if it rips me more, I want him inside me, I want to remember it this time and not be asleep.

He starts peppering my skin with kisses, worshipping me. It feels incredible to just lie there and let him, to feel so calm, so safe, so utterly loved.

He grabs my leg, pulling it aside so that I'm wide open and as I shut my eyes and prepare for the feel of his fingers forcing their way into me, something wet, something entirely different sweeps between my labia.

I jolt, staring down and he's there, twisted round, running his tongue up and down with long languid strokes.

Last time he ate me out it was like he was under some sort of countdown, like he was racing to get me off as quickly as possible. This time it's so different. He's teasing, sucking, licking like he's got all day to get me off. I let out a moan, grabbing hold of his hair, it's so damn good. How does this man even know how to use his mouth like that?

His fingers hold my entrance open and he slips his tongue in, fucking me so incredibly slowly.

"Oh god," I gasp.

He doesn't respond. He just keeps going, keeps pleasuring me on and on and on.

I don't know if he can feel the tear but the way he's thrusting makes it feel so much better. It's like he's doing it on purpose, kissing the part of me that he hurt.

"Koen," I moan. I want to come. I need to come. I'm not that close but I'm already a desperate, horny mess.

He shakes his head, fixing me with a look before he reluctantly withdraws his mouth. "You come when I'm ready for you to." He states.

"But I thought this was about me getting pleasure?" I reply.

He grins. "Are you not enjoying yourself, is that it? Are you saying that you want me to stop?"

"No," I gasp.

The bastard lets out a chuckle before adjusting his grip. "You're my plaything, Sofia, so I'll play with you however I choose and you won't complain, do you understand?"

I nod quickly despite the fact that I still want to argue. That's his kink, isn't it. He likes control. He likes to be in charge. He's given me what I want enough times, I won't ruin this for him.

He returns to pleasuring me, sucking, teasing until I'm such a sweaty needy mess I can't even think straight.

When he finally lets me come it's like an actual explosion goes off in my head. I kick out, I scream, my limbs seem to find some sort of life of their own and he has to pretty much hold me down to keep me there for as long as possible.

I collapse back into the mattress. I need a shower, I need a serious wash and yet right now I don't want to move, I want to lay here, content in the afterglow of my orgasm.

Koen lies back, putting one tattooed arm behind his head, letting me curl into him. I run my fingers across his chest, tracing all that ink.

"What made you get them?" I ask because I need something safe, something okay to say.

He drops his gaze, staring at his body. "I've always been into them."

"Are there any you regret?"

He grins, pointing to where a skull covers his right peck. "I had a tribal one done when I was seventeen. Everything about it was shit. This is a coverup but a good one."

"So you thought a skull was better?"

He laughs. "A skull is more me."

Yeah, I'd say that again.

His hand skims my body, his fingers brush where those words are carved into my flesh. "Were you never tempted to cover these?" He asks.

"I'm not sure they can be covered." I reply. The scar tissue is deep, even if they were fully inked, the skin would still be raised enough for the letters to still show. "Besides, I'd have to show someone them. That in itself feels impossible."

"If you want to, I can be by your side." The way he says that makes my heart flip but I also don't know how to reply. Covering them won't hide what is there, and even if Koen was beside me, another stranger would still see my body.

"Maybe." I murmur, lowering my gaze, scanning his tattoos once more.

He's completely covered, right down to roughly where his boxers would sit. Most of them are interconnected, skulls, guns, exactly what you'd expect the king of the underworld to have permanently drawn on his skin.

My eyes pause when I see a name scrawled in fancy letters on his arm, a woman's name. Is it a past girlfriend? Some woman he loved and lost? Suddenly my jealousy spikes and before I can stop myself, I ask. "Who is Aaliyah?"

CHAPTER

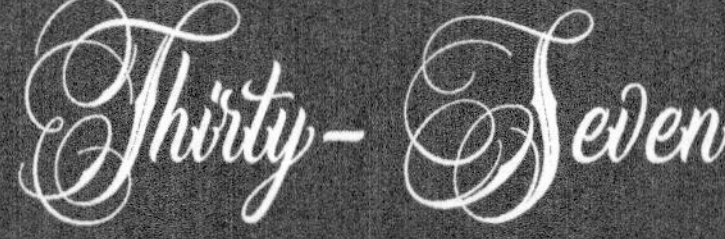

KOEN

My body tenses. I feel that flash of pain that even now, after so many years is just as cutting as the day I realised she was gone.

Her face is fading now. I just remember her bright smile, her blue eyes, and the fact that she always had a smart answer for everything.

"She's my sister." I say before correcting myself. "She was my sister."

Sofia relaxes, that spark of what I know is jealousy instantly dies. "What happened to her?"

I shake my head, grabbing her body, tightening my hands around her curves as if I need her close to fight the wave of grief and anger that hits me. “Darius.” I growl. “Darius fucking happened.”

Her face reacts. A flash of horror morphs her beautiful features into something pained. Perhaps it would be better not to speak of this, but then, she was the one who brought it up. And besides, I won’t pretend Aaliyah doesn’t exist. I won’t disrespect her memory like that.

“She got in with the wrong crowd.” I state like that explains it all. Like it was that damned simple. She was always outgoing, confident, and it didn’t help that our parents were so bloody religious. Of course, they were convinced she was full of sin and made her see a therapist, for all the good that did.

“She started using drugs. Started running away. And then she vanished.”

Sofia frowns, tightening her jaw, just listening to me without interrupting and for that I’m grateful because I don’t think I’d be able to continue if I stopped. I’m not used to feeling vulnerable, to pouring my heart out but right now, I want her to know, I want her to understand.

“I tracked her movements, spoke to everyone that’d seen her and it turns out someone picked her up, they took her right off the fucking streets.”

“Where?” She whispers.

I don’t know if Roman told her everything that Darius and the Capulets were up to. If she truly knows about their little money making scheme, the fact that they trafficked people, chopped them up, sold their organs on the black-market for those who had the money to pay millions for the privilege of life-saving transplants.

I meet her gaze as I say the words. “The barn.”

“No,” She gasps, covering her mouth.

So she does know then.

“I hunted them down.” I growl, as a memory flashes in my head, as I see the man who took her heart, cowering in his bed before I carved it back out his chest. "Every single person I could find who profited from her death, I hunted them down and I took her organs back."

She gulps, her face turning queasy.

"I…" She shakes her head, burying her face like she has something to hide. "My father took me there," She whispers.

"To the barn?" I ask confused. Why the fuck would he have done that?

She nods, clearly forcing herself to face me. "I, I was a child. If I'd known, if I'd realised…"

My body tenses as understanding dawns on me. She wasn't just visiting it. She benefitted from it.

"What was wrong with you?" I snap, unable to keep the anger from my voice, despite the fact she wasn't exactly old enough to be held accountable for her actions.

She takes in a long deep breath, pulling away entirely, shifting so that our bodies are no longer together, no longer touching. "I, I,"

Christ, I can see her shutting down, like she's about to admit something terrible. Did she have some sort of illness? Something that meant she needed a new heart, or lung, or something? She doesn't have any scars that would suggest it. Nothing beyond the awful ones across her belly. What the fuck was wrong with her?

"It's called Mayer-Rokitansky-Küster-Hauser syndrome." She sounds like a zombie, emotionless, disconnected as she speaks. "It's a genetic thing, I, I was born without a womb."

I try not to react. I guess that resolves the whole birth control issue but it still doesn't make sense. "Why did he take you to the barn?"

She shudders, "He thought he could make me normal. He thought he could fix me. It was experimental, at least, it was at the time. Now it's more mainstream…"

She's got her arms wrapped around herself, wrapped around her stomach, as if she can still feel whatever pain they put her through.

"What did they do?" I ask.

I can see the tears pouring down her face, I can see the guilt and the remorse etched there. "They tried transplants. Womb transplants. Only, they all failed."

They? So more than one woman suffered for this? It's hard to define how I feel, on some level Sofia had no control over this and yet, women were cut up for her, cut up to try and fix her, as if her potential to procreate was worth more than their entire lives.

"How many?" I snap.

"Three times."

Three? Three fucking women?

"Koen, I didn't want it." She gasps staring into my face, clearly seeing my reaction written there. "I didn't even understand what it was. I was nine years of age. My father just kept saying it would make me normal, it would make me useful, worthwhile."

She's pleading, begging me as if I have any right to judge her.

I hold my arm out and she crawls back into my embrace, sobbing more.

"You are normal." I growl. "Whether you can have children or not, it doesn't bear any relevance on your worth as a person."

She sniffs, wiping her face.

"My father would disagree with you there." She whispers so quietly. "And after Roman got everyone out, I went back there. I had to see it for myself. I had to see what he'd done, what I'd been a part of. And I was also trying to convince myself that what we were doing was right. That what I was doing was necessary."

My face hardens. "You mean with Otto?"

She gulps, nodding. "He, he attacked me, after a date, he pinned me down in his car and his chauffeur just sat there, watching, doing nothing."

"Why the fuck didn't you just stop?" I growl.

"I was naïve, fucking stupid." She admits. "I wanted to help and this felt like the only way. Everyone else was risking their lives, I could hardly expect to stay in my nice ivory tower…"

I shake my head, tightening my grip. "You have nothing to prove."

"It felt like I did. My entire life I've never been good enough, never been worthy enough. It felt like if I did this then maybe it might absolve some of my sins. Three women died because of me. Me."

"You were a child." I state. "You weren't responsible. And whatever your father made you believe, you are enough."

She let out a bitter laugh. "Not for a Montague. I can't carry on our line. As far as he was concerned I should have been locked away, hidden away. It was shameful for someone of his great lineage to have such flawed genes."

"Do you want children?" I ask her.

She gulps, shaking her head, stumbling over her words. "No. I, I never wanted, I've never, even if I could, I wouldn't want to be a mother, it's just not me."

"And does it affect you in any other way?"

Again, she shakes her head. "No, apart from that, I'm fine. Healthy."

"Then fuck what he said." I growl. "Your father was a piece of shit and he was lucky he managed to die quietly in his bed."

She gives me a crooked smile. "He had heart failure." She replies. "He wanted a transplant, paid Darius for it and everything, only they kept putting the surgery back. Turns out Darius didn't want him to live either."

I don't know how to respond to that, thank fuck another person wasn't murdered for Horace Fucking Montague.

As I drop my gaze I realise we're still naked, still in bed, that the turn of conversation has distracted me from taking care of her.

I get up, leave her there, and go to pour a bath.

When I come back in she's watching me warily, like her confessions might make me change my mind. That they might alter how I view her, how I feel about her.

"Come on, Little Devil," I say, holding out my hand. "Let's get you cleaned up."

CHAPTER
Thirty-Eight

SOFIA

I blink back at him, wondering if I misheard him. Cleaned up?

As I glance down at myself I know I'm not dirty. But then, he fucked me last night didn't he, and after what we did earlier, maybe I do need a shower.

He scoops me up into his arms and carries me into the bathroom – and that action alone seems to make my brain short circuit. When I told him the truth, when I confessed my dark, dirty, little secret I expected him to throw me out, to kick me out. Especially considering what happened to his sister.

For a second I'd feared that her womb had been put inside me, but the timings don't work. Thank fuck the timings don't. If she'd died for me, if I'd been responsible, I know that would have sealed my fate – and rightly so.

And yet still, he's acting like he still wants this, still wants me. I'll admit my head is doing somersaults trying to figure out why.

He sees my face and smirks. "You had your fun in there." He says. "This is part of mine."

My eyes widen. What the fuck does that mean? He's put bubbles in the water, steams already filling the room. It feels like I've just fallen asleep and woken up in a spa.

"This is called after-care." Koen says bending over, placing me so gently into the water, "This is as important as ensuring you enjoy yourself while we play."

"Why?" I reply. It's not like he's bathed me before. But he did shower me, didn't he? When I was too tired from my orgasm to protest.

Koen picks up a sponge and he pours some fancy smelling body cream onto it, squeezing it to lather it up. "Arms." He orders.

"Excuse me?"

"Trust me, Sofia." He replies fixing me with that no nonsense look of his. "Let me take care of you my way."

I don't even know why I'm protesting. Koen wants to scrub me down? He wants to wash me clean? Fine, I'm too shocked to put up any sort of fight.

I guess he sees the resignation in my face because he murmurs, "Good girl," before taking my hand.

It's so odd to let him do it. I just lie there, letting him clean me, letting him wash my hair – like that even got dirty, and then he's massaging my feet and I swear I've just died and gone to heaven.

"How does that feel?"

"Fucking incredible." I gasp.

He chuckles that deep sexy laugh of his.

He's there, kneeling beside the bath, and I can't help but drool at his body, at how toned he is, at all those tattoos that adorn his skin, and make his actually look like King of the Underworld.

He's so damn gorgeous. He's breathtaking. This man oozes danger and destruction in a way that makes you want to throw yourself off the cliff and willingly die for him. I understand now why all his men are so loyal. Why they look like they'd lay down their lives without question.

He could have anyone he wants – I know that. I've been more than aware of that, and up until now I haven't wanted to explore the reasons why he's so set on me. What it is he sees in me that makes me worthy of his attention.

That voice in my head stirs. Those words that my father whispered so long ago, words that took root, that spread, that latched themselves around my soul and leeched into every dream, every hope, every conscious moment.

"Am I not disgusting to you?" I ask.

He freezes.

His eyes meet mine and they're not soft, not gentle, they're hard.

"Why would you be?" He growls.

I gulp, forcing myself to be brave, to just spit it out. "I can't have children." I state. "I can't give you a family, if that's what you're after. And more than that, after what they did, my body isn't something anyone would…"

His hand silences me. He slaps it over my mouth, forcing those words to stop.

My eyes widen, I freeze as my adrenaline spikes.

"You want to know why I made that deal?" He asks, "You want to know why I snuck into your bedroom night after night, why I sat in that damned hotel for months on end, hoping just to get a glimpse of you as you walked by…?"

He did that? He was at the hotel too? What the fuck? How on earth did I not notice? God I'm so stupid sometimes.

"I want you, Sofia, I've always wanted you. From the moment I held you in my arms, I knew you were it. And I also knew I would do whatever was necessary to get you."

"You tricked me." I state. That deal I made, he was always going to say yes, he was always going to let me stay here, and yet I handed myself over to him on a silver platter.

He laughs. Just a little. "Oh, Little Devil," He murmurs. "You have no idea the lengths I would go to keep you with me."

Those words should scare the shit out of me. They should send me running for the hills.

Only they don't.

As I stare back at him all I want more than anything is to show that I feel the same. That I am falling so hard for this man.

"I want to touch you." I blurt out, as my cheeks burn. "I want to..."

I can't finish that sentence but I know he knows.

His lips curl in amusement. "Is that right, Sofia? You want to make me come?"

I know I technically have; he's used my mouth already but it was on his terms. I want to explore with him, play with him, not always simply be taking what he gives like I'm a greedy selfish bitch.

"Isn't it only fair?" I reply. "You've played with me enough times. Don't I deserve to play with you?"

"Alright, Little Devil, later I'll let you touch me." The way he says it is like he's granting me some great honour. Bestowing some award.

But I can't deny how my body reacts. I can't deny how much I actually want it.

CHAPTER *Thirty- Nine*

KOEN

I take my time taking care of her, washing her body, drying her off, brushing her hair too. She's like my perfect little toy right now. Maybe that orgasm made her docile. It's certainly silenced the bratty side of her.

She's watching me carefully, studying me like she's expecting me to get my cock out at any moment, and though I'm more than happy to do just that, we can't spend the entire day in bed. At least, I can't.

She sits on the barstool, watching me prepare what is now a very late breakfast and we exchange a few words. I like that she's not over the top chatty, desperately trying to fill the silence. I like that instead she seems content to just be in this moment.

She eats more than her usual and when I point this out she mutters under her breath about someone making her extra hungry.

And then my phone pings.

I pick it up, grunting at the intrusion. Only, Sofia's phone goes off. Not just once, but over and over.

I narrow my eyes glancing from her to the screen, reading the message from Tia before I open up the social media app.

A strange, strangled sort of cry escapes Sofia's mouth but I see the images, I see the video anyway.

She's lying there, exposed, clearly high off something. There's no one else in view. If you didn't know better you'd think she'd gone on an all-night bender, that she'd lost all sense of reality.

It's been posted to her account, it's like she's uploaded a library's worth of content and I flick from one image to the next.

"What is this?" I ask.

Sofia throws her phone, actually launches it across the room. Her face is ghostly pale, she looks like she might just pass out.

"Sofia?"

"I, I didn't post that." She says quickly, like I'd think otherwise, like she'd even have had the time. "Someone's hacked my account."

"Why?"

She covers her face, shrinking back into that awful scared creature she becomes when her trauma takes her. "They did it."

"Who?"

"You have to believe me."

Christ, the way she says that it's like she expects me to just turf her out. To call her an addict and wash my hands of her.

"Who did it?" I growl, grabbing her hands, forcing her to look at me.

"I, I don't know." She says. "I know that sounds like bullshit, I know how it looks…"

"I don't give a fuck how it looks." I snap. "Tell me what is going on."

She sniffs, wiping her face. Her voice is so quiet now, so small, and I fucking hate it. "They keep setting me up. They made it look like I crashed that car, they were the ones who drugged me back at the Montague House, at the ruins..."

"And now they've hacked your account." I murmur.

"Please, Koen, please believe me."

"Why the fuck would I not?" I ask and she blinks like my words make no sense. "Sofia, you've spent the entire night and morning with me. What moment would you have had to do this? And why would you?"

I run my hands through my hair, thinking it over. Of course it's a stitch up. Sofia's been here, away, safely out of the public eye for weeks now. I bet her moving in here wrecked all their plans.

I grab my phone, staring at the images again.

"Please don't look." She says wincing.

"You were with Otto when these were taken." I guess, though in truth, it's not hard. I recognise the background, the lighting. It's not the exact same space as the videos I saw on Danny Campball's phone but it's a close enough match.

"Yes," She whispers.

"So whoever is behind this was either there, or has copies."

She doesn't reply beyond scowling.

"Has anyone ever contacted you, tried to blackmail you?" I ask.

"No, and I don't think that's what they want. It's not about getting money. They're trying to destroy me. To make me look like an alcoholic. To make me look like a drug addict. Hastings thinks it's to discredit me in court, but..."

"You know something." I state cutting across her.

She balks, shaking her head and she starts trembling worse than ever. "I don't."

"No, you do. That's what this is about. They're trying to make you look like a crack-whore so no one will take you seriously."

"But I don't know anything." She suddenly screams. "I barely remember anything."

I take her hands, leading her over to the couch and she almost collapses onto it.

"Sofia, when you dream, what do you see?"

She whimpers, shutting her eyes, like just the thought is horrific.

"Sofia,"

"Please don't. Please," She begs. "Martin tries this all the time, he keeps asking what I remember, as if any of it will help."

"But you *do* remember bits?" I say.

"Flashbacks. Moments. Nothing that makes sense."

"Did Otto ever say anything, is there anything that sticks out?"

"You mean beyond the rape and torture?" She replies.

Christ, that look in her face, that pain, I grab her wrapping my arms so tightly like they're a wall.

"There's nothing, Koen, I don't know anything."

"It's okay." I murmur.

But in my head, my thoughts are racing. If it is some deep-state Brethren shit, if Sofia does know something and doesn't realise it, then they won't back down. They won't stop.

They'll want her silenced. They'll want her dead.

CHAPTER *Forty*

SOFIA

I spend the entire day beside Tia, watching her take down one video and then another, and another, like it's endless.

And in a way it is.

It's been forwarded, copied, duplicated so many times it's out of control.

We both know there's no shutting the door on this but the fact that she's trying to help makes me feel a tiny bit better.

Every time I see that image flash up I cringe. It's bad enough that those events happened, bad enough that I lived through it but for the entirety of Verona to watch, to gawp, to revel in it. I know they have no idea what they're seeing but it feels like a dagger tearing right into me.

Roman calls. But of course he does. I can't even face talking to him so Tia takes it, answering his questions patiently.

My lawyers call as well. They go off about how this won't help the case, like that's where my head is at. Like I really care two shits about the damned legal battle I'm still embroiled in.

I've shut down my social media. Shut down every account. Tia put a statement up saying I'd been hacked and that those images were not real. I don't think anyone believes it but at this stage I just don't care.

Maybe if I lay low for a few years, just hide out here, eventually everyone will forget that Sofia Montague even exists.

When the buzzer on the gate goes, the whole house seems to stiffen. I can hear half the security team reacting.

And then Rose walks through the front door, her eyes searching for me amongst what feels like an army of men Koen left to protect me.

"What, what are you doing here?" I stammer.

She gives me a look that says it all and shakes her head slightly. "Did you expect me just to take Roman's word for it that you're okay?" She asks.

"You didn't have to come." I say quickly.

She huffs, putting her hands on her hips and that tiny bump pokes out under her clothes. She's definitely noticeable now. I bet she had to fight Roman to be allowed out.

"You're my sister-in-law." She states. "And even if you weren't, I would still be here."

Tia mutters about making tea and she disappears off down to the kitchen while Rose and I settle in the living room.

It's north facing, shaded, with a massive fireplace and two huge corner couches that face one another. The fire is crackling merrily away and as we sit down it feels so cosy despite the situation.

"How are you?" Rose asks.

"Could be better."

She snorts. “I know that feeling.”

“Koen is out.” I don’t know why I said that but it feels like I need to explain his absence.

She nods, glancing around. “I’ll admit his house is far more homey that I imagined it to be.” She says and that makes me laugh.

“What did you imagine?” I ask.

“Oh, I don’t know,” She grins. “Maybe rifles up on all the walls. Skulls above the hearth, that sort of thing.”

“He’s not a psycho.” I gasp.

She laughs more. “Well, you would know better than me, Sofia.”

Tia walks in, placing the tray down, acting like she’s some sort of waitress and, though we ask her to stay, she makes an excuse before disappearing off.

“How is it here?” Rose asks, “Is it better, do you feel happier being here?”

I shrug. “I feel more grounded. I can’t explain why but I do.”

“Sure it doesn’t have anything to do with a certain tattooed hunk?”

I shoot her a look before making a show of pouring out the tea. Hers is decaf and she pulls a face as she sips it, complaining that you can taste the difference.

I’d personally rather have coffee but I’m not going to be so rude as to state that when Tia was kind enough to make this.

“You look better. You look healthier.” Rose says running her eyes over me. “You look more like the old you.”

“I doubt I’ll ever be the old me.” I mutter before I think.

Rose reaches across, squeezing my hand. “Neither will I. But you know, I like who I am now, scars and all. I like the fact that after spending an entire life bending and breaking for other people I now know my strength. I know when push comes to shove, I can be just as ruthless, just as merciless as anyone else in this damned city.”

Is that why I feel the need for revenge so much? Not just because they've done me wrong, not just because they put me through things no human should ever have to endure, but is it because I need to prove something to myself?

"Sofia?"

"Sorry, I was just thinking." I say quickly.

"I didn't mean…"

"It's okay." I smile. "I'm just trying to figure some things in my head."

She gives me a wary look but thankfully lets it go.

"How's Lara?" I haven't asked about her in ages. Roman sends me videos of her being cheeky, or naughty, or just playing with Bella.

"She's good." Rose grins. "She's starting to go on and on about how she wants a little sister and will be really angry if I have a boy."

I laugh. "Oh dear."

"I'm hoping it is a boy." Rose says. "Because it will be a good learning opportunity for her."

I snort back. I don't doubt Lara will have an absolute paddy if it is a boy.

"Ben's been watching her a lot." Rose adds and I wince.

"Is he, is he okay?" I ask gingerly.

"He's fine." She replies but I hear the hint of something in her voice.

"Has he said anything, about me being here?"

She frowns for a second. "No, at least not to me. Maybe he's spoken to Roman. But he wants the best for you. That's all Ben wants."

"I know." I murmur. But that doesn't ease the guilt, does it?

"So, you and Koen?" Rose says nudging me.

"I," God I blush like a teenager. "It's very early days." I state, like he isn't already fucking my brains out.

"But you like him?" She asks.

"He's, well, he's Koen, isn't he?" I reply.

She sniggers. "Is he all growly and possessive with you?"

"Sometimes." I laugh. "But he's also really helping. He listens. He doesn't seem to judge. He just, when I'm with him I don't feel like a complete waste of space."

"Why would you ever feel like that?" Rose frowns.

"Because," I turn my face away sighing for a second. "Roman was our father's favourite." I explain. "He could never do anything wrong, but me…"

She nods, like she gets it. "You were never good enough." She guesses.

"No,"

"Yeah, my parents were like that too. It messes with your head."

"Maybe if my mother had lived, if she didn't die so young." I sigh.

Rose winces, ducking her gaze and that makes me pause.

"What is it?" I ask narrowing my eyes.

"It's not, I shouldn't be the one to tell you." She replies quietly.

"Rose?"

She holds her hands up, like she's surrendering. "Before we handed my mother over to Hastings she told us that she and Darius had your mother killed."

"What?"

"They were having an affair, my mother and Darius, somehow your mum found out so they silenced her."

I should feel more than I do at those words. I should feel pain, sorrow, grief even. Maybe it's because I don't remember her, maybe it's because I have no memories whatsoever, but all I feel is numb. So numb.

When I was little, I'd convinced myself that my childhood would have been better, so much better, if my mother hadn't died. I have no idea if that was actually the case or just some fantasy

I'd woven for myself. Maybe she would have been as disappointed in me as my father was. Maybe it's better she died when she did, better that I could at least pretend one of my parents would have loved me.

"I'm so sorry." Rose says.

"It's not your fault." I reply. "But thank you for telling me."

"We wanted to tell you sooner but Roman was afraid of how you might react."

I can't help the scowl. I know he meant well but once again Roman has treated me like a victim, like someone that needs to be shielded, to be protected.

Rose studies my face for a moment before taking another sip of her tea.

"We should do dinner, the four of us." She says. "I think it might help Roman come around to the idea of you and Koen being together."

The idea catches me off guard. "I'm not sure." I reply. Besides, from the way Koen reacts when I mention my brother's name, I don't think he'll be happy to be in the same room as him right now.

"Okay, well, maybe it can be just us, you and me." She says smiling gently. "We can meet for coffee and catch up until things calm down."

CHAPTER
Forty-One

SOFIA

When Koen comes back, I'm already in bed. I didn't eat dinner. I didn't have any appetite. I just took myself off and decided to curl up into a ball and hide.

I feel him sliding into the bed beside me and I'll admit, I feel so relieved that he's here.

"How are you doing?" He asks.

"Great. A real ray of sunshine."

He grunts back, pulling me around so that I'm now laying on him. I'm once more in one of his t-shirts and he, as usual, is wearing nothing. He feels so warm, so hard, so utterly indestructible.

"Where did you go?" I ask.

He narrows his eyes like he's considering how much to divulge. "I had to see Hastings."

"About me?"

"About the videos, about everything that's been going on."

"He already knows." I state.

He doesn't reply beyond stroking my hair, watching my face like he now knows something I don't.

"What is it?" I ask.

He shakes his head. "Nothing."

"Don't lie to me." I snap. I'm so sick of everyone lying to me, treating me like I'm breakable, like I have to be protected.

He grabs my jaw, forcing me to still. "I told you to trust me, Sofia." He growls.

"Trust is a lot to ask for when you're the one holding all the cards."

His eyebrows raise. "You think I'm tricking you?"

I take in a deep inhale. "No," I admit. I just don't know what I do think. I woke up this morning feeling like a new person, like all that dark shit was in my past and now it feels like the rug has been yanked out right from under my feet and I'm back there, in that room.

Like there's a chain once more around my neck. That I'm surrounded, trapped, and those eyes, those blue eyes…

"What is it?" Koen asks as I tense up.

"I," I shake my head trying to clear the fog. It felt like a memory but I know it's more than that.

"There was someone there." I whisper.

"Where?" Koen growls, like he thinks I mean now and he's ready to smash down every wall.

"Before," I say. "At Otto's. He…"

My voice dies as I see it, that flash of metal. As I feel it smashing into my ribs. My hands wrap around myself, at where those ribs were broken and are no healed.

"He had blue eyes. Dead eyes." I force the words out. "He tortured me because he thought I knew something."

Koen's lying so still now, studying my face like he's waiting for me to divulge more.

"I saw him before." I state. "When I was a child. He visited my father and I walked in on them."

His eyebrows raise in surprise. He sits up just a little. "He visited your father?" He repeats.

"I think he threatened me, I just don't really remember." I reply.

"What did your father do? Did he say anything after?"

I wince, dropping my gaze, not wanting to admit it but I'm also not going to lie. "He beat me."

"Your father did?" He growls.

I shrug, acting like it's nothing because in a way it is. My father is dead. It doesn't matter anymore. None of it does. "I was snooping. I broke the rules."

"Did he hurt you often?"

My lips curl into a bitter smile. "Yes."

"Did he beat your brother too?"

It feels like he already knows the answer to that. It feels like he's asked that on purpose. I mean, I already told him Roman was the golden child, surely that says enough?

"Sofia…"

"It's okay." I reply, using that same reassuring line he's used with me. "My father was not a nice man. I knew that. I accepted that."

He cups my cheek, before planting a soft kiss on my lips. I still can't figure out how a man as physically strong as him can be so gentle.

I drop my gaze, deciding that I'm done talking, done going over this. I want a distraction. I want an escape.

I raise my hand, running it over those dark tattoos I've studied so much. Koen shifts, holding himself perfectly still like he doesn't understand what I'm doing.

His skin is so smooth. He must wax because he has zero chest hair. I run my hand over his nipple, the one he pierced and he takes in a sharp breath of air. Do men have sensitive nipples too? I guess so.

"Sofia," He murmurs.

"I just want to touch you." I say quickly. Though that doesn't explain it. I don't want to just touch him. I'm dying to. When we left this room this morning it was all I could think about and then everything went to shit.

He grunts, lying flatter, like he's somehow giving me permission.

We work out together most days and yet I suspect he does more, he has extra sessions when I'm not there because there's no way him just lifting a few weights and holding a punch bag for me is enough to keep him in this condition.

My hand slides down his abs. Every single one is so pronounced. I've never been particularly into muscly men. The only guy I willingly slept with before Koen was skinny, gangly, nothing like the man I now know intimately.

When I reach his boxers he seems to tense more. I slide my hand under but he's quick to grab me, to stop me.

"Sofia, you've had one hell of a day, how about we quit while we're ahead?"

Something in me snaps. Something in me makes me lash out. I'm up on my knees, glaring at him. "I'm not a child." I hiss. "I'm sick of everyone trying to protect me, acting like I need it."

"I'm not…"

I don't let him finish. My anger right now is blinding me to everything. "I am not a victim." I scream. "I'm so sick of everyone always seeing that, just treating me as that."

His face reacts, he grabs me, pulling me down, pinning me to the bed and while the old me would crumple up in fear, I'm not that girl anymore.

"I don't see you as that." Koen states. "I never have."

"You hunt those men down, why? Because you think I'm not capable of doing it?" I snap back.

His lips curl like he's actually enjoying this, like he doesn't mind being spoken to like this. Like me challenging him right now is turning him on. "Oh, you're more than capable." He growls in a voice that's far more seductive than it should be. "But I don't hunt them for you. I hunt them for me."

"What?"

"They touched you when the only person who has any right to do so is me."

I blink, staring dumbfounded. Did he really just say that?

"You are mine, Sofia, you always have been. I hunt them down because they offend *me*. I hunt them down because they hurt you and still lived to tell the tale."

"I'm not yours." I gasp, more in defiance then because I really don't want to be.

His lips curl more. "Did you forget you gave yourself to me?"

I did, didn't I? I handed myself over to him willingly in exchange for revenge. I didn't think about anything beyond that, I didn't think about the future, how it would feel once all those men were dead.

Will I be content to be Koen's plaything in ten years' time? Will I be content to live my entire life like this? Maybe I'm a fool because some part of me is shouting yes, so loudly I can barely hear anything else.

"Fine." I mutter. "If I am yours then it works the other way too."

His lips curl and he watches my face, as if waiting for me to declare it.

"You are mine." I state. "That means I can touch you whenever I want."

"You want free reign too, Little Devil?" He growls so softly. "Is that what you need? Will I wake up to find you riding my cock, getting yourself off because you couldn't resist it?"

My cheeks blush. I doubt I'd do that but I nod anyway.

He lets out a low chuckle, taking my hand and he wraps it around his dick.

"Go on then, Little Devil. You're so eager to make these big bold statements, but you know you have to back it up with action."

"Tell me how you like it." I whisper. I've never touched a man, not willingly. It wasn't like Otto or any of his cronies every paid that much heed to foreplay. The closest I got was having their dicks down my throat.

But this, this is so different. I want to do this right, I want Koen to enjoy this, I want him to realise how much I want this. How much I like pleasuring him.

He grunts, tightening his grip and starts moving it up and down, showing me the exact speed that he wants.

His skin is so soft, velvety, it contrasts to much with the hardness of the rest of him.

As I work away he groans more, rocking his hips, only it feels like he's still holding back, like he's still trying to restrain himself.

I let out a huff, and without thinking I shift, lowering my mouth and slide him over my lips.

The effect is instantaneous. That caged up beast seems to erupt. He growls, grabbing my hair. And he's thrusting, sliding his dick in and out, faster and faster.

"Is this what you want?" He groans. "Me to fuck this pretty little mouth?"

I can feel my drool slipping down my chin.

I murmur back. Finally he's behaving the way I expected. The way I need. He's hitting the back of my throat so hard I almost choke. But he doesn't stop, he doesn't slow, he just keeps going. It's like he's waited so long for this moment that now he can't hold back.

"I'm going to come down your throat, Little Devil." He says. "And you're going to swallow every drop."

I look up, meeting his gaze, begging him with me eyes.

My hand reaches up and I fondle his balls, tease them.

"Fuck," He groans. "You're so fucking perfect, taking my cock like a good girl."

I can't take my eyes off him. I can't look away. I want this moment seared into my memories forever.

He holds my gaze, gripping my head, staring at me as his come pours down my throat.

As he slides himself out, I lick my lips, and then quickly wipe the drool.

"Such a good girl." He says, pulling me back up, letting me curl contentedly into his arms.

CHAPTER
Forty-Two

KOEN

She fell asleep in my arms. Right where she belongs.

And I lay there, watching her, unable to switch off the whirling thoughts in my head.

When I left this morning I wasn't sure if she did know something, I wasn't sure that wasn't just a notion I'd come up with to try to explain everything, but after what she revealed tonight, that that man tortured her, that he'd been there, with her father first and now - it's too convenient.

I don't want to press her. I don't want to push her.

I saw enough on the videos and hell, my imagination can fill in enough of the gaps to understand why her mind has blanked it all out. In many ways it is better if she doesn't remember, it's easier for her that way.

But her remembering might just save her arse.

No, I will be there, I will save her if that's what it comes to. I'll kill every damned person in this city, I'll fucking annihilate them all if that's what it takes.

She murmurs, rolling slightly, shifting like she needs to get more comfortable. I can see those burn marks on her arm, the way someone put out dozens of cigarettes on her skin for the sheer fun of it.

The next man I take, the next we capture will suffer the same treatment. I'll cover his skin with burns. I'll sear her name into his flesh over and over. And hopefully my Little Devil will be watching the entire time. Truly understanding the justice I'm delivering.

CHAPTER
Forty- Three

KOEN

I need a distraction.

Sofia needs a distraction too.

I can see it in her eyes as she watches me making her breakfast. I can see that questioning look, like she's doesn't think she's worth it, worth all the effort I'm going to.

I don't know what shit her therapist talks about but he clearly doesn't bother addressing her self-esteem because that's rock fucking bottom, despite my best efforts.

"We're going out." I state once we've eaten and I've cleared the plates.

Her eyebrows rise. "Where?"

"For a ride."

"I'm not good enough to be out on the streets." She replies quickly.

My lips quirk. I wouldn't risk her out there, not yet anyway.

"You'll be on my bike." I say. "Up front, where I can keep you safe."

She rolls her eyes, takes a final swig of her coffee and mutters about needing to be appropriately dressed in that case. When she comes back down she's wearing new leathers, ones she must have bought. If I thought the old ones made her look good these are something else.

"Turn around." I bark.

She bites her lip like she knows exactly what she's up to and she turns slowly, showing that perfect bubble butt.

I groan before I can stop myself. Yeah, one day soon I am going to take a real bite out of that arse whether she likes it or not.

THE ENGINE ROARS BENEATH ME.

Sofia is upfront, sat perfectly between my thighs. Her hands and gripping the bike beneath her and I know in many ways she'd be more comfortable behind me with her arms wrapped around my body.

Only, I won't be comfortable like that. I want her arse pressed into me, I want her body flat against mine. If she's at my back it'll be harder to pay attention to her behaviour, harder to recognise if she suddenly freaks out.

A dozen or so bikes are around us.

We look like a swarm as we ride out into the busy Verona streets.

My blood seems to hum in my veins. I tighten my grip and speed up, revelling in the flash of freedom that hits me.

Sofia clings to me, her hands grip tightly to my thighs. Last time we didn't go half as fast but I'm not being reckless. I'd never risk her safety, not like this. And besides, under that innocent exterior, I know she gets off on the adrenaline. That's half the reason she picks those fights with me, she likes the feeling of fear pumping in her veins.

She hates that she likes it.

She's ashamed that she does. And yet it gets her off.

Me scaring the shit out of her gets her more horny than anything else. I know if I truly force her, if I pin her down and take her the way I've imagined, forced, violent, unforgivingly, she'd come even harder than she has to date.

She'd come all of my cock.

I groan, shifting my hips, grinding myself against her. Maybe I should do it. Pick a fight, instigate some sort of situation to make her blow up and finally give me an excuse to cross that line.

It wouldn't exactly be hard. I know her pressure points, her triggers. All I have to do is act like she's fragile, precious, not strong enough and she'll fly right off the handle at me.

And yet, would I be satisfied with that? Surely it would feel better for the moment to arise by her own hand. To let her seal her own fate and then suffer the brutal consequences.

My lips curl at that notion.

Yeah it would be better. Much better. Maybe I'll even taunt her about that as I'm ramming my cock into her. Telling her how she asked for it. How she pushed for it. How she deserves it.

"Boss..."

I hear Reid's voice just as something catches my eye. A car veers in front of us. I swerve to the left, only just missing the nearside of it.

"Fucking arsehole." I growl.

All that blood that's been racing to my groin suddenly shifts. Reluctantly it returns to where I need it more.

He had no reason to pull such a manoeuvre, no reason to cut us up. Stupid fuck needs to learn to check his blind-spot.

But something whizzes past my ear. Something that changes this entirely.

I turn my head, seeing the weapon pointed out of the window, seeing the barrels aimed right at me.

This isn't a fluke. This isn't some dumb arse driver, this is intentional.

"Colt." I bellow; but he's seen him already, and he's pulled his own pistol and started taking shots.

I can hear Sofia, gasping, I can feel her hands clenching my legs so tightly.

Are they here to kill her, or me, or both?

I guess we'll never find that out because neither of us is dying today.

"Take positions." I order, not looking back.

I know my men will do what they must but right now I need to get Sofia out of here, I need to get us both away.

CHAPTER
Forty-Four

KOEN

We dart in and out of the traffic. Cars slam on their brakes. Enough beep their horns but I don't give a fuck.

Colt is to my right, Reid is behind me and I know they're creating a block, ensuring there's enough of a distance for me and Sofia to get ahead.

As we turn a corner, I hear the screech of tyres and then that inevitable crunch of metal.

I glance back seeing the carnage we've left in our wake. One car has smashed into a lorry causing it to jackknife across the entire road. Colt whips out, slipping through the tiny gap left between its smashed-up backend and the barrier.

Seconds later Reid follows him and then the rest of our men ride out. There's no way in hell any car is getting through that.

"Job done." Reid says with a smirk. Stupid bastard is the only one reckless enough to not be wearing a full face helmet.

I grunt in reply. Just because we've shaken them off doesn't mean we can relax now. We're still a good half hour from the house.

I hit the gas, and the engine roars beneath us. We speed off, racing once more, only this time it feels more controlled.

Around me my men create a wall.

But I can hear Sofia's breathing, I can feel the way her body is reacting. I call her name through the mic and she doesn't respond.

She's gone into full panic mode. She's practically folded in on herself as her fear as taken over. I order the others to switch the channel, making sure only me and Sofia are now linked through our headsets.

"You're alright." I say. "They're gone now."

She gasps my name, sobs it out. If I could, I'd pull over but there's no time. We can't stop now or we risk those arseholes catching up and putting a bullet in our heads.

No, I need to distract her some other way. I need to pull her out of her own head, give her something else to focus on.

"Take the handlebars." I growl.

Sofia shakes her head.

"Do it." I order. She reaches out, her hands look so tiny as she grasps them. I know she won't have the strength to hold the full weight of this bike so I keep my left hand on it, ensuring we don't crash.

I yank my glove off, tucking it under my thigh to keep it safe.

And then I slide my right down her body, down beneath her trousers and into her panties.

She gasps, jolting and the bike jerks ever so slightly. It's a good warning that if I fuck this up we'll both end up face first on the tarmac.

"Eyes on the road, Princess," I say.

"Koen," She tries to object but her words turn to mush as I slide my finger deep inside her.

She's so wet, so warm, so fucking perfect. I start slow, it's not about making her come, it's about bringing her back out of her trauma.

Her body must be pumped with adrenaline, I'll use that, I'll turn her into a needy, horny little slut for me instead of the petrified creature she currently is.

I can feel the vibrations of the engine beneath us. She starts to lean back into me then realises she can't without making us crash.

I slip a second finger inside. Her body clings to me and I start pumping away, relaxing her the only way I can.

She lets out a long moan.

"There's a good girl." I reply. I don't give a fuck that we're surrounded, I don't give a fuck that any one of my men could turn their heads and see what I'm doing to her. This is about calming her down, about making her feel safe.

"Koen, I can't, I can't come." She gasps.

My lips curl at that desperate tone of her voice. "You'll do exactly as you're told." I reply.

"We'll crash."

"Don't you want to come, Sofia? Don't you want me to pleasure this pretty pussy of yours enough that you come right here on the highway?"

I know I can't see her face, I know the helmet is hiding her expression but I'd put money on her blushing right now. She arches her back, her body giving me every sign that she needs more.

"Tell me, Sofia, tell me what you want."

"I want…" She gulps, her hips rocking and the bike jerks a little once more.

I let out a low laugh that's almost cruel. "You want it, don't you, sweetheart?" I murmur. "You want to come right here?"

"Koen," She gasps.

"Look around, look where you are."

I hear her sharp intake of breath as she realises how vulnerable she actually is. The Sofia I first knew would never have let herself get in this situation, it's a mark of how far she's come, how much of her trauma she's overcome. And how much she's given herself over to me.

"It doesn't matter what these fuckers think, it doesn't matter what anyone thinks. This is about you. About what you want." I state. "So tell me, do you want to come or do you want me to pull my fingers out, to leave your poor pussy unloved and desperate?"

I pinch her clit, giving her that tiny hit of pain that I know she'll love.

"I want, god, Koen, please, I want to come. I don't care, I want…" Her begging turns to a moan as I curl up deep inside her again.

She arches her back, she slams her head back and her helmet crashes into mine. Her muscles clench around me, her screams fill the mic and it takes all I have to keep the bike steady.

"There's a good girl." I growl. "Showing the whole of Verona that you're mine."

Arousal pours out of her, she slumps back and I reluctantly remove my hand, wiping it on my jeans.

I don't say another word, I just let her lean against me until we get back, until we ride through the gates and they shut behind us.

She's barely off my bike before I've picked her up and hauled her arse all the way up to our room.

It might have been about calming her before, but now, now it's about something else entirely. I need to dominate her, to prove to us both that we're alive.

My own adrenaline is pumping around my body and I have to get it out, to channel it, and fucking Sofia senseless seems like a damned good way of achieving that.

I dump her onto the bed. She's still got her helmet on and as she struggles with the strap I leave her to it, striding into the closest, and I come back with my arms full.

She's curled up, on her hands and knees, still half caught in her panic and that won't do. That won't do at all. The helmet is on the floor by the bed but she's still fully clothed.

"Strip." I order.

She gulps, only just meeting my gaze but she doesn't move.

"Get out of your clothes or I will tear them from your body."

That seems to do the trick. She fumbles to get the leather trousers off, ends up half kicking them off her feet. Then she yanks her top up over her head and tosses it before she turns to face me again.

"They tried to kill us." She whispers.

I grunt back, unclasping the bottle of lube.

"Koen,"

My eyes silence her. I don't want her to talk about it. I don't want her to think about it. Right now all I want is to focus her attention on me, on pleasure, and forget that any of the last couple of hours ever existed.

I grab her ankles, pulling her down the bed harshly till she's right in front of me. Her cunt is glistening, taunting me. Clearly it's desperate for attention, even if her mind is distracted.

I pour some lube over her, ensuring she's nice and wet, and then I slather my cock in it. She's not prepped, not ready at all but I don't care. I need her cunt, I need her body, I need all of her.

And I know she needs this too.

"Koen," She gasps but it turns to a scream as I push myself inside her, as I force her body to accommodate me.

"You can take it." I groan. I know she can. She just needs to relax, to remember that it's me, that she likes this.

Her hands grapple at the sheets, she claws at them, sobbing as I slam myself into her over and over.

"Fuck," Maybe this moment is about me. Maybe this is my selfishness twisting it all but I need to come, I need to claim her, to prove that we're still here, that we're still breathing, that I still have her.

Her muscles spasm, her whole body jerks but she doesn't do anything more than cry.

She's so tight it hurts. I screw my face up, pushing her legs wide enough that I can witness every brutal second of this.

She's squelching, flushed, her pussy is obviously bruised from how I'm essentially assaulting her but I don't feel guilty. I only feel that need, that hunger.

"Sofia," I growl.

She arches her back, she tries to move, to shift in a way to make it more bearable but I refuse to give her an inch. I'm taking her my way. I'm having her on my terms.

My hands dig into her flesh, I grip that perfect arse of hers as I pour myself into her and when I slump, I don't care that my weight covers her, I don't care that I'm overwhelming her.

She whimpers beneath me, but she lays perfectly still.

And as I lift my head to see if she's okay, she claims my lips. She wraps her hands around my neck and she kisses me as if I'm not a monster at all.

As if I'm her very own Prince Charming, the person she's always dreamed of.

CHAPTER

Forty-Five

SOFIA

Oh, I know what I've done.

As he's slamming into me, as he's tearing my insides, mercilessly claiming me, I know exactly what I've created.

And right now I don't care that it hurts, I don't care that it's so close to all that horrific trauma. I just know that I need it. I want it.

That him and me like this, him using me, and me allowing it; it makes me feel powerful. It makes me feel incredible.

As fucked up as that no doubt sounds.

My cheeks are flushed with shame. My pussy is drenched and I know it has nothing to do with the copious amounts of lube he smeared over me. I'm so close to coming. So close to completely and utterly losing it but before I can topple over, he's there, he's filling me up, pouring his come into me and he collapses as though he's just spent his very life force.

His sweat covers my skin. His breath is a ragged as mine.

As he raises his head and I see that concern in his eyes, I narrow mine. I don't want him to worry, to feel guilt, to question this. I don't want him to second guess his actions, to worry he's taken things too far.

I want him to use me. I want him to hurt me. I want this. All of this.

He opens his mouth but before he can speak, I pucker my lips and I claim his. I don't want to hear apologies. I don't want to hear concern. I want him feral. I want him domineering.

In a fucked up way, I like him like this, I like this passion and this aggression and this anger because it proves something, it shows that I matter, that I am something to him.

I know he could fuck other women, I know he could walk out of here and have anyone he choose. But he wants me. He *wants* me.

My heart swells as I repeat that over and over. He wants me. As damaged and as broken, and as pathetic as I am, Koen Diaz chooses me.

And I'll welcome him, I'll worship him, I'll take whatever he offers me, no matter how depraved, no matter how savage, how brutal.

His hand cups my cheek. His kisses are always so gentle, so loving.

But the way he's holding me, that way he's cradling me, I know we're not done. That we're not even close.

He pulls himself out, drags his fingers through the mess of us both that remains between our thighs.

"Too rough?" He asks, and I hear the hint, the test.

"No," I reply.

His eyebrows raise. His eyes darken and I swear I've just waved a red flag in front of a raging bull but I don't care, I don't have regrets. If he wants to spend the rest of today and all of tonight brutally claiming me then I'll take it with no complaints beyond my tears.

His fingers spear me, two of them slide deep inside and he spreads them wide like he wants to see how far he can make me stretch. For a few seconds that's all he does, stretch me, manipulate me, like my pussy is some mould he can manipulate into the perfect fit.

"I liked making you come for the entire city to see." He mutters, sliding a third into me. "My only regret is they didn't get to hear you screaming my name."

I gulp back, nodding because some sordid part of me wishes they'd heard it too. Wishes his men had heard. That Reid in particular had heard what Koen was doing, that even with death snapping at our heels, the only thing Koen considered was me, my body, my pleasure.

"How about we make up for that?" He says. "How about we spend the next few hours making you scream loud enough that every one hears?"

God I'm a whore for how I react, how my body leaks arousal. I wince, knowing it's already trickling down his hand and he chuckles.

"Such a good girl." He groans. "I've got you so well trained now."

When he slides his fingers out, I whimper, but evidently he has bigger plans, better plans. He picks me up, places me face down on my knees so my arse is in the air and my face is in the mattress.

"Don't move." He states, like I'd even consider it.

For a second I hear nothing. I just stay, waiting, literally dripping with anticipation and then something hard touches me.

"This is going to hurt."

That's the only warning I get, the only words he says before he's putting those clamps on my nipples, tightening them more than last time, tightening so much I really do start crying.

Koen sits back on his haunches, placing himself behind me where no doubt he has a great view of whatever the hell he has planned.

He places one hand on my back, holding me still, and then he does what he's been threatening so many times, what he's taunted me with. He clamps my clit.

I jerk, I jolt. I freeze from the sudden shock of pain. In my head this seemed far sexier, far more appealing. But all I can feel is agony.

"You look so good." He murmurs before planting a kiss on my arse cheek. "So fucking beautiful."

I shut my eyes, trying not to imagine the view he has. I'm bent over, my entire privates are on display. Though I've never seen a clit clamp in my life I can imagine what it looks like, and from how my nipples are engorged, I don't doubt it's doing the exact same thing down south.

He slides a finger into me, then another, and another, until it feels like he's got his entire hand forced into my pussy. I can't breathe. I can't think.

My face is covered by my tears and I sob, shaking, forcing myself to be compliant.

"You're going to enjoy this, Sofia," He reassures. "I promise you. You're going to love this as much as everything else I've done."

I want to believe him. I so badly do. Maybe I'm an idiot to put my trust in this man, to let myself end up in such a vulnerable situation but I'm here now, there's no getting away from it. I nod, shutting my eyes, praying that he's telling the truth.

Slowly he pulls his hand out, clenches his fingers together and forces it back inside me.

I swear my eyes bulge. I scream in shock and pain.

He's fisting me? What the fuck?

He starts groaning, growling, his hot breath lands on my back and I can tell from the proximity that he's got his face right there, up close, like he doesn't want to blink and miss it.

"It's too much." I gasp. My nipples are agony. My clit is throbbing in protest. Blood is ringing in my ears like it doesn't know where to go.

"You can handle this, Sofia." Koen replies. "Don't you want to be a good girl for me?"

"Yesss," I sob. I do. I really do. But it hurts.

He sighs, picking up speed like that's what I need.

"You should see yourself, Sofia, you should see how greedily your cunt accepts this," He growls. "How it enjoys this."

I can hear the squelching, I can hear that sound of his hand punching inside me over and over. My legs are trembling. I don't know how I haven't collapsed but if I do that will only increase the pressure on my nipples.

"She's grown so used to my cock that a few fingers aren't enough to satisfy her anymore." He taunts.

My cheeks flame -but my body responds. To my horror all that pain, and that adrenaline that's been racing around my body seems to turn to arousal, to lust, to insanity too, if I admit it.

I moan, I shake, I try to bite down the sound and Koen slaps me hard across the arse.

"Don't you dare." He snaps. "I told you I wanted to hear you scream, and I meant it."

"Please," I whimper. I just need a little mercy.

If he hears me, he doesn't give any indication. He just grabs my head forcing my face into the mattress and he starts fisting me harder.

I scream, I cry, I sob, but it's not all pain now, it's some heady, confused mess. I can't think. I can't breathe. I'm his prisoner right now, trapped in his grasp and as my orgasm threatens to take over

I know that my body is once more submitting exactly the way he wants it to.

Suddenly that pressure around my clit disappears. Blood flushes to it. I gasp, moaning with relief.

His hand moves from my head to between my thighs and he starts pleasuring me. Teasing my clit. I'm so sensitive from the clamp that it barely takes a second before I explode. I combust. I completely and utterly lose all control.

His fist is still buried deep inside me. My insides slam down around his wrist and I scream until my throat goes hoarse. I scream until I swear the blood vessels in my eyes burst.

So much liquid pours out. It drenches me. It feels like I've pissed myself and as I collapse onto the sheets I don't even have the strength to care if I have.

"Fuck," Koen groans, sliding his hand out, rolling me over so that I'm now flat on my back.

I lay still, I lay docile, trying to just breathe, trying to get oxygen in.

"You squirted." He says, brushing the hair off my face. "You actually squirted."

I don't know what that means. I can barely register the words but from the look on his face it's clearly a good thing.

My pussy is throbbing, my nipples are still caught in those metal clamps. He lifts a finger, circling one engorged nipple and then the other and though I know it's madness, insanity, I arch my back, ignoring that searing pain, seeking more, needing more.

"You're doing so good, Sofia," He praises.

I gulp, staring back at him because that phrase tells me everything. That we're not done yet. That he's going to fuck me more, hurt me more. Does he get off on the pain as much as I do? Is that what this is? Or is it that he knows I enjoy it and that's where his head is at? Giving me what he thinks I want.

I shift, wincing as I remember the literal pool beneath me.

Koen picks me up, ignoring my hiss and he lays me flat on my back with my head right off the end of the bed. As I stare up at him he slowly removes his clothes, revealing that body that makes all rational thoughts leave my head.

I open my lips wide, stick out my tongue, ready to accept him the way I know he wants and he grins.

"Fuck, you're so perfect."

His dick slides into my mouth before I can reply. He's not slamming into me the way he claimed my pussy but he's not being gentle either. He's so big that within seconds his cock is there, pushing at the back of my throat, forcing it's way down and I'm taking in huge breaths through my nose, doing everything I can not to choke.

His hand grips my hair, he's cradling my head to ensure I can take him at the best angle for his pleasure.

I suck him like my life depends upon it, I swirl my tongue around, worshipping his cock, ignoring that searing pain of my poor nipples. My eyes are streaming. I must look an absolute state and yet Koen is telling me that I'm beautiful, gorgeous, utterly breathtaking.

He reaches down, right over my body, pinching my clit, teasing it, and I jerk, keeping my legs spread wide for him to appreciate me fully.

He's watching me so intently, clearly enjoying the view of his cock sinking into my mouth over and over.

As he starts to tease, that pain inside me turns to something else. Oh, it still hurts, it hurts like hell but the tease of his fingers, the way he's now pleasuring me turns everything into one heady mess of emotions.

I sob, I moan, I completely lose all sense of time, of consciousness. I forget that it's his cock down my throat, I forget that I'm practically choking on him. I'm too aroused, too needy. I raise my hips, riding his fingers in rhythm to the constant slamming of his dick.

But it's me who comes first. Me who topples over the edge. He's quick to slide out of my mouth, to give me the precious air I need as I start screaming, writhing, rolling about like a thing possessed.

I'm still half jerking, half caught in my orgasm as he spins me around and he lifts my legs up, placing them against his chest.

"I'm going to make you feel good, Sofia." He groans.

I can't process those words. I already feel good. I feel like I've actually died and gone to heaven. Every nerve ending in my body is euphoric, and yet underneath it, that pain in my chest persists.

He tilts he up, my breasts heave, and as I glance at my nipples I gasp at how truly dark they are from the lack of blood flow.

He grins, reaching down to cup them, to pinch them. They're numb, tingling with pins and needles. But god, what I wouldn't give for him to suck them, to tease them, to make them feel good.

He pulls my legs apart, stares directly down to where my pussy is, and places his thumb and finger to spread my lower lips wide, as if this is some sort of inspection, as if he wants to see the very damage he's caused.

"You're so bruised." He murmurs. "This poor pussy is battered."

I shouldn't feel like I'm proud. I shouldn't feel like I've earnt those words.

"I think filling you with my come would make it better, don't you?"

I nod quickly. Yes. Yes, that would help. That would be a start.

He chuckles, like he knew this would be my response, like he understands what a needy little bitch I'm becoming.

This time when he slides into me, it's so controlled, so slow. If I could imagine the way he takes me when I'm asleep, I'd say it's like this, considerate. He's not gentle, but he's measured, like he wants to witness the evidence of every inch of my body he's taking, written there on my face.

I arch my back, I grip the sheets so tightly, moaning with pleasure and delight.

"Touch yourself." He orders. "Pinch your clit, make yourself come while I watch."

I don't hesitate to move, to do it. my right hand snakes down, finding my poor battered clit and I tease myself carefully, slowly circling, running my fingertips up and down while Koen holds himself still, buried inside me.

Fuck, the look in his eyes, the way he's watching this. I can't explain how my heart flips, how it races. Maybe I should do this more often, maybe one day I should tie him down and put on a show, pleasure myself for him to watch. I'd drive him to distraction. I'd tease him until he lost all control and then let him completely and utterly break my body when he finally got loose.

"Don't be gentle." He growls. "Make it hurt. You know you like pain, so don't hide from it."

My heart picks up. He wants me to hurt myself? He truly wants that? Then fine.

My left hand reaches up to my breasts. He traces the movement, he narrows his eyes, not missing a second as I pinch and squeeze my nipples. My tears start streaming down my cheeks but around his cock I'm clenching so tightly.

"That's it." He groans. "That's fucking beautiful."

I can't formulate words. I can't do anything but keep going, keeping pleasuring my clit while hurting my breasts. Koen starts thrusting again, rocking my body and if anything that heightens all of this.

"Oh god," I gasp. I'm not sure I can even come again. I'm not sure I have anything left in me to come. But I want to do it. I want to give him everything he deserves, and he deserves this. He deserves every inch of my body, every second of me.

"Koen," I scream.

"That's it." He growls, slapping my breast.

Fuck it hurts. It hurts too much.

My adrenaline suddenly spikes, my eyes lose focus and I lose all control. I spasm, I jerk, I come one final time but no noise leaves my mouth. It's like my voice is broken, like I'm too exhausted to scream.

He digs his hands into my hips, he growls out, pumping into me, before he too slumps down onto the bed.

I stare at him, wanting so desperately to get these clamps off but I won't make the move. It's his decision. If he decides I have to wear these from now until eternity then I'll do it. I'll wear them with pride.

He leans over as if reading my mind, and he starts lathering my breasts with attention, licking them, kissing them, caressing them. One by one he undoes the metal and as that awful sensation starts rushing back he fixes himself between my thighs, resting on his elbows, kissing them better.

CHAPTER

Forty-Six

KOEN

"They're taking their sweet time." Colt grumbles beside me.

I smirk, staring into the distance, at where the road is still obviously devoid of traffic.

He's not wrong. They are late. But then Barnaby Smith was never good at time keeping.

Roman dropped off the supplies two days ago. It took eight trucks to transport it all here. But this deal ensures our success for years to come. This deal will make us very rich men.

The wind howls around us. When the snow comes it will bring its own problems. No doubt we'll have to rely on the tunnels more, will have to expand them further.

"How's Sofia after the other day?" Colt asks.

"Fine." I state. Though that's not true. She's on edge, jumpy. I may have fucked her brains out but I didn't fuck the memory out of her head. Every noise makes her jump. Every move she's not expecting makes her look like she's about to have a full blown panic attack.

I've dealt with it my way. The only way I can think. By trying to override her brain with so many orgasms she can't focus on anything else.

And yet still, she woke up screaming. She woke up in a complete panic last night and the only way to shut her up was to shove my cock down her throat.

"Reid is on it." I add. He's been going through all the footage, trying to work out where the fuck they came from. It felt like a good task to set him, a good way to ensure he's out of the way too because I know he and Sofia haven't exactly gotten on up until now.

"Is he still spouting that cursed shit?" I ask.

Colt shifts, wincing just enough for me to see.

Fucking great.

"There is some truth to it." Colt states.

"In what way?"

I don't mean to grab him, I don't mean to pin him against the damned door but I do.

He doesn't fight, perhaps he knows that I'm not exactly thinking straight when it comes to Sofia, the evidence certainly seems to suggest that.

I let him go, let him find his footing but I don't move back. I don't give him space.

The men around us shift but they keep their mouths shut.

"You know what they had, Koen." Colt says. "You know what her father had."

"It's bullshit."

"Is it? Doesn't it answer everything?"

I narrow my eyes. Colt was never one for superstition, at least he wasn't until Reid started spurting all his bullshit.

But the diamond is a rumour. A myth. If Horace Montague really had a jewel that valuable he would have used it to his advantage. He wouldn't have turned into a weak, miserly old man.

"Darius knew." Colt states. "He had to have known. That's probably why they had a falling out…"

"Enough." I growl, seeing the movement from the corner of my eye. Our friends are here. And the last thing I want is to be discussing the Devil's Heart diamond within their earshot.

Five armoured trucks speed down the track. It's a good thing it's spitting or the dust cloud they're producing would be engulf us all.

Barnaby gets out first. He's clearly excited to see his new wares.

He's got ten years on me. And he looks every day of it and more. His face is etched with as many scars as he has wrinkles. Every inch of his skin is covered in thick, fading tattoos.

I make a point of showing the surface-to-air missile first. The damned thing took an entire truck by itself. His eyes glint as he stares at it, like he's already imagining all the chaos he's going to create.

When we'd first spoken, he sounded doubtful that we'd be able to get this. I like the look of surprise on his face now that we've proven him wrong.

He takes his time inspecting the other weapons. The boring stuff. Rifles, ammo, drones. All of them necessities but they don't exactly get your blood pumping.

With a nod of his head, his banker pulls out his phone and mutters into it. A second later I hear the ping that tells me we just got paid.

"Load it up." He orders.

I hold out the keys to the truck with the missile. The damned thing weighed a ton. It's easier if they just have it as an extra than bother with trying to shift it over.

He inclines his head like I've done him some sort of favour.

"I'll need more." He says in that whispered, strained voice that's more haunting than you could imagine. The bastard had throat cancer and even though he's beaten it, his voice box will never recover. If anything it makes him more haunting.

"Whatever you need." I reply.

He grins, knowing now that those aren't empty words. That I really can deliver everything he can dream of.

As they drive away, Colt lets out a breath that sounds almost like relief.

"Didn't think you scared so easily." I taunt.

He shakes his head, struts away, and starts barking orders for everyone to get moving.

We have to take the backstreets into the city, the quiet streets. What we're doing is legit, technically, but neither Roman nor I want to start airing our dirty laundry in public. No, the glitzy elite like to think themselves above this, that all that gold they shit out of their arses is untainted. They don't want to admit that this is how the world really works, that at our core, we're all savages.

We pull up to a drive through. Colt's always a cranky bastard when he's hungry and besides, I figure Sofia won't complain if I bring her back something sweet.

As I sit there, watching the traffic idle-by my mind flickers back to the Brethren. To the danger Sofia is in. I don't have contacts but I can't imagine it'd be hard to track someone down. But would that help? I doubt men such as they are, are the kind who like to sit around and negotiate after they've already declared war.

And that's what this is. The moves they're making, all these attacks, it is war. A clever, tactical play. Sofia had all but disappeared from the board, she'd all but gone cold and yet they still weren't happy. They still decided to poke the beast.

I shake my head. I need to get her to remember. I need to get her to focus, but how? If I force the issue she won't thank me for it. And in my heart, I fear she might truly have a breakdown.

"You ready?"

I look up, seeing Colt stood, coffee in hand, squinting at the sun. The rest of us stayed outside, after all, we didn't want the place to turn to panic if all twenty of us barged our way in.

"Sure."

He passes me the pastry. I open the paper bag, inspect the contents then grunt. It's Sofia's favourite. Peacan Pie. I wonder what I can ask for in exchange for this? Maybe I'll smear some of it on my cock and have her lick it off.

The thought makes me smirk. I doubt I'd have to go that far, she's always so eager for me, eager to please. Maybe I should test that, see how far I can truly push her.

Colt reaches the cab, unlocks the doors and gets in.

I jump into the drivers seat and turn the ignition, only it doesn't start. Instead it makes a strange choking noise.

"What the…?"

Smoke starts to fizzle out from underneath the bonnet.

In the seconds it takes for us to spring out the entire thing explodes and we're thrown back, onto our arses, landing on the concrete pavement.

Colt immediately pulls his gun, taking position, expecting a full blown ambush.

I get up, dusting myself down, as I take in the metre high flames. Someone blew my car up? Someone blew my *fucking* car up.

I snarl, turning my rage onto a nearby rubbish bin and kick it till it's nothing more than a crumple mass of metal.

"This isn't a coincidence." Colt spits.

"Of course it's not a fucking coincidence." I growl back.

Two days after they tried to shoot us down, they blow my car up? They want me out of the way apparently. Whatever this shit is with Sofia, I'm clearly a threat.

"Put Reid on alert." I order.

Colt grunts, grabbing his phone, dialling Reid's number and then mine vibrates in my pocket.

I yank it out, seeing the message flash up from Sofia, and I freeze. What the fuck is going on? Was this planned? They take me out and make a move against Sofia all at the same time?

"Get to the house." I bellow. "Get Reid in there now."

Colt stares back at me before repeating it down the phone.

I need to get back there. I need to make sure she's safe.

I run to one of the other trucks, pulling out the driver and take his seat. Colt barely has time to get in beside me before I'm hitting the gas.

"What's going on?" He asks.

I toss my phone at him. Let him read the message that she's in trouble. That she needs my help.

"Fucking hell." He groans.

We're a good ten minutes out. Anything could happen in that time. Anything could go down. Sofia could be taken, could be killed.

A light turns red but I don't stop, I just plough right through narrowly missing the car in the wrong direction.

I don't have time for this shit. I don't have time for anything.

CHAPTER
Forty- Seven

KOEN

I storm into the house. I didn't even switch the engine off.

My gun is out, Colt is hot on my tails.

As we reach the second floor I can't hear a damned thing. It's like nobody is here. Like whatever fight has already happened long ago.

When I get to our room, I see movement.

"Sofia?" I call, tightening my grip. If anyone is in there, I'll blow their fucking heads off.

"In here."

It's not her who answers. It's Reid and he sounds pissed. What the fuck is going on?

I storm in, there's four men. My men, all stood, looking more than a little sheepish. Reid is shaking his head, glaring.

And Sofia, fuck me, Sofia is there, a sheet pressed to her chest and her face bright red, as she stares at the floor in front of her.

"What the…?" Colt says behind me.

"Apparently your woman likes to play games." Reid states looking unamused. "Apparently there isn't enough drama in her life already."

She winces, dropping her gaze further, mumbling some sort of apology. She's clearly wearing nothing but underwear. And my men, they're all stood gawping, like she's some damn art exhibition.

"Get out." I order.

Thankfully they know better than to be told twice, but Reid makes a point of smirking at me as he struts past. He's damn lucky I don't put a bullet in his head for that.

Once it's just us, just me and her she lets out a small sigh. "I'm so sorry…"

"Drop the sheet." I say.

She gulps, pulling it down. I swear my eyes almost pop out of my head. That's new lingerie. More new lingerie. I'd know if she already had that. Has she got a whole store's worth stashed away for me?

"I was bored."

She sounds so quiet. So embarrassed.

I let out a laugh that's more relief than anything else.

"You're not mad?" She asks.

"Oh, I'm fucking furious." I state. "But not at you."

"I didn't realise…" She shakes her head. "Reid told me they attacked you again."

I know why he said that, why he no doubt berated her. He's trying to push her out, doing everything he can to get rid of her. But my Little Devil is going nowhere.

"So you got bored and decided to have a little fun?" I taunt.

She nods quickly. "I didn't think…"

"No, you didn't." I agree. "And now I'm going to have to punish you for it."

"Pppunish me?" Her eyes widen. She stares up at me as if she expects me to actually start hurting her. And I will, but not in a way where she won't be enjoying every second of it.

"Turn around, lie on your face, put your arse in the air." I order.

She does it quickly, whimpering all the same.

I don't think to check if she'll be okay with this, I don't really care if she isn't. I've got shit to do. I can't be thinking about what she's up to while I'm needing to focus on who the fuck is trying to have me killed.

I grab the rope, wrap it around the headboard and secure both her wrists up above her head.

She doesn't try to argue so I guess she isn't too bothered by being tied down. That's good to know. I grab her ankles, cross them over one another then tie them together. I know it'll hurt. I know it won't be comfortable but, she'll have enough to focus her pleasure on, that this should help balance it out.

Once they're properly secured to the other end of the bed I stand back, and admire my handiwork.

She's still wearing that black lacey little set. And Christ, am I going to enjoy ripping it apart later.

I ease the thong down.

She tenses and I can see she's already wet. Yeah, my Little Devil does get off on dominance. On being overpowered.

As I run my fingers through her cunt, she lets out a long moan.

"This isn't about giving you orgasms. At least not yet." I state.

She turns her head as much as she can and frowns at me, obviously confused. My fingers find her arsehole. Slowly, I start circling it and she gulps.

"Have you been fucked here, before?" I ask, somehow keeping the excitement from my voice. I've been dying to fill that tight little hole from the moment I laid eyes on her.

"Yes." The way she says it, the resignation tells me that none of her encounters previously were consensual.

I nod, storing that information. In that case I'll go slow this time, I'll prep her properly, build her up till I can fuck her arse as brutally as I can claim the rest of her body.

I walk out, come back with the toys I need and I pour enough lube over her to make her skin shine. She sniffs, holding her body still, like she expects me to just shove my cock into her. As if that's her punishment. As if I'd be that unimaginative.

I pour some lube onto the plug. It's big, not too big, but big enough that she'll open up and welcome me in, in a few hours' time.

She protests as I force it in. She jerks, tries to move her body away but the way the rope holds her means she can't get far.

Once it's almost home, I slap her arse and she bucks, securing it in place with a pretty little jewel glinting back at me.

"Good girl." I say though she doesn't understand she just did exactly what I wanted.

I run my hands back over her.

"I'd say five will do it."

"Five what?" She stammers.

My lips grin. I could warn her. I could tell her what my plan is but then where would be the fun? I raise my hand, straighten my fingers, then bring it down on her left cheek.

She gasps in shock but before she has time to recover I slap her right.

"No." She sobs.

"You will take this." I state.

"Please..."

Fuck, I love the way she begs, I love the pitiful sound in her voice when she knows she's been naughty and yet she so desperately wants a reprieve.

My response is to slap her again.

She starts crying, whimpering into the sheets. I'm not going easy on her. I'm hitting her hard enough that she *should* be crying. When I'm done her skin is bright red. I can see my very fingers stretched out over her.

I pick up the second toy and slide it inside. She shakes her head but her body accepts it readily enough, greedy little thing that it is.

"Take your punishment." I growl.

"Koen…"

I tut, running my hand back over her sensitive flesh. She thinks this will all be pain but I'm about to leave her squirming with pleasure.

I flick the remote on. The way the egg is buried means I can't hear the buzz but I know it's working from the way she reacts.

The way her body quivers. She gasps, clenching her hands tightly against the restraints.

I take it up one notch and she groans, burying her face in the mattress.

"You're going to stay here." I state. "You're going to be a good girl and wait for me to come back."

I don't wait for her reply. I just turn around and leave her there, heading down to the basement.

CHAPTER
Forty-Eight

SOFIA

I can't think. I can't move. I can't do anything.

The toy inside me is vibrating enough that I can feel my body thrumming, feel my heart slamming into my chest and damn does my pussy throb.

I want more. I need more.

Whatever this is, it isn't enough.

But then, that's the point, isn't it? I work that out after the first hour of waiting desperately for his return.

He's left me here, immobile, with a plug in my arse and something getting me so close to coming but never close enough.

I squirm, I fidget, I rub my thighs together and do everything I can to try to relieve the pressure and it does fuck all.

I know when he comes back he's going to take my arse. I know that's been on the books for a while.

In a way I'm more afraid of that than I was him fucking me vaginally. At least that was good, at least that felt good. I don't see how anal sex can do anything for a woman except cause pain, and I'm fearful of the flashbacks, of the memories that might raise their ugly head, once we embark down this path.

I'm so thirsty I could cry. I swear my throat is drying up and if he came back and decided he wanted me to suck him off then I doubt I'd be able to manage it.

When I do finally hear the sound of footsteps, I tense. My nerves feel shredded, my body is already over sensitised and exhausted. I doubt I'll survive what he has planned. No, I'm certain I won't.

He stalks into the room, coming to a stop right by the bed.

I can sense his smirk and though I'd love to say something clever, I don't dare.

He holds something out, and then instantly that thing inside me picks up a beat.

I moan, I whimper, my hips rock instinctively back and forth trying to give some sort of reprieve.

And the bastard laughs.

He kneels of the bed, placing himself so his knees touch my crossed feet.

"You're dripping, Sofia." He taunts. "There's a puddle right under you. Are you that desperate?"

I gulp, biting my tongue. He knows I'm desperate. He's made me desperate.

His hand strikes my arse.

I scream out, partly in shock and partly because he's already spanked me so many times it really does hurt.

He grabs my hips, pulling me back and that tension on my wrists increases. I feel like one of those medieval spies, tied up, being stretched out on a rack and any minute my joints are going to pop free.

He eases the plug out. It's done so slowly that he makes it feel like my body doesn't want to relinquish it.

"I'm going to fuck you now." He says, lowering his body, positioning his cock and I can feel it already, pushing to be let in.

A sob slips from my lips. I shake my head. I don't want this. I don't want any of this.

I'm too tired, too desperate, and too afraid of how much it's going to hurt.

"Sofia," He growls.

I don't reply. I just bury my face, resigning myself to my fate.

He slaps me again and that thing inside me almost hits my g-spot. Almost.

"Tell me how eager you are."

"No."

I don't mean to say it, I don't mean to speak but the word comes out anyway.

He groans, leaning forward, gripping my skull by my hair.

"You gave me free use, remember? You said I could fuck you anyway I wished."

I did say that. I stupidly said that when I was weak, and vulnerable and not understanding how far he would go.

He pushes himself into me. I try to fight but there's nowhere to go.

He practically snarls as he works his entire length into my arse.

"Fuck," He gasps. "If I'd known your arse would feel this good I might have given your pussy a day off, earlier."

I can't say anything back. I can barely breathe. I feel too stuffed. I feel like as soon as he starts thrusting he's going to tear me in half.

His hand twists around, he finds my clit, and once again, I shake my head.

"You're going to come." He states. "You're going to behave. And you're going to enjoy it."

"Please," I gasp.

He pinches my clit so hard I start sobbing.

"This is your punishment." He says right into my ear. "Now, take it like a good girl or I'll spank you more."

I want to fight. I want to scream out but he's right, he has all the power right now, there's nothing I can do but endure this and let him use me.

He starts circling, teasing, running his fingers up and down my pussy, spreading the shameful amount of arousal I've leaked out.

I try to stay still, to not grind my arse but within seconds I lose any other thought beyond the screaming voice in my head that's demanding a release from all this pressure.

As soon as I do it, as soon as I start enjoying it, he makes his move. He eases himself out, then slides back into me.

It hurts. It really fucking hurts. I feel like I'm on the verge of a panic attack, I feel like my body is trembling so much the entire bed is shaking.

"Relax." He murmurs. "Let yourself enjoy this."

I can't. I can't relax. I can't do anything.

He hisses, clearly annoyed at my response and he starts teasing me more, forcing my body to focus on my impending orgasm.

And then that thing inside me goes off. He must hit some turbo button because it's like everything goes mad. I cry out, I sob, my body heaves with the desperate need for this to be over.

He starts groaning, picking up his pace.

I can feel the rope burning with every thrust. I can feel my skin starting to tear.

"You're doing so good," He praises but I can barely hear him over the sound of my own tears.

His hips are slamming into mine. He's not being gentle. Maybe that plug opened me up a bit but he's still far too big for this.

"Come for me, Little Devil. Be a good girl and behave."

I don't want to. I know if I do I'm going to jerk, to twist, that these bindings are going to hurt me more.

He slaps my arse harder than ever and I scream out.

"Come." He demands, pinching my clit, forcing me right over the edge.

My body freezes, my head seems to lose all thoughts. Stars prick my vision but I'm screaming, bucking, losing what little control I still had.

He's groaning, fucking me just as hard and then he pours himself into me, pours himself into my arse before slumping down onto the bed.

I'm forced to lay there, to stay bent over with my arse in the air as his come starts to leak out.

When he gets up, he's tilting his head, examining me like I'm a science project, before he's pulling that damned toy out of my pussy.

My body physically deflates, I let out a low breath, trying to calm my rapidly beating heart.

"Untie me." I whisper. My throat feels so hoarse, I wouldn't be surprised if I lost my voice after all of this.

He tuts, shaking his head. "You think that was the only punishment you're getting?"

My eyes widen, I start whimpering more.

He gets up, disappears then comes back in with something I can't make out. But my mind can already guess where this is headed.

"I can't," I sob, "I can't."

"You will."

"Koen, please…"

He tightens his jaw, reaching down to undo the ties around my wrists. Only, I'm still bound by my ankles so it doesn't help all that much.

"I didn't mean," I begin. "I was just…"

"Just what?"

I sniff, wiping my face, wiping the tears. "I thought you might like it."

His eyebrows raise. "You thought I might like you showing yourself off to all my men?"

Oh shit. Is that what the issue is?

"But that wasn't my intention." I reply. "I wanted to surprise you."

He grins, flashing that golden tooth. "Oh, you did," He states, leaning down, cupping my breasts in my new bra, pulling them out so that they both sit on top of the lace and are entirely exposed.

"Any other day you would have been fine." He adds.

"But not today?"

He shakes his head. "Not today."

So what, it's my bad luck that someone tried to kill him the same day I decided to play a game of seducing him?

"It's just a case of bad timing." He chuckles.

"But that's, that's unfair." I stammer.

He runs his hand over my arse, soothing the tender flesh that he's beaten so many times I know it will bruise. "Life is unfair, princess, you have to take what it gives you."

I tense as I feel his fingers opening me up wider and then something pressing against me. Something hard. Something unforgiving.

"If you relax this will feel better."

"I can't." I gasp. I'm too wound up, too tired, too mentally drained.

"More's the pity."

I barely hear the words before whatever it is is shoved into me.

And I scream. I bury my face into the mattress and I scream over and over.

He fucks me like he really is punishing me. He must get arm ache from the speed. There's nothing sexy about this, nothing romantic. He's brutalising my body once more.

But I can feel myself growing wet. I can feel my body demanding more.

"Tell me you like this." He growls. "Tell me you like being used like this."

"I do," I cry, feeling every bit the traitor that I am. Every bit the whore that I am too.

He groans, taking in deep breaths like he's trying to get himself under control and then he's sliding that thing back out.

For a second I can convince myself that that's it. That he's had his fun and we're done here. Only that's not Koen, is it? He forces something new into me, something that feels equally as strange.

He lights a cigarette, leans down over my body and I swear to god he's going to burn me, just the way Otto did.

"No," I cry.

But I don't feel that pain. I don't feel that heat. When he sits back up he's grinning.

What the… my mind registers the pain, the momentary feeling of what is unmistakably hot wax. He shoved a candle in me? What the fuck?

He moves back around to my face, props me up on my elbows and holds a shot gun like it's some sort of gift. It's barrel is long but obviously missing half.

"Your pussy seemed to welcome this just now." He states and I gasp.

He fucking fucked me with a sawn-off shotgun? What kind of psycho would even think to do that?

He meets my gaze and then says, "Lick it."

"Excuse me?"

"You've got until the candle burns out to get it all clean."

I stare up at him, seeing the serious look in his eyes. He's not joking. He's not fucking around.

If I disobey, if I turn him down, what else will he do to punish me?

"Why?" I ask the question more out of habit than because I want an answer.

His lips curl, he drags the metal across my lips and I can feel my juices, I can taste myself on it.

"This weapon is all that stands between you and whoever is trying to kill you. The least you can do is show your gratitude."

Gratitude? He wants gratitude?

I shift, feeling that candle move. If I relax my inner muscles too much will it slip out and set fire to the bed? To be honest, I'm not sure I want to know the answer to that. I extend my tongue, glaring up at Koen as I do and slowly take one lick.

He doesn't react. He just stays there, kneeling, holding the Berretta perfectly still. And bit by bit I run my tongue along the metal, tasting myself as I lick it clean.

Every few seconds a drop of wax hits my skin and I wince.

It's so hard to do it, to move my mouth without moving my lower half.

Once the outside is practically spotless Koen turns the barrel, pointing it at my face and he taps my mouth.

No. Not a fucking chance.

"Open up, princess."

I shake my head, only that rocking motion makes my whole body move and I drip even more wax on myself.

I hiss at the burn and the bastard glances down and laughs before his face turns deadly.

"Open wide or I will force this between your lips."

He's not joking. I can see it in his face. I part my lips, shouting every curse word I know in my head.

"Now, imagine it's my cock." He taunts. "You've enjoyed sucking that off enough times."

I hate that I do it. I hate that in some perverse way this is turning me on, but I shut my eyes and suck it.

He groans like it really is his cock, and he starts moving it in and out.

"Touch yourself." He orders.

I shake my head, if I do that I'll burn myself, I know it. I only just manage to blurt those words out as he fucks my mouth.

"I don't give a shit." He replies. "Touch yourself, make yourself come."

He's a bastard. An absolute bastard.

I have to shift around awkwardly to do it but my fingers find my clit and I can feel how disgustingly wet I am. Turns out I really am fucked up then. I really am as twisted in the head as I feared.

I start circling it, teasing myself, maybe if I can eek this out then the candle will be done before I climax.

Koen's got his eyes darting between my legs and where my mouth is still granting his gun pleasure like it's not an inanimate object, but evidently he hasn't gotten a good enough view, because he forces me up, makes my kneel. My ankles are still bound so I can't get away even if I wanted to.

I honestly have no idea how the pair of us are not on fire but more wax covers my skin. I can feel the heat of the flame too close to where my thighs are.

But the adrenaline pumping through me is making me reckless. And the look in his eyes, that feral, wild look, it's turning me on far too much to be rational.

When a moan escapes my mouth, he grins, placing his finger and thumb so that he can spread my lower lips wide and he can see every second of my own handiwork.

"Such a pretty pussy." He states. "When you're done I'm going to fuck you one more time."

I blink, trying not to register those words, to contemplate it. I can feel my body hurtling towards another orgasm. I can feel my forehead growing drenched with sweat. I don't think I can last. No, I know I can't.

I whimper, I shake my head and mercifully Koen pulls the shotgun from my mouth as I lose all control. I scream, I jerk out. At some point he must remove the candle but I don't notice, I'm too lost in my euphoria. I'm too exhausted from how long this delicious torture has held me within its grasp.

I collapse face first into the bed. Panting. Heaving. Feel a pool of my own arousal beneath me.

Koen undoes my legs, soothes where the rope has torn my skin and then he places himself right behind me.

"You've been so good, Sofia. You've done me so proud."

I can hear from that tone that he's all wound up again, that he's going to do exactly what he promised and he's going to fuck me again. Only, I can't move. I can't do anything. I lay there, like we're back at my house and I'm fast asleep, and he's about to have his wicked way with me.

He slides his cock into me and it hurts, it burns, it fucking kills.

I hiss, clenching my jaw. Every muscle in my body protests. Every bone aches.

"You can take this," He states. "I know you can."

He clearly has far more belief in me than I do myself right now.

He picks up my hips, pressing me to him.

"You're so wet." He groans. "I think you're pussy enjoyed being fucked like that, I think it likes being abused as much as I enjoy doing it."

Maybe it does, maybe I do get off on it, but right now I'm too ashamed to admit it.

He starts off gentle, hitting that spot inside me that makes me moan, and stretch and writhe despite my pathetic state.

But then that feral monster I'm getting used to comes out to play. He tightens his grip, he picks up his pace, fucking me like he's trying to break me. And I lay there. I stay still, I let him use me like I'm a fuck-toy solely built for his pleasure.

My eyes grow hazy, my body feels too heavy.

I don't mean to do it but I pass out, I fall unconscious before he can finish.

Before he can force me to give him any more orgasms.

CHAPTER

Forty- Nine

KOEN

She passed out.

She fucking passed out.

I don't know whether to feel frustrated or enthralled.

She's laying there, face down in the mattress, still with my cock buried in her cunt.

A voice in my head says I should stop. That I need to stop.

But she's not dying. She's fine.

I pinch her clit, seeing if that will wake her but it does nothing.

Apparently I've exhausted her entirely then.

But I'm not exhausted, tired yes, but not exhausted.

I pull out, turn her over. In that new bra, her tits look so good. Her mouth is slightly ajar. She's got a tiny huff of air coming in and out. Christ, she looks so peaceful right now, so angelic.

And I'm the devil ruining her.

I force myself back inside her, lowering my mouth over her body and I take my time devouring each of her breasts. I knead them, pinch them, slap them. She's definitely getting plump now. She's really turning into my pampered little plaything.

I force her legs wider, shove them out so I've got the best view of my cock as I slam into her. Her muscles are still gripping me so well. Her body is begging me to end this, to finish this, to use her as I see fit.

I drag my nails down her ribs, I trace those awful scars on her belly. She's majestic right now. She's resplendent.

With every thrust I make, her entire body heaves.

I'm so close I can't even think straight. I grab her throat, tightening my grip, and I whisper into her ear that she's mine, that she will always be mine and then I pour myself into her, I fill her up, the way she deserves.

Her face doesn't react. Her body greedily accepts what I give but she lays there, immobile.

As I ease my cock back out, I take my time studying her, pulling those battered lips of her cunt apart. She's dripping out my seed. She looks red, sore. Every inch of her pussy has clearly been abused. Poor thing, I didn't mean to be so rough, I didn't mean to be so hard on her, but when the opportunity presented itself, who was I to deny it?

Besides, I warned her, I told her I would ruin her.

Did she think those words were just that, words?

Did she convince herself I wouldn't follow through?

I run my thumb through the mess, using it like a lubricant. Oh, I know I'll have to clean her up, and I will, I'll bathe her down, I'll wash every inch of her, but right now I'm enjoying this moment. I'm enjoying her lying still, being obedient, letting me touch wherever I want.

I plunge a finger inside her, twisting it around. I can feel all the little tears in her flesh, I can feel exactly where the Berretta nicked at her skin.

I'm going to do that again. I'm going to have her fuck herself with a pistol next. I'm going to sit there, in a chair, watching as she gets herself off while those lovely tits of hers bounce merrily the entire time.

When I pull my finger back out I can see the smear of blood. There's not much but enough to tell me I truly hurt her. Maybe next time I'll let her use a little lube. I don't want to be mean, after all.

Silently, I get to my feet and I go to the closet, grabbing the tiny box I stashed away. I'd originally been planning to use this after sneaking into her house, only the opportunity hadn't presented itself. I'd contemplated it again right after I made that deal but some part of me didn't want to muddy the water, I wanted her to come to me, and if I did this with her knowledge she would run. Her trauma would rear its ugly head and she'd be all the harder to win over.

The clips snap open loudly as I unlock the case. The gun is small, plastic, nothing like the real thing if you know what you're looking at. I drop the tiny chip into the chamber then roll her onto her side, pressing it into the nape of her neck.

Tomorrow, she'll have a bit of pain but she won't understand why.

As I pull the trigger, the tracker embeds itself just under her skin.

But in my head it's like a chorus of trumpets go off. From now on I'll always know where she is.

She'll never be able to escape me.

She'll never be able to truly hide if I don't choose to let her.

I own Sofia Montague the way the devil owns a soul.
And I will possess every part of her just as much.

CHAPTER

SOFIA

I wake with a groan. My neck hurts. My head hurts. My entire body feels drained.

As the memory of what happened yesterday comes hurtling back, I spring up.

Only there's no one beside me.

Koen is gone. The bed is empty.

It's hard to ignore the pang in my chest at that realisation.

I stare at the clock registering the time, that half the day has passed. Apparently getting off the way I did has consequences then. Maybe it's a good lesson for my body, maybe if it hadn't have been such a slut then I wouldn't have slept away the entire morning.

As I get out of the bed, my legs actually shake.

There's a note on the bedside table and I snatch it up, reading over the words. Koen tells me to rest, to take it easy, that he'll cook me a nice dinner tonight. The way he says it makes him sound like the perfect gentleman. No one would see this and believe that man fucked me with his shotgun last night.

My pussy clenches at the thought, and god, does it hurt.

I know from the way my hair is plaited that he washed me after I passed out. I still can't quite get my head around how I feel about that. On the one hand he's been taking care of me, looking after me, treating me like a real princess. And on the other, well, he almost certainly continued fucking me after I fell unconscious.

He used me like a toy.

I should hate that. I really should.

And yet the only thing I feel is the shame that I don't.

I head down to the pool for a swim, easing out some of that lingering self-reproach and then I wander the house, from room to room. It's so big I could probably hide out and no one would know where I was. Only I don't want to do that. I'm done hiding. I'm done merely existing.

I haven't seen Tia in a few days, and though I know she's probably busy, and though I know I swore to Koen I wouldn't do it, I decide to head down, to go look for her in the basement.

It's not that big a deal.

I mean, I've been here enough times with Koen, and I'm not going to go snooping, I'm just going to find Tia and that's it.

To my surprise no one says anything, no one tries to stop me. I walk down the long corridor on the first floor and though a few of Koen's men glance at me, they keep their mouths shut. Maybe this was a test, maybe Koen only said I wasn't allowed down here because he wanted me to push boundaries? Yeah, somehow I doubt that.

I drop another level. It's busier here. I know most of the sleeping quarters come off this part and I hope I don't accidentally stumble into anything.

Ahead, I spot Colt, though he definitely does not spot me. I flatten myself, trying to think quickly. He'll know I'm not allowed down here, he'll know I'm breaking the rules. Part of me thinks I should just fess up, get him to help me find Tia but a cowardly part wants to duck and run and I make the split decision to hide. There's a door barely a metre from me and I practically sprint to it and shut it behind hoping I'm not seen.

My heart is pumping in my chest, my breathing feels erratic and though I know I'm being ridiculous I can't seem to calm down.

And then I turn. I turn and see what's there. What's all around me.

My heart stops. My brain takes a good second to register it. It's me. Print offs. Images. Awful, horrific moments all plastered across the walls.

I step up, scanning the photos. I know they must come from multiple videos, I even recognise some of my abusers faces because they're pinned up, clear as day alongside me.

What the fuck is this? What the fuck is this room?

My body starts shaking, my adrenaline spikes.

Why the fuck would Koen have a room like this? Has he seen those videos, then? Has he watched them? Did he get some perverse sort of pleasure from truly knowing what they did to me and then he'd comfort me, hold me, pretend to care?

I shut my eyes, then force them open as my stomach twists. Have I made a horrible mistake in trusting this man?

God, Sofia, you absolutely idiot, you did it again, you got yourself stuck in a situation you have no way of escaping.

Behind me the door suddenly opens.

I spin around and my eyes meet Colt's. He frowns for a second before it sinks in exactly what's going on.

"Sofia,"

I don't wait to hear it, I don't *want* to hear. Whatever the fuck this is, I have to get out of here, right now.

I race from the room. Colt tries to grab at me and I swing wide, swing hard, and punch him right in the face.

I run back towards the stairwell, back towards above ground. I'm not really thinking about where I'm headed, just that I can't be here.

But this place is a maze. I must take a wrong turn, go down the wrong damned corridor, because I very rapidly realise I'm completely lost.

When I come to a stop, I expect to hear footsteps, I expect there to be people following me, chasing me, but there's nothing. I turn, staring back the way I came and I gulp as I realise I'm all alone. There's no guards, nobody.

I should go back, I should try to retrace my steps – except, what will I do then, what will I say when they find me? How will I explain why I'm here, and more importantly, what lies are they going to whisper to explain what the fuck that room was?

But I can't stay here, I can't hide down here forever.

I draw in a deep breath. These tunnels used to connect up to the city. That's how they rescued me from Otto, they literally burst out of the ground. Is it possible that I could get out that way? That I could somehow find a route through? What would I do then? I'm not stupid enough to think I could simply walk the streets of Verona. That I'd be safe to do that. Whoever is after me is out there.

I don't know what's going on in the city but I'm more than aware of the fact Koen has doubled security, that I'm never alone and unwatched.

But then, what if he's just done that to make me paranoid, to make me trust him more? What if all of this is mind games? Did he have those images posted to social media as part of some sort of trick?

No, he looked as surprised as I did when that happened. But that could have been a rouse. It could have been.

I gulp, palming my face with my hands, I'm so damn confused, I'm so damn conflicted.

It feels like whatever decision I make will be wrong because that's my life, isn't it, I never get dealt the good cards, I never end up with anything good. Maybe I really am cursed.

My heart sinks at that thought. I don't want to cry, I'm so sick of crying but I feel my tears streaming down my cheeks. I'm pathetic. Just like always. Poor little Sofia Montague. It would have been better if I just died. If I'd never made it out of that house.

No.

I refuse to accept that. I refuse to be that person.

I'm not giving in. I'm not going to crawl up and die because that would be too damn easy for them – that's what they want, and I didn't survive everything just to be defeated now.

I clench my fists, determined that whatever the hell this is, I will have answers. I'm not that scared little girl anymore. I'm not going to be beaten down, lied to, manipulated and controlled. I'm done playing that part. I am done being the victim.

I strut back down the corridor, repeating that over and over.

I am so done.

I climb a staircase – it's not the one I came down but I figure if I keep making my way up then I'll eventually get back to where I need to be.

When I spot Reid up ahead, I have a good mind to give him a mouthful. But he's not alone. He's with a bunch of men, guards, and they're laughing, drinking, clearly having a good time.

I'm not stupid enough to rock the boat so I pause, planning to walk right by them.

Only what I see next makes my actual jaw drop.

There's a woman, no, a group of women. All scantily clad. All laughing and flirting, and the music, the sounds, they're having a party.

I sneak up to the door. Staring in.

Jesus fucking Christ, it's not a party. It's a damned orgy.

My head seems to register it, the sounds, the moans, the way their bodies move. Some distant memory threatens to take over but I force it back down. These women are not being forced. None of this is forced.

I shouldn't look, I shouldn't watch, I should not damn well be here.

I turn to go, spinning on my heel just as a massive shadow falls on me.

"What the fuck are you doing down here?"

CHAPTER Fifty-One

KOEN

I barely get the words out before I register what *is* happening. That Reid and a few others have blatantly ignored my orders. My anger flares more. Did they think I wouldn't find out? Did they think I would just let it go?

I force those thoughts down, focusing on Sofia. I doubt witnessing any of that will help her headspace.

Only, as our eyes meet, she doesn't look scared, she doesn't look in the midst of a panic attack. She looks furious.

She curls her fist, slamming it right into my jaw. Turns out I taught her to punch pretty damn well.

I groan, grabbing her hand, stopping her from hitting me again.

"You bastard." She screams. "You utter bastard."

I don't understand what the hell is making her react like this but I don't have time to deal with everything. Colt messaged to say she was in the tunnels - alone. That she'd freaked out and he'd lost her in the older, less organised passageways.

She slams her other hand into my chest, clearly not backing down.

I shouldn't do it. I know I shouldn't but right now, her anger, her strength, it's making my brain short circuit. It's making my dick come to life. I grab her jaw, slamming my lips into hers.

Her eyes widen. She goes to knee me in the balls and I realise she's not calming down anytime soon.

God, is this not the moment I've been dreaming of? The moment I've been waiting for. Imagining over and over.

"You want a fight?" I growl. "You want to delve out some of that pent-up energy?"

She practically snarls back at me like she really is a devil and not human at all. I glance behind, seeing the darkening corridor. It's too perfect to resist. It's like she's laid herself out for me on a platter.

"Run, Sofia." I say releasing my hold. "You've got two minutes before I come and find you."

Her eyes widen, she steps back like she's unsure if I'm serious or not and then she clearly thinks better of it. She spins on her heel, running as fast as she can, while I stand there, watching, counting down the seconds in my head.

Oh, I know could be cruel. I could cut the time, cheat, but where would be the fun in that? I could also pull up my phone, open the app, use the tracker I planted in her neck and it'd tell me exactly where she is.

But again, that would rather ruin all of this, wouldn't it?

I flare my nostrils. Waiting. Feeling my cock harden with anticipation.

She said she wanted to be forced. She said she wanted to play this game, and what better way of doing it than hunting her down, forcing her to submit when she's this beautifully angry?

As the silent counter hits time, I click my neck, stretch my back. Turns out I'm enjoying this more than I could ever imagine.

I start running, keeping my footsteps light. I don't want her to hear me coming, I want to stalk my prey, attack right when she thinks she's safe.

Besides, she can't get far. I know two of the corridors off this one lead to a dead end. I've studied every part of the tunnels. I know it like the back of my hand. It's like I can see the path ahead of me and I'm there, panting, practically drooling with what's about to happen.

My Little Devil thinks she's gotten away. She thinks she'll be safe if she hides in the shadows, but she doesn't understand that I know exactly where to find her.

I see a flash, a hint of movement and I pause. Waiting.

I'm a cruel bastard but I truly want my capture to be unexpected. I want her to feel hope, joy, to believe she's outwitted me before the truth suddenly hits her.

If she went down the corridor I think she did, then she's stuffed. There's no back turn. Nothing but a few empty rooms. I make a feint of heading the other way, of pretending not to realise that she's there.

I can practically feel the tension, the way she's holding her breath.

Is she aroused right now? Is she as turned on as I am? Or is she convincing herself that this is wrong, that what she's feeling is shameful? Either way she'll be coming all over my cock so it doesn't really matter.

I tuck myself in, flatten myself against the wall.

A shadow moves, a flicker of light gives her away. I hear the tiny sound of one foot being planted ever so carefully, and then it's followed by another. I can hear how fast she's breathing, the way she's trying to keep that noise under wraps.

She pauses, waits. And just as she steps past me I make a grab.

Her scream rings out.

She jerks. She kicks. But I hold her tight.

"You can't escape me, Sofia." I growl right into her ear. "You're never going to escape me."

CHAPTER

Fifty-Two

SOFIA

Fear engulfs me. Fear incapacitates me.

I try to fight. I dig my nails into his arms. I scream, I kick, I do everything I can to get free but he's too strong. Far too strong.

His words echo in my head. That I'm trapped. That I can't escape.

A sob escapes my mouth and on some level I really am petrified, but I'm desperate too. Needy.

He's trained my body, manipulated it and now all I want, all I need is him. I can't even begin to explain the conflicting emotions. I just know that this here, it's make-belief, I know Koen isn't going to rape me for real, and yet I want to act like he is, I need to.

I need this fear, and this panic, and all of this.

I need it so badly.

He slams me back into the wall. I groan as my body takes the full impact and then he's yanking me down, forcing me down.

I kick out more, I fight harder. One of his hands wraps around my neck, pining me down and the other starts ripping at my clothes.

I whimper, trembling, but I can't deny how much I want this. How much his aggression is turning me on.

He shoves one hand into my underwear. There's no tease here, no gentleness. There's no way you can misconstrue this as simply heavy lovemaking. This is Koen taking what he wants, not giving a fuck.

"You're so wet, Sofia." He growls. "How long have been there, hiding in the dark, dreaming of my cock?"

"Fuck you," I spit back.

He smirks, wiping where the saliva lands on his cheek.

"Such a foul mouth for such a pretty girl."

He leans down, claiming my lips, forcing his tongue into my mouth and I moan against him despite myself. There's something about the way Koen kisses, something about the way he dominates me. Nothing else in the world compares to it. Nothing in the world comes even close.

He starts undoing his jeans, pulling his cock out. I shake my head, fighting harder, but he's forcing it into my mouth, forcing me to suck him.

He groans, gripping my hair. "That's it." He says. "Let my cock tame that attitude of yours."

I'm tempted to bite him, to snap my teeth shut, but his hand grips my jaw in such a way that I can't do it. He's using me, just like last time. Fucking my mouth, punishing me.

His cock slams into the back of my throat. I can barely get air in. I try to push him off, to get free but he refuses to let go of me.

"Fuck, your mouth is so good." He growls before he's pulling out, gripping his cock in his hand, slapping me around the face with it.

I blink, half shocked as I stare up at him. I don't know what I expected. I don't know how I imagined this would go, but Koen right now, in so many ways he's petrifying. He's exactly as he is in my twisted little dreams. Possessive, dominant. He's taking what he wants and he doesn't give a damn if I fight him or not.

"You've made me nice and wet for you." He states pulling my around, lining himself up.

I play still, I let him think I'm submitting and just as he leans down I shove my fist into his jaw. He crumples, more from the shock than because I've done any lasting damage.

And I'm up, scurrying away. My feet slam into the concrete. My heart pounds into my chest. If I'm fast enough I'll make it back to where everyone else is. But then, would he fuck me there? Would he hold me down and fuck me in front of everyone?

I don't have time to contemplate how that would make me feel because he's caught up, he's yanked me back down, and now I'm lying on my face, lying in the dirt with his weight on top of me.

"You're a sneaky thing." He murmurs. "I'll need to remember that for next time."

I whimper but those words set my core aflame. Next time? So we'd do this again?

He grabs my arse, spreading my cheeks, and he slams himself into me. It's brutal. It's absolute agony after last night. But I arch my back and love it all the same.

"I'm going to fuck you now," He says, "I'm going to fuck this tight little pussy until you're begging me to let you come."

"I don't want to." I gasp. It's true. Right now I want to be used, I don't want it to be about me.

He laughs, grabbing a fistful of my hair. "I don't give a fuck what you want, Sofia. You'll do as you're told. You'll be exactly what I want, like the good girl I know you are."

He pulls himself out, my body physically deflates and then he slams himself back inside. Another cry escapes my lips. My tears start to stream down my cheeks. I doubt I'll be able to walk straight after this.

"Fuck," He groans, doing it again, sliding out, slamming back in. "This cunt. I just can't get enough." He accentuates every word with one devastating thrust after another.

I can't move from how he holds me but the sheer force is making my body rock all the same.

He somehow manages to get his hand in between my body and the floor and he's pinching my clit, squeezing it.

"Please," I whimper. I don't even know what I'm asking for. This feels so wrong and yet I don't give a shit.

"You're enjoying this, Sofia. Just like you enjoyed my gun last night." He taunts. "Your sweet little cunt is squeezing me so tightly, like it can't get enough."

I shut my eyes, feeling a wave of shame.

As if he knows, as if he can read my mind, his hand comes down and he slaps my arse. "None of that." He growls. "You want to be fucked, you want to be used. You asked for this. I'm just the lucky bastard who gets to do it, aren't I?"

I nod, drawing in one haggard breath after another.

He's stopped torturing my clit now, he's started teasing it, pleasuring me in a way that feels completely opposite to how he's fucking me.

I can't help the moan, I can't help the pool of arousal that leaks out. I'm getting off on this far more than is reasonable.

"Fuck, Sofia," Koen growls and I can tell he's close. "I'm going to come. I'm going to fill you up and leave you dripping out everywhere. But you want that, don't you?"

I shake my head.

He snarls, slapping my arse again. "You want that, don't you, Sofia?"

I gulp, biting my lips, refusing to admit it. He pinches my clit, he pinches so hard I scream. And as his cock slides into me it's too much, far too much. I dig my nails into the concrete, feeling them snap, I arch my back and I scream out my release.

"That's my good girl." Koen says, stroking my hair.

I lie still, panting, wondering why he's stopped, why Koen is no longer fucking me. He's pulled out. He's studying me. And then he flips me over, onto my back before he slides back in.

"When I come I want to see your face." He states. "I want to watch your reaction as I pour myself inside you. As I ruin this pretty little cunt for everyone else but me."

I stare up at him, seeing how impossible dark his eyes are. He is enjoying this. He's loving every second.

This is turning him on just as much as it is me.

He plants his hands either side of my head. Right where they feel like a threat. And then he's thrusting, using just his hips to push himself inside me, over and over.

I lay still, barely breathing, letting him use me.

As his face seems to harden, as his arms lock, I realise he's close. He's coming. He grabs my throat, pulling me up, out of the dirt and he slams his lips into mine, right as he climaxes. Right as he pours himself inside me.

I can't breathe. The way he holds my neck cuts off all my air flow. For two seconds I full on panic and then he slumps down and that oxygen rushes back down my throat.

I can feel him leaking out of me, I can the freezing cold concrete practically biting into my skin.

He rolls over, taking hold of my arm like he's expecting me to flee again. And then I remember why I ran in the first place.

My anger comes rushing back.

My fury burns away any post orgasm haze.

"You saw them, you watched them." I snarl. "Did you enjoy it? Huh? Did you? Did you find it funny to see what they did to me? Did you want to remember it so much that you made print outs?"

His eyes react. His face switches instantly.

"You found the ops room." He murmurs.

"Ops?"

He takes in a deep breath as understanding clearly hits him. "I had to do it." I reply. "I needed their faces."

"Stop lying to me." I go to smack him around the face and he catches my hand, holding it still.

"I'm not lying." He growls. "You think I wanted to see? You think I wanted to know? Just imagining what you went through is bad enough but to see it played out…"

"You had no right." I cry and it echoes around us. Swirls around us.

He pulls me into his chest, let's me bury my face into the strength of his muscles. "I had every right. I had to make them pay. I had to do something. This was the only way I could ensure none of them got away with it."

"Who else has seen it?" I ask. "Who else watched those videos?"

I can see him hesitate. I see that flicker as he tries to decide whether he should lie or not. "Colt." He says, and my shoulders slump at that admission. "No one else. He found the videos, that's why. I've made sure they're destroyed. That no one else will ever see them."

I swallow, pushing myself away from him a tiny bit. "Someone else has copies." I say like we don't both know it.

"I should have told you." He replies.

I sniff, wiping my face. "Why didn't you?"

"It's complicated." He sighs. "I didn't want you to look at me and second guess my behaviour, I didn't want you to think that because I knew I was treating you differently."

"But you knew enough." I murmur. "This whole damn city knows."

He cups my cheek, lifting my face to look at him properly. "Fuck what this city thinks it knows. You're the only thing that matters. Do you understand?"

I don't reply, at least not with words.

I slam my mouth into his, kissing him with that same demand that he kissed me earlier. And those words echo in my head like they're some sort of declaration of love.

His hands wrap around me, he pulls me onto like he hasn't already fucked the life out of me. I groan, needing more, needing so much more.

But he just breaks it off, doing his trousers up, covering me like I'm not able to do it myself and then we're walking back up to world above us.

As if none of this happened. As if he didn't just hunt me down like an animal.

CHAPTER Fifty-Three

SOFIA

The next day I go to see my lawyers. Koen doesn't accompany me but he sends enough men that it feels like I have an entire army with me.

Colt sits beside me in the back of what looks like an armoured truck.

Apparently, we aren't hiding the fact we're at war.

I don't know what to say to him, how to speak to him really. His nose is bruised from where I hit him but thankfully it isn't broken. Whenever our eyes connect I feel a pang of guilt that's hard to ignore.

He's not exactly standoffish but he keeps glancing at me like he's got something on his mind but doesn't have the guts to say whatever it is to my face.

"Will you just spit it out." I snap.

He tenses, glancing at the two men up front. The driver and the man in full body armour, holding an actual assault rifle. How they get away with it, I don't know. If Hastings sees this I don't doubt he'll have an absolute hissy fit.

"It's not my place…" Colt begins, only that makes me laugh. If he's thinking it, then he can damn well say it.

"If you're worried I'm going to go running back to Koen…"

"It's not that." He cuts across me. "Well, maybe a little." The sheepish grin he gives me actually relieves some of the tension.

"Look, I'm not a psycho." I state. "And I don't want you to only see me as his…" I stumble over the word. Am I his girlfriend? His partner? We've never defined what we are, what labels to call ourselves. I sold my soul to the man, what terminology best fits that, slave?

No, I won't be called that. I can't be called that.

I dig my nails into my palms forcing down the momentary panic at that very notion.

"What do you know of the Devil's Heart diamond?" He asks.

That seems to steal away all thoughts of a panic attack.

"The what diamond?"

"The Devil's Heart diamond." He repeats.

What the fuck is that? What would I know about some particular diamond? Do I look like a jewellery expert?

"They say your father had it. It was in his possession and then he died..." He trails off giving me a look like I know all the world's secrets.

"What's so great about this diamond?" I reply. Oh, there has to be something, doesn't there? No way it's just a fancy piece of jewellery.

He narrows his eyes, clearly weighing up the consequences of this conversation. "It's cursed."

I shouldn't react. I shouldn't feel the flash of fear that seems to clench around my gut, around my chest. "Is that why Reid says I'm cursed?" I ask.

He nods. "It's part of it."

"What is this curse? Tell me what you know."

He once more glances ahead before obviously lowering his voice. "The diamond belonged to Marie Antoinette, then some Sultan had it and he lost his throne, then someone else got hold of it and they were murdered."

"I get it." I say cutting across him. Apparently this damned diamond is a death stone. "But who says my father had it?"

"It's the rumour."

I shake my head. "If my father had such a thing, don't you think my brother would know?" I doubt he'd tell me but he wouldn't hide it from his golden son.

He shrugs, "Maybe he hid it away. Maybe he stashed it somewhere."

Stashed.

Why does that word bring up a memory? Blue Eyes spoke about a jewel being stashed, surely he didn't believe this tale? Why would Otto have handed it over anyway? Why wouldn't he have made a play for it himself?

Unless it really is cursed.

No, that's ridiculous. There's no such thing as a damned curse.

I draw in a long breath. One that sounds panicked.

"I didn't mean to scare you." Colt says quickly.

"It's fine," I lie. Besides, I'd rather he was honest. I'd rather he tell me the truth than treat me like I can't handle it.

We fall to silence. Strained, awkward silence. I contemplate messaging Roman, asking what he knows but I'm not in the right headspace to actually have such a conversation.

When we pull up outside the fancy offices it's almost a relief.

Though when I get inside it feels anything but.

I sit there, mute, like a robot as these overpaid suits go on and on about how my recent escapades haven't helped my cause. How my current reputation is doing nothing to sway the judge. When I lose my temper and shout out for the millionth time that I don't want any of my dead husband's money, they all just shake their heads, like I'm the one deranged. Like I'm too stupid to understand any of this.

"Maybe we should speak with her brother." One of them has the audacity to say.

"You know what?" I reply, rising to my feet. "You speak with Roman, but it makes no difference. You're fired. All of you are."

They gasp, they splutter. I doubt anyone has ever fired them before in their entire privileged little lives. But I don't give a shit how good they are. They haven't listened to me once. In fact they've gone completely against my wishes. Have ignored everything I've said up until now. I'm done sitting by, playing the mute, compliant idiot they all view me as.

I storm out into the hall. Colt jumps up from the uncomfortable looking leather seat he's been occupying.

"We're done?" He asks.

"We are so done." I state, folding my arms, heading towards the ridiculous glass lifts.

The sooner I'm back at Koen's house the better.

CHAPTER
Fifty-Four

SOFIA

I all but sneak back into the house, feeling like I don't want company, that I just need some alone time.

And then I spend hours looking up that jewel. Googling it. The image that appears makes my heart stop. It's not clear, it's not see-through, it's nothing like any other diamond I've ever seen before. It's black, pure black, with a tiny red centre.

The photo is clearly old, from the days when they'd only just invented colour photography so it's not exactly a perfect image but it's clear enough.

The stone is the size of an apricot. It's bloody huge. Surely if my father had such a thing I would have known? He wasn't that good at keeping secrets.

It's late afternoon when Koen comes to find me. For a man as big as he is, he knows how to be quiet when he wants to.

"What are you looking at?" He asks.

I shriek, slamming the screen shut which obviously gets his attention.

"It's nothing." I say quickly.

"Nothing?" He repeats.

I put on my biggest, most bashful smile. "I was just looking at underwear." I lie.

He narrows his eyes and for a second I think he might call me out on it, but instead he drops his gaze, staring at my chest, at where my top dips low enough to show my cleavage. "Don't you think you have enough?"

"Do you?" I reply, moving to stand. "You seem to enjoy ripping it off me so I figured I should buy some especially for that for purpose."

He growls, grabbing me so quickly I barely see the movement. My heart slams into my chest. I'm still so damn painful from what feels like day after day of his abuse but if he wants me again I won't refuse him. I'll get on my knees and I'll beg for his cock.

"I have a present for you." He whispers in my ear.

"What present?" I gasp.

He carries me over to the bed, pushes me down flat on my face with my arse in the air, then slides my leggings down.

If this is it, I'm not complaining, if he spent the day eagerly waiting for my return then I'm only sorry he didn't find me sooner.

His slams his mouth against my pussy, eating me out like he's been thinking of nothing else for hours.

I writhe, I moan, I rub myself against his stubbled lips, smearing my arousal over him as if I'm marking him with my juices.

"Fuck," He groans, forcing himself to stand.

His dick pushes against me, I spread my legs wider, giving every indication I can that I'm ready for this, ready for this gift.

As he slides in, he growls, digging his fingers so deep into my hips I know they'll leave bruises.

"I wanted you fill you up." He states. "I want you to walk down with me and to know that for the entire time, my come is going to be dripping from your cunt."

I gasp, rocking backwards, encouraging him and yet not quite understanding it. Walking where? Going where? He talked of gifts, is this not it?

He lowers his mouth to my ear as he picks up pace. One hand wraps around my waist, claiming my clit and the other he places over my hand so that our fingers are intwined. He slams into me so deliciously and I moan as my eyes roll back in my head.

"Fuck, Koen," I moan. "Yes, like that, just like that."

I gyrate against him, taking every punishing thrust.

"I brought you another sacrifice." He whispers. "I brought you another victim. And this time, I want you to do it. I want you prove to me, to everyone how strong you now are."

Fear grasps my heart, turning that hazy lust to something chilling. But I swallow it down, force it down.

And I nod. I'm not that scared little girl anymore, I'm not the creature who first came to hide out here.

I'm Koen's Little Devil. I'm his whore. And I will do it, I will do whatever he asks.

WELL, HE GOT WHAT HE WANTED.

That's the thought that keeps repeating in my head as we walk hand in hand down the cold, concrete steps to the underworld.

I put on a simple dress, one I wouldn't mind getting trashed but one that made me feel like this would truly be a performance.

And with every step I take, I can feel it, his come, dripping, pooling in my panties. My eyes dart to his face. He's got his fixed ahead with that hard, intense look of his but I swear he's licking his lips like he can still taste me on them.

Maybe that's why he was eating me out so purposefully. He wanted a little piece of me too.

Colt is there waiting as we reach the bottom. He glances from Koen, to me, then back to Koen.

"They're ready." He says.

Koen grunts.

As we continue on, I remind myself that I'm going to be strong, that I'm not going to let him down. That no matter what it takes, this will end the way I want.

But as we reach that huge, imposing door I feel myself tremble.

"Sofia."

I shake my head, trying to force back the impending attack.

"Sofia," Koen growls more.

"I can do this." I hiss.

He places his hands on my shoulders and that touch, that grip, it seems to pull me out of the spiral.

"I didn't say you couldn't." He smiles.

I stare back at him, mouth open, convinced that he was about to call this whole thing off, that he was about to pull the same stunt that everyone else does, to treat me like I'm fragile.

Behind us someone clears their throat. I turn, spotting Reid there, arms crossed, openly glaring. So I jerk my chin up, glare back and then push open the doors as if I truly am the queen here, as if I command even Koen himself.

And I swear I hear him growl. I swear I hear him groan the way he does when he's stripped me down and is about to devour me. Does me being haughty turn him on?

I cast my eye over my shoulder and he's got his gaze focused solely on me. That look, that fierce, all-consuming look feels like it sets my soul ablaze.

"I can do this." I whisper. I can do this.

There's a man hanging in the centre. Just like last time. He's not making any sounds and as I approach him, I figure he must be unconscious.

Around the perimeter are a dozen of Koen's, men. Most I know by face but a few I've learnt their names. Colt, of course. And Reid. And Collins, and Fabian.

It's Fabian who hands me the knife. I stare at it, feeling that same repeat of last time. Only, so much has changed. I might still feel my heart hammering, I might still have that panic fluttering, but I'm in control of it and not the other way around.

"Take your time." Koen says quietly.

I step up to the man, take in a deep breath and then drag it down, from his right shoulder diagonally across his chest to his hip.

He jerks, coming to life with a scream.

His brown eyes connect with mine and that pain and confusion turns to horror as he realises it's me.

"No," He splutters. "No, I, no, please, I didn't mean, I didn't…"

"Didn't what?" I hiss.

Suddenly all that pain is there, all that anger, every moment of fury, of fear, it's twisting inside me, begging to be let out.

"He said we could. He said you liked it."

I snarl, slicing him again, carving into his skin the way he carved into mine.

His blood splatters, it covers my hand, my face and I gasp, wiping it with my sleeve. I know Koen is stood directly behind me, I can feel his presence, I feel his shadow. Like he's my guard, ensuring nothing comes between me and my vengeance

He said before he hurt these men because they offended him. That he hunted them because I was his and he needed to make them pay for it. In this moment I get it, I truly do. I am his, and these men not only took from me, they took from Koen, they stole from both of us.

Something in me snaps. Some feral part breaks loose. I stop thinking about anything beyond those moments, those memories, every awful thing Otto and his mates forced me to endure. Every time they broke my bones, every time they raped me, every time they beat me, and tortured me and laughed at my pain like I was a joke. Like I was nothing.

Well, who is nothing now? Who got their revenge? Otto is dead. Darius is dead too. I know Koen has hunted enough of the men who hurt me but here, right here, I truly am getting my vengeance. I'm claiming my strength back. I'm claiming my power back. Koen might have offered it, he might have shown me the way, but this here; it's all me.

Every cut, every slice, every drop of blood I claim. It's mine.

My wrath. My vengeance.

By the time I'm done I don't know if he's alive or dead. I don't know if he even has any flesh left on his body. I've hacked and I've cut, and I've screamed as I did it, purging myself, purging every awful emotion.

And as I dropped the knife and stepped back, my exhaustion swept over me like relief. Like some part of my soul was finally sated, finally at peace.

CHAPTER

Fifty- Five

KOEN

I stare at my phone, frowning at the words.

The message itself isn't unusual but this feels more than a little out of character considering Roman and I don't usually meet. At least not often. We both know our strengths and face-to-face contact does not end well for either of us.

Something in my gut churns. I shake my head, run my hands through my hair, loosening the knot that keeps it out of my face.

"Reid," I shout. The bastard is meant to be around here somewhere.

He pokes his head around the door within seconds.

"Get the bikes ready, we're heading out." I state.

He grunts back before disappearing once more.

I left Sofia up in the house. She's got a bullshit appointment with her therapist today and was already more than grumpy about it. I'll admit, I'm rather hoping after the other night that this is it. Her therapy is done. Nothing that man can say will have more effect than the power that one night of meeting out revenge can.

Perhaps by the time I get back she'll have sent him on his way and we can shut up another reminder of her past.

I grab my jacket, yank it on, then stalk out to where everyone is now waiting.

"You know the drill?" I say.

They nod, all in unison, like good little dogs.

Ever since that shootout and attempted assassination we've come up with new rules, a new way of working. I'm not happy about it but it is what it is. And we need to be smart. Smarter than the people hunting us.

I clamber onto the bike, kicking the engine on by the foot pedal.

Reid rides up front, taking on what is my usual position. I don't like him putting himself in danger but I'm also not going to be a fucking idiot when there's a potential target on my back.

We ride out through the gates and it doesn't take long to notice the car tailing us.

Oh, he's doing his best, tucking in, trying to be inconspicuous. We make a right, then a left, cutting through the busy streets and off to where it's quieter.

When we pull up at the supposed meeting spot, I expect an ambush. We all do. But there's no one there. The car park is deserted. The only sound is the noise of our bikes idling away.

The car that was tailing us has all but disappeared and I'm not sure what to make of it. Were they checking to make sure we took the bait or did they plan an attack and then decided against it?

"This is fucking joke." Reid mutters through the mic. I can't say I disagree with that.

We wait a few more minutes before I call it. On any ordinary day I wouldn't be standing around like this so it's pointless to do it today.

We hit the road, taking the same winding streets back.

But it's clear from the moment we start moving that something is up. That this is what they're after.

We've got three cars on our tails.

I keep back, making sure Reid is up front. Collins is at the back, giving everyone a blow by blow of which car is where, ensuring we can all anticipate how this is going to go down.

And then the car slams into Reid's bike. My bike technically. I see it go sideways. I see him come off and thank fuck he's been forced to wear a helmet to hide who he really is because if he didn't, his brains would be all over the damned tarmac.

He skids along, coming to a stop but none of us have time to check on him.

Behind me, Collins and Fabian are dealing with the two other vehicles, ensuring they don't get far.

I speed up, taking my gun and use it to smash through the glass of the one that took out Reid. Whoever the fuck it is evidently thought we'd been too concerned about my supposed demise to take any other action.

I hear the shout as I grab hold of the door and force my body in through the gap.

They thought they could simply eliminate me? They thought that I'd just roll over and die, just like that? Not a fucking chance.

The driver yells something out. I use my helmet to bash the face in of the fucker in the back and then I open the door and push his unconscious body out. I don't give a shit if he dies. I don't give a shit if someone runs him over and spreads his fucking organs all over the road.

The bikes all slip back. I know one of them has now come to a stop, that someone is seeing to Reid.

I grab the gun, stick it right into the neck of the man behind the wheel and remove my helmet.

"Drive." I order. "Return to your mistress."

He blinks at me in shock. Like I was too damned stupid to work it all out.

"If you give the game away, if you do anything to alert them, I'll blow your fucking brains out." I threaten.

He nods quickly, obviously complying. I guess he's a hired hand. A mercenary. Whatever this vendetta is, he's not got any skin in the game, he's not interested in anything but the pay-check and you can hardly spend that when you're dead, can you?

We slow down, return to what looks like a normal speed. I can't help the fact the window is out but I fold my body, cramming it as low as someone as physically big as I am can go.

I just need to get inside. Nothing more.

Houses whizz past. I can tell from the size of them that we're in the Bay District. Somewhere close to where Roman resides.

We make a right, then another right, the roads are winding here, deliberately designed so that all these grand palaces have enough space around that they all look like mini Versailles.

As we pull up to the huge security gates

I ram the gun into the driver's ribs. If he fucks this up he'll have a bullet in his gut before he can finish uttering his sentence.

He mutters something. The guard grunts back and then those massive black gates open.

Behind it is a pale pink, Italian style villa complex. It's more glass than walls. The front has more columns than the Parthenon.

The main door opens, she practically runs out, clicking her high heels as she skips down the fourteen steps to the sweeping drive.

"Well?" She cooes, like she's asking about a designer's half-price sale and not whether someone is dead.

"It went well." The driver says, getting out slowly.

"Well?" She repeats, glancing at the window and frowning. Perhaps she's wondering where the other two cars are, perhaps she's not smart enough to realise their absence.

I ease the door open, keeping the weapon in my grasp.

"I'd say it went very well." I state.

She gasps, covering her mouth, stepping back but those stupid heels she's in are so high she practically falls over.

I reach out, quickly grabbing her wrist and yank her to me, ramming the gun into her pearl wrapped throat.

Of course her security respond, a dozen or so rifles point at me, but we all know they won't pull the trigger.

"Open the gates." I bark.

"No," The bitch cries like she's still in charge.

I tighten my grip, feeling that fine silk dress she's got on ripping in my hands.

Someone rushes over and starts arguing with the gatehouse.

"You really think they'll let you walk out of here?" She sneers. And I'll admit I'm surprised she still has the gall.

"Oh, I don't think they'll have much of a choice." I grin as those black gates roll aside and a dozen or so of my men ride right in.

She snarls, she fights, I backhand her with the gun and that seems to knock some sense into her.

I know she's going to be a fucking nightmare to transport but, as that realisation hits me, I lay eyes on the fancy Roller she has, gleaming on the driveway.

I pick her up, toss her into the boot and slam it shut.

I'd much prefer to be on my bike right now but the fuckers destroyed it when they took Reid out.

"How is he?" I ask.

Collins pauses, keeping his gun trained on the perimeter but he meets my eyes as he says, "He'll be fine. Medics are with him now,"

I grunt. We padded him out, made him wear enough protection gear that it should have taken most of the impact. His body had to resemble mine from a quick glance so the extra padding helped on both counts.

I stalk to the front of the car, get in and turn it on. It's a thing of beauty, I can't deny that, but it's not to my taste. I'd rather be in a beat up old banger than something as fragile as this feels.

"Let's go." I shout out.

This standoff has lasted long enough. We've probably got minutes left before the cops arrive and everything goes to shit.

I hit the gas, screech out of the drive, and slam the car to the right. I know that bitch will feel every turn, every pause, every move I make and I intend to make her suffer.

Blue lights trail behind us.

It makes me laugh as I glance in my rear view mirror. The bikes create a blockage keeping them back but we're also creating a scene.

When we get to the Governor's House, it feels like everyone seems to breathe a sigh of relief.

I'd normally take her home, take her to the basement and make her pay for the months of torture and bullshit she's put Sofia through. But I'm not a fucking idiot.

If I do that, it might backfire on Sofia.

No, this is the smart move. The logical move.

The Roller comes to a stop right out front.

This place used to have high walls, an country's worth of security, when Darius was in charge but Hastings is trying hard to give off a different image.

I can see his exasperated face as he stalks out to meet me.

"What the fuck is this?" He hisses.

The cops are keeping the crowds back, keeping as many as they can back, while they keep their guns trained on me.

I grin, getting out of the car.

"Jesus, Koen." Roman mutters. Of course the fucker was here.

I ignore them both, going to the boot and pop it open.

She hisses, she tries to swing for me only that makes me laugh.

"Let's go." I say grabbing her by her fancy, overpriced dress, hauling her out.

"What the…?" Roman gasps, staring at the hysterical creature in my hands.

"You wanted to know who was behind all this shit." I growl. "Turns out it wasn't what you thought, Hastings."

He shakes his head, staring at Valentina Blumenfeld in shock.

"Turns out it was just one greedy, spiteful, woman." I state.

Hastings draws himself up, clicking his fingers and the guards behind him take her from my hands and drag her inside.

"It wasn't me." She cries. "I'm innocent."

"Innocent of what?" Roman snarls loudly.

"I didn't do it. I would never try to kill anyone." She shrieks.

I can't help but grin at those words. The stupid bitch is literally signing her own death warrant.

"We've got it from here." Hastings mutters.

"What are you going to do with her?" I ask.

"She has to pay." Roman cuts across. "That bitch has to pay for torturing Sofia…"

"And she will." Hastings says. "We'll make sure of that. Just, not while the entirety of Verona is watching this."

I turn my gaze, glancing at the crowd that's only getting bigger.

"I have to go." I state to no one in particular. I need to check on Reid. I need to make sure he really is okay.

But as I walk away, Roman grabs me back. "Where is Sofia? Does she know about this?"

He hasn't seen her in weeks. I know they talk, that they message, but I've not exactly been encouraging the pair of them. Perhaps this will help heal whatever the rift is between them. Perhaps now is the time for me to encourage that.

"Come round later." I state. "She'll need cheering up."

He frowns at that. "Why?"

"She's always a mess after her therapy sessions."

"What?" He gasps.

I tilt my head, "Did you think I'd get in the way of that? You lot were the ones making her see him."

Roman frowns more. "What the fuck are you talking about?"

"Martin." I snap growing more annoyed. "Her fucking therapist."

Hastings comes up beside him, looking at me like I'm talking actual nonsense. "We cancelled all of that months ago. And it wasn't a man we sorted. It was a woman."

I blink, not understanding exactly what they're saying. "A woman?" I repeat.

"Her name was Kate. She saw Sofia two times." Hastings says.

"Then who the fuck is Martin?" I bellow.

But my gut already tells me what it is. What all of this is. Have I been that fucking blind? That stupid?

I grab my phone, dialling Sofia's number. She doesn't pick up. I dial Colt's next. Normally he answers after barely a ring but it takes him almost a whole minute before it connects.

"Boss,"

Jesus, I can hear it in his voice.

"Where is she? What the fuck is happening?"

"Boss, they, they took her. They set off a bomb, fucking hell, Koen…"

I hang up, sliding my fingers across the screen. This can't be happening. This can't be real.

The tracker pops up on the map and I zoom in, staring at the image. At least they didn't know about that.

"What is that?" Roman asks peering over my shoulder. "Where the fuck is my sister?"

I shush him, taking note of the coordinates. There's no way this is a coincidence. No way at all.

I rush to the bikes, shoving aside one of my men, I'll be far quicker on two wheels than four.

"Where the fuck is my sister, Koen?" Roman growls, try to yank me back like I'm the one behind all of this.

I shove the phone in his face and he stares at the screen.

"You, you put a tracker in her?" He splutters.

"Look where she is." I snap. Like it matters how I know right now.

He frowns, and I see the place register in his face. "Why the fuck would she be there?"

I don't try to answer that. I don't really have an answer for that. And yet it feels all too connected. Far too connected.

I spin the bike around, rev the engine and speed off. I don't know how long they've had her, what the hell they might be doing to her, but the sooner I can get there, the sooner I can stop whatever this is.

CHAPTER
Fifty-Six

SOFIA

I can't help the groan of annoyance as he walks in.

He's got that polite smile on his face as though I can be as rude as I like and he doesn't care. Christ, am I itching to test that theory.

"Shall we…?" He says holding his hand to direct me to the study.

I roll my eyes, turning my back on him and stalk through the hallway.

I already prepped the room, put out two glasses of water, removed everything from sight, not that there was all that much in there. Beyond the chairs and the desk it's pretty much empty. Like Koen has no need for such a space. I'll admit that makes me smile. I couldn't imagine how he'd sit behind this desk. How he'd look, tapping away at a computer, acting like the kind of man who wears suits.

I sit down, folding my arms, half tempted to set my own timer because I feel like Martin's sessions seem to be going on forever.

He opens that same damned folder as last time, flicking through the papers before he shuts it up in a dramatic fashion.

"I thought we'd try something a little different today." He says.

"Different how?"

He leans forward, unbuttoning the arm of his right sleeve and methodically he rolls it up, like it's hot in here. He does the same to his other sleeve and then he sits back, fixing me with that gaze.

"We need to work on your memory, Sofia."

"Excuse me?"

"If you want to get past all this, if you want to move on, then you have to face it."

My nails dig into my palms. I can feel myself already reacting, already panicking. "I don't want to go there." I state. "If I open up those wounds, I'll never come back."

"Oh," He says waving his hand at me. "Don't be ridiculous, there are ways we can do this, ways we can peek into your trauma and uncover what we need to know."

"And what exactly do we need to know?" I snap.

He narrows his eyes, takes a long sip of the glass of water beside him as though he's trying to figure out the best plan of attack.

"Tell me, Sofia, are you still having nightmares?"

"Yes."

"And what do they consist of?"

"Flashbacks." I whisper. "I don't see much, I don't remember much, I just…"

His hand slams onto the table beside him and I swear I jump half a foot in the air. "If you focus, you will remember."

I gulp, shaking my head. "I don't, I'm not interested." I say getting to my feet. "Maybe you should go."

"Go?" He says smiling. "But we haven't even gotten started yet."

"I'm done." I'm so fucking done. Maybe me telling the lawyers to shove it sparked some final defiance in me. Maybe I truly have grown up. I don't care about the consequences anymore. I don't give a shit what Hastings says or does. I know Koen will back me on this.

I'm done with therapy, I'm done with it all.

He tuts, getting to his feet and it feels like he's facing me off now. "You know the thing I always found strange," He murmurs. "Even after all this time, all these hours we've spent pretty much locked up, just the two of us, you still don't recognise me, do you?"

I blink, staring back at him as it feels like something takes over my body.

Sheer, utter terror seems to trap me.

"Maybe it's the glasses," He says, pulling them off and tossing them. "Or the hair." He pulls that off too, and his hair changes from that mousy brown, side parting to a dark brown mop that sticks to his forehead from the sweat, morphing his face into something else entirely.

"Who, who are you?" I stammer, taking a step back. If I can get to the door, if I can get out of this room then Koen's men will step in, they'll help.

I'm barely three metres away, almost touching distance. I just have to stay calm, to play this carefully.

He laughs, closing the distance just a little. "You really don't remember?" He taunts. "But we had so much fun together. Well, I had fun. You, not so much."

I scream, I turn and run, but he reaches out, grabbing me by my ponytail, yanking me back.

Before I can do anything, he slaps some fabric over my mouth, and I choke, I splutter, my body goes slack and I slump into his arms.

My head hurts. No, not hurts exactly, just feels heavy, really heavy. I groan, trying to shift to a more comfortable position only my hands don't move. Neither do my legs.

My eyes snap open. I jerk in the chair but all it does is creak in protest.

"Now, now." A voice says gently. "No need to get so worked up."

"No, no, no, no, no," I whimper staring at the man in front of me. Staring at those blue eyes.

He smiles back, leaning forward to sweep my hair back from my face. "It's good to see you too, Sofia."

"What, what do you want?" I gasp.

He steps back, tilting his head, his jaw tightening for a second. "I want what I've always wanted. What your father stole and failed to return."

What the fuck does that mean?

My eyes dart about, to the white blank walls, to the heartrate machine beside me. Am I in a hospital? Is that what this is? Why the fuck would I be in a hospital?

I'm not attached to anything, I'm not connected up, but that doesn't mean much. I shudder, remembering the Barn, how it looked, how it felt before Roman torched the place.

Blue eyes holds up his fingers, clicking in front of my face and I realise I've zoned out.

"I, I don't know anything." I gasp. God, haven't we been through this before?

More footsteps echo. I crane my neck and see Martin walking in, pushing a metal gurney with a tray neatly placed on top of it.

"She's still spouting on about memory loss." He says like I've been putting it on this entire time.

My eyes dart between them and I hate how it's only know that I notice the similarities. The turn of their noses, the eyebrows. They could be brothers. How had I not seen that before?

"It's true." I cry. "I don't know…"

Blue Eyes' hand slaps over my mouth. He shoves something inside and I try to push it out with my tongue but he tapes it in place. "I'm done playing games, Sofia." He says so calmly. Like this is all some simple misunderstanding.

I try to argue but everything I say now is muffled.

Martin starts laying out instruments. Scalpels, what looks like an actual saw. Christ, are they going to torture me again? What good will that do if they've essentially gagged me?

"It took me a long time to work this out." Blue Eyes states. "Of course, it was simple really. Logical. What else would your father do, considering the options he faced?" He pauses, picking up a pair of scissors and he starts cutting away at my clothes, cutting right up the middle so that my entire chest and abdomen are exposed.

"He wasn't going to tell Darius where it was, not after their falling out..."

I stare from him to Martin. Desperately pleading. I know this isn't going to end well. I know however this goes down, they're going to hurt me. I just don't understand why.

Blue Eyes slaps me across the face. "Pay attention when I'm talking to you."

I glare back at him, only that makes him smirk.

"Oh, you do have your mother's defiance, don't you?" He murmurs, like he knew her, like they were intimately acquainted.

"I always thought Otto wanted you simply because of what you were worth. For the Montague fortune, only that wasn't it, was it, Sofia?"

I gulp, trying to calm myself, trying to figure out some way out of this. Surely Koen's men will know I'm missing? How the fuck did Martin even get me past them in the first place? There's no way he killed them all. That's not possible. It can't be possible.

I glance across at him and he's smiling, like he's been imagining whatever's about to unfold for months.

Blue Eyes, grabs my jaw, yanking my face so that I'm forced to look at him. "You don't have a clue, do you?" He says. "You don't realise what your father did all those years ago?"

I shake my head.

I have no idea what he's going on about but I doubt my ignorance will save me.

"Your father stole a very rare, very precious jewel. He and Darius thought they could out manoeuvre me, they thought they could fool me. And when that didn't work, he decided that instead of giving it back, he would hide it somewhere I'd never think to look. Do you know where that is?"

I could laugh. I could seriously laugh at the irony of this. It *is* about the Devil's Heart diamond, isn't it? He's as deluded as everyone else.

But even if my father did take it, how the fuck would I know where it was? Besides, they burnt the house down. They reduced it to rubble. If there is some bloody diamond hidden there it'd take years to shift through all the debris.

His hand traces up my stomach before coming to a stop above my belly button. "He tried to fix you, didn't he? He saw your condition as a failure, a tarnish on your great family name, only the surgery didn't work."

I frown, trying to jerk away. What the fuck does he know about it? What the fuck does that have to do with any of this?

His lips curl like he can read my thoughts. He lowers his face till he's right up in mine and I can taste the foul breath despite the fabric in my mouth.

"Do you know what he did, Sofia? Have you put it all together, yet?"

I shake my head. He's playing with me, taunting me the way a cat does a mouse before they kill it. I hate how powerless I feel. I hate how defenceless I once again am.

"I always wondered why Otto kept you alive, why he kept you close. It would have been so much easier to kill you off and be done with it. But you see, he figured it out. God knows how he did, but he knew. And he was smart enough to wait it out. Turns out he did have patience after all."

Wait what out? What the fuck is he talking about?

He pushes further into my belly, to the point where it really hurts. I try to twist, to get away and the chair starts to scrape back.

He grabs my head, half tearing my hair out of my scalp. "Your father was a smarter man than I gave him credit for." He states. "He knew exactly where to hide it, where to ensure it would be under all our noses and we wouldn't think to look."

I stare back trying to understand what the hell he's getting at.

As he reaches around to undo the ties, I keep still, waiting. Playing docile, playing the scared little creature they all believe me to be.

My hands come lose, then my ankles – though they're still strapped together so not much use if I want to run.

But it's enough.

Blue Eyes tries to carry me over to the bed and I lash out, using my elbow as weapon, slamming it right into his face. He groans, falling backwards. But Martin is there in a flash, he grabs me, shoving me face first into the gurney, pinning me down.

"You stupid slut." He growls. "We were going to play nice, make this as pain free as possible for you, but now…"

I can feel my leggings being wrenched down, I feel freezing cold air hit my skin.

My heart slams into my chest.

I scream out into the gag but it does nothing.

"Do you know what hoops Otto made us all jump through?" He growls, fumbling with his pants. I know he's undoing them, I know exactly where this is headed.

"Do you, Sofia? You think he let just anyone fuck you?"

I curse him, snarling into the fabric. Telling myself that this doesn't matter. That he's had me before, and it didn't make any difference. It won't make any difference this time. I refuse to let it.

He pushes himself into me, forces himself in. I scream more, I jerk, feeling how he tears my muscles, tears my insides, only the sick fuck is groaning like this is pleasurable.

For a moment I can't focus. I can't take it. The pain is too much. Everything grows hazy. Maybe it's the drugs they gave me but I know if I pass out I won't wake up. That that will be it.

And yet I'm okay with that, some part of me feels okay, because I just want it to end. I just want the pain to stop.

But I don't want to die. Not like this. I don't want them to win.

I grit my teeth, forcing myself to mentally fight, to stay present.

I can do this. I can survive this. I know I can.

"I only got to have you once. One fucking time." He spits, thrusting enough that the entire bed we're leant over skids sideways by a few inches. The sound of it rings in my ears, echoes in my head. "But I've got you now…" He taunts.

"Martin…" Blue Eyes snaps behind us.

"You told me I could have this." Martin hollers back.

"I said you could have her when we're done." Blue Eyes retorts.

"What good will she be then?" Martin replies, forcing my face around so that he can look me properly in the eyes. "When we've cut her open. You think I'll want to fuck her corpse then?"

I freeze as much as I can. Cut me open? What the fuck is this?

"You get it now, don't you, Sofia?" Blue Eyes says as Martin continues raping me again. "He hid it inside you. He turned you into a walking safety deposit box."

I can't think. I can't process those words. Martin's groaning, sweating, getting close to coming and I know now what's going to happen once he's finished violating me.

I don't want to cry. I don't want to give in but my tears start streaming down my cheeks.

All the while Blue Eyes is stood, watching this play out, as if he gets off on seeing the act as much as committing it.

Martin pulls out, turns me over, yanking my torn top wide open and he bears my breasts for him to ogle at. My hands are still bound and now all my weight is on them and it hurts so much.

I lift my body, slamming my head into his and he groans before backhanding me.

Blue Eyes moves around the other side, grabbing my hair, pinning me down. Apparently they both want a piece of this game.

Except, they seem to have forgotten what else was on the bed; what is now right under my hands. My fingers fumble, I feel the sharp blade of something slice right through the tips but I don't give a shit, I don't care how much it hurts. I don't care if I have to cut off every digit to achieve this. If I can manoeuvre it right, I might just be able to actually get myself free.

Blue Eyes undoes his trousers, rips the bandage from my mouth and he points a gun at my temple. "Suck." He orders.

I glare back but I don't fight as he pushes his disgusting cock into my mouth. He's not even hard, I'm not sure if this is just because he can do it, or because he's realised this will be his only chance. That once they've gutted me I won't live long enough for anything else to go down.

I don't want to consider that.

I don't want to contemplate that.

I grip the handle, pulling the blade up and though it nicks my skin, it slices right through it, I feel the tape come loose.

Martin's about to finish. It would make sense to deal with him first. But Blue Eyes has the gun to my head – if I do anything to

Martin I don't doubt Blue Eyes will blow my brains out and be done with it.

But then, if he pulls the trigger, surely my mouth would clamp shut right around his dick and he wouldn't want that would he? I could almost laugh at the absurd situation I'm in right now. The options I'm weighing up.

Only, it's not funny. Not for a second.

So I make a split second decision. I twist my hand out, snatch forward and cut Blue Eye's dick right off.

Blood spurts everywhere. It covers my face. The gun goes off almost immediately and I have no idea where the bullet hits but it's not me. Thank god it's not me. Blue Eyes falls back, collapsing against the medical equipment behind us, grasping at where his appendage is no longer present.

Martin doesn't even have time to react before I've sprung forward and rammed that same scalpel right into his throat.

He gurgles, he chokes, falling back on his arse.

I scramble off the bed, my feet are still bound, my leggings and underwear are around my knees and I slip over, falling face first in the pool of blood. But my eyes see the weapon, the gun, and I reach out, snatching it before Blue Eyes can get at it.

I spit the severed part of his dick out of my mouth, scooting away, pushing myself far from them both. I don't know how many bullets this gun has but I know there's enough for what I need.

The door smashes open.

The shock of it makes me jump and my finger pulls the trigger before I even register that it's moved.

The sound echoes in my head. It's like it plays out in slow motion, I see the direction of the gun, I know exactly where it's headed and it hits Martin right between the eyes.

He falls over, landing in a heap, and I train the weapon back on whoever the fuck has now joined us.

CHAPTER

Fifty-Seven

KOEN

Jesus fucking Christ.

It's like a blood bath. She's sat in it, covered in it. Her leggings are by her ankles, her top has been completely sliced into two. She's as good as naked.

But that's not what has my attention.

It's the gun pointed right at me. At us.

"Sofia," Roman says.

He jumped on the back of one of my men's bikes, following in my wake from the Governor's house.

I hold my hand out, stopping him in his tracks. I don't know where her head is at, I don't know if she's lost right now in some traumatic death spiral, but she'd never get over it if she shoots her brother.

She blinks looking between us with a blank expression, like she's not really aware of what the fuck is actually happening. Perhaps they've drugged her. Perhaps she's had a complete breakdown.

"Put the gun down, Princess." I say.

She narrows her eyes, shaking her head.

And then movement in the corner makes us turn and look.

There's one man dead by her feet. The man we witnessed her shooting as we walked in. But another man, an older man is hunched over, holding what looks like his bloodied groin.

Sofia trains the weapon back on him, narrowing her eyes, and then my mind turns to fucking fury as I register what it is lying there, in the blood, in front of all of us.

"He fucking raped you?" I growl because why else would his dick have been out?

Sofia nods, wiping her face on her shoulder but all it does is smear more blood across her skin.

I don't think, I just cross the room, grabbing the bastard and I haul him up by his throat. As our eyes connect it's like a knife twists in my heart. That old wound, one I thought was long buried, stirs and it's so much worse this time.

No.

No fucking way.

"You fucking bastard." I growl.

I thought I'd gotten them all. I thought I'd given Aaliyah all the justice she'd needed.

He stares back at me, his severed cock still spurting blood everywhere.

I pull my knife from my pocket, flip it open and one by one I cut them out. I cut out his eyes, her eyes technically.

No one says a word as I do it. No one moves.

His howls ring out and I'll admit I'll savour that sound, I'll fucking die a happy man now that I've heard it.

Sofia is still there, back pressed against the wall, with that gun held in her hands like she needs to fight.

Everyone else is stood by the door like she's the one who's unhinged.

I let the man go, watch as he collapses at my feet. He'll bleed out soon enough. I doubt he's got more than a few minutes left, judging by the blood flow from his missing cock.

Sofia eyes me warily but I don't hesitate. I prowl towards her, ignoring the weapon entirely and, just as I get within a hairs breath, she flings herself into my arms.

"I've got you." I murmur, holding her so tightly against me. "I've always got you."

She buries her face into my chest. I know she's still holding the gun but it makes no difference to me. I just carry her out, leaving everyone else to deal with this mess.

CHAPTER
Fifty-Eight

SOFIA

I take a shower. I brush my teeth. I scrub myself clean.

I know Koen has questions. I also know that Hastings and Roman are here, downstairs. Waiting.

We're in a hotel. Not the one I lived in before.

Apparently they blew up Koen's house so that at least explains how they got me out so easily.

I huddle up, wrapping the towel around myself, staring at my reflection in the mirror.

They raped me.

I don't understand why I'm not so affected by it. Why I feel so numb this time. Am I so used to trauma now that I don't even respond appropriately?

My hand slips to my stomach, and those words echo; that my father used me as a walking human safe. Is it true? Is that even possible? Wouldn't I know if I had some sort of object inside me for all this time?

A tap at the door makes me yelp in shock. Koen's face appears around it but he does his best to hide the concern there.

"How are you doing?" He asks quietly.

I give him a small smile back. "Good."

His eyebrows raise. "Good?" He repeats obviously unconvinced.

"They're dead Koen, they're all dead."

He grunts, eyeing up the dark bruise on my cheek.

"I've put some clothes out…"

"Stop." I say cutting across him. Even now I can see him trying to retreat. I know he's trying to be considerate, to give me space, but that's not what I need. It's not what I've ever needed from him.

He frowns, watching me carefully, no doubt waiting for me to fall apart.

"I don't want you to go." I say. "I want you here. I feel safer when you're here."

He lets out a low breath, nodding his ascent, and before he can refuse me, I wrap my arms around his waist and curl myself into him.

"Sofia,"

The way he murmurs my name, the way he holds me right now makes my eyes well.

For a second I don't want to move, I just want to stay here, like this.

But my legs are trembling, my body is giving every sign that if I don't lay down, I'm going to pass out again.

In the bedroom, Koen has laid out what looks like leggings and a hoody on the bed. He makes a point of looking away while I get dressed and I'll admit that annoys me. He's seen enough of my body, he's fucked me enough times to be intimately acquainted with every inch of me.

Hell, he fucked me while I was asleep, why now is he acting all respectful?

I want to call him out on it but I'm so exhausted that I can't bear the potential fight.

So I let it go. Let it slide. Maybe he needs to process what happened too. Maybe it's fucked his head to have made so many promises about protecting me and then, when it came down to it, they pretty much waltzed right into his house and stole me away.

I crawl over to the bed.

He doesn't say anything as he watches me. I feel so tired, so damn exhausted but in an entirely different way to how I am after Koen has finished with me.

Koen lays down beside me but he's still keeping that distance.

I shake my head, rolling over, leaning into his body, and then groan as that bruise on my face screams out in protest.

"Do you want to talk about it?" He asks softly.

I shake my head because it still feels like I'm trying to process everything that went down.

"They raped me." I say anyway.

I hear him take a quick inhale.

"They were going to cut me up." I add.

He frowns before wrapping his arms tighter around me like some protective cage.

For a moment I ponder whether I should tell him everything. If Martin and Blue Eyes are dead what does it matter if there's an actual diamond inside me?

But they had resources. I remember Blue Eyes taunting Otto about it. That *they* were letting Otto keep me. What if there are more out there? What if Blue Eyes told them what he suspected? Will they also hunt me down, carve me up just to see if I am hiding this damned diamond?

I tense, palming my face with my hands.

Koen has never let me down. He's never once fucked me over or made me question myself. Sure, he might push my boundaries, might take more from my body than I feel always able to give, but he loves me in his own way.

I gasp at that thought. Does he love me?

"What is it, Little Devil?" He asks gently, as though he's just been laid here watching my body language shift with every wave of new emotion.

"Do you, do you," Christ, just spit it out. "Do you love me?" I ask.

My face is so damned red, I know now is not the time for such a conversation but let's face it, timing has never been one of my virtues.

He snarls, grabbing my hands, yanking them from where they're desperately trying to hide my embarrassment.

"Is that a joke?" He asks. "Have I not made that abundantly clear? From the start I have done everything I could to have you, to keep you, to ensure you belong to me."

"But that isn't love." I snap back. "That's possession."

He chuckles, cupping my cheek with his massive palm. "What do you think love like ours looks like? You think it's roses and chocolates? Us holding hands while we skip merrily down the harbour? No, shit like that is not our kind of love, Sofia. Our souls are too dark, too twisted for such nonsense. Our love is a burning, raging monster, our love is controlling, it's a furious rampage."

"Ours?"

He lowers his mouth, claiming my lips before I can even finish that unspoken word.

"Ours." He states. "You love me just as much as I love you. That's why you enjoy all the filthy depraved things I do to your body."

He's right. The arsehole is right. I just didn't realise this was what I felt because it's been there so long, mixed up in my trauma, twisting around with my confused emotions.

"I need to tell you something." I blurt out.

He tilts his head, waiting.

"They, they put something in me." I whisper. "My father did."

He frowns. "What do you mean?"

I gulp, moving my hand to cover my belly. "He kept pushing the surgeons to try again. And when the transplants failed he must have figured a new way to make me useful." I know I'm waffling, going all about the houses to explain this but to say it out loud, to say those words…

"Tell me, Sofia." He growls softly.

"The Devil's Heart diamond." I whisper. "He put it in me. He hid it in me."

His eyes widen, he drops his gaze, staring at the spot that I'm covering.

"Who told you that?"

"Blue Eyes."

"You can't be sure then…"

"I am." I am certain. I can't explain how I know but in my heart I do. My father was a callous, manipulative piece of shit. Of course he came up with the idea. He was the one who came up with the plan of kidnapping people and selling organs in the first place. Of course, Roman thinks I didn't know that fact but I knew a long time ago, I just didn't understand what it was that I was seeing.

He shakes his head, curling his body up and pulling the covers tighter around me. "We'll deal with it." He says. "Together."

CHAPTER

Fifty- Nine

KOEN

I leave her sleeping.

It's not that I want to but her brother is downstairs, as is the Governor. There's going to be enough of a fallout from today's events. If I can take some of that load, if I can do anything to make the next few weeks easier for Sofia, then I will.

I stalk down the stairs, letting my boots crunch against the immaculate carpet. I've got guards on the door, guards by the lift, men in the kitchens too. I'm not taking any risks, especially considering what Sofia confessed.

Roman is stood a metre from Hastings. They both look in the midst of some sort of debate but they fall silent as I walk in.

"Well?" Roman asks.

"She's asleep." I state.

Hastings huffs. Roman glares at him but I ignore the pair of them.

There's another man here, a man in a suit, standing like he's used to slithering about on the peripheries, getting his hands dirty when no one notices.

"Who the fuck are you?" I growl.

I was very specific about who was to be let in here. Random strangers were definitely not on the list.

"This is Magnus Blake." Hastings says in a tone that puts me even more on edge.

The man smiles politely enough, holding his hand out for me to shake.

"Who the fuck are you?" I repeat.

He glances up the stairs, revealing more in that one action than he probably meant to. "I appreciate this has been somewhat eventful for you all, but this situation must be resolved."

"This situation?" Roman says, taking a step closer, as if he too wants to gut the man.

Hastings shakes his head. "There is no need to fight about this. Let's just discuss this like adults."

"Like his buddies have taken that approach so far," Roman spits. "They kidnapped her, they raped her, no doubt they were going to carve her up like a pumpkin…"

My anger surges, I grab the man by the throat, slamming him back into the wall. So, that's what this is. He's with Blue Eyes and the fake therapist.

"You stay the hell away from her or I'll…" I begin.

"You'll what?" He gasps. "You think you and your little biker gang are any match for us? We are the Brethren. We run this country. We control everything. You think we can't simply have you removed and just take what we want?"

"If you even try…"

"Koen,"

I freeze.

We all freeze at that voice.

Magnus turns his gaze to just over my shoulder and he grins.

"Sofia," Roman snarls, moving to block her but she shifts quickly out of his grasp.

"Put him down." She says gently to me.

"Is that a joke?" I reply. "This man would happily gut you…"

"And if we're smart, then perhaps it won't come to that." Sofia states.

Magnus smiles more. I clench my fist, slamming it into his smug little face and then I let him fall.

Hastings tuts but I can tell Roman approves of my show of aggression. Not that I need his approval.

"You should be resting." I say to Sofia. She's still in those leggings and dressing gown. She looks shattered. Her hair is all over the place and I have no idea why she even got out of bed.

"You weren't there." She says quietly. "You can't expect me to sleep in a bed if you're not beside me."

I huff, feeling like I should feel more complimented that I do right now. Maybe I'll have to handcuff her to the bed when I leave from now on.

She plants a kiss on my cheek then turns her attention on Magnus.

"You want the Devil's Heart diamond, don't you?" She says.

He nods only enough for us to notice. As if extending his head further would be a waste of his precious energy.

"I'll give it to you." She says, holding her hand to silence my splutter. "But on one condition."

"Your father made conditions." Magnus sneers. "And then he failed to honour them, why should we trust his daughter to be any different?

"Because unlike him, I don't give a shit about it." She snaps. "And you can at least hear me out before you make yourself look stupid in turning me down."

Fuck, I love her like this. Full of rage. Full of fury. How my cock doesn't stir in my pants I don't know but it's a good thing. I can hardly stand here with a raging hard on in front her damned brother.

"Go on then." Magnus replies.

"You can have the diamond as long as you agree that Koen is there when you extract it."

"Excuse me?" He blinks like he doesn't understand.

My jaw drops, I shake my head but again she dismisses me, acting like she has sole control of the room.

"The diamond is in me." Sofia says.

All three men react. Roman with horror. Hastings with shock. And Magnus, I can't quite tell what he thinks but he quickly covers it.

"He hid it in your body?" Roman gasps. "How the fuck did he do that?"

Sofia's face turns pained, she drops her eyes, staring at the carpet like she has something to be ashamed about. "You remember all those operations I had as a child?"

Roman nods almost reluctantly.

"He was stealing other women's wombs, transplanting them into me. But it didn't work. So I guess he decided that my lack of ability to be a functioning woman, could be turned into a different use."

"That fucking bastard." Roman growls.

Sofia shrugs. "It's not me you should feel sorry for. It's the three women who died simply to try and fix a fault that never existed."

Fuck, I think I love her more in this moment. To hear her say it, to hear her declare that she is enough, that she is fine just as she is.

"You'll need to cut me open to get it but I want Koen there, I want him to ensure that you don't simply butcher me." She says, clenching her fists.

"We will arrange for the finest surgeons." Magnus smiles.

"Fine." She replies.

I don't know what to think. What to say. She's willing to go through that? To let them cut her open?

She takes my hand, all but strutting out like she's said her piece and she's done with everything.

When we get back to the room I can't help but scowl.

"You don't have to do this." I state.

She snorts. "Yes I do."

"Sofia,"

"You think I want it in me? You think I want to be a walking reminder of every fucked up thing he's ever done?"

I grab her, wrapping my arms around her trembling body.

"If I do this it'll be over." She states. "All the taunts, all the drug attempts, all of it. I'll be free."

I tense realising that she still doesn't know everything.

"It wasn't them." I state. "Those attacks, the way they were setting you up. That was Valentina."

"What?" She gasps.

"She was the one who tried to kill me." I explain. "She was the one behind all of it. She wanted to make you look like a junkie so that she could get her hands on more of Otto's money."

She stills, her body goes so tense. "That fucking bitch." She snarls.

"She's paying for it." I state.

"How?"

I can't help the grin as I meet her furious gaze. "Hastings had her thrown into the county jail. She's going to be locked up for attempted murder."

"Fuck," She half-laughs.

"Fuck indeed."

"I guess karma is a bitch after all."

I scoop her up, carrying her over to the bed. "It is. And you've earnt yourself some rest."

She sighs, leaning into my chest. "Only if you promise to stay here beside me."

"Where else would I want to be?"

CHAPTER

SOFIA

Two days later I have the surgery. I know Koen is still furious about it. I know Roman is ashamed that our father did this in the first place.

But to me, this doesn't feel like a bad thing. Like a travesty.

It feels like I'm ridding myself of the last remnants of Horace Montague. It feels like I'm setting myself free.

Reid said I was cursed and in a way, I agree. I am cursed. My father cursed me. And having this damned diamond cut out will free me from it.

They knock me out entirely. Koen is as good as his word, staying right by my side the whole time and from what I can tell the surgeons are so afraid of him that they barely dared breathe.

I don't get to see the stone. Magnus steals it away before I even come round.

I guess it's better that way. How would it feel to look at it anyway and know that my father valued that one thing more than his own daughter's life?

As I wake up, groggy and in pain, it's Koen who's there, holding my hand, ensuring that I know I'm safe.

I have a piece of plastic in my left hand still from where they pumped me full of meds. My body won't stop shaking from the anaesthetic and it's only Koen's arms holding me tight, keeping me warm, that seems to ease it.

I curl up, desperately thirsty, and Koen grabs a glass, places it to my lips and holds it until I've sipped as much as I can.

Magnus was right with his promise of the best surgeons. We had to fly to New York for the operation. By private jet, naturally. I'll admit the thought of a vacation, of being away from the oppressive atmosphere of Verona is what helped calm me when I started to overthink it all. When I started to panic.

That first night, I get little sleep. I daze in and out, fighting the pain and the constant need to pee. Apparently my bladder did not like the anaesthetic.

As I shift in bed and try to get comfortable, Koen is so careful to hold me in a way that soothes but doesn't constrict.

And when he realises I really am not sleeping, he starts whispering of the future, of what he wants from it, how he sees us building a new home, a bigger one – as if we need that. He promises that this one will have a bigger pool and an actual library and though it hurts to laugh, I do, wiping the happy tears that seem to escape my eyes.

"You'll have it, Sofia." He states. "Everything you've ever wanted, everything you've ever dreamed of."

I smile, curling into him more. He's what I wanted. He's what I needed.

"If you want a wedding, if you want a ring, then say it..."

"No," I gasp. I don't want that. I never want that.

He frowns, brushing my hair from my face. "You don't want to get married?"

"Not..." I gulp, trying to make my brain work, trying to articulate those thoughts. "I don't need that. I don't want to be tied, to be trapped."

He nods like he understands and I pray to god that he does. It's not him that's the issue, it's not that I don't want to be with him, to spend my life with him but I can't go down that route. Not again.

He plants a kiss on my head, gently, lovingly.

"Then no marriage." He murmurs.

My heart seems to ease, relief floods through me. He's not angry, he's not hurt. It clearly doesn't seem to bother him the way I feared it would.

"You don't mind?" I whisper.

He smiles, shaking his head. "I want what you want." He states. "Besides, you sold your soul to me, remember? Isn't that worth far more than a marriage?"

I blink, I almost choke and he chuckles that deep, growly laugh of his, like he knows he's played his trump card.

For the next few days I do little beyond sleep and use the toilet. When I'm well enough to be discharged, Koen has us move into a fancy penthouse looking right over Central Park, and I sit there, staring out past the glass, watching the view below, imagining how it will feel to be free, to explore.

Every day Koen brings me delicious food, fattening me up the way he always promised he would.

And that first day I step outside, I can't help the smile that covers my face. Koen ensures we have enough men around us that

I feel safe, secure, that even though my body isn't fully healed I'm not concerned about anyone accidentally bumping into me in the busy congested streets.

He takes me to a bookstore with so many floors I lose count. And I swear I hear Reid cursing under his breath as he has to carry the huge stack I buy back.

And that night, I stay up, curled up, with a blanket, watching those sparkling street lights while I read.

It's an odd feeling, to feel suddenly at peace, to realise that all that fighting, all that anger and rage, it's gone, it's left me. Maybe I really was cursed. Maybe that diamond was truly a thing of evil but now that it's gone, I feel reborn.

And I'm determined that I'm going to make the most of my life now, that nothing my father did will every haunt me again.

CHAPTER

Sixty-One

KOEN

I left Sofia sleeping. My men are on the doors. I know she's safe now, safer than ever but I still won't take any risks.

As I step out into the park itself, there's barely anyone around. For a city that never sleeps this place feels eerily quiet.

And then I spot why.

"You." I snarl. I thought the bastard was long gone. That he'd gotten his damned diamond and had flown away.

Magnus smirks, stepping out from the shadow of the trees. "We needed a chat."

"Have you been waiting here all this time?" I taunt.

He gives me a deadpan look that I'd wipe off anyone else's face without hesitation.

"You killed Alistair," He states. "Such an act cannot go unpunished."

"Who?" I reply.

His lips quirk and then I realise, Blue Eyes, he's talking about Blue Eyes. That's his real name then.

"He deserved it." I growl. "He raped Sofia, he stole my sister's eyes…"

"I not here to debate his soul." Magnus says dismissively. "I'm here to explain a few facts."

"And what are those?" I sneer.

"The Brethren does not forget. The Brethren does not forgive."

My eyebrows raise, I take a step, closing the distance between us. He might think he had power but right now, I could crush him so easily.

"I'm not afraid of you." I state.

"Then perhaps you should be. You think we wouldn't hesitate to crush you? To kill your men, to wipe you all from the very earth." He glances up, over my shoulder to where the sparkly great skyscrapers are, in the direction of where I know Sofia is. "We'd take her too. She's got some experience as a sex slave from what I hear, I'm sure she'd fit in just fine as she serviced our Lords…"

I snarl, grabbing his throat, slamming him into the bark.

A gun jabs into the back of my neck. I know all logic and reason should mean I relinquish my grip and yet I can't do it. I won't do it.

"You touch one hair on her head…" I begin.

"Very fucking noble." A man behind me spits. "But such declarations mean nothing if you're lying dead on the ground."

"What do you want?" I snarl.

He jabs the gun further into my neck, making a point with that gesture. I reluctantly let Magnus go and he draws in a deep breath before adjusting his coat, brushing off the dirt like that's his only concern.

"We can come to an agreement." Magnus says. "There's no need for such measures."

"You threaten her…"

He holds his hand up tutting. "I don't give a shit about Sofia Montague. You can have her."

"Then what do you want?" I ask.

"You. Roman. I want your businesses. I want your resources. I want it all."

That makes me pause. I step back, and that gun that moments ago was pressed into my neck now finds a new home against my spine.

"You think we'll just hand it all over?" I growl.

Magnus laughs. "You misunderstand, Koen." He says. "We're not looking to *take* from you. We wish to welcome you in."

Welcome us? What the fuck does that mean?

The man behind me drops the weapon moving around to face me full on and my voice seems to die as I realise who it is. Barnaby Smith. Barnaby Fucking Smith?

"You impressed me." He says in a voice so utterly different to the cancer ridden one I heard a month ago. "Such talents deserved to be rewarded."

"You want us to join you?" I repeat. Is this some sort of trick?

"It is not a wish." Magnus says. "It is your only option. You killed one of us. Ordinarily, that crime has one punishment. But we will overlook that in the circumstances if…"

"If we become one of you." I reply.

They both nod. Like fucking dogs.

I look between them, wondering if this is some sort of joke. I've never been one for secret societies, cults, any of that shit. I don't give a damn about politics, or who is President, or anything beyond my own businesses. But what they're offering, what this could mean.

"Have you spoken to Roman?" I ask. Not that it should matter what he says and yet we share this company together. He technically has as much say as I do.

Magnus shakes his head. "We figured you would do the dirty work for us."

I grunt. Fucking typical. Is that how they plan this then, us doing the work and them profiting?

When I voice that they both laugh once more.

"Come to London." Magnus says, handing me a card. "Meet the Brethren, and then you'll truly understand the gift we're offering."

It doesn't sound like an invitation. It sounds exactly what it is. An order. Go and live, refuse and die.

I draw myself up, turn my back on them both and head down the same path I entered by.

When walk into the Penthouse, Sofia is awake, stood, staring out of the windows with a glass of water in her hand and a robe wrapped around herself. She's still not properly healed. She's still fragile, and though I've been dying to touch her, I know I can't, not yet anyway.

She turns, fixing those beautiful eyes on me with a questioning gaze.

"I needed some fresh air." I murmur.

Her lips quirk. "Is that so?"

For a second I contemplate lying, changing the subject, but then, if we're to do this, if we're going to make this work, she has to be in this too. That's what the Brethren is. It's not a one foot in, one foot out. If I join, then Sofia becomes a part of this.

"I met someone." I say.

She freezes, frowning, like I'm about to confess something appalling and I guess in a way I am. "Magnus."

"What?" She gasps.

I hold my hands out, trying to calm her. "Hear me out first." I say. "He wants us to join them, to join the Brethren."

"Is he mad?" She snarls. "Why the fuck would we ever want that?"

I sigh, taking the glass from her hand and I place it on the side. "We might not have a choice."

"How so?"

"I killed Alistair," I state. "Apparently that means I've given myself a death sentence."

"But they'll spare you if you join them?" She guesses.

"Yes. But, it's not all bad." I hate that I'm spinning it like this, but I'm not lying either. Joining the Brethren has perks. Big perks. I've always been a greedy man, an ambitious one, so far I may have only set roots in Verona but I wanted more, I've always wanted more. Darius put paid to a lot of that but joining the Brethren can give me it back, it can give us it all.

And Sofia, if she becomes one of them, she'll be even more protected.

She sighs, studying my face for a moment. "You want to do it." She surmises.

I nod. "But it's not just me, we both have to."

She chews her lip, clearly not liking it. "Will they really kill you if you say no?" She asks.

I nod back. They may not have said the words but I know what the threat was.

"Then what choice do we have?" She replies.

My eyebrows raise. "You make it sound so simple."

She laughs, planting a quick, almost chaste kiss on my lips. "It is simple. I'm not going to do anything that risks your life, and besides, you don't look too pissed about it."

My lips curl, I wrap my arms around her waist, dearly wishing I could claim her the way I so desperately want. By the time we have sex again I doubt I'll be able to last more than a few minutes before I blow my load. It's a good thing I've been fattening her up because she's going to need all that energy for the amount of orgasms she owes me.

"So we'll do it?" I ask.

She sighs, claiming my lips. "Together."

The End

If you liked this book read on for a sneak peek at
Coercion: An Age Gap Mafia Romance…

COERCION

A MAFIA ROMANCE

Her

Five years ago my uncle murdered my family, butchered them in their beds. And I know the only reason I'm alive is because I'm useful, a thing to barter. A thing to sell.

Well, today he'll get his payday. He's made a deal, he's handing me over as a blushing bride to Preston Civello.

I'm meant to be the rubber stamp of a truce between our two warring families but in secret I'm there to bring my new husband down, to bring Nico Morelli down from the inside. To act as a spy.

Only I have an entirely different plan - I'm going to seduce him, to win him to my side. I'll play the good little wife and I'll serve him on my knees if I have to, all the while pretending that my past never happened.

But when all my horrible secrets are revealed, will my husband believe me or will he see me as just a traitor in his bed?

Him

I know her past. I know her history. I'm convinced she's going to be a snake sleeping in my bed but when my Mafia Princess Bride is all but dragged down the aisle and I clap eyes on her tear-stained face, I don't care. Something feral takes over.

She might have been a pawn in her uncle's games but from now on she belongs to me. She's mine.

Only that's not exactly true because of the promise Nico forced me to make- she doesn't know it but she's his god daughter, and I'm not allowed to touch her. Not allowed to claim her. He's made her off limits, a fruit I'm forbidden from tasting and, as each day passes, it's getting harder and harder to resist my tempting little wife. And tempting she is. Dangerously so.

When all the players come out of the woodwork, I'm forced to face a truth I never thought possible, that maybe she's not as loyal as she seems. Maybe she really is the snake I first took her for.

- Things to know about Coercion:
- Mafia with a healthy dose of spice
- Age Gap
- MF
- Jealous / possessive hero
- Strong female with a traumatic backstory
- Dual POV
- Trigger warning list in front of book

Grab your copy here:
https://www.amazon.com/dp/B0CM7MSP5S/

COERCION

Sneak Peak

Preston

ost men don't dream of their wedding day. Most men don't even consider what it will be like, if they even have one.

But then again, most men aren't in the line of business I am. I stand stiffly with Nico beside me. My parents had an arranged marriage, as did my grandparents. It's nothing unusual with our way of life and yet I'd never considered it for myself. Truth be told I'd never imagined getting married at all.

With death stalking your every move it seems a selfish thing to want to build a family, to want to put others at risk.

Maybe that's why I'm so stoic about this. I'm not leaving some loved one behind, I'm not making some grand sacrifice, in reality this decision was pretty easy to make. This is for the good of the Morelli Family, it's the least I can do considering how much Nico's family have sacrificed for me.

As the music begins to play out I let out a low breath. Nico and I have already agreed how we're going to handle this. It's a marriage of convenience, a way to seal the deal and while I'll smile for the cameras that's all this is; a show. I'll pretend until this alliance falls apart, if it falls apart, and if it doesn't well, at least the girl will have a little more freedom at my side, that is, if she deserves it.

Nico shifts beside me. The church is full. Levi has his side packed as though he really does consider Ruby to his actual offspring. All his men have that trademark diamond pinned to their suit pocket. God knows how much those things cost. Each diamond shows the rank of the man wearing it. The bigger the diamond, the higher up the food chain they are, with Gunnar having a full five carat monstrosity that looks almost ridiculous as it glints under the stained glass window.

On short notice it's our men that fill out the pews to the right making this look even more of a shotgun wedding than it already is.

Behind me I can sense them approaching. I can hear the tell-tale ruffles of a wedding dress, but I can hear something else too, above the music, above the merry little tune that's ringing out around us.

She's crying.

My heart twists. I haven't even laid eyes on her and already I feel something akin to sympathy. God, what has this girl gone through?

I wish I could stop this, I wish I could pull her aside and tell her what's really going on but I can't. Besides, it could all be an act, a way to get me on side, while underneath she's Levi's creature through and through.

But she starts fighting harder, giving up all pretence and as we all watch on I realise she's either the best actress I've ever seen in my life or this is real. She really doesn't want this. She really is fighting as if her life depends upon it.

She digs her heels into the thick carpet and he curls his fist clearly wanting to hurt her but he refrains under all our watchful gaze. Instead, he digs his fingers into her arm and jerks hard enough that she stumbles forward and he can haul her down the last bit to where I'm stood.

As they come up beside me it takes all I have not to punch the bastard in the face but then I look at her, at my bride, and my heart seems to stop.

She has a long veil covering her entirety, underneath a satin dress clings to a curvaceous body that makes my mouth water and my dick come to life. I know Levi said she was twenty one but she looks older.

She looks nothing like the blurry photo he showed me on his phone.

But it's the tears streaming down her beautiful face that seem to captivate me in a way I didn't expect.

She keeps her eyes down, refusing to look at any of us. Levi is gripping her arm in a way that I'm certain will bruise badly and I'm quick to pull her free. In less than an hour she'll belong to me anyway. I'm staking my claim, making him see that from now on she's untouchable to him and all his cronies.

His lips curl as he looks at me and then he slinks away off to sit on the front pew beside Gunnar who is scowling like someone has shat on his bed and made him sleep in it.

The ceremony is quick. Someone clearly bribed the priest because he doesn't seem to care that the bride wants no part of this. When it comes to her vows she stumbles, sobbing harder, too distraught to say any articulate words and Levi gets up, slapping his hand over her mouth from behind and speaks them for her as if none of us would care.

Nico gives me a look and the priest acts like this is all perfectly normal, like every blushing bride behaves like this, as if they have a gun pressed to their temple.

Putting the rings on is even worse. I have to wrench her hand open and practically jam the thing down her finger. The diamonds seem to sparkle in jest, their light catches on the tears still streaming down her cheeks. She doesn't make any attempt to pick up the gold band meant for me and in the end I pick it up and put it on myself.

When he says the words 'man and wife' she seems to deflate more. Like it's a death sentence she's just been handed. Like life as she knows it is over.

I take her hand again, trying to ignore how small it feels in my grasp, and we walk back down the aisle while I glare at every man we pass.

We only have to get through the reception now and then this entire charade is over.

LEVI AND GUNNAR ARE DRINKING LIKE THIS REALLY IS A CELEBRATION. Eleri is sat stiff with her eyes continuously darting to Ruby who still hasn't looked up. Her veil is off her face, every few seconds she sniffs. Her makeup, that no doubt was immaculate hours ago, is smeared down her cheeks and a part of me wants to scoop her up and take her away from all the jackals surrounding her.

To her left is Levi and then Gunnar. I'm on her right, our chairs placed close enough that my leg should be touching hers and it takes a lot of effort to keep it twisted at an angle so I'm not. Nico is beside me with Eleri placed on the nearest table to ours. I wonder if they did that on purpose, to try to goad Nico. To insult him.

Eleri doesn't make a fuss. She takes her place beside Blaine and they seem to make conversation. If anything I wish I could join them. I bet they're having a far better time than all of us sat on the top table.

It's a five course meal. Each one seems to drag out. I don't speak, I just eat, wanting this damned day over with. I don't think Ruby has more than a bite the entire time. By the time desert comes, Levi is making blatant innuendos about his niece; comments no decent uncle would say.

"She comes from good breeding stock." Levi says slapping Ruby's thigh as she jolts like she's been hit by lightning. "I expect you to use her well, after all, this is about binding our families together."

Ruby physically recoils, only there's nowhere for her to go; she's caught between the brute to her left and me, a man she's never met before and clearly doesn't trust. If I could I'd say something to placate her, to make her feel safe, but Levi is too close. Besides, I don't know what her reaction would be if I did. I can't risk it. I can't do anything but let this insult continue.

"Her mother was easy to train." Gunnar says leaning right over his plate to look me in the eyes. "In time I'm sure you'll get her to behave exactly the way you want. Turn her into a proper whore for you."

I clench my fists at the way they just spoke about my now wife even though she clearly does not want me as a husband.

"Keep it together." Nico mutters beside me, low enough that only I hear.

"Alright for you." I say back through gritted teeth. "Would you do the same if they spoke of Eleri like that?"

Nico tilts his head, his eyes flashing. "The situation is not the same."

"Eleri is your wife just as Ruby is now mine."

He shakes his head. "No..." He begins but Gunnar cuts across him.

"As a wedding gift from our family to yours we have booked you the honeymoon suite at the Astoria."

My eyes connect with his as I take in the words. "What?" I half snap.

"Come now, Preston." Levi says. "Surely you want this wedding to get off to a good start? Afterall, my niece is used to the finer things in life, I expect you to treat her with respect."

Like they have up until now? They've already stated how much they want me to fuck her brains out. Hardly the words of a respectful family.

It feels like the room tenses.

I can't read the expression on Nico's face as he side eyes me. "The honeymoon suite?" I say acting like I'm suddenly honoured.

Beside me Ruby looks like she's crying again. God, this is fucking awful.

My anger spikes and before I can stop myself I'm on my feet. Levi looks at me like he wants this fight, like this was the entire point of today's proceedings.

My eyes drop to Ruby. She's huddled up like she just wants to disappear entirely and I can't say I blame her.

"Fine." I growl back. If they want to play this game, then I'll meet them head on. I grab Ruby's arm hauling her to her feet more roughly than I mean and she lets out a yelp. "Enjoy the rest of the party." I say before leading her out to what feels like a frat house round of applause.

OTHER BOOKS

by Ellie Sanders

Twisted Love Series – A dark, Romeo & Juliet retelling.

Downfall

Uprising

Reckoning

The Fae Girl Series

A Place of Smoke & Shadows

A Place of Truth & Lies

A Place of Sorcery & Betrayal

A Place of Rage & Ruin

A Place of Crowns & Chains

A Mafia Romance Series

Vendetta: A Mafia Romance

Coercion: An Age Gap Mafia Romance

Sexy Standalones

Good Girl: A Taboo Love Story

ABOUT THE AUTHOR

Ellie Sanders lives in rural Hampshire, in the U.K. with her partner and two troublesome dogs.

She has a BA Hons degree in English and American Literature with Creative Writing and enjoys spending her time when not endlessly writing exploring the countryside around her home.

She is best known for her duet, 'Downfall' and 'Uprising', as well as standalone novels including Good Girl, and Vendetta: A Mafia Romance.

For updates including new books, please follow her Instagram, TikTok, and Twitter @hotsteamywriter.

Authors Note

Thank you so much for reading 'Reckoning'. I hope you enjoyed it as much as I enjoyed conjuring up all the twists and surprises.

There will be more books in the future that feature 'The Brethren' so watch this space…

If you enjoyed this book, why not subscribe to my newsletter where you'll be the first to hear about new releases and any giveaways I'm running. There'll also be bonus chapters released here, including revisits to Rose, Roman, and Sofia's story because who doesn't need more??

I would be eternally grateful if after reading this you left a review. Reviews really are an author's lifeblood, not just because it helps beat back the crazy amount of imposter syndrome we all have but because it helps us get noticed / builds our community on places like amazon and ensures we can continue creating more stories for you to read and indulge in.

Printed in Great Britain
by Amazon

43191253R00255